THE IVY LEAGUERS

THE IVY LEAGUERS

MIKE VAN HORN

THE IVY LEAGUERS

Published in the United States of America

ISBN: 978-1-7339293-7–0

Cover by Lauren Reneau

For Ann,
Whose selfless mind sees only the best in people.
It's up to me to dream up villains for you.
Sorry...and you're welcome.

Something wicked this way comes.

—The Second Witch. Act 4, Scene 1 of Shakespeare's Macbeth

Wherefore take unto you the whole armour of God, that ye may be able to withstand in the evil day, and having done all, to stand.

—Ephesians 6:13, King James Bible

Now remember, when things look bad and it looks like you're not gonna make it, then you gotta get mean. I mean plumb mad-dog mean. Cause if you lose your head and give up then you neither live nor win. That's just the way it is.

—Clint Eastwood as The Outlaw Josey Wales

CHAPTER ONE

Dylan listened to Howard Stern in the mornings. It took him back to his glory days in high school and his abbreviated days at Yale. It reminded him of the East Coast. The acerbic Stern was an asshole to much of Middle America but was beloved by his fanboys. Dylan certainly fell into this category.

But not today.

Dylan needed information on local events, and he was stuck in flyover country. Ohio. Stern had to go. It was just past 6 a.m. on a Monday and Dylan needed to hear the local news.

Dylan Riordan drove his Range Rover Evoque SUV south on the aptly named Country Road, a three-thousand-foot stretch of asphalt that spiked north off of State Route 36 a few miles west of Urbana. He'd just left the rental house that had served as base camp for him and his partners in crime.

He jabbed at the Range Rover's display screen, finally finding his way from Sirius Radio to the FM band.

Where the hell was that local station? What was it called? Hilltopper Radio?

One of the locals at the Depot Coffee House in Urbana— a converted train station—had explained to Dylan that "Hilltoppers" was the nickname of the Urbana High School athletic teams. She didn't know where the name came from, and Dylan, frankly, didn't give a shit. But Hilltoppers it was, and Dylan, after a few seconds, found the station.

He was nearing the stop sign that signaled Country Road's end at Ohio State Route 36 when the signal from Hilltopper Radio fought its way through the Ohio ether to the Range Rover's speakers.

... authorities are asking that anyone with information call the Urbana Police Department... To repeat, a body was found late yesterday on Water Street in Urbana. Reports indicate that it was under the World's Largest Loaf of Bread, a

1

novelty roadside curiosity on Urbana's south side. There are initial indications that the death is suspicious...

Dylan sighed and turned down the radio as the station went to a commercial.

Goddammit.

He came to a stop at Route 36, a two-lane east-west track that bisected Western Ohio. Dylan glanced to his left and noted the lights of Urbana reflecting off of low-hanging clouds. The town—if you could call it that—was home to some 11,000 souls.

Well, more like ten thousand, nine hundred and ninety-nine now.

Dylan smiled.

Not all of the eliminations Dylan and his associates carried out involved emotional investment. Most, he supposed, did not. But that reprobate, Shadow, had it coming, and Dylan had to admit he felt more than a little satisfaction when the weapon discharged.

He began to relive the events of the previous night then noticed headlights approaching in his driver's side mirror. Dylan took one more look to his left, waited for a UPS truck to pass, then turned right and followed it westward.

The lights of Urbana were now quite literally in his rearview mirror, but Dylan knew that he and his crew weren't yet ready to move on. They had selected the house on Country Road—an Airbnb—because of its proximity to multiple target areas. Urbana, in Champaign County, lay to the east while Piqua sat fifteen minutes away to the west. Piqua was located on I-75, a major north-south highway. It, and its neighbor ten miles to the south, Troy, were in Miami County. Another ten miles north of Piqua lay Sidney, in Shelby County.

All of these cities—towns, really—fell precisely within the target profile of Dylan's group. They were small enough to remain just under the radar of the big players but, taken together, were extremely attractive to a group such as Dylan's. This area needed product.

Dylan had it.

The drive to Piqua took Dylan through a series of small towns and villages, only half of which boasted even one stoplight. St. Paris, Lena, Fletcher, Dilbone. They were as unremarkable to Dylan as the people who inhabited them.

They're worker bees...boring, uninspired worker bees. Stolid, yes, able to put in a good day's labor for what they deemed a fair day's pay, but they weren't really living. Their life is just...an existence. They wear cutoff jeans, pay for basic cable, and clip coupons.

Dylan supposed some of them still sent handwritten thank you notes via the United States Postal Service. Was there any wonder that the demand for Dylan's product was increasing at a rate that would be envied by any Fortune 500 company?

Dylan slowed as the UPS truck made a turn outside Lena. It being June, there was no longer a chance that he'd be caught behind a lumbering school bus that made frequent stops to load students. Still, the drive could be tedious. He was accelerating, having just gotten clear of the truck, when an adolescent red squirrel darted onto the road surface from the right. Before he could react, Dylan felt a slight *thump thump* under his passenger side tires. His eyes flashed to the rearview mirror and he saw the body of the creature pancaked on the asphalt, its bushy tail swaying in the morning breeze.

Damn.

Dylan watched for a few seconds as the squirrel's remains faded into the distance, soon, no doubt, to be a meal for the carrion feeders that utilized America's highways and back roads as a buffet.

He shook his head.

Gotta focus.

There was work to do this morning. Now that the situation with Shadow in Urbana had been resolved Dylan could turn his attention to the challenge in the Piqua area. Two members of his organization, Dax and Willie, had already laid the groundwork for the takeover in that area.

Dylan allowed a smile to appear on his lips. They had honed their techniques over the past two years. They found that the most effective method for success was to send two members of their leadership circle to an area as an advance element to make the proper contacts and carry out the fact finding necessary for the next step. Dylan and his Number Two, Min, the Chinese national, then followed up. Dylan and Min would close the deal.

The final result was often a consensual partnership, one that benefitted both Dylan's group and the local operation. Sometimes, though, negotiations weren't fruitful. A hostile takeover was necessary. The result could be bloody.

Shadow had found this out the hard way.

Dylan eased off the accelerator as he neared Fletcher, the largest of the burgs on the way to Piqua. He remembered the information Dax and Willie had learned about the man. Shadow was a mid-level dealer who obtained his product from a number of sources, none of them particularly reliable. He should have easily grasped the opportunity that Dylan's group presented. A consistent source, more inventory than he could've imagined.

But Shadow was obstinate. He would not agree to the proposed division of profits. This, and the fact that Dax and Willie had discovered numerous stories of Shadow's predilection toward underage "partners," made the final resolution an easy call.

Dylan and his associates could not be in business with someone who seemed to go out of his way to attract the attention of law enforcement.

A meeting was arranged. Shadow had been demanding evidence that Dylan could actually provide the amount of product they'd been discussing. Dylan agreed and conveyed to the dealer that the meet should take place somewhere safe from police scrutiny. Shadow could select the site.

Dylan was dumbfounded when Shadow called him with instructions.

"Midnight, Saturday...at the World's Largest Loaf of Bread."

4

Dylan remembered thinking *the World's Largest WHAT?*

But it was true. An online search revealed that Urbana was indeed home to a 30-foot-long, 10-foot-high replica loaf of bread. It sat on the property of a company on the town's south side that manufactured products used in the commercial baking industry. The oddity was constructed of fiberglass and steel. It was painted to look like a loaf covered by clear plastic, its slices clearly visible within. One side even had an oversized twist tie seemingly sealing the loaf, the blue and white end of the "bag" blooming outward for several feet.

Min drove to the meet. The company, American Pan, was situated in a mostly residential section of Urbana. For this reason, Dylan decided that Min should park nearby and quickly extract him once Shadow had been dealt with.

Min steered Dylan's Range Rover past the entrance to American Pan. Thirty-foot-wide stone walls, topped by statues of crouching lions, flanked the entrance. An access drive ran between the walls and slightly uphill for a few hundred feet to a cluster of brick buildings. These structures, built before the Civil War, had previously been home to a gristmill, a woolen factory, and a tool and die company. For the past several decades the current business turned out a steady stream of high-quality products such as commercial pans and mixers.

Min pulled to the curb. Both men scanned the area, looking for signs that area residents had taken notice of their arrival. The neighborhood was comprised of older two-story houses, many of which were shrouded by mature trees. At this late hour there were few lights in the windows and absolutely no sign of people outside of the homes. Traffic on the street was virtually nonexistent.

Dylan turned to Min. "It's go time."

Min responded in his native language. "Yúkuài shòulie."

Dylan, by now used to his top assistant's penchant for sprinkling Mandarin Chinese into conversation, simply tilted his head and gave Min a quizzical look.

Min smiled. "Good hunting."

Dylan exited the Range Rover and stepped to the rear of the vehicle. The Evoque was equipped with a powered tailgate feature—known as Gesture—that allowed a key holder to open the hatch door by simply pantomiming a kick motion to the base of the vehicle. Dylan did so and the hatch released and glided upward. He stood back and watched as his golf bag came into view. Dylan smiled, reached for the bag, and slung it over his right shoulder. He cast a look at Min over the seatback, winked, and made the kick gesture a second time to close the hatch.

Dylan strode wordlessly toward the entrance to the factory complex, consciously keeping his gait smooth so the shafts of the clubs in his golf bag didn't rattle as they contacted each other. He supposed a witness might think it odd that a man was walking down the sidewalk at midnight carrying a golf bag. But Dylan surmised that Shadow was savvy enough to have selected a time and place for the meet that would have a minimal chance of unwanted attention. This was Shadow's territory.

For now.

Dylan slipped past the stone walls and made his way up the drive. The faux loaf of bread was a couple hundred feet ahead. It stood several strides to the right of the drive. Lights installed at the base of the loaf shone up and accentuated the ersatz golden-brown bread slices as well as the white and royal blue "wrapper." Trees at the rear of the display provided a backdrop. The presentation, Dylan noted, was damn near dazzling.

As he approached, Dylan detected movement just off the right side of the loaf. A tall, thin figure materialized out of the darkness and edged furtively into the field of light.

Shadow.

Dylan left the road surface and made his way toward the man, noting his long, stringy, dirty blonde hair and attitude of superiority. Shadow didn't wear either well. His obvious overuse of the various products that were his stock-in-trade had left him the poster child of a drug abuser. On this night he exuded a look of euphoria.

Dylan thought, *he looks high as a kite, hell, he looks high enough to touch Elon Musk's Starlink satellites when they whiz by overhead.*

Shadow spoke. "Yo, D-Man, come show me your goods!"

Dylan fought to keep a frown from his face. The dealer, despite being possibly the whitest man in Ohio, went out of his way to come across as a brother. In their only other face-to-face meeting, Shadow peppered Dylan with street lingo, spending nearly ten minutes expounding on his collection of 80 pairs of Air Jordans.

As Dylan drew closer, Shadow moved more fully into the light. Dylan realized that the taller man was wearing a black hoodie covered with images of basketball sneakers.

It was ridiculous.

Still, hoping to ingratiate himself with the dealer, Dylan managed a compliment.

"Nice hoodie."

Shadow smiled and gestured to his torso with both hands. "Damn straight. This mofo is hip hop."

Dylan let a smile form on his face. His thoughts, though, screamed *this can't end soon enough.*

Apparently noticing the golf bag for the first time, Shadow tilted his head and remarked, "A *golf bag?* Why the hell you bring a *golf bag* to the meet?"

Dylan swung the bag from his shoulder and stood it on the ground between himself and Shadow.

He forced another smile.

"You wanted proof that we could supply you with inventory...I brought proof."

He reached for a zipper that ran down the right side of the bag and pulled it down. Dylan inserted his hand into the compartment and felt for an object inside.

Shadow took a step back, frowning.

"Yo, man, you not here to cap me, right? We partners."

Dylan thought *we're way past that point, you dumbshit. You had a chance to take our deal, but you decided to play Big Man.* But he let his words mollify the dealer.

"No dude, just reaching for our money maker." Dylan's fingers found the object inside and he grinned up at Shadow as he removed it from the bag.

Shadow watched as Dylan withdrew a rectangular box from the zippered pocket. He stared at the box then, confused, turned to Dylan. "Golf balls? What the fuck?"

Dylan held up a finger as if to give the other man pause. "Not just golf balls."

Dylan turned the box toward one of the lights that shined up at the loaf of bread. The box was red. The label showed a lean animal sprinting across its face. Above this, in script, were the words *Running Dog.*

Dylan opened the box to reveal four sleeves holding three balls each.

Shadow frowned. "Okay, a dozen golf balls...so fucking what?"

Dylan responded, "So, a lot of fucking money." He opened the end of one sleeve and removed a ball. It gleamed white in the artificial light. The same red Running Dog logo that was on the box was stamped on one side.

Dylan flipped it to Shadow. The dealer snatched it from the air.

"Depending how you cut what's inside that ball, Shadow, you're holding about a thousand dollars of street value drugs in your hands. That ball is filled with carfentanil. Elephant tranquilizer."

Shadow's eyes widened as he stared at the ball with fresh eyes. "Nooo shit."

He said it not as a question, but as a statement of appreciation.

Dylan rested his hands on top of the clubs in his bag and leaned in. "We bring these balls into the country from China by the pallet." He let that sink in.

Shadow, his mind racing, shot a look at Dylan. "No shit? *NO SHIT?*"

As Dylan smiled, his hands, unnoticed by Shadow, worked at something with one of the clubs.

Shadow pushed the stringy hair back from his forehead and leered at Dylan.

"We gonna be millionaires."

Dylan raised his right hand and positioned it next to Shadow's forehead, then responded.

"One of us will be."

Shadow saw what was coming at the last instant and turned his head quickly to the right.

POP.

Dylan watched the dealer spasm and drop to the ground. He returned the weapon to its place before glancing down at the man at his feet. The body was twitching violently. A rivulet of blood appeared behind his left ear.

Can't have an asshole like you in our organization.

Shadow laid on the concrete pad that supported the fake bread loaf. He was exposed to the spotlights and, Dylan realized, would be easy to spot in the light of day. Dylan did a quick assessment of the area and for the first time realized the loaf was elevated a foot or two off the concrete. He knelt and scanned the area. Steel beams rose from the four corners of the concrete and acted as supports for the loaf. A low line of shrubs was strategically planted in such a way as to hide the beams.

Dylan grabbed the body—which was still convulsing—and dragged it headfirst to the base of the structure. He bent, took a deep breath, and snatched the golf ball from Shadow's hand before pushing the body as far as possible under the loaf. He stood and gathered the golf bag before making his way back to the street.

One little pop, that's all. Shouldn't draw too much attention.

Dylan spotted the Range Rover—Min had materialized at the curb as if by magic—and moved quickly to the vehicle. Before tossing the bag into the SUV he cast a look back to the meeting place.

Shadow's Air Jordans protruded from the base of the loaf. A thought took shape in Dylan's head. He remembered watching *The Wizard of Oz* as a young boy with his maternal grandmother. In his mind's eye he saw the feet of the dead Wicked Witch of the East sticking out from under Dorothy's house.

Dylan smiled.

Dylan came out of his revelry as he entered the Piqua city limits early on Monday morning. Shadow's body had been discovered but it was time to move on. As he neared the I-75 interchange Dylan looked to his right and recognized Winans Coffee & Chocolate. It sat a short distance down Looney Road, the last turn before reaching the highway. The shop was part of a regional chain that he'd come to appreciate. He pulled in.

He entered the store and placed his order—a 24-ounce latte with a shot of hazelnut—with the barista. She was a pleasant young woman with a name tag that read "Phoebe."

She asked him for a name to put on the order.

Dylan always gave the same name in these situations.

"Eli."

This was the nickname given to graduates of Yale, one of the crown jewels of the Ivy League, located in New Haven, Connecticut. He'd been railroaded out of the school. He'd claim the honor of the name for himself...he didn't give a shit what anyone thought.

While waiting, Dylan sketched out the rest of his morning. Min would be meeting him in an hour right back here at Winans. They would sit down with the pair of brothers that dominated the drug scene in the Piqua-Sidney-Troy area.

In the meantime, Dylan would take his latte across town and hit some balls at the practice range of the local municipal course, Echo Hills. The coffee was always too damn hot. He'd leave the cup in his Range Rover Evoque to cool, stripe some drives down the middle of the range, and plan the next step for his organization.

Dylan's mind wandered, finally focusing on the recent death that gave him some guilt.

Damn shame about that little red squirrel.

Phoebe called out.

"Eli?"

CHAPTER TWO

Dylan swung his Ping i530 8 iron. He made perfect contact with the range ball and propelled it toward a flagstick 150 yards distant on the Echo Hills practice range. The ball arced majestically before landing twenty feet from the flag. It bounced once before coming to a stop. This was the third ball he'd hit, and Dylan noted with satisfaction that all three came to rest in a grouping no larger than a standard parking space.

Swinging it well today.

He smiled. Maybe things were looking up. The morning had started with news of the discovery of Shadow's body. This could complicate things for Dylan's organization, but he knew it was inevitable.

We knew it was only a matter of time. We assumed it would happen. Maybe not this soon, but we can navigate through this.

They'd done it before. Dylan absentmindedly used the toe of his 8 iron to pull another range ball from the green basket that lay on its side. Balls spilled from it, giving it the look of a horn of plenty, a cornucopia. He did a quick tally and noted that this was the eighth murder they'd committed since launching their enterprise.

My fourth...two for Min...one each for Dax and Willie.

Dylan lined up his shot. His swing was fluid. The ball came off the clubface exactly as the previous three. He watched it settle in the center of the group. Hitting golf balls helped him focus. He needed to take advantage of this quick session to assess the situation before his next meeting.

Dax and Willie are in a hotel outside of Dayton. They would've been up late last night, putting eyeballs on some of the street dealers that work the area. I need to message them...let them know Shadow's body has been found.

Dylan made another perfect swing with his 8 iron and held his follow through, watching the flight of the ball.

I need to stay out of Urbana. Min too. We won't go any closer to the town than the rental house. It should be safe for Dax and Willie to go back—if they're careful—and meet with Shadow's people...let them know we're their new source. A couple of them already had it figured out before I took care of their boss.

A pair of senior golfers approached, carrying their own baskets. Like Dylan, they wanted to take advantage of the range, which, as long as you fed tokens into the ball dispenser, was open from dawn to dusk. They stopped to watch Dylan hit a couple balls. One made a comment.

"Nice swing, young man."

Dylan turned to the pair, nodded, and winked. They moved on, found a spot to set up, and began stretching.

Next up, the Shortridge brothers.

Dylan pulled his phone from the pocket of his Lululemon golf shorts and checked the time. It was 6:55.

Just enough time to finish this basket and get back to the coffee shop for the meet.

Dylan stepped back to his golf bag. It was made of fine white leather. The Running Dog logo, in fire engine red, was visible on the front and two sides. Officially he was the company's Managing Director of North American Business Development, though hitting golf balls was the closest he came to expanding Running Dog's legitimate product line.

He wiped the clubface of the 8 iron with a towel—also bearing the logo—that hung from one side of the bag. He then returned the club to its proper slot before selecting his driver. Removing the head cover, he smiled.

Those old guys are about to see some SHIT!

He unzipped another pocket, this one near the top of the bag, and reached in to retrieve some tees. His hand first encountered the dimpled surface of a golf ball, reminding Dylan that he'd stashed it there after prying it from Shadow's hand two nights earlier. His fingers pushed past the ball and grabbed a few tees.

The driver was a Titleist GT3. It represented decades of technological advances in engineering and materials. It had cost Dylan nearly $900, but, in his opinion, was worth every penny. When it came to golf, money was no object. Dylan spent for quality. Quality equipment, quality experiences.

He'd played over a dozen of the top 100 courses as ranked by Golf Digest. He'd even played numbers four and ten in China. Both—Shenzhen and Mission Hills—were in Guangdong Province, which also happened to be the base of operations for Running Dog.

His favorite, he supposed, was Pebble Beach, the iconic venue on the California coast.

Great vistas. Epic ocean views.

He frowned slightly remembering the two strokes he lost there with a double bogey on number 10. He shot 74 for the day and would've finished with an even par 72 without that hiccup. He'd overcompensated with his tee shot, trying to stay away from the beach on the right that ran along that entire side of the hole leading to Carmel Bay, and landed in a bunker on the left side of the fairway. It still bothered him.

Dylan took a moment to remove his black Cutter & Buck windproof vest. The temperature had reached 75 degrees and the swings he'd taken with his iron had generated just the slightest bit of perspiration. He popped the collar of his flamingo pink polo, making it stand up straight. The shirt was made by a Charlottesville, Virginia company called Rhoback. Dylan supposed it might seem a bit preppy for Ohio, but...

Fuck em.

He tucked a loose fold of the shirt into his belt and was faintly annoyed that he'd begun to develop a slight paunch that stretched the fabric.

Five foot ten...pushing two hundred pounds. Only twenty-six years old. Gotta get a handle on that.

Dylan stepped back to his position on the practice area, bent to put a tee in the ground, and placed a range ball on top. He stood, pushed his black hair from his eyes, and took a practice swing. In his periphery he noted that the two seniors had stopped stretching and were watching him. Dylan addressed the ball before delivering a buttery-smooth swing to it. It flew well beyond the 250-yard marker, straight down the middle. He turned to the older men and winked again. One of the men nodded knowingly before they both turned away to take swings of their own.

The Shortridge brothers...Garrett and Gerard. Garrett has the brains, Gerard has the...what? He certainly can't contribute much to the operation when it comes to developing their business model or hiding profits. I guess he could be a bit of an enforcer if necessary. He DOES come across as a bully. Min definitely got that vibe.

Dylan smiled, remembering Min bristling after their first face-to-face meeting with the brothers the previous week. It had taken place at the same coffee shop that they would utilize this morning, Winans. The four men took a table and exchanged handshakes. Gerard held Min's hand a beat too long and, grinning, said, "I woulda bet all the tea in China that you Ivy League boys woulda been regular white guys. I guess you're the one called Min?" His pronunciation rhymed with tin.

Dylan interjected, "It's pronounced *Mean...Mean Shee-aan.*"

Gerard's grin widened as he looked fixedly at Min.

"You don't look so *mean.*"

Min Xian's face had remained impassive. Dylan, however, knew his partner well and sensed a rage building in the man.

Garrett broke in.

"Cool it Gerard."

He turned to Dylan and Min.

"Let's talk business."

The meeting didn't go particularly well. The Shortridges flatly turned down the first proposal that Dylan put forward. The four agreed to a second meeting. Dylan had become quite adept at reading people in these situations. He'd reconsidered his offer and, since the first meet, had decided to lower his asking price to twenty percent. But he wasn't confident that the brothers would accept.

They didn't realize that they really did not have a choice. The Shortridge enterprise would not continue to operate in its current form. They would agree to Dylan's offer or they would experience a hostile takeover.

We'll roll over them.

Dylan began to shape shots with his driver, alternating between hitting draws—ball flights that moved slightly to the left—and fades—flights that moved to the right. He noted with satisfaction that only low handicap players like him could do this. Lesser players sprayed shots with similar paths.

But not on purpose.

Dylan hit the last of the balls before securing his driver. *I hit it well today. Still...could use a bit more draw.*

The driver could be easily modified to change the loft and angle of the head with the use of a small tool called the SureFit torque wrench. Dylan made a mental note to tinker with the club's setup when he had time. He checked his phone.

Fifteen minutes before the meet. Perfect.

Min, who had spent the night in Columbus with a woman, would join him.

Dylan shouldered the bag and made his way toward the Range Rover, stopping for a few seconds to watch one of the seniors hit the top of a range ball with his 3 wood. The ball skittered 50 feet and came to rest.

Dylan smirked and walked away without a word. The senior noted the smirk out of the corner of his eye and turned to his partner.

"Cocky SOB, ain't he?"

Dylan settled behind the wheel of his SUV. He wanted to make sure that the entire leadership group was aware of Shadow's discovery. He opened the email application on his phone. He and his colleagues used a simple but effective method of communicating important information. They'd set up an email address with a mutually agreed upon password that all of them possessed. When they wanted to communicate, they could compose an email and save it to the drafts folder. The other password holders could simply log in and read the draft. After each subsequent user read the message, they would add a code word—Dylan's was Eli—with the last reader deleting the draft. Because the draft was never sent, there was no electronic trail to be traced and retrieved.

Dylan took a sip of his coffee.

Perfect...just a little over room temperature.

He was odd, he supposed. He didn't want his coffee too hot, and he sure as hell didn't want iced coffee—the other extreme. He almost always let his cup sit for several minutes before enjoying it. Once he started, he drank it fast. He calculated that he would need a refill by the time he arrived back at Winans to meet the Shortridges and Min.

Min Xian took the State Route 36 exit ramp off of I-75. His Evoque was an exact clone of Dylan's, both in Eiger Grey. Min hadn't heard the word Eiger before being presented with the vehicle and had to search online. It referred to a mountain in Switzerland. Apparently, the American actor Clint Eastwood had starred in a movie in which it was featured. Min allowed a hint of a smile to cross his lips.

There's a man that takes care of business.

After Shadow had been dealt with, Min told Dylan he'd like to make the drive to Columbus on Sunday. He wanted to check out the bar scene around the campus of The Ohio State University.

Dylan had smiled, knowing the effect a good-looking man with an international background and a wad of cash would have on coeds ten years his junior.

"No problem. Just as long as you're back in time for the meet in Piqua Monday morning."

Min came to a stop at the top of the ramp. He made a right turn on red. His thoughts drifted to the previous night, spent in the apartment of an International Studies major. She was a former high school cheerleader who told Min she'd once visited Hong Kong. She was obviously attracted to him and wasted no time inviting him to come home with her.

Those campus bars aren't exactly KTVs—the widely accepted term in China for karaoke bars masquerading as brothels—*but they serve the same purpose.*

Min made a left and signaled to make the turn into the coffee shop parking lot. Dylan was there, standing next to his Evoque. The smirk on his face told Min that Dylan knew exactly how things had gone in Columbus.

Min returned the smirk.

CHAPTER THREE

At that moment, some 500 miles to the east, four men piled into a Dodge Ram 1500. The truck had rear seating and accommodated the men easily. It had been a workhorse for its owner, Mike McClary, having pulled his camper—dubbed the Bourbon Trail'r—to over twenty states in the continental United States.

This morning found the truck at the Capitol KOA campground in Anne Arundel County, Maryland. The campground was more or less centrally located between Baltimore—some twenty minutes north—and Washington D.C., a few minutes more than that to the southwest. This made it perfectly situated for activities the men had planned for the trip.

On Saturday morning they'd visited the Fort McHenry National Monument and Historical Shrine on Baltimore's south side. Next, they drove several blocks north to a large urban cemetery, Green Mount. They then found a watering hole—Pickle's Bar—across the street from Oriole Park at Camden Yards and downed several adult beverages before making the short walk to the ballpark to watch the Orioles host the New York Yankees.

They returned to the KOA after the game, enjoyed a campfire, cigars, and a nightcap, then turned in.

They began their Sunday with sausage, eggs, and coffee at the site then drove 15 miles southeast to Annapolis. They visited the historic sites, toured the United States Naval Academy, and ate fresh seafood a stone's throw from Annapolis Harbor at the Federal House Bar & Grille. They then drove back up to Baltimore to catch another Orioles-Yankees game.

Guys, doing guy things.

This day, Monday, promised to be just as enjoyable. The Washington Nationals were hosting the New York Mets in the last of a four game wraparound series. That is, a series that starts on a Friday, extends through the weekend, and concludes on a Monday, generally a travel day in Major League Baseball. First pitch would be at 12:05, which would allow for an early departure for both teams afterward. Each would be playing road games the following day.

McClary started the truck and wove his way through the campground. He stood six feet four and was still solid despite nearing retirement age. A former minor league pitcher, Mike often had insights to the game that eluded his colleagues.

"We might see some runs scored today, guys. I never liked early starts like this when I was playing. It throws off your internal clock...makes it hard for a pitcher to get loose on time."

The rider in the front passenger seat, Paul Hull, looked up from his phone with a bit of a frown.

"Just what we need. We're starting a rookie on the mound. We'll need all the help we can get."

Paul was 51 and, like Mike, was a New York Mets fan. Both men grew up north of New York City. It wasn't until decades later, though, that they met—unsurprisingly at a baseball game. The odds were long, however, that the game would be in Dayton, Ohio. They, and their wives, were sitting a row apart at the Dayton Dragons minor league stadium. They struck up a conversation and began a friendship that night that would last the remainder of their lives.

A deep voice rose from behind Paul. "Don't start that *we* B.S. I don't think you'll be suiting up for the Mets today, Sticks."

The voice came from Gatewood "Woody" Dowdell.

A few years older than Paul and, at six foot one, an inch taller, Gatewood differed from the younger man in several ways. Gatewood was a black man; Paul was white. Gatewood was active duty military, while Paul was retired. And Woody had a prosthetic lower leg—his left—while Paul did not.

This last difference had nearly been negated when Paul sustained a badly injured right leg in a parachute training accident. The leg was saved but it ended his military career.

And what a career.

Paul was the recipient of four Bronze Stars with the "V" device for valor. They constituted the top decorations on the chest rack of ribbons hanging in the closet of his home in Troy, Ohio. The chest rack was eight rows deep and represented more awards than he'd cared to count. Paul had been an Air Force Combat Controller, a key component of the United States Joint Special Operations Command. Referred to as CCT, Combat Controllers specialized in coordinating and directing combat aircraft. They were also highly capable warriors on the ground. They were typically assigned in small numbers to forward units of the Army, Navy, and Marine Corps. CCT referred to these as their "customer units."

Paul earned the right to call himself a CCT after graduating from the grueling two-year training program known as "The Pipeline." One of his instructors during that period had been Gatewood, a fellow CCT who was also highly decorated. Both men had reached the apex of Air Force Special Operations. That is, they'd been selected to become part of the 24th Special Tactics Squadron. "The Two-Four," as it was known, assigned individuals or small teams of CCTs to the nation's Tier One units, such as the Navy's SEAL Team Six and the Army's Delta Force, creating extremely capable—and deadly—entities.

Gatewood had similarly impressive awards in his service file. Though his days as a Combat Controller were effectively ended by the IED explosion in Iraq that cost him his lower leg, he remained in the Air Force and was now the senior enlisted member of the unit responsible for security at Wright-Patterson Air Force Base just outside Dayton.

The fourth man in the truck piped up. "Woody, I always wondered, why the hell do you call my man Paul 'Sticks?'"

The question came from Sebastian Tzortzakakis, a former Army Ranger first sergeant who had served with both Paul and Gatewood. Tzortzakakis, now a civilian, looked as if he could still pass as active duty. His black t-shirt, accentuated by the word *RANGER* across the chest, clung to a muscular upper body. The left sleeve of his shirt barely covered a tattoo of the same word. His dark hair was cut short, though perhaps not to Army Grooming Standard AR 670-1. At five feet, ten inches Tzortzakakis still managed to appear imposing.

Dowdell assumed a mock tone of condescension.

"To bring you up to speed, First Sergeant, the designation 'Sticks' was pinned on former Master Sergeant Hull because when he prints his last name the 'L's come out looking like hockey sticks, see? That, and the fact that he has the same last name as a couple old time hockey stars."

Gatewood cocked his head at the retired Ranger.

"Anyway, why would a well-known Pogue such as yourself be so concerned about someone else's nickname? Don't you have enough on your own plate?"

"Pogue" was derogatory military slang for a soldier that stayed on base, never venturing to the front lines and seeing combat.

The comment drew a volley of laughter from everyone in the truck, including Tzortzakakis. There were two reasons for this. First, the former Ranger was the furthest thing from a rear echelon member of the military. Like Paul and Gatewood, he was highly decorated, having had a reputation in the special operations community as a hard charger.

Secondly, his last name had been the basis for an endless stream of jokes since his first day of boot camp.

Paul turned in his seat.

"I like 'Eye Chart,' it has a nice ring to it.

Gatewood shook his head.

"No, Sticks, the best one is 'Scrabble.' Do you realize that his last name is worth 38 points?"

McClary, despite having just met Tzortzakakis two days earlier when they'd picked up the former Ranger from Baltimore/Washington International Airport, offered a comment.

"And that's not even with a double or triple word score!"

"Scrabble" held up his hands in surrender.

"Okay, okay. I guess I went down a road I should've avoided. I get it. My last name might not be so strange in Greece, but here..."

They were on US-50 now, nearing the halfway point of the drive to the stadium. The volume of vehicles picked up as ballgame traffic was added to the normal morning rush hour.

After leaving the Army, Scrabble, his wife, and two kids had settled just outside of Savannah, Georgia. He'd stayed in touch with Paul and Gatewood, who had invited him to join them and Mike for several days of camping. The trip was planned to coincide with home games by the Orioles and the Nationals. Scrabble accepted the invitation and flew into BWI. The timing was perfect. The other three men were able to make the drive from Ohio pulling the trailer and set up at the KOA before heading to the airport.

Scrabble served 20 years in the Army before getting out nearly four years ago. After boot camp he spent some time with the 4th Infantry Division at Fort Carson, Colorado, deploying with them to Afghanistan. After getting a taste of combat, he volunteered for the Ranger Assessment and Selection Program, then completed Ranger School, one of the toughest tests in the Army. He was assigned to the 1st Battalion of the fabled 75th Ranger Regiment, based at Hunter Army Airfield just south of downtown Savannah.

The Rangers were considered an elite light infantry force specializing in a number of tasks. These include direct action raids and airfield seizures. During the War on Terror they became adept at supporting units such as Navy SEALs and Delta Force in operations to kill or capture high-value targets. It was in this capacity that he came to know Gatewood and Paul.

Tzortzakakis developed a reputation as an extremely effective Ranger. He seemed to have a sixth sense in the field. He often noticed things on missions that no other member of his platoon picked up—and these were some of the best infantrymen on the planet. His battalion commander paid him a supreme compliment after Scrabble sniffed out an enemy ambush one dark night in Afghanistan's Zabul Province.

"First Sergeant Scrabble, you would've made a damn fine Indian scout in the Old West."

This comment was slightly ironic, seeing as how Scrabble was a lifelong bow hunter, had his wife ship a compound bow and several dozen arrows to him while on the deployment, and had jokingly asked to carry the weapon on missions.

At least his buddies *thought* he'd been joking.

Since leaving the Army, Scrabble had become a fixture at archery competitions. Just last year he'd finished third in the North American Field Archery Championships in Clarkston, Michigan.

Scrabble decided to change the subject.

"Alright Paul, how the hell did you come across the location of John Wilkes Booth's grave? I googled it last night and you had more information than the entire internet."

The trip to Green Mount Cemetery on Saturday was Paul's idea. He had a quirky hobby. He liked to visit interesting graves. They were generally the final resting places of historical figures, often military men. Sometimes these visits resulted in a bit more than Paul bargained for. Sitting around a campfire at the KOA Saturday night, Scrabble listened intently while Gatewood and McClary described incidents over the previous two years relating to Paul and cemeteries. Paul—staring thoughtfully into the fire—had allowed his friends to carry the conversation. The stories involved murder, kidnapping, the graves of the Wright brothers, and a World War Two hero named Alex Drabik. If these tales had come from another source, Scrabble may have dismissed them. But Woody and Mike had been serious.

Paul now turned to Scrabble and explained. "I came across the information in an old Civil War magazine that focused on the final days of Abraham Lincoln. It detailed the assassination, Booth's escape, his capture, and his execution. At the end of the article there was a description of the burial site." Paul continued, "The Booth family had a plot in Green Mount. They secretly buried the assassin and put an unmarked stone above the burial site. That's the site we found Saturday."

Gatewood grinned, "And the site that family was checking out when we got there."

All four men chuckled, remembering the couple with two young children that had been at the plot when the men arrived. The father and his son—who looked to be four or five years old—were standing above Booth's grave. They appeared to be relieving themselves. Mom stood off to the side with an older daughter and captured the scene with her cellphone camera.

"Yeah," said Paul, "that was classic."

The men were in a good mood. They would visit Arlington National Cemetery the following day to pay their respects to fallen comrades in Section 60. This promised to be somber. For now, though, they would enjoy the day.

The foursome was now inside the I-495 beltway and traffic had grown more congested. Brake lights appeared in front of them more than once, occasionally slowing them to a crawl.

McClary, losing patience with the pace, tilted his head to the right and asserted, "I've done this drive in traffic before. There's a short-cut coming up. We can get off at the exit for RFK Stadium and cut southwest on surface streets."

"You're the boss." Paul realized that his comment could be taken quite literally. Mike McClary—and his wife, Marge—were, in fact, his bosses. They owned and operated a business called Jasper Spirit Consulting. They'd talked Paul into coming on board with them the previous year. Paul had been pleasantly surprised that he'd taken to the job. It was, he supposed, a good thing. He suspected his wife, Lauren, was growing concerned with his lack of purpose after leaving the military. He conceded that she was probably right to be troubled.

Mike signaled and moved toward an exit ramp. Traffic was light for several blocks before increasing as they progressed toward Nationals Park. Twice they were forced to wait through two complete cycles of a stoplight before passing through the intersections. The truck was in the left lane of C Street NE, a two-lane, one-way street, waiting to turn left.

Scrabble had just commented—"Good to get this trip in before next week...big tropical storm brewing in the Atlantic"—when a car flashed past them on the right. It was quickly followed by several more. The first vehicle—a black ten-year-old Mercedes with chrome spinners—reached the lead car in the left lane and swung in front of it, blocking its path.

Charlie Braddock sat in his Ford Thunderbird waiting for the red light to change. His T-Bird was the 2005 model, the last year the iconic vehicle was manufactured. It was a convertible painted torch red. When parking in the city, as he would do today, Charlie drove it with the optional hardtop. He liked to get to the ballpark early. Especially when accompanied by his best buddy. That, of course, was his seven-year-old grandson, Baker. The boy had blonde hair that always looked as if it had been mussed by an adult family member—sometimes it had—bright eyes, and a love for sports.

Charlie, now 71, had spent a lifetime following local professional sports teams. As a kid in Severn, Maryland he lived and died with the Baltimore Colts and Orioles. Third baseman Brooks Robinson was his favorite athlete. Charlie had met the man at the old All-Star Chevrolet dealership in Elkridge and was gratified to confirm what he'd suspected.

Brooksie was a damn fine human being.

Brooks was gone now. Hell, the car dealership was gone. But Charlie would do all he could in the time he had left to encourage his grandson's love of sports. It was in the boy's blood. Wasn't his middle name, Charles, after his grandpa?

Grandpa Charlie was now retired, still living in Severn. Whenever possible he would drive down to his daughter and son-in-law's place in Greenbelt, just northeast of the capital city, and take his grandson to a Nats game. He hadn't been able to turn the boy into an O's fan, but a ballgame was a ballgame. He generally picked up Baker early enough to enter the ballpark and watch batting practice. They found a souvenir stand outside the park that sold plastic batting helmets. Charlie bought the helmet of a different team for his grandson each time they visited. Baker hoped to collect one for every team. With today's game having an early start Charlie knew that both teams would skip batting practice. He knew of a nice little breakfast joint a few blocks north of the park. He and Baker would load up on pancakes then head to the game.

"So, what helmet are you gonna get today?"

Baker looked at his grandpa, deliberated for a beat, and responded.

"Well, I have the whole National League East. I think I'll start on another division, one in the American League. Prob'ly the West. Mmmm, maybe the Astros or Rangers or Angels."

Charlie smiled at his grandson, no longer astounded at his ability to accumulate and categorize sports facts. He caught movement to his right and shifted his gaze. A dark car, a Mercedes, quickly drew alongside before cutting in front of the Thunderbird and jamming its brakes. Charlie realized that a black mask was pulled down over the face of the driver. The front of the mask bore the image of a white skull. He quickly determined that the other three occupants of the vehicle were wearing the same mask. The rider in the front passenger side, apparently a female, was hanging out of the car. Her legs were inside the vehicle while her elbows were braced on top of the roof. She held a cellphone in her right hand and moved it back and forth, capturing the scene as more vehicles edged past the Mercedes. Every person appeared to be wearing a similar skull mask.

Charlie's heart rate spiked. He realized he could not pull forward and he was blocked from behind by a long row of traffic. A fleeting thought went through his head. A story in the Baltimore Sun weeks earlier mentioned that this group—he assumed it was this group—was randomly barging through congested areas of both Baltimore and Washington D.C. They were composed of teens and young adults. So far as anyone could tell, the group had no political statement to make, wasn't protesting anything, and was just snarling traffic as a form of entertainment. They were disrupting to disrupt.

They were just assholes.

Charlie saw Baker turn to the Mercedes. A look of alarm immediately appeared in the boy's eyes. As the protective instinct kicked in, he reached across his grandson's body and pushed down the passenger door lock.

Gotta keep Baker safe...get him away from these assholes.

Charlie's eyes flicked to the left. He tried to calculate whether there was a way to maneuver around the Mercedes and escape. He eyed the rearview mirror to see if there was any room to back up. There was a subcompact car a few feet behind the T-Bird. Charlie saw a larger grey pickup truck looming behind the car. He knew there would be several more vehicles in line behind the truck.

Maybe if I throw it in reverse, cut the wheel and back a foot or two, I can get enough of an angle to swing past the Mercedes and go up over the curb...get around it.

"Hold on Baker!" The boy, he realized, was paralyzed with fear as he gaped at the skull masks.

Charlie swung the steering wheel to the right before easing the Thunderbird backward slightly. He cranked the wheel back left with a quick hand-over-hand motion and eased his foot off the brake pedal. The T-Bird moved barely a foot before Charlie realized he wouldn't safely clear the blocking vehicle. The front headlight of Charlie's car was now just inches from the front left quarter panel of the Mercedes.

Not only had the attempt to escape been unsuccessful, Charlie realized it had attracted the attention of the occupants of the Mercedes. He saw the driver turn to the back seat and say something, the lower part of his mask stretching grotesquely as his jaw rose and fell. The individual riding behind the driver threw open his door.

Oh shit!

Once the rider stepped from the Mercedes, Charlie saw that it was a large male. He was several inches over six feet, wide at the shoulders, wider around the midsection. The man wore a long sleeve shirt and, Charlie realized, tight black gloves that also exhibited the white bones of a skeleton. Instantly Charlie realized that everyone in the Mercedes was dressed the same way, as were the occupants of the cars—mostly beaters—that had rushed past the Mercedes into the intersection and blocked the other lanes of traffic.

The figure leaned toward the passenger window and screamed, "Stay the fuck back from our ride!" He loomed over the window before leaning in toward Baker. The mask seemed to leer at the boy. Baker cringed.

Sonofabitch. Charlie put the Thunderbird in park and threw open his door. "Stay the hell away from that boy and get that car out of my way...what the hell is *wrong* with you people?"

Charlie's reaction did not have the desired effect. He watched as the other rear door, and then the driver's door opened. The female with the cellphone remained sitting on her door and began panning back and forth. Charlie realized with growing alarm that all of the cars that had arrived with the Mercedes had stopped. Doors opened on these vehicles and skull-masked occupants emerged.

It's like a goddamned bad movie.

Paul and his companions watched from two vehicles behind the Thunderbird. He saw masked figures emerge and press toward it. An older man had stepped from the T-Bird and was gesturing for the offenders to move. His words weren't discernible, but his intent was—a young boy was just visible in the passenger side of the car.

He's trying to keep the boy safe.

Paul decided to act. He reached for the door handle. Before he could push it open, he heard both rear doors of the truck slam shut. Gatewood and Scrabble, having had the same thought, had exited the rear seats. As Paul jumped out, he perceived McClary's door opening as well.

Gatewood turned toward Mike.

"Stay in the truck. You'll have to move through when we clear this up."

Gatewood, Tzortzakakis, and Paul strode forward toward the head of the column. The skull-masked female in the Mercedes swung her phone toward them, as did a similarly dressed rider in a worn-out Nissan Versa beside it.

The men walked on.

Charlie felt the press of bodies closing around his car. He noted that there seemed to be a few cellphones poking above them from behind.

They're filming this? What the hell is wrong with these people?

There was movement to his right.

More of them?

He shot a look toward Baker then turned to the newcomers. Three men moved toward the Mercedes. Though they were not dressed as skeletons their faces, Charlie realized, were just as striking.

Charlie allowed just a trace of a smile to form on his face.

Gatewood, his prosthetic leg clearly visible, came to a stop a few feet from the men who had spilled from the Mercedes. Tzortzakakis was to Woody's left, the left side of his body nearly touching the Thunderbird. Paul, on the other side, turned slightly to the right to face the riders of the trailing cars that were approaching from that direction.

Gatewood held his hands at chest level, palms out.

"Whoa, whoa, whoa...you don't want to do this, son. Let's everybody back away and go on about our day."

The driver of the Mercedes, standing slightly to the rear of his larger running mate, turned to the three newcomers and stared. He didn't appear to be irritated with the men's arrival, just slightly befuddled. He and his crew had been joyriding for weeks, having their way, unchallenged by other drivers or, for that matter, even the police.

The large man from the back seat had a different reaction. He faced the three party crashers and narrowed his eyes.

"I'm not your fucking son, old man." Eyeing Gatewood's prosthesis he continued. "You better get your gimp ass outta here. And take your boys with you."

After a beat, Scrabble spoke. "He's right, Woody. A better term for this guy would probably be 'delinquent.'" He squared his body to the larger man, slightly tensing his upper body. "What do you say, big guy, want to upgrade to 'victim?'"

A few seconds passed as all parties considered their next move. Through his mask the big man's brow appeared to furrow. The cellphones, their unsaid purpose to record the group's disregard for the rules of society, continued to film. The resulting video would no doubt be posted online.

Scrabble doubled down.

"It'd be a damn shame to have to post video of the day you got your ass kicked by three old guys." He smiled.

The big man, taken aback, turned quickly to the leader, who was assessing the situation, seeming to calculate possible outcomes. He looked at the three challengers, first eyeing the man on his left before sweeping across to the man on the right. His gaze stopped on this man's t-shirt. One of the trio had an artificial leg, sure, but all three had the look of hard men who were confident in their capabilities. There was a steely look on their faces. The leader came to a quick decision.

"Let's roll."

He turned to the surrounding riders and twirled an index finger in the air. "Saddle up, let's roll!"

The surrounding riders turned to each other in confusion. The big man was incredulous.

"What?!? There's only three of them!"

The man in the RANGER shirt looked him dead in the eye and spoke.

"You're outgunned, partner."

As the riders returned to their vehicles and began to clear the intersection, Charlie Braddock slid back behind the wheel of the Thunderbird. His grandson, who had a front row view of the altercation looked over with a question.

"That man outside my window was wearing a shirt that said 'RANGER.' I've checked out the logos for all the Major League Baseball teams. That one didn't look like the one on the Texas Rangers' jerseys...and it didn't have an 'S' on the end." He stared at Charlie quizzically.

Charlie grinned. "I'm pretty sure that man was on a different Ranger team."

CHAPTER FOUR

Dylan held out his fist as Min, in a tight-fitting plain black t-shirt and black jeans, approached the front door of the coffee shop. Min smiled and bumped knuckles.

Dylan commented, "You look refreshed, Min. I trust everything went as planned in Columbus?"

His colleague nodded once. "Very successful. I'm back and...how do you say? Bright-eyed and bushy-tailed."

Dylan tilted his head. "Well *I* sure as hell don't say things like that. Sounds more like something our prospective partners might say." His eyes slid from Min's and focused on the driveway in front of Winans. "Here comes the dynamic duo now."

A black Lexus LX sport utility vehicle eased onto the property. It rolled past the two Range Rovers and tucked into a space a few spots from the front corner of the lot.

Dylan and Min watched as two men emerged from the front doors. The driver, Garrett, was dressed in blue jeans and a short-sleeved button-down denim shirt. His brother Gerard wore cargo shorts and a t-shirt with the sleeves cut off. When they recognized Dylan and Min at the entrance Gerard leaned into his brother and whispered a comment. Both brothers laughed. Dylan was certain that one of the words the man spoke was *Chinaman*.

Dylan felt a tug on his sleeve and turned to Min.

"If we have to kill these two, I get the fat man."

Dylan nodded to his partner and turned to the approaching Shortridge brothers. "Welcome gentlemen, glad you could make it."

Gerard spoke. "Hey, check this out." He pointed to the image on the front of his shirt. It showed Auguste Rodin's *The Thinker* sitting on a commode. Underneath was the phrase *Process of Elimination*.

"You get it?" He looked at them expectantly.

Dylan nodded and forced a smile. Min remained expressionless. Dylan held the door and allowed the brothers to pass. Min followed. He hesitated as he brushed past his partner, turned to him, and narrowed his eyes to a menacing glare. Dylan stifled a laugh.

The four men entered Winans and got in line. The shop was busier than earlier in the morning when Dylan had stopped. A number of cars were in the drive-thru as customers queued for their morning caffeine fix. Phoebe, the barista that waited on Dylan earlier, was now taking care of customers in the drive-thru line. A pretty middle-aged woman with dark, curly hair handled the walk-in business. Dylan approached and duplicated his order from an hour before, adding a scone. He looked at the woman's name tag and was initially confused. It read "Cledith, Manager."

Dylan shrugged. *Hmmm, never heard that name before.*

He gave her a name for the order—Eli—removed some bills from his wallet, and motioned to the three men behind him.

"I got all three of these guys."

Cledith nodded and took their orders.

The foursome spotted a table in a corner of the shop and drifted over, each carrying a scone or muffin. They made small talk until their drinks were ready to be picked up, then returned with them to the table. Settled in, Garrett got down to business.

"So, we are definitely interested in sourcing from you. If your access to the product is what you say, we can move it for you...at least a good bit of it. But the numbers you talk about, well, they just don't cut the pie."

Garrett had the body of a working man. He stood a shade under six feet, two inches and weighed 220 pounds. He had strawberry blonde hair, cut short, and a ruddy complexion. The specific shade of his greenish eyes was often described by acquaintances with words such as olive, moss, or sage. They shone with intelligence.

36

Dylan nodded as if in sympathy with Shortridge. He removed the plastic lid from his latte to let it cool. The cup had a maroon sleeve around its midsection bearing the Winans logo. Dylan began to spin it slowly around the cup.

"We understand that—"

He was cut off by Gerard who, an inch taller and 30 pounds heavier than his brother, leaned forward to emphasize his point. His hair was the same shade as Garrett's, but longish. A strand fell in front of his eyes as he bent toward Dylan. Eyes, both Dylan and Min would wager, that had never been described as intelligent.

"I don't think you *do* understand. *We* have the distribution network here. *We* own our own pill presses and can convert the raw product. Hell, *we* even have a source inside the Miami County Sheriff's Office letting us know when their people start sniffing around."

Both Dylan and Min saw Garrett wince when his brother mentioned the source in the sheriff's office. They were sure that was something Garrett would've liked to keep secret.

Gerard continued, "We've been supplying the area with high speed chicken feed for six years and you two dandies waltz in and ask for twenty percent of our profits? Just because you *say* you can furnish an unlimited supply of the stuff. I'd say your terms are pretty re-goddamned-diculous." He leaned back, pleased with himself.

Min sipped his cappuccino and silently studied Gerard, as if trying to determine where to place a bullet. Dylan took a deep breath, forced a smile, and tried again.

"Twenty percent is very reasonable. With the increase in sales volume you will see, your earnings will jump significantly. The nature of the opioid-dependent condition drives the user to reliable sources. The crisis isn't going away. Your business will grow, as will," he paused to look each brother in the eyes, "your profits."

Gerard frowned and began to speak. Garrett raised a finger. It was clear that he was in charge of the Shortridge operation, despite his brother's bluster.

"And you," he nodded in the direction of Dylan first, then Min, "will earn profit on the sale of the...product to us in the first place. I'm afraid an additional twenty percent is out of the question." He leaned back slightly before sipping his coffee.

Gerard added, "Damn straight. Asking for twenty percent of *our* money is just," he struggled for words for a beat, then added, "science friction."

Min, who was taking another sip of cappuccino, nearly spit it through his nose. The big man's mispronunciation of "fiction" hung in the air. He glanced at Dylan, who purposefully avoided his gaze.

The four men sat in silence for a few seconds before Garrett filled the void.

"Look, we've talked about this," a thumb poked toward Gerard, "and decided we could do five. But twenty...no way. And we definitely need some proof that you can provide the inventory."

With that, both Min and Dylan knew, the Shortridge brothers had sealed their fate. The brothers were unaware that Dax and Willie had succeeded in putting together a fairly comprehensive assessment of their operation. They knew where the pill presses were located and who operated them. They had identified the dealers who moved the product to customers, at least most of them. Hell, they had even identified the source in the sheriff's department. It hadn't been that hard. Once they were onto the dealers it was just a matter of following them to customers. One transaction even occurred a short distance from the sheriff's office with the buyer returning to the building afterward.

The Shortridge brothers were not relevant to their own operation. They were disposable.

Dylan nodded slowly and assumed a facial expression that he hoped projected understanding. "Your concern about the percentage is justifiable. Min and I will discuss this with our partners and consider a...counterproposal." He turned to his colleague, expecting a nod of agreement. Instead, Min looked unblinkingly at Gerard.

38

Dylan was both amused and annoyed. *For Christ's sake, Min. You might as well just tell these guys we're going to kill them.* He shifted gears, turning to Garrett.

"I suggest we set up a meet where we put our cards on the table. We show you the product. Once you see it, you'll realize we really can handle all your volume...and more. Pick someplace safe, out of the way." Dylan cocked his head to Gerard. "No weapons, of course."

Gerard smiled and leaned in. "Don't you worry your pretty little head." His smile could've been mistaken as a snarl.

Dylan considered. *Jesus, this guy might not've been born...he might've been TRAPPED.*

Garrett added, "We'll be in touch later today. We'll do the meet tonight, tomorrow night at the latest." He opened his cellphone to check the time before taking a long pull on his coffee. "Anybody got anything else?"

Dylan and Min shook their heads. Gerard pointed to Dylan's latte, still untouched with the lid removed. "Ain't you gonna drink that?"

"Too hot for me."

Gerard smirked, pushed his chair back, and made for the door.

Miami County Detective Amos Bunker sat in a nondescript grey Chevy Malibu on the far side of the Winans parking lot sipping coffee. From his vantage point he could just make out the table where the Shortridge brothers and two strangers sat. The brothers had been on the radar of local law enforcement for some time. Whispers had reached both the Miami and Shelby County Sheriff's Departments as well as Piqua and Sidney Police Departments. A fair amount of illegal opioids were being moved in the area and Garrett and his brother Gerard were at the top of the list of suspects.

Bunker was 43 and of average height. His official department physical examination measured him at 5'11" and one-half inches. The Bureau of Motor Vehicles allowed you to provide your own height, however, so Bunker's driver's license showed that he was an even six feet. This was perhaps the only speck of vanity in his entire persona. He had prematurely grey hair, pale blue eyes that missed little, and a predilection for law and order that most viewed as healthy. Some, admittedly, would better describe it as over-the-top. One member of the department staff was fond of saying Bunker is "so square he is divisible by four."

Whenever possible for the past few weeks Bunker had devoted fragments of his time to surveilling one or both of the brothers. This effort had been very hit-and-miss due to the responsibilities of a detective in a small department. Bunker was bounced around the county on a myriad of mostly mundane tasks on a daily basis. Whenever he had a spare hour or two, though, he devoted it to the Shortridges. On this Monday he was free until a 9:30 a.m. meeting at the sheriff's office in downtown Troy. He got an early start at 6:30 and rolled the dice, hoping to catch one of the brothers starting their week. He'd found a seldom used lane a half mile from their farm and pulled in. When a big SUV cruised up their lane Bunker lifted his binoculars and confirmed that both Garrett and Gerard were inside. He put the Malibu in gear.

The Shortridge farm was located on Miami Shelby Road, the dividing line between the two counties. The farm sat on the south side of the road in the Piqua School District. Properties directly across the road were in the Sidney District. Three generations of the Shortridge family had raised corn and soybeans on the property. Two years earlier the sons' father, Grant, died suddenly of a heart attack. Three months later Gwen, their mother, suffered a debilitating stroke. She lasted less than six months in a Sidney nursing home before quietly passing.

Garrett, who lived a mile from the farm and was separated from his wife and three kids, and Gerard, who was single and lived in a Piqua apartment, both moved back to the homestead. They quickly sold most of the land to a farming corporation. They soon attracted attention by throwing around money. They bought cars, trucks, and a $90,000 Yamaha 252XE 24-foot Wake Series boat they kept at Indian Lake, a summer vacation locale some thirty miles northeast of the farm. Rumor had it that they were in negotiations to close on a half-million-dollar house on the same lake.

Bunker had researched the property sale and knew that the boys had done well. He also knew that despite what the Shortridge brothers proclaimed to acquaintances, they hadn't done *that* well. But they had money coming in. Lots of it.

Bunker thought about the opioid problem in the area and the possible role played by the brothers.

Lives ruined. People dying.

He turned to look at the Law Enforcement Fentanyl Response Kit in the go-bag resting on the floor of the back seat. These kits were now required equipment in every department vehicle. The uniformed deputies were the most likely to employ the kits due to the nature of their jobs, but even the handful of detectives on staff had occasion to break them out. Bunker had done so twice. He hoped he would never need to do it again. He realized this was a forlorn hope.

The SUV—it was a Lexus—turned west on Miami Shelby and through his binoculars Bunker was able to tell that Garrett was behind the wheel. He gave the brothers a quarter mile then pulled out and followed. Two miles on, at County Road 25A, the Lexus turned left and headed toward Piqua. There was more traffic as they neared the east side of town, so Bunker closed the gap a bit. He didn't want to tip the Shortridges to the fact that they'd drawn the interest of investigators, but he also didn't want to lose sight of them. He saw them signal and turn right into Winans, a successful local coffee and chocolate shop that had over twenty locations in West Central Ohio.

Bunker slowed as he watched the Lexus ease into a parking spot. By the time he'd reached the turn for the shop, the brothers were out of their vehicle and walking to the front door. He saw Gerard lean into his brother and say something. This was followed by laughter from both of them. Bunker then noticed that two men appeared to be waiting for them in front of the shop.

Damn, should've had my phone ready to take a picture.

41

Bunker pulled into the drive-thru line which was several vehicles long. For once he didn't care. It gave him the perfect position to maintain scrutiny. He quickly picked up his phone and opened the camera app. He snapped a quick picture as the four men entered the shop. Bunker expanded the view on the phone's screen. The Shortridge brothers were passing through the door while the newcomers brought up the rear. They were facing each other. The shot was taken from some forty feet away. As Bunker pinch-zoomed, the sharpness of the image degraded. He concentrated on the trailing men.

The clearest view was of the man on the left. He looked as though he was dressed to tee off at a country club. He wore a pinkish golf shirt with expensive shorts. Bunker guessed him to be 5'10", around 200 pounds, dark-haired, and thirtyish. He had a bit of a spare tire around his midsection.

The second man was shorter, slighter, and had jet black hair. The picture was able to capture just a portion of the side of his face. Bunker studied it closely.

Japanese?

A car horn honked, and Bunker looked up. A gap had formed in front of the Malibu as the line progressed. Bunker gave the car behind him a half wave. Gradually he made it to the order window and requested a large coffee with cream and a shot of caramel flavoring. He surreptitiously peeked through the window to try to locate the men but couldn't see them from this angle. When his order came, he pulled around the building and found a parking spot that gave him a good view of the Lexus and a limited view of the four men at their table inside Winans. He sipped his coffee.

Bunker took note of the other vehicles in the lot. Two of them drew his attention. They were nearly identical Range Rovers. One had Connecticut plates, the other New York. Bunker ran the plates and found that both were registered to something called Running Dog Enterprises.

Well isn't that interesting? What the hell is Running Dog Enterprises?

After less than twenty minutes, the meeting—it certainly had the appearance of a meeting to Bunker—broke up. Garrett and Gerard exited carrying coffee cups and made for the Lexus. The strangers followed and, as Bunker suspected, walked toward the Range Rovers. Bunker eased his phone above the top of his passenger door to take another picture, but the shorter man turned his head in the direction of the Malibu at that instant. Bunker lowered the phone.

No picture, but Bunker had gotten a good look. The man *was* Asian. There were a number of Japanese-owned companies in the area. Honda had a massive engine plant employing nearly 10,000 people—they called them *associates* —north of Sidney, outside of the small town of Anna. There were numerous Japanese-owned satellite companies spread throughout the region that manufactured components for the auto giant. It was not uncommon to see Japanese people in area shops and restaurants.

But not on a Monday morning in casual clothes. They usually wear their white work uniforms.

Bunker watched as the Asian man got in the Range Rover with New York plates and his companion entered the second SUV.

Who to follow?

He'd set out to shadow the Shortridge brothers, but this new pair was intriguing. Bunker decided if the three SUVs went in different directions, he would tail the Range Rovers, or one of them if they split up.

I can always find the brothers. These two might be new players we need to know about.

The Lexus turned left onto Looney Road and headed north, the direction of the Shortridge farm. Both Range Rovers turned right before easing into the left turn lane. This would put them on State Route 36 heading east. Bunker made a mental note to circle back to the coffee shop and talk to the staff to see if they could shed any light on the meeting he'd witnessed. He allowed a car to pass and get between his Malibu and the Range Rovers before pulling out.

The Range Rovers stayed together, leading Bunker out of Piqua and through flat farming country. His thoughts turned again to the drug problem. The opioid of choice seemed to be fentanyl. Unintentional drug overdose deaths had exploded in recent years across the country. A neighboring state, West Virginia, had the highest death rate per 100,000 people. But the Mountain State's 1,500 annual deaths paled in comparison to the 5,000 that occurred each year in Ohio, a more populated state.

Bunker glanced at the dash clock and realized he wouldn't be able to follow the two vehicles for much more than fifteen minutes if he was to make it to the meeting in Troy on time. He considered calling the dispatcher, Millie, and asking her to notify the sheriff that he'd be late but decided against it. The text he'd received Sunday night about the meeting made it clear it was important to attend.

He trailed the Range Rovers for several minutes, passing through a number of villages and the small town of Fletcher. He entered Champaign county just past Lena. He was considering turning back a short time later when the Range Rovers slowed and signaled left turns. A road with lines of residential homes appeared, slightly incongruous, surrounded by farmland. It connected with State Route 36 but went no further. Bunker, using discretion, allowed the SUVs to turn without following. He noted the name on the road sign—Country Road.

He smiled. *Go figure.*

Bunker accelerated to the next farm lane, made a K-turn, and sped back to Country Road. He could just make out the dark grey vehicles in the distance. He followed now but hung back. Two-story homes—some of them fairly expansive—lined both sides of the road. Less than a half mile into the drive there was a small roundabout, unusual since there was no crossroad. It was apparently put there to curtail speeding. Bunker noted that the speed limit was just 35 miles per hour. The Range Rovers continued through the circle and pulled into the driveway of the second house beyond on the left. They disappeared into the garage. Bunker made a note of the address and continued on. Though he'd intended to swing back past the house before heading to Troy, it turned out he had no choice. Country Road ended in a cul-de-sac another quarter mile north of the circle.

Bunker coasted around the cul-de-sac and cruised back past the house. There was no sign of the men. He looked at his watch.

Gotta hightail it to Troy.

He searched his memory for the subject of the meeting.

Something about a murder over the weekend in Urbana.

CHAPTER FIVE

As Paul, Gatewood, and Scrabble returned to McClary's truck, traffic began to flow once again through the intersection. A number of drivers smiled and gave the men thumbs up. Several honked their horns as if to celebrate a victory for the Good Guys.

Mike watched his friends climb back into the truck and cracked, "So, what do you guys call yourselves? I think 'The Avengers' is taken."

The three former special operators chuckled. Woody answered, "Just trying to get to a ballgame on time."

And they did. The Mets, to the satisfaction of Mike and Paul, won a back and forth contest 8-7. The foursome left the ballpark, walked a few steps beyond the left field exit to a bar named Tap99, and allowed the traffic to clear out. It was a self-pour tap house that, as the name suggests, offered 99 types of beer, wine, and cider. Mike, the driver, nursed a beer while his companions sampled a number of the offerings, including several that were locally brewed.

On Tuesday, after a hearty camp breakfast, the men made the trek back toward the capital city. They arrived at Arlington National Cemetery a few minutes after 10 a.m. for what could best be described as an informal gathering of American warriors. Weeks earlier Gatewood answered his phone at Wright-Patt and was delighted to hear the voice of a former helicopter pilot from the Army's 160th Special Operations Aviation Regiment. This unit, known as the Night Stalkers, was the premier helicopter combat unit in the world. They worked exclusively with the country's Tier One combat units, taking on the toughest missions, generally at night. The pilot explained to Woody that he and a few comrades planned to visit Arlington in the near future. They wanted to pay their respects to unit members lost in the Global War on Terror. One of the men had the idea to invite others from the special operations community.

Not surprisingly the idea took off. Many of the former servicemen contacted quickly agreed to join in. The result was a gathering of some of the most accomplished—and often unsung—individuals in the history of the United States military. Some came alone. Many came with friends or family members. There were representatives from every branch of service. They came to pay their respects, to shed tears, and to tell funny stories. Paul, Woody, and Scrabble were reunited with a number of men, and a few women, they hadn't seen in years.

They congregated at Section 60 on the eastern side of the cemetery grounds, the final resting place of nearly 900 service members who perished fighting the war on terror. A significant number of them were special operations personnel.

Tzortzakakis made it a point to find the final resting place of Captain Russell Rippetoe, the first Ranger KIA from Operation Iraqi Freedom to be buried at Arlington. Scrabble hadn't served with him but knew others in the 75th Ranger Regiment that had. Rippetoe was killed 18 kilometers southwest of the Hadithah Dam by an improvised explosive device in April of 2003.

Gatewood was intent on visiting Staff Sergeant Dylan Elchin, a Pennsylvania boy and fellow CCT who made an impression on everyone he met. Elchin was also killed by an IED.

Paul, walking amongst the sobering field of white marble headstones, happened upon the grave of Senior Chief Thomas Valentine. "Tommy V" lost his life in a parachute training accident in Arizona in 2008. Paul remembered him as being one of the standout members of SEAL Team Six. He'd made several combat deployments to Afghanistan in leadership roles before the accident.

Paul read the dates on the headstone: December 28, 1970 to February 13, 2008. Valentine was killed the day before Valentine's Day. Paul shook his head.

I remember him. He was one of the hardened vets everybody looked up to...just 37 years old.

48

Mementos were left on or next to the stones. There were unit insignias and coins on top, poems and photos leaning on the fronts and sides. There was a baseball with a child's writing proudly proclaiming, "This is my first home run ball, Daddy." The stark white of one stone was punctuated by the perfect impression of a kiss in bright red lipstick. There were beer and whiskey bottles left behind by comrades who'd come to share a drink.

It was thought-provoking, smile-inducing, and heartbreaking.

It was that kind of day. Every marker represented a husband, a father, a daughter, a son. They were torn from their family members, many of whom made the trip this day and visited their personal fallen hero.

A few minutes after noon a group coalesced at what was informally known as the "Extortion 17 Row." The June sun was directly overhead in a cloudless sky. Both the temperature and humidity had risen to uncomfortable levels. A dozen or so sets of eyes studied the line of headstones.

Extortion 17 was the call sign of a CH-47D Chinook twin-rotor helicopter that was rushing a Quick Reaction Force to the support of an element from the 75th Ranger Regiment that had requested assistance. They were in Wardak Province, eastern Afghanistan, in the early morning of August 6, 2011. The rocket propelled grenade round that reached up out of the darkness gave the pilot no time to react, it struck one of the rear rotor blades, severing ten feet of it off. The Chinook went into a violent clockwise spin and fell from the sky. The crash killed everyone aboard. This included the crew, several technical specialists, eight Afghan Special Forces, and 17 Navy SEALs, 15 of whom were members of SEAL Team Six's Gold Assault Squadron. In all, 38 personnel and a combat dog were erased from existence.

Most of the SEALs and some of the other casualties were interred in one row here in Section 60. It was a sobering sight. A marker nearby spoke to the violence of the crash.
HERE LIES THE UNIDENTIFIED REMAINS OF EXTORTION 17

49

Paul and his companions stared at the row for a full minute before slowly walking its length.

After nearly three hours the four friends trudged toward the truck. Mike, the only one of the foursome who hadn't served in the military, broke the silence.

"I don't know about you guys... but I could use a drink."

Scrabble wiped his brow and spoke for the rest of the group.

"Roger that."

A woman walking in a group a few feet away overhead them and volunteered a suggestion.

"A few of us are heading over to Alexandria to a nice Irish bar, Murphy's Pub. Great place. Good food. I think some of the other folks"—she motioned toward a few of them streaming toward the parking lot—"are coming too."

Mike tried to inject some levity into the day by adding an exaggerated lilt to his tone.

"An Irish bar you say...hmmm...we McClarys generally steer clear of such places...but if you twist my arm..."

Paul laughed, "Get in the damn truck. Let's find this pub."

Find it they did. Murphy's Grand Irish Pub was located on King Street in Old Town Alexandria, a historic district on the Potomac River waterfront a few short miles southeast of Arlington.

Upon opening the heavy wooden door, the men were greeted with the sight of a long, polished wood bar on the left. Multiple taps were visible with selections such as Guinness Stout, Kilkenny Red, and Harp Lager. A large fireplace was visible deeper into the interior. A good percentage of the wall space as well as the rustic wooden beams on the ceiling were covered with cloth patches. Closer examination revealed they bore the emblems of military, fire, and police units from all over the United States.

McClary stood, seemingly frozen, taking it all in. His father had been the proverbial Irish cop in New York City. A wide grin appeared on his face.

Paul noticed this. He held out his hand to his friend.

"Give me the keys to the truck, I'll drive back to the campsite tonight."

They ate a selection of Irish dishes, including bangers and mash, shepherd's pie, and hearty Irish stew. Enough people from Arlington had made the drive to Murphy's to fill four tables. Conversation and good Irish beer flowed. Toasts were made to honor lives that had been extinguished in their prime.

Woody asked to talk to the manager and promised to send patches from the 24th Special Tactics Squadron as well as the 88th Security Forces Squadron, his current unit at Wright-Patt. Minutes later, a waitress brought a round of drinks to their table with her boss's compliments.

As afternoon turned to evening Mike commented, "What a great place! Reminds me of a couple pubs in New York City. Only thing is...well..."

Paul tilted his head. "Well, what?"

"Well, it's the name. Aren't there already enough Irish pubs out there called 'Murphy's'? I mean, seems like a place like this could have a more distinctive name, something that sets it apart."

Paul ventured a guess. "You mean like McClary's?"

Mike touched his nose with his index finger, pointed at Paul, and winked.

"Time to go, gents." Paul reached for the truck keys in his pocket.

The men began their Wednesday with another camp breakfast. They would be leaving the KOA the next morning so Mike, the primary cook, scrambled the last of the eggs and fried the remaining sausage links. Over coffee they discussed options for the morning. Thanks to a suggestion by the manager of Murphy's the day before, the men planned to visit the National Museum of the Marine Corps south of Washington in the afternoon.

Mike had a Zoom call at 10 a.m. with his wife and business partner, Marge. They would be joined by a client from the Chicago area. Scrabble, scrolling on his phone, hinted

51

that he might be interested in visiting a shop that offered a fair amount of archery supplies.

"It's a half hour east, across the Chesapeake Bay Bridge at a place called Kent Island. Maybe I could get an Uber."

Mike tossed him the keys to the truck. "No sense spending for that. The truck will just sit here all morning."

Scrabble thanked him and turned to the former Combat Controllers. "You guys wanna tag along?"

Woody answered, "Sticks and I are going for a hike. I want to see if he can keep up with a one-legged old man. I'm thinkin' he'll have a rough time."

Paul nodded and stroked his chin. "I'm pretty sure I can carry him back to camp after he crashes and burns."

Gatewood flipped a glob of scrambled eggs at Paul. It hit him on the forehead and stuck for a few seconds. Woody, Scrabble, and Mike roared with laughter.

The morning activities were completed successfully. Scrabble bought some accessories at the outdoor shop. Woody and Paul hiked for an hour and a half and returned to the campsite covered in perspiration. Mike's Zoom call went well but would require a follow up that might involve Paul when they returned to Ohio.

The afternoon was spent in Triangle, Virginia just outside the sprawling Marine Corps base at Quantico. The museum, they agreed, was spectacular. The highlight was seeing the actual flag that was raised on Iwo Jima's Mt. Suribachi and photographed by Associated Press photographer Joe Rosenthal. The shot of six Marines straining to plant and raise the flag was arguably the most famous photo ever taken.

They made a fire on their last night at the campsite. Paul activated a chemlight—a plastic tube filled with chemicals that every former ground soldier seemed to have scrounged from their unit—and held it aloft while Mike configured the wood and paper. After the fire got going Mike broke out a bottle of bourbon and four rocks glasses.

"Gotta have some bourbon on a Bourbon Trail'r trip."

Scrabble eyed the odd-looking bottle. "Is that shaped like a book?"

Mike nodded as he splashed some liquor in each glass and passed them around.

"Sure is, and our boy Paul here had the idea that created it...he's my number one employee at Jasper Spirit Consulting. Well, maybe number two behind Marge."

Scrabble looked at Paul and raised his eyebrows.

Paul shrugged, "Long story." He held out his glass.

"Cheers, gents."

They packed Thursday morning under Mike's watchful eye, taking care of the various steps necessary to secure a trailer for travel. Scrabble had a morning flight out of BWI and would grab breakfast at the airport. Mike, Paul, and Woody would pick up something along the way to eat in the truck.

When they dropped Scrabble at the airport all four men got out of the truck and hugs were exchanged. It had been an enjoyable few days. Woody said, "We gotta do this again."

The guys all nodded, as guys will do at times like this, but they meant it.

The drive to Ohio was not fun. They ran into construction slowdowns and were delayed by two serious accidents. Combined with fuel stops—the truck got barely 10 miles per gallon when pulling the trailer—they would not reach the lot where Mike stored the trailer until nearly 8 p.m. They had intended to then drop Gatewood at his house before heading to the McClary house in Dayton's South Park neighborhood. Paul had left his vehicle—a new Honda Pilot SUV painted modern steel metallic—parked on the street in front of Mike's house. He would have another 30-plus minute drive to make it home from there.

As they neared Dayton, Mike made a suggestion.

"Maybe you should just stay at our place tonight Paul. We'll take Woody home first like we planned. The Chicago distillery would like you on the follow-up Zoom call tomorrow. You could crash in our spare bedroom and we can do the call together."

Paul considered. "No, I want to get back, see Lauren."

Paul dragged himself to his home on Polecat Road, north of Troy, just before 9:30 p.m. Thursday. He was tired but happy to be home. Lauren was on the phone with her mother, who lived in New Mexico. Chappy, their chubby orange cat, greeted him with a where-the-hell-have-you-been look. Paul smiled and scratched Chappy under an ear.

Lauren wrapped up her call and gave Paul a hug and a quick kiss.

Paul asked, "Any news from the agency?"

Lauren, with a touch of melancholy, shook her head. "Not a thing."

Paul made an effort to sound upbeat. "Hey, that's not *bad* news, right? We haven't been turned down. It just means that no decision has been made on our application."

Lauren gave a hesitant smile and changed the subject. "How was the trip?"

Paul recounted the last several days, giving special emphasis to the one spent at Arlington National Cemetery.

Lauren smiled warmly, "Sounds like you guys really enjoyed yourselves."

Paul agreed, "Yep, we had a really good week." Then, "How'd it go here? Did I miss anything?"

Lauren looked thoughtful. "Well, things were busy at work...the guy came to the house to fix the air conditioner Saturday...Oh, I almost forgot. Two men were murdered outside of Piqua. Their bodies were found this morning."

Paul looked at her with a stupefied expression.

CHAPTER SIX

On Tuesday afternoon Min guided his Range Rover north on I-75. He was returning to the rental house outside of Urbana, 40 minutes away. He looked at the small package on the passenger seat and fought an urge to grin. The business he'd just left, Olde English Outfitters, was a wonder. It was a dual-building complex packed with anything and everything the modern American shooting "enthusiast" could ever desire.

Dylan had received a text from Garrett Shortridge that morning. Though the initial contact between the two parties was initiated using personal phones, all subsequent calls and texts were carried out with disposables—"burners"—basic tradecraft in the illegal drug world. Shortridge gave the time for the meet—11 p.m. Wednesday night—and the location.

Min and Dylan brought up the site on Google Earth and were delighted. They could not have picked a better location for what they had in mind. Min spent several minutes examining the overhead view and came to a conclusion. He turned to Dylan.

"I've found the spot, my friend. I will use the rifle. The distance is not great...but it would be helpful to have better"—he searched for the word—"*capabilities* in the dark. I wonder if I can find a proper device in this area?"

He could. A quick search online revealed that Olde English Outfitters, one of the most outstanding gun shops in the Midwest, was less than an hour's drive from the rental house in the small community of Ginghamsburg, south of Troy. Min left immediately.

He stood for a second in wonder upon entering the business. The lines of weapons and aisles stocked with accessories were foreign to nearly all Chinese. He forced himself to push forward into the shop.

Min found the perfect item less than five minutes after entering. A friendly clerk showed him to a case holding an array of optics. Min spotted the small device and asked to examine it more closely. The clerk removed it from the case and handed it to him.

It was a Romeo MSR 1X20MM Red Dot sight. Made by the Swiss firm SIG Sauer, the unit was barely three inches long. Its housing was aircraft grade aluminum. It was battery-operated and boasted ten daytime and two night vision settings. It was intended to be mounted on shotguns, air rifles, or—Min observed with satisfaction—carbines. It cost barely $100 and came with no requirement of buyer identification or registration.

It was perfect.

After making the purchase with cash, Min took a few minutes to browse the store. He'd always had two passions. One, photography, had led to him being awarded the Sanyu Scholarship to Yale, which had been established to support Chinese students of art. The second was guns. This interest was virtually impossible to pursue in China, a country with some of the most restrictive gun laws in the world. Min had always thought it ironic that his native country went to great lengths to keep weapons out of the hands of its citizens while at the same time devoting nearly $500 billion annually to its military.

He'd spent hours watching American action movies, fantasizing about his second interest, weapons. Two months into his studies in New Haven he learned of the Rifle and Pistol Team. He began shooting with them and found to his satisfaction that he had a talent. They shot with intricate-looking small bore .22 caliber rifles, similar to those used in Olympic competition. Min was, he supposed, a rising star in the organization.

Right up until I pointed my rifle at that fucking Beau Tinker...What kind of a name is that anyway? BEAU!

They were part of a group practicing on the 50-foot range, working at their craft and, Min had thought, studiously ignoring each other. He'd found that he was mistaken when, after missing a shot slightly to the right of the bullseye, he heard Tinker laugh. Min's rage flared instantly. Without thinking he swung his weapon toward Tinker and shouted, "You think that's funny? Cao ni ma!"

He'd shouted the "fuck your mother" insult in Mandarin in the heat of the moment. Tinker, Min realized later, didn't understand the words, but the vehemence in which they were spoken conveyed the proper meaning. Tinker froze, his eyes on the barrel of the gun. A .22 caliber bullet was small but if delivered to a critical part of the human anatomy would be deadly. Min and his partners had made this abundantly clear to several opioid dealers in the last two years.

The confrontation lasted just a few seconds. Tinker turned pale and backed away, palms up. Min watched him with satisfaction. Two days later he was summoned to appear before the Yale College Executive Committee. He was not particularly worried. He was the recipient of a coveted scholarship and was a foreign student in a hyper-progressive university. Min believed his status would outweigh any witness statements made against him.

He was wrong.

Min found out the hard way that there were hidden video cameras on the range. He'd lied to the Committee, claiming the witness statements were exaggerated, and was caught red-handed. His desultory academic performance hadn't helped. His time in New Haven was over. Two years later Yale ended the entire shooting program due to anti-gun sentiment by current and former students. Min learned that Tinker was one of the most crestfallen members. This gave him little satisfaction. By then Min was back in China, working on a way to get back to the U.S.

Min walked down a row of long guns that stood vertically in an open display rack. His eyes were drawn to one rifle. It was identical to his own. It was a Patriot P-15 Minuteman, a semi-automatic carbine with a desert-brown ventilated rail that covered most of the barrel. It fired 5.56 millimeter rounds that were significantly larger than the little .22s of the Yale target rifles. It looked complicated—Min was enamored by intricate designs—but actually functioned quite simply.

Min checked the price tag and saw the rifle could be purchased here—after a proper waiting period and review of any criminal record—for $1,600.

Hmmm, $900 less than I paid the illegal dealer in New York City. Of course, there was no waiting period, and no registration. What was the American saying? You get what you pay for.

Min was gratified to see that the SIG Sauer Romeo sight would attach easily to the top of the Patriot's rail. He left the shop, intent on making it back to the house and attaching the sight.

Now, just minutes from the rental, he kept an eye trained on the countryside, looking for a place to test fire the weapon after the optics were in place.

On Country Road, Min saw that Dylan's Evoque was parked in the center of the drive, effectively blocking access to the garage. The overhead door was down.

Dylan must be at work in the garage.

He let himself into the two-story house through the front door. After setting the gunsight on the kitchen table he strode to the door to the garage. He heard a high-pitched whine from the other side, confirming his suspicions. He opened the door a foot or two and looked inside. Dylan was standing over a workbench, working a small battery-operated Dremel tool over an object that was clamped into a vise. His back was to Min.

As I thought...hard at work. The Range Rover is positioned in such a way that I—or Dax and Willie if they come back to this place today—wouldn't be tempted to open the door.

Had that happened Dylan, wearing a full-body yellow Dupont protective suit, would be visible to passersby. Very few things would draw more attention. The suit featured a head covering with a clear plastic front. It would not have been out of place in a science fiction movie.

Min reached through the opening and flipped the light switch off and on to get Dylan's attention. He was careful to

58

not inhale when his head entered the garage space. He noticed a bottle designed for nasal spray was on the workbench within reach of Dylan. Min knew it contained naloxone; an opioid antagonist used to combat overdoses. The men always had a bottle nearby when working on the loaded golf balls.

Dylan switched off the Dremel and turned. He shouted through the face covering.

"Did you get the sight?"

Min nodded and gave a thumb's up.

"How's it coming here?"

Dylan twisted to look at the vise before turning back.

"Almost done. I'm through the cover and just have a quarter inch or so to go before the two sides of the cut come together. I think I'll leave it that way until we're with the brothers. Prying the cover off can take a minute or two. It'll give you more time to line up your shot if you need it."

Min nodded, unconsciously narrowing the opening of the door and leaning backwards. The lethality of the carfentanil was not lost on him.

Dylan noticed. "Let me finish here then we'll open up the garage and let it air out."

Min gave another thumbs-up and quickly closed the door. He stepped away and took a deep breath.

I can't believe people intentionally put that shit in their bodies. Crazy!

He made his way to his upstairs bedroom. He wanted to get started on the installation of the sight.

Dylan turned from the door and switched on the Dremel. He examined the golf ball. He'd started the cut just under the red Running Dog logo and worked until he no longer had a good angle. At that point he loosened the vise and repositioned the ball until he was again able to apply pressure at a downward angle. He'd repeated this process a handful of times before Min flicked the garage light switch.

The attachment that seemed to work best—he'd tried them all over the last two years—was the 420 Cut-Off Wheel. Roughly the size of a fifty-cent piece, it was brown, shaped like a round wafer, and had a small hole in the center that allowed it to fit over the Dremel's spinning shaft. This shaft rotated at a speed that was variable, turning at 5,000 to 35,000 rpm. Dylan found that something in the 25,000 rpm range worked best for this task. The wheel's edge—ostensibly used to cut slots in bolts or to saw through protruding nails—did an excellent job on the Surlyn material that Running Dog used.

Dylan concentrated on the last quarter inch and was gratified to see the two ends of the cut nearly met. He shut down the Dremel and examined his handiwork.

Not bad. Not my straightest cut, but not bad.

He loosened the vise with one gloved hand and with the other removed the ball and dropped it into a plastic bag. After double-checking the bag's seal, he dropped it onto the workbench. There was a standard size door to the rear of the garage that led to the backyard. Dylan pushed it open and stepped outside. He could remove the suit here without being seen by the neighbors or passengers of any vehicles that happened past. As he did so his mind wandered back to the beginning of the enterprise.

Dylan had been two years removed from the debacle at Yale—something he avoided thinking about—when he received a call out of the blue from a former New Haven acquaintance.

It was Min Xian, a Chinese national he'd met at Rudy's Bar, a pre-World War Two brick structure on Chapel Street near campus, his junior year. Dylan was 21—barely—and was drowning his sorrows, drinking—perhaps for one of the last times—in a happening place near the institution that he considered the intellectual center of the world.

That day at Rudy's, Min had been just 19. He sauntered up to the bar and, in a don't-give-a-shit fashion, ordered a Budweiser. The bartender, rather than asking for an ID, shrugged and filled a mug from the tap. Min sat next to Dylan, who watched with an amused look on his face.

"Just like that, huh? You just roll in and order alcohol and get served? You can't be 21." Dylan had a buzz on and a bit of a don't-give-a-shit attitude himself.

Min turned to him, a solemn look in his eye. "What the hell are they gonna do to me? Kick me out of the country? I'm leaving anyway."

Dylan concentrated on the Chinese and it came to him. "Hey, didn't I see you in the hallway today outside of the Executive Committee room?"

He had.

Both men had sat through disciplinary committee reviews that day. Neither was confident in their ability to survive the outcome. Both had been right. They sat at the bar together for a long time that night commiserating. It was the first night that Dylan had heard the word gānbēi, the Chinese word for cheers. He'd heard it many times in the ensuing years.

They were on their second beer together before either took the trouble to introduce themselves. Dylan extended his hand.

"Dylan Riordan, I'm from Vermont." He studied the Asiatic features of the man on the adjoining stool, noting that his English was excellent. "You must be from somewhere farther away, right? Hmmm, I'm guessing Kentucky...maybe Arkansas?" He smirked.

Min was confused for a second before a wide grin appeared on his face.

"Ahh, a joke. I am Min Xian, from Shenzhen, China."

He sipped his Budweiser, seeming to contemplate.

"Actually, my name is Xian Min. In China, the family surname comes first, given name last. We sometimes reverse this when we come to America to"—he searched for a word— "adhere to your customs. I've only been here for a few months, but I'm used to it now. It is agreeable."

After their fourth beer Min allowed Chinese clichés to creep into his speech. He was at times sullen, muttering *"Mei ban fa"*—there's nothing we can do—in its defeatist form. When beer number five arrived, however, he rallied.

"Hē pijiǔ, hao shuijiao." Drink beer, sleep well.

The pair gravitated toward each other in the ensuing weeks. It was a friendship fed by a mutual sense of being unfairly oppressed.

Min left the country more or less voluntarily after the ruling was made on his case. He didn't want his F-1 student visa to be revoked—something that would harm his chances of returning to the United States. He'd come to enjoy this country and its many freedoms.

Dylan, for his part, fought to the bitter end to stay enrolled. His father, once his biggest backer, had withdrawn all support. Without the clout of his reputation—and money—Dylan was cooked.

He'd assumed he would never see Min again. He was wrong.

Dylan was toiling at a job selling cars in Vermont, clipping the occasional $100 bill from oblivious golfers at the local course, when his cellphone rang. It was Min.

He had a proposition.

CHAPTER SEVEN

Min returned to China in shame. The Sanyu Scholarship represented a rare opportunity for a Chinese student. It was first established by Swiss American photographer Robert Frank to honor the integrity, work, and memory of his friend, Chang Yu, a talented artist from China. In America, Chang Yu was known simply as Sanyu. The scholarship was awarded to Chinese that showed promise in the fields of photography, video, film, and other visual arts.

Min fit this profile exactly with his background as a teen. His photographs of Chinese landscapes outside the city of Shenzhen drew praise from important people in the region. Local officials vouched for him and even assisted in the application process. He spoke English, which seemed to be a huge hurdle that he'd already overcome. After being selected, Min left his homeland, knowing full well that his parents were apprehensive. But Min was excited. He was going to America.

He experienced too much America, too soon. The abundant choices available in shops and restaurants, the women, the *freedom*! Min was drawn to the excesses, unable to limit himself to moderation. Photography and classwork became an afterthought. Nightlife, and shooting rifles, became his passion.

When he returned, his parents were happy to have him back, but humiliated. Min, as are most Chinese of his generation, was an only child. China has a cultural preference for sons. Male children grow up as the absolute center of their parents' and grandparents' universe. They are known as "Little Emperors." The fall of an emperor can be a crushing event. His parents had selected his name purposefully. Min means "quick" and "clever." Until the trouble in America their son had lived up to the name.

Now back in Shenzhen, Min was despondent. He stayed in his room for nearly a week upon returning. His parents were at a loss. It was an uncle who reached out offering a job.

63

He was a mid-level manager at a new manufacturing facility in Shenzhen, which is located just north of Hong Kong in Guangdong Province. The company sought to have the same success as a much larger business on the other side of the city, Shenzhen Greenswing Golf Supplies. Greenswing had been in business since 2014 and was rapidly becoming a leader in the production of ancillary golf products such as tees, scorecard pencils, towels, and logo golf balls. The new company, Min's uncle boasted, was hoping to challenge Greenswing.

It was called Running Dog.

The name was a joke, really. "Running dog" is a pejorative term in China. If you're called a running dog in that country it means you are a yes-man, a lackey. The term often creeps into political speech, having negative connotations. In March of 2021, for example, a Chinese diplomat verbally attacked Canada as America's "running dog" when prime minister Justin Trudeau joined the United States in criticizing alleged human rights abuses in Xinjiang province.

A high percentage of golf-related products from China find their way to the United States. The founder of Running Dog, Zhang Chu, thought it would be ironic, comical even, to export truckloads of products stamped with logos that were an insult to America, a country that most surely was a rival in trade and, quite possibly, a future military adversary.

Min first went to work on the production line. Within a year he was selected to replace a retiring worker in the department responsible for artwork. He was told this was due to his background in photography. Running Dog had begun to manufacture customized logo balls, a growing part of the business, and Min's talents were becoming indispensable. He appreciated the promotion but lamented the fact that his life was not what it could have been.

A year ago, I was in America, at Yale. Now...this!

Two more years went by. Two years helping turn blocks of cedar into 85 millimeter pencils and gelatinous slabs of polybutadiene into golf balls with ridiculous logos. Well, not all of them ridiculous. The Running Dog logo, with its eponymous sprinting canine, was carving out a niche in the golf world. While the brand had nowhere near the sales of giants like Titleist, TaylorMade, or Callaway, Running Dog's price point and—to Americans at least—compelling logo, had the Shenzhen factory working around the clock. They maintained steady sales of items with custom emblems, but the company logo had taken prominence.

Min remembered that it was a Saturday when he was approached by a company staffer and asked to report to the office of Mr. Chu. Min was surprised that the big boss was working on a weekend but shrugged and complied. He was admitted to the office, which was permeated by the odor of Chunghwa cigarette smoke, Chu's preferred brand. A slight man in his sixties, Chu waved at a seat. When Min settled in Chu got right to the point.

"You have noticed the R&D area in B-wing, yes?"

Min nodded. "Of course, Mr. Chu."

It would have been impossible to miss. The area comprised nearly 10,000 square feet. It was off limits to most employees. Min thought it odd that a company such as Running Dog would even *have* a research and development department, let alone one so extensive.

"I am bringing you into the inner circle today, Min. That area is actually involved in an undertaking much more important than R&D. It is an activity that will enrich Running Dog while at the same time help China grow stronger. We are at a point where we believe your experience will be helpful."

Min was intrigued. There were rumors. Some claimed to have seen newcomers in protective suits in the area. Production equipment had been moved into the space. Min had assumed this was for testing purposes, though none of the equipment seemed to return to the main floor of the plant. An associate in the art department claimed to have heard a dog barking behind the closed door. *What the hell was going on in R&D?*

Chu continued, "Obviously you would be honored to take part in such a project, no?"

Min realized that he wasn't being asked to join this special project. Neither was he being forced. Mr. Chu simply assumed that he would be privileged to become part of an effort that would benefit the country. He nodded his agreement to the older man.

"Good! We are about to flood the capitalists with an extremely powerful version of the opioids they seem to covet. We've perfected a way to produce carfentanil, a version 100 times more powerful than typical fentanyl, in a pliable state that can be shaped to fit into the presses that are used to stamp the cores of our golf balls."

Min stared at him dumbly.

Chu smiled and continued. "We treat the spheres with a thin layer of odor counteractant gel before sending them to a standard compression mold that adds the cover and the dimples. All that's left to do at that point is to stamp our logo." He sat back in his chair, satisfied, and lit another Chunghwa.

Min was stunned, hardly able to believe that this project was going on virtually under his nose. But he was fascinated.

He asked, "The odor defeating material helps prevent detection?"

Chu appeared pleased with the question.

Young Min grasps the salient aspects of the operation. He appears untroubled by the ramifications for the Americans.

"Correct, carfentanil has no odor—to humans—but we are taking precautions to avoid discovery by trained dogs. It seems that progress has been made in the field of fentanyl detection. We've brought drug-sniffing dogs into R&D and put them to work. Once the drug core is coated with the material, then sealed with the cover, it is virtually impossible for the dogs to detect it. And that is before we add the standard Running Dog packaging and shrink-wrap the pallets. We are now producing the...special product in limited quantities. Soon we will be ready to export."

Like all Chinese, Min was aware that the penalty in his country for drug crimes was death. The penalty can be handed out for possessing more than one kilogram of opium or 50 grams of heroin. It is not known how many executions are carried out annually—the government does not release the number—but it is believed to be in the thousands. Min, whose drug of choice was alcohol, thought it ironic that the method of state executions was lethal injection.

If Running Dog was producing illegal opioids in such quantity, it was obviously with the approval of the government. Chu's description of the project touched on it being good for the country. This almost certainly meant that it was designed to help weaken the United States, the one country that challenged China both economically, and more importantly, in the dispute over Taiwan, the wayward Chinese province that much of the world mistakenly looks upon as a sovereign country. Min enjoyed living in America—until the unfortunate ouster that cut short his stay—and felt no desire to do it harm, but if becoming part of the project enriched his prestige and bank account, he was interested.

Min was in it for Min.

Despite not yet knowing his role in the enterprise, Min smiled and said a single word in Chinese. It was a word whose American version had been ubiquitous during his time at Yale.

"*Bàng.*"

Awesome.

Min was able to install the optics on his rifle in less than half an hour. He sat on his bed and brought the weapon to his shoulder. He sighted out the rear-facing bedroom window, mindful to stay a few feet back so he didn't attract attention. The houses in this rural neighborhood were spaced well apart, but he didn't want to run the risk of a random set of eyes detecting suspicious behavior.

Dylan was finished with his work in the garage. He came up the stairs wearing shorts and a t-shirt that showed signs of perspiration. He poked his head into Min's room.

"You got it mounted already?"

Min nodded. "All set...just have to take a few shots with it to make sure it's zeroed in. Shouldn't take much. From the look at the meeting area that we got on Google Earth; the shot will not be difficult."

"Where can you practice?"

Min cocked his head to the rear wall, indicating a westerly direction. "I passed a lane a few miles back on my way here. It should work. I'll only need five minutes...just a few shots."

Dylan nodded. "I talked to Dax. He and Willie are staying in Dayton again tonight, maybe tomorrow night too. He says he thinks the dealer they're watching will visit clubs the next two nights, deliver to some customers. He figures it'll be an excellent chance to piece together info on the customer base...just in case."

Min grinned. "Just in case something bad happens to the dealer and we take over?"

Dylan pointed at his partner. "Bingo. By the way, he's thinking the Dayton guy is not going to deal, just like the Shortridge brothers. Good chance he and Willie will need the weapon after we do the brothers. Dax is thinking probably sometime in the next few days."

Min gestured to the Patriot P-15 Minuteman. "My rifle?"

"No, the other one...in the golf bag."

Min nodded in understanding.

They had casually discussed the impending murder of three more people with no more emotion than they put into any other mundane task. They could've been talking about brushing their teeth. Offhandedly, Min moved to another subject.

"I'm confused...why would a bodyguard for the father of your country be buried in such a forgotten place? In China, such a man would be remembered. His, uh..."—he searched for the word 'grave' unsuccessfully and momentarily slipped into Mandarin—"*fén mù* would be much visited."

Dylan, as he often did when Min resorted to his native language, interpreted the meaning of the unfamiliar word from its context. He shrugged.

"No idea, but Garrett sure knew about it."

CHAPTER EIGHT

Garrett Shortridge steered the Lexus through the darkness Wednesday night. It was 10:30 p.m., a half hour before the scheduled meeting with their potential new supplier. He glanced up at the sky and noted that stars hung there in most of his field of vision. Here and there a few of them winked out momentarily before reappearing, indicating their light was blocked by wispy clouds flowing overhead. A 10 to 12 mile per hour evening breeze, rare for a night with no forecast of storms, pushed in from the southwest.

Gerard leaned forward and craned his neck.

"Got some moon tonight. Should be good for us. Can't say I really trust these guys. Glad we brought insurance."

Garrett's eyes were back on the road. He was always cautious in situations like this, aware of the dangers of in-person transactions in the world of illegal drugs. In this case, though, he and Gerard were not bringing any inventory to the meet. There was really no reason for the Ivy Leaguers to do them harm. The proposed deal would benefit both parties. Their leader, Dylan Riordan, would seem to have more reason to be wary. He was bringing the carfentanil, or so he'd said.

Still, the Shortridge brothers hadn't reached the top of the mountain in the opioid trade in their area by being naive. Both were carrying hidden pistols, despite their assurance to Riordan that they would be unarmed.

Gerard spoke, "So, the Chinaman won't be there tonight?"

Garrett shook his head. "Nope, Riordan says he has a girl in Columbus...wanted to hook up with her one more time before they head out. That's where he was coming from Monday morning when we met them at Winans."

Gerard smirked, "He's a sly dog, that Chinaman...not so *mean* though." He was sure his repeated play on Min's name was clever and was mildly disappointed that his brother didn't laugh.

69

Garrett redirected the conversation.

"Just be sure to follow the plan. I don't think there's much chance we have anything to worry about tonight but let's be smart."

Garrett's main concern was surveillance by law enforcement. He knew that any of their customers could use knowledge of illegal activities by the Shortridge brothers as a bargaining chip to escape or reduce penalties. Any one of a hundred buyers of their product could make a deal to set them up.

It was a short drive for the pair. After traveling a few miles west on Miami Shelby Road from their farm they slowed at a dip and turned right at a road that connected with Miami Shelby from the north. This was Brown Road, a narrow track that ran north through trees on either side.

Garrett crept along at 35 miles per hour, his eyes scanning forward.

"Okay, it's right up here. I'm gonna make a pass. Look for anything that seems odd."

The Lexus rolled toward a clearing on the right, barely one thousand feet north of Miami Shelby Road. The men saw a white metal sign fixed to a lone steel post a few yards back from the road.

WESLEY CHAPEL CEMETERY

As the Lexus cruised past the sign, just enough light from the headlights spilled into the open terrain to cause shadows to dance among the headstones. Garrett accelerated slightly and pulled past the cemetery. Brown Road sloped gently downward to a short bridge that spanned a creek. Garrett crossed the bridge and accelerated again as the asphalt surface sloped back upward. The road then followed a series of curves before coming to an end barely two miles north, intersecting with an east-west road closer to Sidney.

There were few houses along this stretch of road. Garrett drove until the bend in the road made the Lexus impossible to see from the cemetery. He ducked into a long gravel driveway, stopping just a few feet inside, and turned to Gerard.

"See anything?"

Gerard shook his head. "Nope, not a thing."

Garrett backed out of the drive and pointed the Lexus back in the direction of the cemetery. Nearing the site, he slowed. The front of the cemetery was lined by a series of wooden posts, stationed 20 feet apart. Though it was invisible in the darkness, the brothers knew there was a steel cable that ran the entire length of the posts, passing through holes drilled through each of them. A level grassy space that served as a pull-over area for vehicles was wedged between the posts and the surface of Brown Road. Garrett turned the wheel and the Lexus eased to the left. Headlight beams now arced directly across the south section of the cemetery, illuminating the aging headstones, and throwing jagged shadows on a line of trees at the rear of the property. Both brothers peered into the interior of the grounds, searching for anything out of place.

Gerard, still scrutinizing the area, commented.

"Looks clear."

Without turning to his brother, Garrett nodded. He put the Lexus in reverse and backed slowly onto the road before turning the wheel to the left again and easing off the brake pedal. The north portion of the grounds was now revealed as the light swept through. Garrett guided the Lexus to a stop on the level grass, facing north, and put the vehicle in park.

"What time you got?"

Gerard checked his phone. "Not quite a quarter till."

Garrett nodded. "Okay, I'll walk on back. You stay here and wait for him. Bring him back when he gets here." He took another quick look in every direction before getting out.

Gerard watched his brother disappear into the forgotten cemetery.

Dylan navigated his Range Rover through the twists and turns of Brown Road, working his way south in the darkness toward the cemetery.

This place is definitely off the beaten path.

It was an odd stretch of road, winding, just a couple miles long, and terminating on both ends by intersecting with comparatively larger rural roads. To Dylan there didn't appear to be a good reason for the road to exist.

He and Min had examined it on maps.

It doesn't really GO anywhere.

Except, he supposed, to an old cemetery.

There was the occasional house on both sides. They ranged from smallish one-story structures that were not much more than shacks to enormous two-story creations that, Dylan thought, seemed excessive for the location.

Looks like some of the well-heeled locals bought up property and built their McMansions. I wonder if any of them are our future customers?

He came around the last bend and followed the road as it descended to a small bridge. Dylan glanced to the left at the bridge, smiled knowingly, then pushed up the gentle grade that took him the last few yards to the cemetery. He saw the Shortridge's black Lexus LX SUV parked just off the left side of the road. It faced him and he could see one occupant on the passenger side through its windshield. Dylan pulled up next to the Lexus and stopped.

Gerard Shortridge leaned toward the open driver's side window. He jerked a thumb toward the rear of the Lexus.

"Hey there Riordan, you can park behind us."

Dylan nodded and eased forward. He saw that the Lexus was parked on a flat area of grass just large enough for two vehicles. He angled into the spot and reversed so the two SUVs were parked back-to-back. He pulled forward as far as possible without dipping into a ditch. He allowed enough clearance to open the rear hatch door of the Range Rover.

So technically I'm parked illegally, facing the wrong direction...but if a cop comes along that'll be the least of my worries.

He exited the vehicle and walked toward the rear. Gerard was there.

"Follow me Riordan, Garrett's waiting." He gestured to the dark interior of the cemetery with a nod of his head.

Dylan flicked his eyes to the darkness then back to Gerard. "You guys aren't trying to pull something, are you?

Wouldn't make sense for you to rob me of a fraction of the stuff we can supply you."

"Nah, we weren't sure we could trust you. Garrett figured we'd split up until we knew it was safe...didn't want you to be able to take out both of us at the same time." He added, "Garrett's smart like that." He touched his temple with an index finger.

Dylan fought to keep from rolling his eyes. "Hold on." He stepped to the hatch door of the Range Rover and opened it. Out of the corner of his eye he saw Gerard reach behind his back and rest his right hand on something.

So you came armed, huh Gerard? Big bro probably did too. Against the rules we agreed on but can't say I blame you.

Dylan leaned into the cargo area and slid out the white Running Dog golf bag.

A tenseness drained from Gerard as he eyed the bag, bewildered. "What in the fuck?"

Dylan worked an arm through the bag's shoulder strap and hefted it to his back. He turned to Shortridge.

"This is your home course, Gerard, lead the way."

Gerard eyed the bag with its red Running Dog logo with confusion. He shrugged. "Follow me." He stepped to the steel cable that lined the front of the property and raised it so Dylan could duck under. The pair walked through a large area that was clear of headstones. It struck Dylan that this could have been where a building once stood. The name of the cemetery, he theorized, must've been derived from a chapel that once stood here.

After a hundred feet they neared the first line of stones. Most appeared to be marble, the engraved names on their facings faded and weathered. The rows were uneven. It seemed to Dylan that the graves had been placed in a haphazard fashion. Many of the headstones had collapsed. Most of those still upright were crooked.

Gerard led him through the first line of markers then angled left. The form of his brother materialized ahead from the darkness. Garrett was standing next to a grave that was more intricate than others in the cemetery. Two knee-high marble markers stood roughly six feet apart. They were located inside a thin stone rectangle that was visible just above the height of the grass. A flat granite marker was situated in the center of the rectangle. Dylan saw that this marker appeared to be considerably newer than the other parts of the memorial. He looked up from the marker and spoke to Garrett.

"This is it, huh? George Washington's bodyguard?" He spoke in a neutral tone, careful not to appear doubtful of the importance of the man buried below.

Garrett nodded. "Yep, me'n Gerard used to ride our bikes over here as kids...play army."

Gerard added, "Had some great shootouts in this place."

A laugh strained to rise from Dylan's throat. He was able to wrestle it down before it escaped. He coughed to hide any trace that may have leaked out.

You're about to have one more, big fella.

Garrett got down to business.

"I assume the golf bag has something to do with the inventory you claim to have?"

Dylan unslung the bag and stood it on the ground next to the bodyguard's plot. The white leather gleamed in the moonlight.

"Let me show you."

He unzipped one of the tall side pockets of the bag and reached in. He removed a pair of thick rubber gloves and slipped them on, pulling them partway up his forearms. Reaching back inside he removed a clear plastic bag. It contained a small screwdriver and the golf ball he worked on the previous day with the Dremel. The Shortridge brothers looked on, transfixed. Dylan slowly swung the bag toward them.

"This, gentlemen, is your future. The core of this ball is pure carfentanil. It can be combined with any cutting agent you like. You can form it into pills with your presses or sell it a half dozen other ways. We bring them in from China by the pallet. They are undetectable at customs due to the cover—and some other things we've added." He checked the wind direction and shifted a step to his left.

"You do *not* want to be downwind of this when I open the bag." Both Shortridges took a step back. Dylan removed the screwdriver, keeping the ball inside the bag. With the fingers of his left hand securing the ball, he reached inside the bag with the screwdriver and pried its flat end into the cut made by the Dremel. After a few seconds half of the cover popped off. A gooey substance was revealed, which Dylan removed by pinching through the plastic. Below the goo was an off-white orb.

Dylan held the bag aloft as if it were the Holy Grail.

"Pure carfentanil." He repeated the words for emphasis.

Gerard, not the brightest crayon in the box, managed "No fuckin' way!"

Garrett, considerably shrewder than his younger brother, had one question.

"How many balls per pallet?"

A grin appeared on Dylan's face.

"Eighteen thousand."

CHAPTER NINE

Min knelt on the scrub grass inside the tree line. He was dressed in his customary black jeans and t-shirt, making him nearly invisible. The waterproof boots that he wore, as it turned out, weren't. Dylan had dropped him off 90 minutes earlier north of the bridge on Brown Road. He'd slipped into the woods, splashed across the shallow creek, and made his way up the south bank. He picked his way through the dark, angling east, then south again until he was in position. He was 20 feet from the eastern edge of Wesley Chapel Cemetery. He could see the entire graveyard as well as Brown Road beyond.

The moisture that had seeped into his boots was an irritation, one that normally would have infuriated him. But Min was soothed this night by something that is cherished in China. It was the sound of crickets. Min found himself momentarily taken back to his native country where his fellow Chinese treasured the lifestyle connected to the land and nature. The trill of the insects helped remind them of a rural existence. This was especially true of city dwellers. They yearned for reminders of the simpler life.

Beginning in the Tang Dynasty, from 618 to 907 AD, many Chinese kept crickets as pets inside small, intricately designed wooden cages. Traditionally gourds, a symbol of good luck in China, were also used to house the creatures. The gourds were specially grown for this use, often resulting in unusual shapes. They were emptied of pulp then dried and lacquered to form a warm heat-retaining cocoon. Crickets rested on a bed of lime and loam. On cold nights they might also receive a cotton pad. The exterior of the gourds was often developed into a striking art form. Heated metal needles were used to carve intricate designs. Though wooden cages and cricket gourds are still used today, many of them have been replaced by modern plastic structures.

Min was reminded that another tradition from the Tang Dynasty had survived to modern times—cricket fighting. The crickets—always males—are weighed to the closest hundredth of a gram. Two that are in the same weight class are placed in a clear plastic ring the size of a dinner plate. The ring has a dividing wall that separates the two insects. The owners then lightly brush the crickets with a frayed reed stick. This agitates them and goads them into fighting. The dividing wall is removed, and the crickets go at it. They never fight to the death and there are seldom serious injuries. When one cricket retreats, he is declared the loser.

Often these matches are held in smoke-filled backrooms. But there are highly visible televised affairs in the eastern city of Hangzhou and in Tianjin near the Bohai Sea in northern China. Though gambling is technically illegal, it is an open secret that large sums of money change hands based on the outcomes.

Min shared the positive view of crickets held by most of his countrymen. He watched the televised matches while growing up. His parents kept their crickets in wooden cages, generally paying 35 to 70 yuan—about five to ten dollars—to trappers who made a profit selling to those living in urban areas. He fell asleep most nights to the song of the family's crickets. Here in the woods he forced himself to stay vigilant and not be lulled to carelessness.

He had work to do.

After waiting more than an hour, he saw the Shortridge Lexus come into view. It crossed his field of vision traveling left-to-right before continuing out of view to the north. Minutes later it returned and swept its headlights across the entire length of the cemetery. Min resisted the urge to flatten himself to the ground, knowing there was a slim chance that the movement might be detected. Immobile, in dark clothing, he was just another small puzzle piece of the dark jigsaw that was Wesley Chapel Cemetery.

The Lexus parked at the front of the property. After a short time, the driver's door opened. Min could make out Gerard sitting in the passenger seat. The door closed and the driver—it had to be Garrett—walked away from the vehicle and picked his way through the headstones. He came to a stop near a plot that seemed to have two markers, roughly 200 feet from Min's position. Though Min and Dylan hadn't known the exact location of the grave the Shortridges had designated as the meeting place, fate had seemed to smile on them.

Min would have a clear shot. He'd zeroed in the new sight late that afternoon by firing a dozen rounds through it in a woods a few miles west of the Airbnb. He raised the Patriot carbine with his gloved hands and rested it on a low branch of a young maple tree before easing into a firing position.

Dylan watched the Shortridge brothers. He saw in Garrett's eyes that the older brother immediately grasped the potential financial windfall that this new source represented. Gerard was slower on the uptake, but realization seemed to be creeping in.

Even this dolt can figure out we're offering an unlimited supply. I can practically see cartoon dollar signs forming in his eyes.

Garrett spoke. "Of course, we will want to test it...make sure it's what you say it is."

Dylan nodded. "Of course. I'll leave you this bag."

Gerard took a half step closer to get a better view of the bag. "And even if this is the real stuff, how do we know you won't screw us by sending us regular golf balls? I mean, if the cover is the same there's no way we could tell until we cut into 'em."

Dylan fought to hide a grin. The imbecile had set him up perfectly for the next step.

"Great question. You're no dummy. Let me show you."

Dylan lowered the bag to the grass and turned to the golf bag. Reaching into a pocket, he removed a small box. The low light conditions made it difficult to discern that the dark portion of the box was, in fact, red. But the white Running Dog logo stood out. He removed the top of the box to reveal four sleeves of golf balls. He turned the box top upside down and deftly inserted the bottom of the box that held the sleeves back into it. He held the box in his left hand, so the four sleeves were displayed. This made Dylan feel a bit like a salesman presenting his product which, he supposed, he was.

"The shipments will come to you just like this. There is an easy way to see that you're not getting regular balls. You're familiar with the amount of bounce that you get when a golf ball is dropped on a hard surface?"

Dylan considered diving into a detailed explanation of a golf ball's coefficient of restitution, the property that allowed it to absorb energy, change its shape upon impact, and snap back to its original form while changing direction. In golf this relates to the transfer of energy from the face of a club to the ball itself. He knew that the COR of regular Running Dog balls was 0.5 while the version with carfentanil cores was barely 0.1. He considered this, believing Garrett would grasp the concept.

Then he turned to Gerard and saw the face of a dullard.

Better keep it simple.

He selected the sleeve that held just two balls, the missing third ball being the one in the plastic bag that he'd cut open with the Dremel. He leaned down and laid the box on the grass next to the plastic bag, then turned the sleeve so that one of the balls rolled into his right hand. As he did so Gerard piped up.

"Yeah, they bounce like super balls. I used to hit them across the road toward old man Barhorst's house with a baseball bat...hit the house on the fly a couple times." A wistful look appeared on his face. Dylan noticed.

He remembers it like it was a crowning achievement... it's not exactly like splitting the atom, for Christ's sake.

Dylan held out the ball and turned it slowly. The Running Dog logo came into view, twisted away, and appeared again. The brothers watched.

"Looks like a regular golf ball, right?"

Both Garrett and Gerard nodded.

Dylan pinched the ball between his thumb and index finger at waist height and positioned it directly over the flat granite marker in the center of the plot. He glanced at the brothers.

Garrett slightly to my left, Gerard to my right, closest to the wood line. Perfect.

He mimicked the Shortridges nods. "Well, would a normal golf ball do this?"

Dylan dropped the ball. It fell three feet, struck the granite with a *pap* sound, and bounced up an inch or two before settling back to the surface. Dylan looked at the brothers.

"Pretty easy to tell the core of this ball is something other than polybutadiene, huh? If we ship you balls that bounce, you'll know they're not filled with the good stuff."

Garrett caught on at once. He rubbed his chin, appearing to run computations in his head.

Gerard queried, "Poly-*what?*"

Dylan bent to retrieve the ball, thinking, *this fucking hayseed Gerard...Min will be doing the world a favor.*

Picking up the ball was the prearranged signal to Min to prepare to fire. Dylan's hand closed over the ball and he was about to stand up when, for the first time, he noticed the engraving on the granite marker. It read:

*LEWIS BOYER
PVT   DRAGOON
INDPT TRP OF HORSE
REVOLUTIONARY WAR
1755   1843*

Revolutionary War? Maybe this cat really WAS George Washington's bodyguard.

Dylan squeezed the ball, reached for the box that rested on the grass nearby, and stood. He inserted the dropped ball back into its sleeve then tucked the sleeve back into the box it came from. He then turned casually to the golf bag and slipped the entire box back into its pocket before zipping it shut. He rested his right hand on top of one of the clubs protruding from the bag—the putter—and turned to the brothers.

"What do you think, guys? Are you satisfied that we can safely get product to you in volume?"

81

Gerard spoke first.

"It sure as shit looks like it. Damn! This is perfect!" He turned to his brother. "Right Garrett?"

The elder Shortridge sought to dampen his brother's excitement.

"It's good, don't get me wrong. We might even consider raising our offer of five percent of the profits. We need to think about this, maybe take a day or two."

Garrett did not fool Dylan. The man clearly lusted for a steady supply of opioids and the profits they represented. He didn't need time to decide whether to jump in bed with Dylan and his partners. He was simply trying to work an angle that was more beneficial to him and his dumbshit brother.

Dylan casually lifted the putter from its slot in the golf bag. The head cover was yellow and displayed the words "Breakfast Ball." He removed the cover to reveal a blade-style head that reflected a bit of the light from the moon and stars. He took a stance and pantomimed tapping in a putt as he responded.

"If you can't commit right now maybe we need to move on and deal with someone else. There are plenty of other people out there dealing this stuff." Dylan raised the putter with his left arm and rested his right hand on its head as he peered at Garrett.

Rubbing his chin again, Garrett appeared to consider. "Hold on now, we want to do business with you. We'll bump our offer to seven percent of the profits...now that's on top of what you clear on the sales you make to us. What do you say?"

Dylan gripped the blade of the putter with his right hand. His left went to an area a few inches above the blade where the hosel and shaft came together. He quickly turned his left wrist and the shaft disengaged from the rest of the club. Both brothers, intent on the negotiation and still somewhat overwhelmed by the massive opportunity before them, were slow to react, or even to suspect a problem. At the last second Garrett noticed a piece of metal flip out of the hosel. A part of his brain identified it at the same instant that Dylan's hand rose toward him.

It was a trigger.

Dylan spoke. "Here's our counteroffer." He swung the weapon to Garrett's forehead and in one motion jerked back the trigger. A hollow pop sounded across the cemetery as a small black hole appeared between Garrett's raised eyebrows. He dropped to the ground like a sack of meat.

Momentarily stunned, Gerard reached behind his back for his hidden pistol. Dylan had time to recognize rage on the man's face through a thin blue haze of gunpowder smoke. As Gerard's hand whipped back with the pistol Dylan had just enough time for one thought.

Come on Min!

Gerard's head snapped backward as a spray of liquid filled the air to his rear. He collapsed on top of his brother. The sound of the bodies impacting was drowned out by the reverberating crack of the rifle from the woods.

Min had told Dylan that the fat man was his.

He was correct.

CHAPTER TEN

Paul sat at the desk in his home late Thursday. The space had been converted from a third bedroom by the home's previous owner and he and Lauren, who was now preparing for bed in the master bathroom, had continued to use it for that purpose. He noted that there was a yellow legal pad on the desk next to the computer and idly observed writing in Lauren's hand.

He opened his laptop with the intention of catching up on work emails. When the screen brightened Paul saw that a browser was open. It displayed the last page viewed. It was the foster and adoption page from the State of Ohio website. Lauren, obviously, had been using the laptop while he was gone.

Paul blinked. He and Lauren had been unable to have children. The doctors—there had been several—explained that the fault was with a combination of issues between both him and Lauren. Before hearing this explanation, Paul assumed that infertility was due to circumstances present in one partner or the other. He learned that fully one-third of cases are due to a combination of conditions between the two partners.

Paul brought up his email and began the process of deleting the junk that had found its way to his inbox the last several days. That done, he began to examine the remainder that were pertinent to his job. Most were follow ups from clients of Jasper Spirit Consulting. Some messages contained scheduling information put together by Mike McClary's wife, Marge. After scrolling through several, Paul's mind wandered.

What was this about a double murder?

He went online and searched local news sources. The most comprehensive seemed to be the Dayton Daily News, which reported that a farmer living on Brown Road in rural Shelby County drove past a country cemetery in the early morning hours and noticed a vehicle parked there. Two hours later he returned from breakfast at a Cracker Barrel restaurant

85

in Piqua and saw the same vehicle—a Lexus SUV. He thought he recognized it as being owned by another farmer that lived nearby. Thinking the owner may have had a mechanical problem, he parked near the Lexus and approached it, looking for a note or to see if he could offer assistance. It was at this point that he noticed a flock of turkey vultures overhead. He investigated, walked into the cemetery, and discovered the bodies of two men. He then dialed 9-1-1. The Shelby County Sheriff's Office responded first. They were soon aided by units of the Miami County Sheriff's Office.

Paul scanned back through the article to see the name of the cemetery where the men—not yet publicly identified— had been found. Something about the mention of Brown Road had tickled his memory. He found it—Wesley Chapel Cemetery.

I've been there.

One of the methods Paul used to keep in shape was cycling. Bike rides were an excellent low impact workout and fit into the rehab program he'd adhered to after the parachute injury that ended his military career. The distance of the rides increased to the point that he was logging twenty-plus miles on almost a daily basis, topping out on a few at more than 50. He remembered ranging several miles south of their Troy home on a pleasant fall day the previous October and turning down an unfamiliar road. He'd noticed a forgotten cemetery tucked into a wooded stretch. When he returned from the ride, he went online to check it out.

This seemingly unusual action was not at all out of character for Paul. He'd always had an interest in cemeteries. It was, he supposed, a bit disturbing to some, but fortunately Lauren had no problems with it. Most of his interest was in significant people who were interred in these resting places. His recent visit to Arlington National Cemetery was a prime example. But Paul also found it compelling when he came across little-known memorials that had a story to tell. On occasion his curiosity had led to much more than a simple inquisitive visit. The previous year he'd been involved in an altercation in a Toledo cemetery with a bank robbery gang that had nearly cost him and Lauren their lives.

A few months after the October bike ride on Brown Road, Paul returned to the cemetery for a longer visit. For Christmas, Lauren gave Paul a drone. It was small but packed with features, including still picture and video capabilities. Paul spent a few weeks at their Polecat Road property growing familiar with the unit. When he felt confident with its operation he began to branch out. He flew it over the homes of friends and neighbors, snapping pictures that he later emailed to them. He dabbled with the drone's "Follow Me Mode," which allowed the unit to track and follow a person or object while keeping them in focus. He found that videos recorded using this feature during his bike rides were almost hypnotic. He limited his use of this mode to rides on bike paths where there was little chance of disturbing others or intruding on private property. He also traversed the area to get the drone's eye view of interesting geography or public structures.

One of these—probably his favorite—was the Big Four Railroad Bridge located on the southern edge of the city of Sidney. Construction began on this massive concrete structure in 1923. Built across the Miami River Valley, the bridge is 780 feet long and over 100 feet tall. It supports two lengths of track and can easily bear the weight of fully loaded trains moving in opposite directions—one east, one west—at the same time. Four gigantic concrete supports, or piers, anchor the bridge's five main spans. It dominates the view of motorists coming to or going from Sidney on County Road 25A which, like the river itself, passes below.

The bridge had a fascinating history. Hundreds of laborers worked to build it. Five people were killed during its construction including, it was rumored, one worker who fell into one of the concrete piers before it had hardened and was left to become an unplanned component of the edifice.

One aspect that definitely *was* planned are the vertical openings that run from the top of the arches nearly to the track surface above. These openings are semi-circular at their peak. There are 49 in total, all being nine feet, nine inches wide.

They vary in height from more than 40 feet on the low sides of the arches to barely ten feet at their centers. This design, known as open spandrel, gave the bridge a nearly art deco look.

It had been mid-January when Paul took his drone to the Big Four. He parked just north of the bridge along Riverside Park and flew the craft to an altitude of over 200 feet, twice the height of the bridge. From this vantage point Paul was able to capture some stunning images. There were two inches of snow on the ground and it was a bright, clear day. He passed over the length of the bridge while using the unit's panoramic mode. He later enlarged one of these photos and framed it, hanging it in their home near pictures of hot air balloons, some of Lauren's favorites. He was even able to record video of an eastbound blue and yellow CSX engine pulling more than 50 boxcars and autoracks toward cities on the eastern seaboard.

After 45 minutes Paul landed the drone and installed a new battery. He decided to try something a bit more adventuresome. He piloted the drone vertically until it was even with the arch of the second span from the bridge's western edge. He then very carefully steered it into, and through, one of the smaller archways. The resulting video was extraordinary. It wasn't until he watched it closely days later that he saw *"G.S. WAS HERE, 1976"* scratched onto one of the inner walls. He'd wondered, *how in the hell did G.S. get in that chamber nearly 100 feet high almost 50 years ago?*

On his way back to Troy that day Paul stopped off at Wesley Chapel Cemetery. He'd been researching the life and service of Lewis Boyer and wanted to pay his respects. He'd found that Boyer served in a unit officially known as the Commander-In-Chief's Guards, at the time commonly known as Washington's Life Guards. Soldiers were reportedly chosen for this unit on the basis of sobriety, honesty, and good behavior.

Boyer was a dragoon, or mounted soldier, and fought in a number of Revolutionary War engagements including the battle of Yorktown. He was said to be nearly six feet in height, tall for the time. Boyer's obituary stated that he was present at Washington's crossing of the Delaware. His discharge paper was signed by General Washington on December 10, 1783 in Philadelphia, Pennsylvania.

At the beginning of the war there were just 50 Life Guards. Though this number eventually expanded to 250, the unit remained elite throughout the conflict.

Paul found the old soldier's grave and cleared the marker of snow. He then placed a quarter inside the "O" in Boyer with George Washington's profile facing up.

Now, in his office in June, he read about the two bodies found just inches from that same marker. The first story about the murders gave the basic facts of the discovery of the bodies. An update on the Dayton Daily News website written less than an hour ago revealed that the victims had suffered gunshot wounds. It went on to say that there may be similarities to a third murder that occurred over the weekend in Urbana.

Paul wrinkled his brow.

Another murder?

He found himself diving down this rabbit hole. It seemed that this victim, Shane "Shadow" Donald, 37, was found Sunday morning, the apparent victim of a single gunshot wound to the head. It was rumored that Donald dealt cocaine and fentanyl in Champaign County. He'd had two previous drug arrests. His body had been found on the property of a prominent Urbana business under an oddity known as the World's Largest Loaf of Bread.

Paul shook his head.

You've gotta be kidding me.

He'd been out of the loop on local news during the camping trip to the Baltimore-Washington D.C. area. This was the first he'd heard of the Urbana murder, an event that had apparently attracted a modest amount of national attention. Paul, with his well-developed sense of curiosity, had been compelled to make a short stop to see this novelty the previous summer. He'd driven to Springfield, several miles east of Troy, parked, then rode the entire 32-mile length of a bike trail north to Bellefontaine. Completing the round trip gave him his longest ride to date.

The trail was named after legendary frontiersman Simon Kenton, whose exploits were celebrated in a series of classic books by Ohio author Allan Eckert. Paul had read the books, dug into Kenton information online, and discovered that the man, a friend to Daniel Boone, was buried in Urbana. He decided to add some extra length in Urbana on his return trip to Springfield to make the trip 65 miles. This, he supposed, appealed to his sense of order. Perusing possible sights of interest in Urbana during preparations for the ride he learned of the bread-related novelty nearby. He'd thought, *Oh yeah, I definitely have to swing by that thing.*

He had pictures on his phone of both Kenton's grave and the loaf. He'd snapped shots of the latter from the sidewalk several yards away. But he had excellent access to the former in Oakdale Cemetery on Urbana's east side.

Paul thought back to that day, remembering that a life-size statue of Kenton, musket in hand, stood on top of an impressive stone monument. He now remembered that a tablet at the monument's base mentioned Kenton's service in the Revolutionary War.

He was a contemporary of Lewis Boyer.

Paul continued to look for further information on the murders but found nothing that added significant detail. A thought passed through his mind.

The first murder was in Urbana, maybe 25 miles from here. The two bodies off Brown Road were found, what, 15 miles from here?

The events of the past two years, in which he, and more importantly Lauren, had been put in danger by criminal elements, made Paul wary of coincidence. He plotted the murders on a mental map, stared at the screen for a few seconds, then closed the laptop. Whatever this was, it was moving closer. His eyes slid to Lauren's handwriting on the legal pad. He saw several columns with headings that included *Adoption Costs, Adoptive Parent Training,* and *How Adopting Will Change Your Life.*

Paul's eyes locked on the last heading. He rose, suddenly feeling a need to be near his wife.

CHAPTER ELEVEN

Late Thursday afternoon, Amos Bunker sat in a black Miami County Sheriff's Department SUV and stared at the building before him. He decided it was more than a building— a complex, really. Set behind a manicured lawn, the sprawling three-story facility managed to project a pleasant, welcoming appearance despite its purpose.

StoryPoint Troy was a senior facility that offered both independent and assisted living. It featured a number of amenities. These included a cheery lobby with a piano, excellent dining areas, a theater, game rooms, a library, and a retail cafe. It had a hair dressing salon, a garden for the residents, and expansive rooms with views of the surrounding area. The staff was first rate. Yet none of these qualities were what drew Bunker.

StoryPoint also specialized in memory care.

His mother, Dana, began to have issues the previous year. At first it seemed innocuous; misplaced keys, reading glasses that seemed to vanish. Like that. Soon, however, more serious symptoms revealed themselves. She was often drowsy and took long naps during the day. Bunker told himself these were simply a function of his mother's advancing age. At 67, he theorized, these must be natural phenomena.

He grew alarmed when his mother, during one of his frequent visits over the holidays, exhibited disorganized behavior. She removed unwashed cups and plates from her dishwasher and returned them to kitchen cupboards. Friends reported that she made repeated phone calls to them, asking the same questions—and receiving the same answers—several days in a row. Twice Bunker arrived at her Plum Street house and found her wearing mismatched shoes.

The odd behavior reached a new level when Dana began to have visual hallucinations. She would call her son at all hours of the night to frantically report prowlers at her doors and windows. Bunker always responded, driving from his house a few blocks away, and checking her property for signs of intruders. After the second such incident he realized that the problem likely existed solely in his mother's mind. Still, he made the trips. He installed Ring doorbells at her front and back doors, linked the feeds to her cellphone, and explained how they operated. His purpose was not to capture video of a trespasser, but to prove to Dana that her fears were unfounded. It didn't work. The calls persisted.

Finally, in early spring during a period of clarity that seemed to be increasingly rare for Dana, Bunker was able to convince her to seek medical help. What followed were a series of visits and tests at The Ohio State University's Wexner Medical Center in Columbus. The diagnosis was sobering for both mother and son. Dana was in the early stages of Lewy body dementia, a disorder that causes abnormal protein deposits to form in the brain.

Individuals with LBD typically survive just five to seven years after they are diagnosed. Bunker immediately began to investigate possible living facilities. Sometimes Dana participated in this process. More often she barely tolerated it. On occasion, she flatly refused to discuss a move to assisted living. Bunker learned to put off discussions when his mother was going through a period of confusion or apathy, two of the more common signs of the disease. As Dana's symptoms became more frequent and severe, it became increasingly difficult for her to participate in the process.

Now, in June, it was finally going to happen. Bunker had stopped at her house the previous week for coffee before starting work. This was something he'd done virtually every week since his mother moved to Troy six years earlier. The move was prompted after Bunker's father, Alex, died of a heart attack while sitting at his desk in Cape Girardeau, Missouri. This was a calamity for his business, the eponymously named Alex Bunker Insurance Agency. It was devastating for Dana and Amos. The morning cups of coffee and, more importantly, the discussions that accompanied them made a significant mother-son bond even stronger.

Amos supposed he had always been a mama's boy. When he tried out for peewee football it was his mother, not his dad, that attempted to snag his errant passes in the backyard. When it became apparent that Bunker was not cut out to be a quarterback, he and Dana reversed positions. Bunker made the team as a wide receiver. Dana learned to throw a spiral. It was Dana who accepted and encouraged her son's desire to pursue a career in law enforcement. This despite the inherent dangers of the profession and Alex's wish that Bunker join the family insurance business. There was not a prouder mom in the audience on the day that Bunker accepted his diploma for criminal justice at Southeast Missouri State's multi-purpose arena, the Show Me Center.

On the morning that finally moved the needle toward Dana accepting a move to assisted living, Bunker stopped in for coffee. He realized the moment he stepped into the Plum Street kitchen that his mother was having a good day. She looked lucid, even cheerful. Her shoes matched, her clothes were clean—not always the case of late—and the kitchen and dining room were well organized. Bunker smiled.

"Looks like you've been busy, Mom."

Dana returned his smile. "I'm afraid it's hard to keep up with the housekeeping now that I'm living with this sloppy person. She's much more difficult to clean up after than your father ever was...or even you when you were little, for that matter."

Bunker stirred sweetener into his coffee and arched an eyebrow. *Living with another person?* He questioned his earlier assessment that she was having a good day.

Dana saw his confusion. She raised an index finger and theatrically pointed at her chest.

"She's in here, Amos. Sometimes I can see what she's doing, feel what she's thinking. Sometimes she takes over completely. I go somewhere else. When I come back, I have to try to figure out what she's been doing, how she's... embarrassed me." Her smile faded and she dropped her eyes to her own coffee cup.

Bunker felt the heartbreak swell inside of him. His mother, never a large woman, was now rail thin. On the way, he feared, to being emaciated. Her eating habits were hit and miss. She needed a nutrition program that was regulated. She needed so much more.

He tried for low-level humor. "Ahh, it's like a Dr. Jekyll and Mr. Hyde thing, huh?"

She nodded, "I guess it's more like a Dr. Jekyll and *Mrs.* Hyde thing." She removed the spoon from her cup and laid it on a paper towel. Her eyes focused on the inside of the cup where coffee and cream had combined, becoming one. Two elements now fused to form something different.

Bunker watched as the most important person in his life struggled to avoid despondence.

He'd never married. The personality that led him to strictly adhere to rules—laws—served him well in police work. It was less than ideal when it came to relationships with women. His mother accepted him for what he was. But it was difficult to watch her change. Even her hair, always blonde and lustrous, was now mostly grey and seemed unnaturally dry. Bunker had always believed that his mother's hair somehow mixed with his father's male pattern baldness to form a gene pool from which his prematurely white hair sprung. Though she'd made an effort to make herself presentable this morning, the LBD had taken a toll. He thought of the salon at StoryPoint.

Bunker watched as his mother raised her eyes to his.

"I think I'm ready to make the move, Amos. I can't keep putting you through this. We need help."

Bunker didn't know if her use of the word *we* referred to the two of them, or to the dual versions of herself that were struggling inside her brain.

Bunker glanced again through the SUV's windshield at the building before him. The process of transitioning to StoryPoint would take time. The facility was full, and Dana had been put on a waiting list. Fortunately, her husband's business had been successful, so the financial commitment was within her means.

Bunker glanced at his watch—4:39. He'd received a call earlier in the day telling him that a room in the memory care wing of the facility was about to become available. If he could get to the business office before 5 p.m. the paperwork could be finalized. This was good news, signaling that a better life was on the horizon for his mother. At the same time Bunker knew that there was only one way that a room in this area could become available. He shook his head to remove the thought, not wanting to fixate on the inevitable outcome that a move to StoryPoint represented.

Bunker opened the door to the SUV and made his way up the front walk. He wore a beige golf shirt above camel-colored slacks. His medium brown sport coat made him uncomfortable in the June heat, but It hid the Glock 17 pistol in the black leather Aker pancake holster attached to his belt near his right hip. He forced himself to push bleak thoughts from his head, to think of something—anything—but the end of his mother's journey. Fortunately, there was another subject swimming just under the surface.

He'd spent most of the day investigating a double murder in rural Shelby County. Though it was technically out of the jurisdiction of the Miami County Sheriff's Department, Shelby County had reached out for assistance. The bodies had been discovered just a few hundred yards from the county line and the victims—whose names had not been released but who'd been tentatively identified—had been fairly well known in both counties.

A number of vehicles from the neighboring county were on hand when Bunker arrived at Wesley Chapel Cemetery. Two Shelby County deputies stood next to a Lexus SUV at the front of the cemetery.

Bunker recognized the vehicle immediately as belonging to Garrett Shortridge. He'd trailed it on and off for weeks, including three days earlier, Monday, when Garrett and his brother sat with two men at Winans Coffee in Piqua.

Son-of-a-bitch!

Bunker barely had time to introduce himself to his opposite numbers when a second Miami County detective arrived. This was Mike Karabin, the senior member of his county's three-man detective force. Known as Pappy to virtually everyone—including his wife—Karabin was widely respected by members of law enforcement throughout West Central Ohio.

Pappy approached Bunker and the two Shelby County deputies. "Whatta we got?"

Bunker, despite working with Karabin for several years, had not yet figured out how the senior detective felt about him. The man's hard eyes seemed to stare unflinchingly at him during conversations. Karabin did not mince words, often responding to Bunker's queries with truncated answers that were delivered from under his brush mustache. Bunker deferred to one of the deputies.

"Two dead. Gunshots to the heads. Looks like different weapons. We were just about to take your man,"—the deputy jerked a thumb toward Bunker—"back to have a look. They're back by George Washington's bodyguard."

Karabin raised an eyebrow and nodded. "Lead the way."

The foursome ducked under a steel cable and worked their way through the headstones. Bunker noted that almost all of the markers were covered to some degree by lichen, mold, or a combination of the two. Seconds later they approached another group of deputies and plainclothes detectives who were grouped around the far side of an aging gravesite flanked by two time-worn white markers. Bunker took a second to eye a flat rectangle of engraved granite that was situated between the two markers.

LEWIS BOYER.

George Washington's bodyguard?

He returned his attention to the group of law enforcement officials. The bodies of two large men were sprawled between the officers and the grave. One of the bodies was face up. The second was draped over it, face down. The scene gave the impression of two men wrestling, one being pinned by the other.

The lead Shelby County detective, Gary Russell, greeted them.

"Hey Miami County, welcome to the party."

Bunker and Karabin nodded. Karabin repeated his earlier question. "Whatta we got?"

Russell gave the same basic information that his colleague had provided before adding details.

"We ran the plates on the Lexus." He nodded toward the SUV parked near the road. "It's registered to Garrett Shortridge." He knelt and pointed to the body on the bottom. "This would be him."

Bunker recognized Garrett, despite the fact that a small, dark hole was now present a fraction of an inch from the center of his forehead.

A thought occurred to Bunker. *Dead center...literally.* He pushed it away and concentrated on the detective, who continued.

"The body on top is his brother, Gerard. You can see that his wound is different...apparently from a larger caliber weapon. Gerard's entry wound is at his left temple."

Bunker and Karabin sidestepped to their left in order to view the wound.

Karabin stated, "Two shooters."

Bunker, looking closely at Garrett's wound and the hint of dark residue that surrounded it, added, "One from in close, the other from more of a distance." He stood and surveyed the tree line to the rear of the cemetery.

All eyes turned to Bunker, then followed his gaze.

Russell was about to go on when another SUV arrived at the scene, its light bars flashing.

"Looks like the coroner's here. We've got all the pictures we need. As soon as he gives us the high sign, we can roll the bodies...look for exit wounds..." He trailed off. The customary way to finish the sentence—*and look for driver's licenses to make positive IDs*—wasn't necessary. Every member of law enforcement in the two counties knew who the Shortridge brothers were. A number of the detectives had, like Bunker, shadowed one or both of them at some point. It was an open secret that they were major players in the area's drug trade.

The coroner, a short, barrel-chested man wearing a suit, edged his way into the semi-circle. Used to dealing with dead bodies, he appraised the situation. In a laconic tone that mirrored Karabin's, he prodded, "Gimme the story."

Minutes later the coroner gave permission for the bodies to be moved. When the body on top was rolled to the side a Beretta semi-automatic pistol was found. It had been trapped between the two corpses. Karabin let out a low whistle.

"Look here." This from Russell who was pointing to a matching Beretta tucked into the belt of the second body. Everyone present had the same thought.

Drug deal gone bad.

The wallets of both victims were found, and as expected, the identity of each Shortridge brother was positively established. A large exit wound was evident on the right side of Gerard's head.

Karabin exhaled. "A through-and-through. We'll play hell finding the bullet. Anybody's guess what direction it came from."

Russell, examining Garrett's head, remarked, "Better luck here. No exit wound. We'll find this bullet, or rather *he* will." He motioned to the coroner. "Looks like a .22. Up close, GSR evident."

The reference to gunshot residue confirmed what Bunker had noticed earlier.

Russell continued. "Looks like almost a carbon copy of that murder in Urbana a few days ago." He turned to one of the deputies. "Larry, didn't you talk to your brother about that?"

The deputy, whose name tag read "Wick," nodded. "Yep, same kinda thing. Up close shot. The round was a .22 short. Urbana PD has it...should be able to do a comparison."

Russell turned to Bunker and Karabin. "Larry's brother is a police officer in Urbana."

Wick added, "The victim,"—he searched his memory for the name—"Shadow Donald, dealt coke and fentanyl. Two-time loser, a couple short stretches in prison. And get this, two years ago he testified against a partner in order to get a lighter sentence. Put the guy away for 18 months. Guy named Kevin Turner. He just got out three months ago and he hasn't checked in with his parole officer."

Karabin perked up. "Any history with firearms?"

Wick nodded. "Lifelong hunter...or at least he was. Can't own a gun with his felony record."

Russell added, "Not legally anyway."

The entire group stared at the bodies of the Shortridge brothers.

Karabin summarized. "Sounds like a solid lead. Let's find this guy Turner."

Bunker and Karabin stayed at the scene until early afternoon. When they finally walked to their vehicles Bunker mentioned the fact that he'd witnessed the Shortridge brothers sitting with two men from out of the area.

"I think those two are worth checking out, Pappy."

He cited the fact that they had out-of-state plates and their vehicles were registered to a business. He finished by revealing that he'd followed the pair to a house west of Urbana. As he listened to himself, Bunker felt a feeling grow that the two unnamed subjects may very well be involved.

Karabin looked dubious.

"I don't know Amos...the fact that this Kevin Turner guy is out of prison and seems to be missing, well...I think it's too much of a coincidence to not be related." He continued, "Look into the strangers if you want, but don't lose track of the obvious. What do they call it, Occam's razor?"

Bunker was familiar with the theory; the most obvious answer is often the right one. He nodded grudgingly.

Karabin reached for the door handle of his SUV before turning back to Bunker.

"Let's find this guy Turner."

Bunker watched the senior detective drive off, not quite understanding why his information on the strangers hadn't held more sway with the man. He reached for his own door handle. He checked his watch, knowing that he had paperwork on his desk at the Miami County Safety Building in Troy to complete before heading to the business office at StoryPoint.

I need to find out more about this Running Dog company.

CHAPTER TWELVE

Dylan sat at the kitchen table in the rental house at 7 a.m. Friday morning. He was checking his phone for updates on the discovery of the bodies on Brown Road. A mug of coffee sat untouched and cooling on the table. He looked up as Min padded down the hall rubbing his eyes. Though barefoot, the former Sanyu Scholarship recipient again wore a black t-shirt with black jeans.

Min spoke. "Heyyy bossman, everything good?"

Dylan looked up as his associate shuffled to the cupboard and selected a mug. He smirked slightly, realizing that Min had again gone with the all-black combo.

"That's starting to be like a uniform for you, isn't it?" He gestured to Min's clothes.

Min grinned and poured coffee into his mug. "It's very Jet Li. The ladies love it, especially the American ladies."

The reference to the Chinese-born martial artist and actor seemed appropriate to Dylan. He'd always thought his colleague resembled the man.

"I get it. Has to be pretty damn warm on these hot Ohio days though."

Min sipped from his mug. "Yes...the humidity makes it uncomfortable, but the...benefits make it worthwhile. I believe I have my priorities in order." He reached toward Dylan to clink mugs.

Dylan picked up his own mug and tapped Min's then took a sip. He frowned slightly.

Min cocked his head. "Your problems with heat come from inside your cup, not from the weather. Let me guess, still too warm?"

Dylan nodded. "Still too warm. Has to be just the right temperature."

One side of Min's mouth curled upward. He sat across from Dylan and asked, "What's the latest?"

"Not much more than we saw online yesterday. Bodies found. Public appalled. Cops working diligently, etcetera, etcetera. No indication that we have anything to worry about, not that they would mention specifics to the press at this point." Dylan's eyes turned back to his phone. He looked thoughtful. "Still, seems best that we lay low for a while."

Min sipped. "Three murders in what, five days?"

Dylan nodded, well aware that the attention the murders generated threatened the entire operation. It was sometimes necessary to take out the local dealers in order to pave the way for expansion. Yet the murders brought increased scrutiny from law enforcement. It was a bit of a chicken and egg scenario, he supposed. Dylan had another nagging thought. They had operated for nearly two years and killed seven people. In the last five days they'd eliminated three more. He remembered a lecture at Yale on abnormal psychology. The professor described how psychopathic killers gradually lose their sense of self-control and turn more and more to violent acts that can lead to their discovery and apprehension. He was determined that this wouldn't happen with him.

I'm no psychopath.

He looked at Min. "Probably best that we get back to convincing these dealers to do business with us, not killing them...unless we have absolutely no choice, of course."

Min smiled. "Of course." He took another sip, remembering what it was like living under a totalitarian regime where the citizenry did its utmost to avoid the attention of the government. "We have a saying in China; 'Man should fear fame like pigs fear getting fat.'"

"Wise words, Min." Dylan looped an index finger through the handle of his mug and tried another sip. He nodded. *Better, the temperature's lower.* Then, "I'm calling Dax and Willie, gotta talk to them so we're all on the same page going forward."

An hour later Dylan was in his Range Rover headed to Dayton. He'd decided to meet in person with the two partners.

Their work in that city had reached a critical phase and it made more sense to Dylan for him to go to them than the other way around.

The pair was staying in a Home2 Suites hotel in Centerville, a suburb southeast of Dayton. Dylan called Dax first, received no answer, left no voicemail, then tried Willie. A fatigued-sounding voice answered after four rings.

"What happened?"

Dylan put an extra level of smart-ass into his tone. "Morning Willie-Boy, glad you're up and at 'em! Get your shit together, we need to meet."

Willie repeated his question, sounding a bit more awake. "What happened?"

"Not on the phone. Go to Dax's room and beat on his door. I called and he didn't pick up." Dylan paused then added, "He's not with a girl, is he?"

Now fully awake, Willie sputtered, "What? Fuck no. We were out until almost three this morning trailing a couple of assholes. We both crashed as soon as we got to the hotel."

"Okay, go get Dax. Take a quick shower. Pack a travel bag. Bring both vehicles, the Evoque and the rental. I'll see you guys at 8:30. I'll text you the address on the burner." He considered, then added, "Dax is a candy guy. Tell him he's having chocolate for breakfast."

"What? Wait...what the fuck happened?"

The line went dead.

Dylan had selected another of the many area Winans Coffee and Chocolate locations for the meeting. This one was on the north side of Dayton on Miller Lane, just off I-75. He'd begun to grow familiar with the chain and had come to realize that a high percentage of the shops' business was done through their drive-thrus. There should be tables available.

He fought the urge to drive to Piqua and swing north for a few miles to cruise past the site of the Shortridge murders. He knew the idea was asinine—*Even these small-town cops were smart enough to know a killer might try that*

—and dismissed it without much consideration. The goal at this point was to assume a lower profile.

He decided to avoid Piqua—the closest point of access to I-75—altogether. He took country roads south from the rental for a few miles before linking up with State Route 55, another two-lane east-west route. The road meandered through farmland for a half hour until Dylan entered Troy. There he turned left on Market Street. He guided the Range Rover to the center of town and a traffic circle that surrounded a picturesque fountain. His navigation system directed him to work his way around the circle until he could exit and continue south. He now had, according to the system, nearly four miles to cover through city streets and a semi-rural area before reaching I-75. From there it was less than 15 minutes of highway driving before reaching Miller Lane.

Dylan steered the Range Rover south, leaving Troy's downtown district. Within a few blocks he was passing through a residential area that featured older homes and tree-shrouded lots. Soon businesses began to appear. He passed a drug store, a truck repair shop, gas stations, and a small church. He was approaching a Chevrolet dealership on his left when he noticed brake lights ahead. An orange sign on the side of the road came into view.

ROAD WORK AHEAD

Damn...construction.

Dylan coasted a short distance to the last car in line and slowed to a stop. He glanced at the clock on the Range Rover's interactive display, did a quick calculation, and determined that even with a short delay he should arrive at the Miller Lane Winans a few minutes before his colleagues. Dylan had found both Dax and Willie to be punctual. This, he theorized, had more to do with their employment history—Dax drove an Uber, Willie trailed subjects for a large private investigative company—than their days as college students, where they no doubt overslept on any number of occasions. It would not be a surprise, though, if the pair drug themselves into the coffee shop a few minutes late. They had been running hard the last several nights and had to be fried.

Dylan's thoughts were interrupted as a slow-moving aircraft came into view in the medium distance above the line of traffic ahead. He watched as the craft banked slightly in his direction and began to descend. He focused on it and could now see that it was a biplane. As it came closer, he could discern the aircraft's color. It was bright yellow. The morning sun glinted off it, leading Dylan to believe its surface was metallic, rather than wood and cloth. It seemed to be angling toward the far side of a cluster of buildings off to Dylan's left.

Seconds later, the biplane, now barely ten feet off the ground, disappeared behind the buildings. It was hidden for just seconds behind the structures before reappearing. Dylan saw it surge from behind the buildings through his driver's side window, moving faster than expected. Its two front wheels, enclosed in some sort of teardrop shaped covers, were just leaving the ground. The yellow surface of the plane flashed through Dylan's field of vision as he turned his head and shoulders to the left in an effort to follow it further. As the biplane disappeared behind some trees Dylan noticed for the first time a bright orange windsock waving from a pole. It was near the flat ground the aircraft had flown past.

Was that a crop duster? What is this place?

He turned back toward the buildings and noticed large white letters painted on the roof of one.

WACO
TROY O

What the hell is WACO?

He reached for his phone and typed *W-A-C-O* into its browser search box. Pages of results appeared referring to the city in Texas. Dylan flicked his eyes forward, confirmed traffic was not yet moving, and added the word *airplanes* to his previous search.

He watched as dozens of results appeared. He quickly skimmed a couple. WACO was apparently an aircraft manufacturer that operated in the area before World War Two. One site mentioned a museum and showed a map. Dylan compared it to the one glowing on the Range Rover's display and saw that they matched.

How about that? A museum for old planes...and they still fly?

He was eyeing the buildings ahead on the left when the brake lights of the car ahead of him went out. The line of vehicles began to inch forward. The Range Rover was still four vehicles from the orange vest-clad worker whose sign had been turned so that it read *SLOW* rather than *STOP* when the yellow plane appeared again to the south. It made the same approach as before. Dylan had to make an effort to pull his eyes away from the plane as he rolled past the worker with the sign and maneuvered past asphalt paving equipment. The Range Rover began to accelerate as it drew even with the entrance to the museum complex.

Dylan glanced back to the biplane and saw that it was very low, approaching the area behind the buildings. He saw that the area was a grass landing strip, flanked by the buildings on the west side and a line of trees on the east. The front wheels touched down and the yellow biplane rolled out of Dylan's line of sight behind the buildings.

He directed his attention back to driving while a part of his mind processed the sight of the biplane.

Damn, really cool looking plane. Beautiful. Struts and wires...looked like two people, a pilot up front and a second person behind in another cockpit...would you call the second seat a cockpit too? Probably not. And those streamlined coverings on the wheels, VERY cool. Made it look classy...like the plane was wearing spats.

The road angled right as it approached the intersection with I-75. Dylan signaled a left turn and waited for an opening. He was soon merging with southbound traffic. He thought again about the plane.

It looked like something out of The Great Gatsby. Something old school cool...something that...

Something internal kicked in, halting his train of thought. He realized that the elegance and vintage nature of the biplane reminded him of Yale. Both the plane and the university served a function, yes, but both did it with more style, more importance.

That goddamn place.

He had 15 minutes left to drive. He allowed himself to be drawn back to what almost was.

CHAPTER THIRTEEN

Paul tipped the skillet and used a wooden spoon to slide scrambled eggs in equal portions onto two plates. He turned to the toaster in time to see two slices of wheat bread appear, golden brown and ready to be buttered. He removed them from the toaster's slots and dropped them onto his plate. He then removed two more pieces from the loaf on the counter and slid them vertically into position. Before depressing the lever, he glanced at the dial that controlled the amount of time that heat would be applied.

Almost forgot.

He reached for the dial and turned it counterclockwise until the time was reduced by half. He'd never figured out why Lauren preferred such light toasting.

Might be her only character flaw.

Paul scratched his chin, smiled, and pushed down the lever. He turned his back to the toaster and leaned on the counter. The cycle for Lauren's toast was so short it made little sense to move on to another task. Besides, everything seemed to be ready. Two steaming cups of coffee sat on the island in the center of the kitchen. Paul had cleared away the bric-a-brac, odd stacks of paper, and pieces of mail that seemed to collect there of their own accord like sand on a towel at the beach.

Paul wanted to make breakfast for Lauren on his first morning back from the trip. Her shift began at 7 a.m., but she'd already had an ambitious start to her day. She was back to doing early morning runs with her jogging partner, Lacey Wells. The two women, both employees at Kettering Health, a medical center in downtown Troy, met at 5:30 at Lacey's new house in a subdivision on the city's north side. Lacey and her husband Matt bought the house a few months after their wedding the past October.

Paul's thoughts turned to injuries that Lacey suffered during a run with Lauren last year, injuries at the hand of an assailant. His eyes were still directed at the coffee cups, but he was seeing troubling events from the past.

It was at this moment that Chappy, their orange tabby, leapt from the opposite side of the island and settled on its surface behind Paul's cup. The cat's appearance perfectly coincided—as if engineered by a Hollywood special effects expert—with the mechanical spring sound that came from the toaster as Lauren's slices popped up. The combination of movement and sound gave the impression that the star of a feline action hero movie had announced his presence on screen.

Paul was not quite startled but was quickly brought back to the present. Chappy was framed in soft morning sunlight that streamed in from the kitchen window. Paul saw small strands of the cat's hair, propelled upward by the leap, float in the glow and alight in his coffee cup.

"Dammit Chappy!"

Paul reached for the cup and snatched it off the island. Some of the hot coffee splashed over the rim and onto his wrist. Chappy's green eyes followed the movement with apparent disinterest.

"Oww, DAMMIT!" He glared at the cat. "You are NOT supposed to be on the island...or the table...or the countertops. You—"

He was cut off by Lauren, who entered the kitchen, showered and dressed for work. "Getting reacquainted with Chappy?"

At the sight of Lauren, the feline immediately jumped down from the island. Paul watched as Chappy padded to her and arched his back against her legs.

"So, he just jumps down now as soon as he sees you? He completely disregards me when I order him down. Am I in a bad reality TV show?" He made an exaggerated turn as if looking for hidden cameras.

Lauren snickered. "You were enlisted, remember? I was a Warrant Officer. Chappy bestows the proper respect to rank." She bent to scratch the top of Chappy's head.

Although Lauren began her career in the Air Force as an enlisted airman, she earned a position as a Warrant Officer while working in the medical field. Technically she had outranked her special operations husband, who was a Master Sergeant when he retired.

She straightened and reached for her coffee cup. "What do you have today? Back to the grind?"

Paul shot a final withering look at Chappy as he emptied his cup into the sink and reached for the pot. "Some emails and calls. Got a Zoom call with the McClarys and a client at ten...might have to go to Chicago sometime in the next few days. Hopefully not, since I haven't even unpacked from the D.C. trip."

"So, laundry today too, huh?"

"Yeah, laundry."

They ate mostly in silence. The thoughts of each of them drifted to the same subject—their application to the state's foster and adoption program. It represented perhaps their last opportunity to be parents. Both were becoming concerned that the delayed response might mean they were turned down. Paul broke the silence, keeping the subject light.

"Good run?"

Lauren nodded, seeming to brighten. "Yeah, Lacey's really bouncing back. Her injuries kept her from running for months. She's only been back at it a couple weeks and I'm already having trouble keeping up. I guess that's what youth will do for you. It would take me twice as long to bounce back to that level." As she completed the last sentence her expression changed.

Paul read her face and realized that Lauren's inadvertent reference to her age seemed to immediately dim her mood. The Hulls had always wanted children. After they accepted that they would never have their own naturally, they prioritized other aspects of life. Paul was in a cycle of combat deployments. Lauren was a medical laboratory technician. She spent time at several locations, some outside of the United States. Though adoption was a consideration, there never seemed to be a convenient time to pursue it seriously. Now, with both of them out of the military and having put down roots in Ohio, the time seemed right.

There was one concern—their age.

Paul, at 52, and Lauren, at 47, realized it would be difficult to be approved by an agency to adopt a baby. Taking in and raising an older child seemed to be a more attainable goal. After discussing the options both were comfortable, even eager, to pursue this alternative.

Still, what Lauren termed "the age thing" was never far from her thoughts. The clock was ticking. She was reminded of this often. Every time she was not asked for her ID in a bar or restaurant, every time she used hair dye to treat grey roots, and, in this case, each time a discussion illuminated the fact that she no longer possessed the same recuperative abilities of a twenty-something.

Paul made an effort to be upbeat.

"I think I'll call the state today...find out what's taking so long."

Lauren offered a thin smile.

Paul worked out in the basement after Lauren left for work. Though they had walked for miles on the camping trip, Paul and his mates hadn't devoted time or effort to strenuous exercise. Paul felt the effects of the layoff almost immediately. Half of the basement space was outfitted with equipment that Paul used regularly. He found the normal number of repetitions more difficult to complete. After nearly an hour he toweled off and headed back upstairs to shower.

I think Lauren was onto something...We're not getting any younger.

After showering he closed the office door on a curious Chappy and spent time at his desk prepping for the Zoom call. The prospective client in Chicago was a craft distillery seeking to take their products—primarily vodka and gin—national. Chicago had a rich history with liquors of all types, something that is often overshadowed by stories of rum-running and whisky smuggling during Prohibition. There were currently at least a dozen craft distillers inside the city limits. If the suburbs were included this number rose to more than 20. Paul reread the correspondence between company officials and Mike and Marge. At 9:50 a notification appeared on his laptop's screen indicating the meeting could be joined.

Paul, Mike, and Marge made small talk until a pair of representatives from Chicago, the president and the head of marketing, joined in. The meeting went well. Mike cautioned the Chicagoans, touching several times on the difficulty of making a local brand, no matter how successful in its home market, successful on a larger scale. The president, a man named Beckert, nodded each time.

After the third such warning from Mike, Beckert asserted, "Look, we know it'll be a hard climb. Frankly, we are coming to Jasper Spirits because of the success of Tutor's Bourbon. We understand your efforts were instrumental in their growth. We want to partner with you."

Paul was gratified to hear this, having worked directly with the fledgling bourbon distiller from Kentucky. At the conclusion of the call, Marge, the planning and logistics whiz at Jasper, agreed to put together a prospective action plan.

As soon as the conference call ended Paul's phone rang. He answered and heard Mike's voice.

"That went well."

Paul concurred. "Yeah, for two reasons; they want to do business with us, and they didn't say anything about me coming to Chicago right away. It won't break my heart to work from home for a while."

"They might not want you there right away, but they're going to want you sooner or later." Mike continued, "The work you did for Tutor's got our foot in the door."

Paul brushed this aside. "Team effort."

When the call ended Paul checked the time and saw it was after 11 o'clock.

Better try the adoption people. I promised Lauren.

He dialed and was mildly surprised when an actual person answered. He explained that he wanted to speak to someone about a pending application and, as he'd expected, was put on hold. A caseworker came on the line two minutes later and Paul gave her his name and explained why he was calling.

"I'm sorry Mr. Hull, but it looks like we still haven't received all of the completed background questionnaires yet. Actually, it looks like we're waiting on just one of them. As soon as we receive it a determination can be made on you and your wife's application." She apologized, saying it usually didn't take this long to receive responses. "Frankly, I'm looking here at your military records and I would think you'd be a shoo-in for approval."

Paul thanked her before hanging up, wondering who in the hell was sitting on a request for information that could influence their entire future. A friend? A former commanding officer? He checked the time again and saw it was past 11:30.

No wonder I'm hungry again.

He opened the office door, nearly tripped over a clearly aggravated Chappy, and turned toward the kitchen to make lunch. He stopped after two steps.

Forgot to start the laundry...crap.

He made an about-face and retrieved his duffel from the master bedroom. He slung it on his shoulder, grabbed the laundry hamper—*might as well do Lauren's too*—and headed to the basement laundry room.

He grabbed handfuls of soiled clothes from the duffel and pitched them into the washer. The second handful included a University of Kentucky hoodie. Gatewood had purchased several of these and gifted them to close friends after his youngest son, Henry, committed to UK as a wide receiver on the football team. When Paul got to the bottom of the duffel, he found a second identical hoodie.

He regarded it with confusion before it hit him.

Gotta be Gatewood's. He and I were both wearing them at the campfire that last night. Don't think Mike took his on the trip. Scrabble doesn't have one.

He remembered Gatewood talking about his sweatshirt at the campfire. "See this hoodie fellas? I was wearing it when Henry made his first collegiate TD catch against Alabama. This hoodie has religious significance."

All four men burst out laughing.

I must've grabbed Woody's hoodie when we were packing up. He's gonna want this back ASAP.

Paul decided to shoot his friend a quick text.

Hey Woody, I have your UK hoodie. Want me to drop it off?

Minutes later he received a response.

Will get it later. Bad day. Storm off coast getting worse. East Coast bases probably sending planes to WPAFB. Also, Henry's buddy Bean died.

Paul stared at the phone's screen.

What the hell?

The mention of the storm and its possible repercussions for Wright-Patterson Air Force Base were not particularly a surprise. East Coast storms, if they reached a certain level of strength, often triggered a little-known phenomenon in the U.S military. Airbases in the threatened area routinely sent their aircraft to bases further inland to protect them from being damaged. Wright-Patt was one of the primary destinations. Gatewood, in his role as the senior enlisted member of the base's security detail, would be knee-deep in the preparations for such an event. Paul knew this. It was the last part of the text that stunned Paul.

Bean died? What the hell happened?

Paul fired off another text asking just that. While waiting for an answer he ruminated. Vernon "Bean" Grissom was the same age as Henry Dowdell. They were both starting wide receivers as sophomores for the Wayne High School Warriors in suburban Dayton. Bean tore an ACL late that season and was never quite the same on the field. Henry went on to stardom and received multiple college offers, eventually choosing Kentucky. Paul had met Bean and spent time around him on a handful of occasions at Gatewood's house. The young man had always seemed upbeat and likable.

The Dowdells must be torn up about this.
Paul's phone buzzed and he looked down.

We're hearing fentanyl overdose. Not confirmed. Henry coming for funeral. Talk later.

Paul read the text several times, always returning to one word.
Fentanyl?!?

CHAPTER FOURTEEN

Traffic was light on I-75 as Dylan completed his merge into the slow lane. He checked his mirrors and waited for a plumber's van to flash past before easing into the passing lane. He watched the van pull away while thinking, *There must be a toilet somewhere in need of an emergency unclogging.* He set the Range Rover's cruise a few ticks over the speed limit and let his thoughts drift back.

Generations of the Riordan family were born and raised in Framingham, Massachusetts, a town of some 70,000 about twenty miles west of downtown Boston. They worked blue collar jobs, followed the Red Sox and Celtics, and strived to get their kids through high school. Most years the family met, by informal tradition, on the third Monday of April near the railroad station on Framingham's Waverly Street. This was Patriots' Day, a legal holiday in Massachusetts and five other states that commemorated the first battles of the Revolutionary War: Lexington, Concord, and Menotomy.

Framingham was situated, more or less, at the six-mile mark of the Boston Marathon course. The Riordans joined hundreds of fellow town residents at the Waverly Street location to cheer runners as they passed by on their way to the towns of Natick and Wellesley, to Heartbreak Hill, and—if all went as hoped—the finish line on Boston's Boylston Street near Copley Square.

Though successive generations of Riordans imagined little chance of a family member someday attending one of the fine Boston area colleges or universities, these institutions were always held in high esteem. They included the University of Massachusetts, Boston College, Boston University, and Harvard University, the particularly unattainable Ivy League school in Cambridge, across the Charles River from Boston.

In the 1960s Dylan's paternal grandparents left Framingham, relocating 100 miles north to the small town of

Charlestown, New Hampshire. His grandfather was attracted by a factory job opportunity, something that had become increasingly rare in Framingham. Dylan's father, Patrick, was born in 1965.

After graduating from Charlestown High School, Patrick went to work at a small car dealership on the edge of town. He started as a general laborer, washing cars on the lot and sweeping floors. After a year he began turning wrenches with the two full-time mechanics. Eventually he worked at every level of the business including sales and bookkeeping. When the owner retired, Patrick was able to secure a loan and bought the business.

Dylan was born in 1995. By the time he entered high school his father owned a string of car dealerships in New Hampshire, Vermont, and Massachusetts. The Riordans were wealthy beyond anything their previous generations could have imagined. It was a foregone conclusion that their only child would become the first member of the family to attend college.

Dylan enjoyed a childhood completely out of step with his family tree, wanting for nothing. He drove new cars from his father's dealerships. He was a junior member at several area golf courses. At no time did he hold a job, even one that was part-time. Rather than go to a public school in Charlestown, Dylan attended Vermont Academy, a private college preparatory school 20 minutes southwest, across the state line. Golf, as it turned out, became the one area where Dylan applied himself.

He did well in youth tournaments. Patrick, who rarely played, indulged his son by having a green as well as a driving range built on their property. Dylan improved to the point that he placed second in the Vermont State High School Golf Championship held at Burlington Country Club his junior year. This put him on the map as a possible college golfer. He began to look at options.

Though he hadn't particularly applied himself academically at Vermont Academy, Dylan was confident in his intelligence and ability to score well on standardized tests. His parents set up private prep sessions for him before taking the SAT and he responded with a score of 1410, an excellent mark that was good enough to get into all but the very top-level schools.

But it was a top-level school upon which Dylan had set his sights.

He was a contrary boy in many ways. He liked to go against the grain. Knowing that Riordans had cheered for the Boston Red Sox for decades, Dylan instead chose their rivals, the New York Yankees, as his favorite team. He did something similar in virtually every aspect of life. This prompted Patrick, several times, to wonder, *Is this kid just TRYING to piss me off?*

When it came to a college to target, Dylan was true to form, telling his father, "I want Yale." Harvard was out of the question.

A visit was arranged to the New Haven, Connecticut campus, two states to the south. Dylan and his parents first met with the golf coach who seemed impressed with the boy's scores but openly wondered, "Have you talked yet with admissions? What about submitting your SAT scores?" Dylan was unconcerned with these details, sure that he was the principal decision maker in any convergence of student and school.

It turned out that he was wrong. Yale had the upper hand in the process. It was awash in applications from good-not-great high school golfers, many of whom had posted better SAT scores than Dylan. And with an endowment north of $40 billion, the university did not particularly need Patrick's money.

Dylan, faced with the possibility of being denied for the first time in his life of something he wanted, pressed his parents—they might've said he whined—until Patrick offered to make a donation to the school that was barely significant to it, while at the same time making an alarming dent in the bank account and investment portfolio held by him and his wife.

Dylan's application was accepted. He was promised a spot as a preferred walk-on to the golf team. He spent his senior year of high school wearing Yale gear whenever possible and putting forth an effort in the classroom that was below par. His performance on the golf course—where below par would've been a *good* thing—was also lacking. He practiced less, complained about course conditions, and was generally a pain in the ass to any and all playing partners. He failed to advance past the district meet and did not earn a chance to equal, or better, his second-place finish as a junior.

Still, he showed up as expected at New Haven. He was cocky, entitled, and spoiled. This did not necessarily differentiate him from a number of incoming freshmen. Most of these, however, came ready to perform.

Dylan had a modicum of success in the classroom. After earning C's on early tests in introductory math and political science courses he bounced back. His 2.4 GPA was unspectacular but acceptable.

It was on the golf course where his underperformance was more noticeable. The poor work ethic he'd displayed as a high school senior carried over. He was shocked at the level of talent it took to be a Division 1 golfer, even at a northern school that generally did not attract the better players from warmer climates. Dylan found himself pressing, which, in a sport that required touch and patience, was calamitous. He failed to make the travel squad in any match. At his post season meeting with the coach he realized he was not part of the team's plan going forward. The exact words used by the coach were, "I'm going to need your roster spot next year for a player coming in from California."

Dylan could quit the team and stay at Yale, or transfer. Either way, he wouldn't be a member of the Yale golf team the following year.

He quit the team.

His parents were furious. Both with his performance and the now seemingly wasteful hit to their net worth after making the donation.

Dylan buckled down as a sophomore in the classroom. He earned an A in a 200-level psychology class and found that he was fascinated with the subject, eventually declaring it as his major. It was in this class that he first set eyes on a willowy blonde from Delaware. The blonde reminded him of a high school conquest, a sexually active 18-year-old who repeatedly gave 16-year-old Dylan "self-guided tours" of her body in any number of convenient parking spots near the Vermont-New Hampshire border. Dylan found himself in the same class with the Delaware blonde at Yale nearly every semester. He went out of his way to be next to her on several occasions, not quite noticing that she retreated whenever possible.

In mid-February each year at Yale, some members of the junior class are chosen to become members of one of Yale's secret societies. Some of these societies are famous, with a list of prominent past members who became well known. The inner workings of these societies are shielded, almost mysterious. A number of conspiracy theories blame—or credit—these organizations for being a driving force behind how true power is apportioned not only in the United States, but the world as a whole. Skull and Bones, founded in 1832, was perhaps the most famous, having a past membership that was sprinkled with names such as Vanderbilt and Rockefeller and even included three presidents: William Howard Taft and both George Bushes.

Dylan saw the societies as an opportunity for advancement, as fraternities on steroids. Yes, they were populated by a number of wealthy sons and daughters of privilege who believed they were above the rules, but, damn it, he wanted in.

The day that those chosen for societies are notified is known as "Tap Day." In the 1870s students rioted over the selection process used by the societies. Tap Day was instituted in 1879. Yale juniors crowded into Branford Court near the center of the Old Campus with hopes of being tapped on the shoulder by a member of one of the societies. A "tapped" man was one who had received an offer to join. There are stories of members of different societies racing to tap the most desirable candidates.

Over the years the process continued to evolve. Rather than it being a single day of membership offers and induction ceremonies, an intricate system of interviews, pre-taps, and initiations occurs in the weeks leading up to the actual day. Since the official tap now generally takes place in the evening, many at Yale now refer to the event as Tap Night.

Having an expectation of being chosen and being passed over can be crushing. Being tapped was validating, affirming, even life changing. That some also considered it ridiculous did not diminish its allure to Dylan.

He *really* wanted in.

Dylan's first contact with the societies happened just before he went home his junior year for Christmas break, or more accurately winter break, the term Yale used so as to not offend anyone. He was walking outside of Harkness Tower, having finished classes for the day, and thinking about where he might hit some golf balls. It was an unseasonably warm December day. Despite no longer being a member of the golf team Dylan retained his love of the game. Driving ranges in New Haven were closed for the season.

He stopped and stared absentmindedly up at the iconic tower. It stood 216 feet tall and featured a crenellated design that wouldn't be out of place in Monty Python's *Holy Grail* or any of the Harry Potter movies. A famous picture of John F. Kennedy giving a speech in front of the tower in 1962 hung on the walls of several Yale professors. Dylan's favorite story about the tower involved the famous architect Frank Lloyd Wright who, when visiting the campus, was said to ask for a room in a particular guest suite because it was the only location in New Haven from which Harkness Tower could *not* be seen. Dylan was watching a bird circle the tower and flare its wings to land when he heard his name.

"You're Dylan Riordan, right?"

It was an athletic, blonde, young man. He was slightly taller than Dylan. His winning smile and palpable confidence made it obvious to Dylan that this was another Yale student.

"Yeah, I'm Dylan."

"Fred Fisher." A hand was extended and Dylan shook it without consideration.

"I'll cut to the chase. I'm with Fence Club. You're being considered for membership. We'd like to talk to you...you know, an interview. Maybe right after winter break?"

Dylan fought to keep a grin from his face. Fence Club, though not one of the more fabled societies on campus, drew significant interest during spring rush. An invitation to the organization would make many envious. He squared his shoulders and projected a look of disinterest.

"Sure, we can talk."

Fisher nodded and backed away. "Okay, we'll be in touch then." He turned and appeared to be looking for his next target.

Dylan dropped his attitude of indifference as quickly as he'd assumed it. "Wait, don't you need my number?" He held up his cellphone, realizing as he did so that he must've looked like the neediest son-of-a-bitch in Connecticut.

Fisher smiled. "We already have it. Remember, we're a secret society." He winked and strode off.

An even more gratifying possibility occurred in early January after Dylan returned from spending the holidays at home. The time off had been welcome but the constant harping by his parents, particularly his dad, spoiled the break. *What are you gonna do with a psychology degree? What about golf? Maybe transfer somewhere where you can make the team. You know your mother and I have INVESTED*—the word dripped with sarcasm—*a shitload of money in this Yale thing and it doesn't look like it's panning out. Maybe just come back and work at one of our dealerships?*

He'd been back to campus for just two days when he received a text from an unknown number.

Can you meet tonight in regards to Tap?

Dylan was sitting on the couch in his off-campus apartment eating ramen noodles and scrolling on his phone when the message popped onto the screen.

He brightened. *Gotta be from that guy Fisher. This is Fence Club!*

He quickly typed, *Absolutely! Where & when?*

Before hitting send he reconsidered his response. It seemed a bit too eager. He deleted it and retyped. **Will make it work. Text me the deets.**

In seconds, a new message appeared.

10pm Sterling Library. Philosophy Reading Room, 6th Floor.

Dylan responded with a thumbs up emoji and returned to his noodles, secure in the belief that he was one step closer to membership in a society.

He arrived at Sterling Library several minutes early. Located at the heart of central campus, Sterling was the largest of Yale's 15 libraries. Built in a style known as Collegiate Gothic, it boasted 14 floors of book stacks and seven floors of study area. For years it housed Yale's copy of the Gutenberg Bible, one of just 49 in existence. The bible, donated by the same Harkness family whose name is attached to the tower, was now displayed at Beinecke Rare Book & Manuscript Library nearby. Dylan remembered being walked through both libraries on a campus visit after being accepted. The student leading the group seemed to be impressed by the 600-year-old bible as well as a 1,250-year old print of Buddhist prayers on display at Beinecke. Dylan, a Yankees fan, was more fascinated that the original manuscript of Babe Ruth's autobiography was housed there. After the tour, Dylan and his parents visited the campus bookstore. While waiting for his father to pay for the $800 worth of gear they'd selected, Dylan saw a framed black and white photo of an aging Ruth presenting the manuscript to Yale's baseball captain and first baseman, George Bush Sr. The thought of Bush, a Bonesman, refocused Dylan on the task at hand—meeting with Fred Fisher.

But it wasn't Fisher.

Dylan got off the elevator on the 6th floor and followed the signs to the Philosophy Reading Room. He halted outside the door and glanced down, checking himself to make sure nothing was out of place. He wore a striped polo, Tommy Bahama khaki slacks, and a pair of Sebago docksiders with no socks. Confirming that all was in order and he was sufficiently preppy cool, he entered.

The room was not large. There were a few long oval walnut tables surrounded by common office chairs. Desk lamps rested on both ends of each table. A wooden bookshelf filled one wall while the others were bare, aside from coats of bland beige paint. A young man with reddish hair sat alone in the room at one of the tables. He wore frameless glasses and a knowing smile. He stood.

"You're probably wondering why we chose this room to meet." He continued, not waiting for an answer. "We need privacy and, well, it *is* the philosophy room. Who the hell is going to be using it...even at Yale, right?" He gestured to a seat across the table.

Dylan allowed one corner of his mouth to curl upward and moved to the chair. Settling in he asked, "Where's Fred?"

The other man sat back down and allowed his knowing smile to grow wider. "Ahh, Fred Fisher of Fence Club. Rolls off the tongue doesn't it? I'm afraid he will have nothing to do with our discussion. You see, I'm not with Fence Club."

Dylan looked at the man, confusion now showing on his face.

"No Dylan, I'm with Mace and Chain." He sat back, allowing his words to sink in.

Dylan was dumbstruck.

If Mace and Chain was a step below Skull and Bones and a handful of other secret societies, it was a small step. Mace and Chain was founded in 1956 and was one of just eight such groups at Yale that is "landed," meaning it has its own clubhouse. Dylan, like all Yale students, had heard that the societies met on Thursdays and Sundays at their buildings, which were also known as "tombs." The Mace and Chain tomb was located on Trumbull Street in downtown New Haven and was rumored to have been built with materials salvaged from Benedict Arnold's home.

The redheaded young man put his elbows on the table and steepled his fingers. It was a gesture that Dylan would have thought pretentious if this wasn't the most pretentious moment of his life.

"You've heard of us, of course?"

"Of-of course," Dylan managed.

"We tap just 15 juniors each year. You are part of a group of 25 that we are considering. I'll be frank with you, your top attributes seem to be that you are from a family that is a donor to the university, and—you might think this ironic—that you lost a spot on the golf team but have seemingly recovered from this with no ill will to the team and coaching staff. You also seem to have plugged away academically and shown continual improvement almost every semester since freshman year."

Dylan nodded, attempting to look self-deprecating. In truth he had done more than his fair share of badmouthing Yale Golf in the bars near campus. He also knew that the chances of any further donations from the Riordan clan were roughly the same as Dylan spontaneously bursting in flames right there in the Philosophy Reading Room.

He cleared his throat. "Well I...appreciate your interest. This is certainly a great opportunity." He suddenly remembered that the name Mace and Chain was supposedly chosen after the original members had a number of discussions about chivalry, something that Dylan did not give two shits about. Still, he gave the redheaded young man what he thought sounded right. "I hear you develop leaders who go on to great things. That's what I want out of the Yale experience, to be a proper Eli."

The man was barely older than Dylan, but he seemed to exist at the Ivy League institution on a completely different plane. Which, Dylan believed, he actually did thanks to his association with the important secret society. Dylan hoped he was hiding his actual thoughts.

Being tapped by Mace and Chain would be career-making. I'd be tied into a powerful alumni network. Beats the shit out of sitting at a desk at one of Patrick Riordan's dealerships.

The young redheaded man narrowed his eyes slightly as if assessing Dylan. He then nodded and stood.

"This was simply an introductory meet. Our membership will evaluate all candidates. Be prepared to do a more in-depth sit-down between now and Tap Day in February." He stepped to the door and opened it.

Dylan quickly stood and asked anxiously, "Do I need your contact info?"

The young redheaded man smiled.

"You do not. This is not a negotiation. It is a selection process. We decide who is in and how they are chosen."

He stepped through the doorway.

Dylan watched him disappear.

What a prick...

Then, *I want in!*

Dylan waited a full minute before leaving the room. He didn't want to give the Mace and Chain representative the impression that he was being followed. After allowing the time to pass he stepped into the corridor and made his way to the elevator. He caught a reflection of himself in a window and realized he was beaming.

Gotta get a grip on myself.

He tried to reconfigure his face into a more subdued expression but was only partially successful. Reaching the elevator, he pushed the down button. He tried to remember when he'd last been this giddy.

The elevator dinged and the door slid open. It was empty. Dylan stepped inside and selected the ground floor, then stood looking back at the sixth-floor corridor. He watched fellow students amble across his field of vision. He made a supreme effort to put a bored look on his face, again with limited success. As soon as the door slid closed, he pumped his fist.

"YES!!!" He cried out, not caring that his voice would've carried through the door to the corridor beyond. He was going to be a "Made Man." His life's path was altered. As the elevator began to descend, Dylan's brain, catching up, supplied him with two possible answers to when he'd last been this jazzed: the first time he got laid or his first hole in one.

Ha! You could describe both events as a hole in one!

He was laughing at his own wit when the elevator door opened on four and she got on.

It was the willowy blonde from Delaware.

CHAPTER FIFTEEN

Dylan nearly missed the exit. He forced himself to leave his memories of Yale and come back to the present. After exiting the highway, he found his way to Miller Lane and spotted the Winans ahead on the left. He entered the lot and was not surprised that there was no evidence of his colleague's vehicles.

This Winans, despite having a different configuration than the Piqua shop, did exhibit the same maroon on black color scheme. Dylan parked and strode to the door, which displayed a help wanted sign. Entering the shop, he noted with satisfaction that there were just a handful of patrons inside. This despite the fact that there were several vehicles queuing outside in the drive-thru. He waited for a woman to place her order—*why did this always take so long in a coffee shop?*—then stepped forward.

"Large latte, shot of hazelnut please...name is Eli."

The barista, a harried-looking middle-aged man, nodded and, after Dylan paid, reached for a cup and jotted E-L-I on it before turning to the espresso maker. Dylan turned and selected a table in the corner. He sat and waited for both his partners and his drink, wondering faintly which would appear first.

The barista called his name three minutes later and Dylan rose to retrieve the cup. As he turned back to the table, he saw two bedraggled men enter the shop. Dylan gave a short wave, pointed them to the counter, then indicated he would be at the table in the corner. The first man was short and pudgy and wore dark-framed glasses below black hair that was tightly curled. The second was taller at 6'3" and had shoulder-length straw-colored hair. Both nodded without enthusiasm and shuffled to the counter to place their orders.

Two minutes later William Pace "Willie" Wiley, the shorter dark-haired man, approached the table. Seeing the lid removed from Dylan's cup and level of coffee near its top he asserted, "Still too hot for you, right?"

Dylan grinned and nodded.

Willie was dressed in a grey tee covered by a well-worn flannel shirt. He wore dark green shorts. His pale legs were supported by feet clad in a pair of sandals that looked like they would be at home at a Grateful Dead concert in 1968. He sat and rubbed his eyes.

"God, I am fucking tired." He looked at Dylan. "What the fuck happened? What—"

Dylan held up a finger and nodded toward Dax who was making his way toward their table.

As he pulled out a chair, Dax, whose given name was Keenan Devereaux, cracked a smile, checked over both shoulders, then breathed, "Did you and Min really leave Shadow under a giant loaf of bread?"

"Seemed like the thing to do at the time."

Dax grinned. He wore a lightweight button-down sky-blue shirt with cream-colored microfiber shorts and flip-flops. His exposed skin was tan, the direct opposite of Willie's.

"I never really liked that guy. Too much of a poser. Who took the shot, Min?"

"Nope. Yours truly." Dylan slid his cup closer and blew lightly, rippling the surface of the latte. He recounted how the killing went down in Urbana, stopping only when the barista called Dax and Willie back to the counter to pick up their drinks. Dax returned with a cup of chai tea. Willie had both a small serving of espresso and a large cup of regular coffee loaded down with sugar.

"Okay, so why are we meeting?" Willie sipped the espresso.

Dylan noticed for the first time that Willie's t-shirt bore the message *HISTORY BUFF: I'd be more interested in you if you were dead.* He remembered that the man had been a history major at Brown.

"We have a lot going on at the same time. The Shortridge thing the other night—don't get me wrong, it had to be done—but it is *really* drawing a lot of attention since it happened so soon after we did Shadow."

Willie tilted his head toward Dax and met his eyes. The unspoken message was *Well, who the hell's fault was THAT?*

Dylan continued.

"We have things going in three different areas now and we have to make sure we think things through...check all the boxes."

Dax stirred his tea and leaned in. "So, we're getting down to the short strokes with this thing in Dayton. Do we need to shift gears?"

Dylan picked up his cup and tipped it until the liquid touched his lips. He frowned and set it down. "Let's start there and work backwards. What's the latest with that?"

Dax and Willie had been surveilling several people in the Dayton area. They'd identified street-level sellers who moved a variety of illegal drugs, the majority of which were opioids.

Willie spoke. "The hookups—the mules out making the deliveries—are low-level. They get their stuff from a guy named Barnes...tough guy, former football player or some shit."

Dax jumped in. "Yeah, Barnes says he had a tryout with the Cowboys. Supposedly a big high school star somewhere down south. Went to some nowhere college that nobody's ever heard of. Ended up in Dayton. We contacted him, set up a meet. He's a big talker, kinda reminds me of Shadow that way. Anyway—"

Willie interrupted. "Anyway, we thought he was the source, the guy we had to sell. The meeting didn't go well."

Dax grinned. "He called Willie a fucking dweeb."

Willie's face reddened. "Yeah, well he called *you* a fucking surfer dude."

"But I kinda like being called a surfer dude...doesn't bug me." Dax turned to Dylan. "Willie's right, it didn't go well. That's when we contacted you to say there was a good chance we would need to take this Barnes guy out."

Willie, his face still red, added, "He could use a nice dose of .22 short from our putter right between the eyes."

Dax made an effort to hold back a grin and continued the narrative. "So, we put a microscope to Barnes...try to see where he is sourcing his stuff. Long story short—and it *is* a long story, we've been working our asses off—Barnes is getting opioids from some doctor named Mahmud. He's getting his blow and some meth from other sources but we—"

Willie again took over. "But we don't give a shit about that...just the opioids. The doctor is legit...well, he's a real doctor, he's just writing more illegitimate scripts than the quack that was supplying Michael Jackson."

"So, we need to make a deal with this doctor... Mahmud?" Dylan was pretty much up to speed on the network up to and including Barnes since Dax and Willie had posted updates in the mutually accessible drafts folder they utilized, but the revelation about the doctor was new information.

Dax answered. "We're about 90 percent on that. Thing is, it looks like he wrote so many bogus scripts that he's being looked at by the Dayton cops and the DEA...maybe even the FBI. So, he's been trying to back off on that and he's got a new source. We're hearing the doc should be getting a shipment any day from whoever that is. Willie and I are hoping to identify who is now supplying Mahmud." He stopped his briefing long enough to sip his tea. Willie took over.

"If Mahmud is buying from some shit-kickers from Tennessee or wherever, he should jump all over our offer. He'd take one look at the carfentanil in the golf balls and jump in bed with us. But if his stuff is coming from the Venezuelans or the Russians..."

He didn't have to finish. All three men knew their business plan was to target independent operations in more rural areas. They had no desire to butt heads with the violent cartels or organized crime that operated in large cities. That got messy. It resulted in lots of bodies. More, even, than Dylan and his crew were generating. Right now, the only victims were the dealers that didn't fall in line. Taking business from MS-13, or gangs like it, came with great personal risk.

Dylan nodded. "Got it. We need to ID Mahmud's supplier. If his source isn't a threat, we do a meet with him... sounds like he'll deal. If it becomes critical that we need info on how much heat is on Mahmud from the cops, I can check with our source in the FBI. I'd rather not do that—he can be expensive—but I will if I have to. If the doc's source is too much of a threat to us, we pull the plug on Dayton. This is exactly the kind of shit Min and I were afraid of when we put this thing together."

At the mention of their fourth partner Willie asked, "Speaking of which, where the hell *is* mini-Jet Li?"

Dylan lifted his cup, slowly moved it in a circle to swirl its contents, and again brought it to his lips. He took a small sip, made a *not bad* expression, and set it down to cool a bit more.

"He's back at the rental, prepping the Running Dog golf bag and cleaning the guns. Nice segue Willie. Let's talk about what we need to do back in Urbana and Piqua. You guys did a nice job setting up things in both areas. What we need now, and pretty damn quick, is to circle back to both areas and meet with the people who are replacing Shadow and the Shortridge brothers. Both of you know those people. Min and I should probably lay low in both areas...for obvious reasons."

He did not need to spell it out. He and Min had killed three dealers in the past few days. They didn't believe that anyone had witnessed the killings, but the smart play was to keep a low profile until their business in the area was complete and they'd moved on to safer areas.

Dax asked, "So you want us to go back today and line up things with the replacements?"

"Just one of you, in the rental car. That's why I had both of you drive here this morning. The other one can stay and work the Dayton thing. Your choice who stays and who goes."

The car was a nondescript grey Nissan Sentra sedan that had been rented in Dayton and had not been driven in Urbana or Miami County. The second vehicle that Dax and Willie were using was a Range Rover Evoque, leased by Running Dog, that looked exactly like those driven by Dylan and Min. Dylan knew that his colleagues had not yet used the Range Rover to surveil the Dayton network. It could actually be advantageous to use it now. The possibility always existed that someone had noticed the Sentra.

Dax and Willie looked at each other. Both would rather stick with the undertaking in Dayton. It had taken a significant effort to reach the position they were currently in and they were about to achieve a breakthrough. Willie had an additional reason to stay in Dayton—he hated to drive.

Dax turned to Willie. "Whattaya think Mr. College Graduate...rock, paper, scissors...loser drives the Sentra back to the middle of nowhere?"

Willie sighed.

He chose scissors.

Dax chose rock.

CHAPTER SIXTEEN

Detective Amos Bunker began Friday morning with a mental checklist of tasks to accomplish. Before tackling them, he decided to stop to see his mom.

She won't have many more days at the house.

It struck him that the morning routine they'd developed would be ending with her move to StoryPoint.

She's gonna miss me stopping by in the mornings... Hell, I'LL miss stopping by in the mornings.

He resolved to continue the visits once she was set up in the facility. Any familiar routine that could be carried over to StoryPoint, he reasoned, would be comforting. She was going to be away from the house she'd lived in for years, away from most of her possessions.

It was depressing to Bunker. He could only imagine how depressing it might be to his mother. He shook his head.

Have to focus on the positives...she'll be getting better care.

Bunker was driving a department SUV today. He had several official tasks to accomplish and did not anticipate the need to drive an unmarked car. He pulled into the driveway on Plum Street and walked up to the front door. For years he would simply go to the back door, knock once, and let himself in. When his mother began to imagine prowlers, he ended the practice. He didn't want to alarm her any more than necessary. Ringing the front doorbell could be distressing if she was having a bad day, but it was a lower risk.

It took nearly a minute for her to reach the door. After 30 seconds he rang a second time. He was growing concerned and was about to reach for his copy of her house key when he saw her face appear in one of the small windows beside the door. He knew immediately that she was having a bad day. She peered out at him with a fearful look on her face. Bunker saw that her hair was disheveled.

Ahhh, man.

After several seconds, a spark of recognition seemed to appear in her eyes. She unlocked the door and stepped aside as he entered. Bunker made a conscious effort to be upbeat.

"Morning Mom, what does a guy have to do to get a cup of coffee in this joint?"

She looked at him blankly for a beat. Finally, a smile appeared on her face. "Follow me Amos...I could use a cup myself." She led him to the kitchen. Once there, she busied herself with the preparation.

With her back turned to him, Bunker surveyed the kitchen. It was a mess. A full trash bag leaned up against the refrigerator, it's open top revealed an egg carton. Several eggshells were on the floor below the bag. It appeared that one of the shells had been stepped on. A half-full jar of pickles sat on the counter, its lid laying nearby. He noticed a fork on the floor.

Oh boy.

Bunker made small talk with his mom while he tidied up the kitchen. He tried to do it inconspicuously, hoping not to embarrass her.

"Sounds like your apartment will be ready soon, Mom. They're getting it spiffed up for you. I think the walls are getting repainted tomorrow."

She finished prepping the coffee maker and turned, seemingly intent on another task. She stood for a second, appearing to struggle to remember what it was, then opened a cupboard to retrieve two mugs. She managed, "That's nice."

Minutes later they sat across from each other at the table. Bunker continued the small talk. He'd put a new bag in the trash can, tossed the pickle jar inside, and picked up the fork. The notepad that his mother used to write grocery lists was on the table between them. From Bunker's angle the writing was upside down. He pulled it toward himself and turned it.

"Do you need some groceries? I'm working in the area today and can swing by the store for you." He made a mental note to add pickles to the list. But when he saw what was written on the pad he was confused.

Estelle Getty, Tom Seaver, Robin Williams.

He looked up and saw that his mom's face had brightened. It seemed that a switch had been thrown somewhere in her mind.

"I always liked Estelle Getty in *The Golden Girls*. Did you know that she played Bea Arthur's mother in the show, but she was actually a year younger than Bea in real life? They used wigs and makeup to make her look older."

Bunker stared at her, astonished that she seemed, at least temporarily, to have returned to her old self.

"Well, no. I didn't know that." He tilted his head from his mother to the notepad, and back. "What's with this list? Looks like a really random group."

Dana's expression turned melancholy.

"It's a list of people that had Lewy body dementia. I was on the computer last night reading about it and came across these names."

Bunker stared at the list. He knew that *The Golden Girls* was one of his mom's two favorite shows, the other being *Murder, She Wrote*. He had no idea that one of its stars had suffered from the affliction. He remembered that Seaver, the Hall of Fame baseball pitcher, had to withdraw from public life in his 70s due to memory loss and other factors. Williams, a comedic genius, was affected in his early 60s.

Dana continued, "Your father thought highly of Tom Seaver...said he was intelligent. Did you know he owned a vineyard that made award-winning wine? And that Robin...so funny in *Mork & Mindy*..." She chuckled. "And *Mrs. Doubtfire*...I *loved* that movie."

Bunker allowed a slight smile to cross his face as he looked again at the list. He realized that all three people were deceased and that one, Williams, had taken his own life.

His smile disappeared.

Bunker walked into the Piqua Winans 45 minutes later. Thoughts of his mom lingered, and he made a conscious effort to push them to the back of his mind. He wanted to look deeper into the Running Dog connection and the meeting he'd witnessed from the Winans parking lot on Monday morning seemed to be his only lead. The shop was busy, with three customers in line at the counter and vehicles waiting at the drive-thru. The thought crossed his mind that he should perhaps come back when it wasn't as busy. He decided to wait in line, allow those in front of him to order, then ask for the manager when he reached the counter.

Doesn't seem right to cut in front and tie up their people when they're this busy.

When it was his turn Bunker, who wore a navy sport coat over grey slacks, produced his badge and asked to speak to the manager. The barista, a young woman, opened her eyes a shade wider as she peered at the badge. She nodded.

"Yes sir, officer."

Bunker, a stickler, responded. "Detective." Realizing he sounded like a jerk, and quickly added, "No worries." He made an effort to put a pleasant look on his face to show he wasn't offended.

The barista walked to the drive-thru window where two more female employees were working. She touched the shoulder of the one who seemed to be in charge, a petite dark-haired woman, then leaned in to say a few words. Both women then turned to look at Bunker. The petite woman nodded before turning to the other drive-thru attendant and speaking for a few seconds. She made her way to the front counter.

"What can I do for you uh...officer?

"Detective." Bunker couldn't help it.

She blushed. "Sorry...detective."

Bunker waved it off, annoyed with himself for his near fanaticism about being precise. He held out his hand while at the same time shooting a glance at her name tag. It read "Cledith." He had never seen that name before.

"Amos Bunker. Thanks for taking a few minutes ma'am."

"Call me Cledith, Cledith Roosa." She pronounced it "Clee-dith."

Bunker was relieved to hear the name verbalized. He made a mental note to remember it.

"Can I get you anything to drink, detective? Maybe a muffin?"

He declined. "No, I appreciate the offer, but I just had coffee...with my mom, actually."

Her face brightened. "That's nice."

She was in her mid-fifties and had bright blue-grey eyes with a quick smile. Bunker thought she seemed like a great boss, someone who was meticulous when it came to training an employee. He hoped she was also observant of customers who came into the shop.

Cledith led Bunker to an open table and they both took chairs. "How can I help you? I hope this isn't about one of my employees." She used "my" rather than "our," leading Bunker to believe she was invested in each worker. This was another plus in Bunker's book.

"No, nothing like that. I'm actually looking for information on some men that met here in the shop Monday morning."

Her face took on a puzzled look.

Bunker continued. "I'm sure you've heard about the two men found shot to death near the county line earlier this week?"

Cledith's eyes grew large. "The Shortridge brothers...oh my God, yes. They were actually customers here from time to time."

Bunker nodded. "Yes—"

She cut him off. "Wait, I remember...they were here a few days ago. Was that Monday?"

"It was. They were sitting right over there."

He pointed to the table in the corner, which was empty. She turned her head to look and quickly turned back. Her eyes appeared to look inward as if searching her memory.

"Can you give me any information about their visit that morning? If it helps, we know that they met with two other men. Anything you can remember about the men would—"

Cledith's back straightened. Her upper body went rigid. "Did *they* do it? Were the murderers right here in our shop?" Her eyes shot back to the table in the corner.

141

Bunker tried to downplay the Monday meeting, though his suspicions echoed those of the manager.

"No ma'am. We have no reason to think that. We're just trying to reconstruct the victims' movements the last few days before the shooting."

This seemed to mollify her. Her shoulders relaxed. "Well, let me think. Monday morning? Well, I was working the drive-thru—it's always busy in the morning—I'm afraid I paid almost no attention to our dining area."

"What about video? I see a camera up there." He looked up at a camera mounted above the serving counter.

Cledith nodded. "Yes, we'll have video from that camera. I'll get it for you of course. It is a high angle so I'm not sure how good of a look it'll give you of their faces...and the table in the corner is the furthest one from the camera."

"I'd appreciate getting that." Bunker said this knowing the photo he was about to show Cledith, despite its so-so quality, was probably better than any images he would get from the shop's video system. He pulled out his phone and opened the photo app, bringing up the picture he'd taken from the parking lot of Garrett and Gerard exiting the building with the two strangers with ties to Running Dog. He turned the screen to her.

"Here is a shot of the four men walking out. Do you remember ever seeing either of these two before?" He pointed to the two men next to the Shortridges.

She shook her head, appearing disappointed she couldn't be more helpful. Then almost immediately a thought seemed to come to her.

"Wait, Phoebe would've been working that day! She had the front counter. She might be able to help." She rose. "Let me go get her."

"So, she's here today?" Bunker realized it was a stupid question as soon as it left his lips.

"Oh yeah, she's here almost every day." She leaned toward Bunker and lowered her voice. "She's my *best* worker. Don't tell any of the others." She turned and rushed away from the table.

Phoebe Faris, as it turned out, was the young woman who had been behind the counter when Bunker walked in. She was a pretty brunette who looked to be in her late teens or early twenties. She walked toward Bunker with obvious trepidation.

"Cledith sent me over." She looked back toward the counter where Cledith, who had taken her place, paused while taking an order from a customer and wiggled her fingers at both of them.

Bunker tried to put her at ease. "Yes, nothing serious Phoebe...can I call you Phoebe?"

"Sure, sir."

"Detective Bunker." He couldn't help himself when it came to formality. He managed a smile and gestured to a chair. "We're trying to identify anyone who came into contact with Garrett and Gerard Shortridge in the days leading up to their murders."

Phoebe sat and nodded. "Cledith told me. I do remember them being here a few days ago."

Bunker tapped his phone. Before turning the screen to her he said, "Anything you might be able to tell me about the two men with the Shortridge brothers in the picture I'm about to show you would be extremely helpful."

Phoebe, looking doubtful, watched as Bunker turned his phone. A look of recognition appeared on her face.

"Oh...YEAH!" She pointed to the oriental man. "I don't remember much about this guy..." She shifted her finger to the slightly larger man wearing a pink golf shirt.

"But *this* guy," she said triumphantly, "is named Eli."

CHAPTER SEVENTEEN

Min sat in the dining room at the rental house west of Urbana. He'd found a blanket in a hall closet and spread it over the table. His P-15 Minuteman rifle lay in pieces on the blanket. He'd disassembled it and meticulously cleaned every component with gun oil, cleaning patches, and dry washcloths from the kitchen. On the chair next to him his cellphone fed a steady stream of music via Bluetooth connection to his earbuds. He wore disposable gloves to keep his fingerprints from appearing anywhere on the weapon.

Can't be too careful.

He knew that the FBI rivaled China's PAP—People's Armed Police—and MPS—Ministry of Public Security—in effectiveness. If he had to ditch the rifle at some point he wanted to leave as few clues behind as possible. He began to reassemble the P-15, remembering the thrill that coursed through his body as Gerard Shortridge's head filled the sight.

Not laughing now, are you fat man?

A look of satisfaction appeared on his face. Gerard had embodied two aspects of America that Min had experienced in his relatively brief time in the country. On one hand the deceased drug dealer and his brother personified the American spirit. They were adventurous. They took what they saw as theirs.

What phrases did the Americans use? Go for broke! Grab the brass ring!

In this way they perfectly reflected the capitalistic spirit of their country. Min admired this about the Americans. Though he would never consider admitting it to officials from his country—or even to Mr. Chu at Running Dog—he had come to believe that the American style of capitalism was probably superior to the socialist market economy of China.

The second trait that the Shortridges personified—arrogance—was their undoing. The brothers simply refused to accept an arrangement that would add greatly to their wealth.

Not only were they unreasonable, they—at least Gerard—were insulting. This, Min thought, was also very American.

I did what was necessary. Just as China will do what is necessary when the inevitable military confrontation occurs between the two countries.

A niggling thought swam into Min's head.

Making that shot was FUN!

He pushed the thought away and concentrated on the last steps of the reassembly. The situation, he supposed, was complicated. Min enjoyed America. Yale, until he was asked to leave, had been an enjoyable—even enlightening—experience. He had been fortunate enough to get a second chance through Running Dog and found America, if anything, even more fascinating.

Such a paradox. I enjoy this country, yet I am here to harm it. A situation worthy of Confucius.

Min shrugged as he reached for the final component, the Romeo Red Dot sight. He hesitated before attaching it, realizing that the rifle, without the sight, looked exactly like it did when he first used it to eliminate an obstacle that stood in the way of him and his colleagues.

Wellsboro, Pennsylvania was in Tioga County near the state's northern border. Barely 15 miles separate it from the New York State line. Wellsboro is the county seat and home to 3,500 people. Its relative isolation—a four hour drive from both Pittsburgh to the southwest and Philadelphia to the southeast, and a three hour drive from Buffalo to the northwest and Syracuse to the northeast—and its rural nature made it an excellent target area for the Ivy Leaguers.

They arrived in the region fresh from coming to an agreement with a small operation in Western New York, one that was accomplished without bloodshed. Wellsboro would be different.

The main player there was a man named Taggert—Min didn't remember his first name. Taggert was an over-the-road truck driver. He was an independent, meaning he owned his own truck, a dark red 2022 Freightliner Cascadia. Both the truck and Taggert were large and loud. When angered—which was often—Taggert's face turned the same color as the Freightliner's cab.

Taggert traveled all over the United States and Canada on legitimate runs. He'd made contacts in multiple states that could supply him with an array of illegal merchandise. He bought cases of cigarettes with no tax stamps in Minnesota, stacks of cellphones stolen from West Coast ports in California, and handguns from Virginia and Tennessee. He also bought and sold opioids, typically acquiring them in Texas from a seller who brought them into the states from Mexico.

Min and his partners approached Taggert the previous November after determining that he was the contact in the area who could disseminate the most product. Taggert had no interest. They met with him three times after first gathering significant information on his distribution network. At the third meeting they showed him one of the golf balls that had been cut open. Taggert was unmoved.

Dylan, with his psychology background from Yale, theorized to the group that Taggert had an overdeveloped hunter-gatherer identity and he felt validation when he was able to leave home, go on a quest, and return with a prize. Willie thought Taggert just liked to drive, unlike himself.

Whatever the case, Taggert wouldn't deal. He would have to go. The little .22 from the golf bag couldn't be used since Taggert refused to meet again. It would have to be done from a distance. That meant Min and the rifle. But how? Where?

Discreet conversations in Wellsboro's bars and restaurants yielded information on the trucker. Much of it was marginally helpful. Taggert, who had been divorced twice, was purportedly having affairs with women in three different states and—if Mona at the Gas Light Bar and Grill could be believed—men in two others. He supposedly had a tattoo of each state he'd visited strategically placed on various parts of his body. Most agreed that an outline of Texas enveloped his butt cheeks. There seemed to be no agreement on which state adorned his male genitalia. Some said California, others Rhode Island.

They heard stories about his trucking business, his high school athletic career—which was erratic—and his disdain for the police. It wasn't until late in the month when deer season was about to open that they learned that Taggert never missed opening day.

Min credited Dylan with coming up with the plan. Taggert's favorite hunting spot was well known to every hunter in town. It was located ten miles west of town on private property just outside the Tioga State Forest. The forest was home to Pine Creek Gorge, typically referred to as the Grand Canyon of Pennsylvania, which was 45 miles long and whose depths reached nearly 1,500 feet. Thousands of deer lived in this vast tract of wilderness, many trophy sized. Taggert knew this and chose his spot with the intention of bagging a large buck that strayed from the park's boundaries. Most years he was successful.

At 4:30 a.m. the foursome from Running Dog parked down the street from Taggert's house. Dax drove a rented Chevy Suburban with Willie in the passenger seat. Min rode with Dylan, who drove his Range Rover. Their research had revealed that legal hunting hours in Pennsylvania began 30 minutes before sunrise and ended 30 minutes after sunset. The state—or more accurately, the Commonwealth—of Pennsylvania published exact times for each county. For Tioga County that meant hunters could discharge their weapons starting at 6:47 a.m. They assumed Taggert would want to get set up early and found they'd guessed right when he loaded gear into a pickup truck at 5:45 and set off westbound on State Route 6.

The Range Rover and Suburban followed. Dylan pulled off to the side of the road after a few miles to allow Dax to take the lead. When Taggert drew closer to the forest he made a right turn. Dax then pulled over and Dylan again took the point. They watched as Taggert's truck rounded a bend, braked, and swung left into a farm lane. Min, who was speaking to Willie on his burner phone, relayed the information.

"He turned into a lane on the left. We'll drive past and find a place to stop. Drive slowly past the lane and look for him. Try not to be too obvious."

Willie spoke less than two minutes later. "We got a good look. He's walking to the left...that would be, what, the south? Just like we figured when we looked at it on Google Earth. The tree line Dylan picked out is maybe a hundred yards from his truck. You should be able to double back past the lane and duck into the woods behind him."

Min checked the time on the Range Rover's display screen. It was 6:19. He turned to Dylan.

"Go back past the lane and drop me off."

Their plan was for Min to walk from the road to the line of trees where they believed Taggert would be set up in a tree stand. The two SUVs would pull off to the side of the road about a quarter of a mile apart, one on either side of Min's entry point. Min, after doing the deed, would find his way back to the road then quickly make his way to whichever vehicle was closest.

The Range Rover and Suburban were now approaching each other slowly, the Suburban having just passed the lane where Taggert's truck was parked, the Range Rover heading back toward it. Both SUVs headlights were on, and as they passed each other Min and Willie could see one another while they spoke on their phones.

Willie, concern on his face, looked across at Min and mouthed, "Careful, he's carrying a long gun."

Min saw Willie's lips moving while hearing his friend's words through the phone at the same time. It was surreal. He grinned at Willie as the vehicles slid past each other.

In a reassuring voice he stated, "So am I."

The Range Rover cruised back past the lane. Seeing nothing unexpected, Dylan crept along another hundred yards and stopped.

"Go get him, Min. It'll be just like your days in the Yale Rifle & Pistol Club."

149

Min, remembering having the asshole Beau Tinker in his sights that day on the shooting range in New Haven, slowly shook his head as he exited the Evoque cradling his rifle.

"No. This time it will be different."

He turned and disappeared into the darkness.

Min had no formal military training. Most of his knowledge of his country's armed services came from a childhood friend, Yang Wei, who was in the navy and, like Min, had no experience with land warfare tactics. Min relied on movies and television shows to guide him as he crept through the brush toward the trees. He moved a few steps at a time before hunkering down to listen for signs of Taggert, then repeated the process.

It was cold. Temperatures were in the low 30s. Min, as usual, wore all black clothing. He'd added a sweatshirt, ski mask, and black nylon coat to his regular attire. He and Dylan had discussed the possibility of Min wearing a blaze orange vest to blend in with hunters but had decided against it.

Min argued, "I think we should rely on stealth, not deception." Dylan agreed.

Only the darkness kept Min from seeing his breath. By the time he reached the tree line an orange haze began to appear behind him as the sun broke the horizon. He crouched on one knee and scanned the trees. Not yet locating Taggert, he dared not dig out his phone to check the time.

CRACK

Min jumped, nearly dropping his rifle. The sound had come from off to his left, perhaps a half mile out.

That can't be Taggert. He couldn't have gotten that far. He—

CRACK

Min swung his head back to the right. This shot had come from that direction and had also seemed too far away for Taggert to have been responsible.

I guess it's 6:47...or close enough to it for these American hunters.

Min peered at the trees. The growing light gradually helping define shapes as the trees, mostly leafless, took shape.

He slowly swiveled his head left to right, then back again. Seconds later he saw movement.

Taggert sat on a tree stand slightly to Min's left, 50 feet away. The stand appeared to consist of a camouflaged chair with a ladder underneath leading down to the ground. As he watched, Taggert—who wore the mandatory orange vest over his head-to-toe camo and had a long gun of some sort resting on his lap—reached into a breast pocket and retrieved a silver flask. He unscrewed the cap and took a short pull before returning it to the pocket.

Min raised the P-15 and brought it to his shoulder. He may not have had a background in military tactics, but he could shoot. He'd proven that at Yale. The rifle's selector switch and safety were both on the right side of the receiver, making them easily accessible to a right-handed shooter like Min. He already had a round in the chamber. All he had to do was flip the safety to the firing position. As he did so an amusing thought came to him.

In researching the various regulations for deer season, he and his partners had learned that of the states that allowed hunting deer with rifles, Pennsylvania was the only one that did not allow *semi-automatic* rifles.

The P-15 Minuteman was semi-automatic. It was illegal to have it out here during deer gun season. Min remembered a saying his grandfather often used when it came to rules from the government.

Shan gao huangdi yuan—The mountain is high and the emperor is far away.

Min shrugged and put the front sight on Taggert's head.

I'm not hunting deer.

He squeezed the trigger. The report of the rifle was no different than dozens of others that echoed across Tioga County that morning.

Min let the memory of the shot wash over him with satisfaction. He finished attaching the Romeo Red Dot sight and laid the freshly cleaned rifle on the table before turning to the leather Running Dog golf bag which stood a few feet away.

Okay, time to get this ready.

He knew that Dylan would be returning from Dayton with either Dax or Willie and that whoever made the trip would be taking it back to Dayton at some point. He made sure the carfentanil balls were in their box and tucked into a tall zippered pocket on the right side of the golf bag, where they joined two identical boxes. Regular Running Dog balls were kept in a similar pocket on the bag's left side. Min found a plastic bag tucked into a small pocket at the top of the golf bag. He saw that it held the ball that Dylan had cut open with the Dremel tool.

He confirmed that the plastic bag was sealed, then quickly zipped the pocket shut.

Fucking elephant tranquilizer...bad shit.

He knew that Dylan had snatched the plastic bag from the ground at Wesley Chapel Cemetery seconds after Min had splattered Gerard's brains. Dylan had hastily gathered the golf bag while Min emerged from his shooting position in the woods. They jogged to the Range Rover and left in a hurry for the rental house.

After confirming that all the pockets were properly configured, Min turned his attention to the putter. He pulled it up and out from its slot in the golf bag and examined the cover that protected the head.

It says 'Breakfast Ball.' What did Dylan say that means? Something about getting to take a free shot that doesn't count against your score?

Min removed the cover to reveal a standard blade-style head. The hosel—the tubular metal that connected the head of the putter to the shaft above—was barely three inches long. Min held the shaft firm in his left hand. With his right he gripped the joint where the hosel and shaft came together. He made a twisting motion with his hands and was satisfied when he felt the head and hosel release from the shaft. He slowly pulled the shaft away and saw a metallic piece snap into position.

It was a trigger.

The weapon had been machined in China by craftsmen in Running Dog's R&D department. The head of the putter acted as a pistol grip. The hosel, machined from high-grade steel, was the barrel. There was a small slot, hidden when the putter was assembled, that allowed for a single .22 caliber short round to be loaded. Rifles and pistols in .22 caliber generally accept all three styles of bullets: .22 long rifle, .22 long, or .22 short. The shorts have the least range and power and are rarely used. They were, however, the only size that the machinists in China could incorporate into the design of this weapon.

Min examined the pistol. It was, effectively, a derringer. Its ability to hide in plain sight had made it extremely effective.

Better get you cleaned up and reloaded. Lots more action coming your way.

CHAPTER EIGHTEEN

Dylan retraced his route back to the rental house. He checked his mirrors frequently to make sure that Willie, in the Sentra, was still following.

How the hell did he keep a job with a private investigator company? He really has a thing against driving. I could've done a paper on him at Yale.

His experience at the university, it seemed, would not leave Dylan's thoughts today. He drifted back to a class his sophomore year that focused on interpersonal relations. The professor spent an entire class period discussing a study done in the 1990s at the University of Michigan. Experiments were set up to examine how norms of a "culture of honor" manifest themselves in the emotions, behaviors, and psychological reactions of Southern White males. Dylan had found it fascinating.

In one exercise, student volunteers who grew up exclusively in either northern or southern states came to U of M's Institute for Social Research. They were informed that the experiment would be about something completely unrelated and that they were to first fill out a demographic questionnaire. They were told to take the finished form to a table at the end of a long, narrow hallway. As the participant walked down the hall, a collaborator with the experimenter walked out of a door marked "Photo Lab" and began working at a file cabinet in the hall. The collaborator had to push the file drawer in to allow the participant to pass by him and drop his paper off at the table. As the participant returned seconds later and walked back down the hall, the collaborator—who had reopened the file drawer—slammed it shut on seeing the participant approach and bumped into him with his shoulder, calling the participant an "asshole." The collaborator then walked back into the Photo Lab.

Observers were posted in the hall, supposedly doing homework and not paying attention to the action. One was seated on the floor where he could look up and see the participant's face. The other was sitting at the end of the hall. Both observers could hear everything the participant said and read his body language. Immediately after the bumping incident the observers rated the participant's emotional reactions based on 7-point scales. The reactions of anger and amusement were the ones of greatest interest, but observers also rated how aroused, flustered, resigned, or wary participants seemed.

The results were telling.

Northerners and Southerners differed in how angry or amused they appeared to be after the bump. Observers rated Northern participants as significantly more amused by the bump than Southern participants. Southerners tended to be angrier.

The study wasn't dependent on subjective observations alone. Saliva samples were taken from the participants. Analysis showed that Southerners showed a significant increase after being bumped in both testosterone and cortisol levels. Cortisol is a steroid hormone produced by the adrenal glands. The amount increases when a person is stressed.

Armed with this information, the experimenters added a new wrinkle. In this version, a 6-foot 3-inch, 250-pound male waited around the corner until the bump occurred. He then entered the hall and walked toward the participant at a good pace on a collision course. In effect, a "chicken" game was set up. Researchers knew that chicken games were important in cultures of honor. Southern participants, as expected, allowed the approaching male to get much closer than Northerners before "chickening out." They also showed more aggression.

Subsequent studies showed that Southerners had more measurable reactions when there were witnesses to them being bumped or insulted. When witnesses were removed from the experiment, Southerners reacted more like Northerners. They seemed to believe their status was hurt in the eyes of the person who saw the insult.

Findings of the experiments as a whole showed that the expectations for what one should do when his honor is insulted are different in the two regions of the country. A male from the South who is insulted but does not retaliate risks having his masculine reputation diminished.

The experiments were summed up in an overview.

We believe the experiments might represent a microcosm of the insult-aggression cycle that is responsible for a good deal of violence in the South and in similar cultures of honor in the United States and elsewhere.

Dylan didn't know what to make of the study while sitting in the classroom in New Haven. He'd spent his entire life in the Northeast and had almost no contact with Southern culture. Now, he had come to buy in to the results of the research. He thought of it as the "Redneck Study." Ohio, and to a lesser extent Pennsylvania, possessed many of the qualities of the South. Certainly, the Shortridge brothers—especially Gerard—fit the mold. Dylan wondered how things would develop as his Running Dog group continued to penetrate deeper into the country.

I'm guessing that fewer and fewer of these people will want to deal...That means we'll have to hit them with our own code of honor.

A look of resolve appeared on his face.

Dylan, with Willie in tow, took the first Troy exit and made his way north toward the traffic circle. He passed the WACO Museum and glanced at its airstrip but saw no evidence of the yellow biplane he'd seen earlier.

A grass airfield. Wonder how many of those are still operating these days? Can't be that many, can there?

At the traffic circle Dylan angled right and proceeded halfway around the circle before exiting and continuing north on Market Street. He checked again to make sure Willie made the turn and realized the rented Sentra had stopped inside the circle. He heard a car honking.

For Christ's sake, Willie. It's not brain surgery. You yield at the circle, wait for an opening, then duck in and roll until you reach your exit.

Dylan pulled the Range Rover to the side of the street and turned in his seat to watch. The Sentra edged forward, braked, and finally lurched ahead. Another horn sounded as Willie finally found his way out of the traffic circle.

There's no way he's going to be able to drive around Miami County by himself meeting the replacement dealers. I'll have to go with him...or Min will. As long as we're in that Sentra instead of a Range Rover we should be okay.

Dylan pulled out as Willie approached and they made their way north on Market before turning right and heading east on State Route 55.

Min, he knew, would have no problems explaining the updated chain of command to the new people running the local drug networks that unexpectedly found themselves buying opioids from Running Dog. He could be quite persuasive, even ruthless. The only negative, so far as Dylan could see, was his inability to blend in when operating in rural America.

Not many Chinese in Podunkville, USA.

Dylan knew this was why Min contacted him in the first place. His superiors at Running Dog formulated the plan that was now adding to the flood of opioids in America. They knew that Min, a clever, ambitious employee in their factory, had connections in the U.S. They brought him into the fold and picked his brain. Did Min have any connections in the States that might assist in this enterprise?

In turned out that yes, he just might know of someone.

Dylan was working at his father Patrick's original dealership in Charlestown, New Hampshire. He was bored stiff. He sold a car every week or two, played a shitload of golf, and tried to avoid his dad. He had no desire to hear the "You screwed the pooch in the Ivy League, boyo, now you have to earn your keep" speech for the umpteenth time.

Two fucking years at that car dealership. How the hell did I do it?

158

Charlestown might've been a quaint town to settle down in if you wanted a wife, three kids, and a 40-hour work week. Dylan didn't particularly want any of these things. At one time the town was marginally famous for being the hometown of Hall of Fame baseball catcher Carlton Fisk.

In Game 6 of the 1975 World Series Fisk, playing for the Boston Red Sox, hit a ball high and deep down the left field line in Fenway Park off Cincinnati Reds' relief pitcher Pat Darcy. He waved his arms, attempting to will the ball fair. When the ball hit the foul pole at 12:33 a.m., the Red Sox had a 7-6 victory and had tied the best-of-seven series at three games apiece.

It was, without a doubt, the most iconic video of a home run ever shot. A camera in the "Green Monster," Fenway's 37-foot left field wall, operated by NBC cameraman Lou Gerard, stayed on Fisk after he made contact with the ball. This was unheard of. Cameramen in 1975 simply did not follow players' reactions. The director of the broadcast, Harry Coyle, told Gerard to follow the ball if Fisk hit it. But there were rats inside the wall where Gerard was stationed.

"I've got a rat on my leg that's as big as a cat. It's staring me in the face." Gerard was unable to move. "How about if we stay with Fisk, see what happens?"

The rest, as they say, is history. The video of Fisk's homer changed sports broadcasting. That the Reds won the next night to clinch the World Series was almost an afterthought.

Another result of the home run occurred in Fisk's hometown. The bells of St. Luke's Episcopal Church, on the corner of Main and Church Streets, 128 miles from Fenway Park, began to ring. A 61-year-old resident named David Conant, whose son played baseball with Fisk at Charlestown High, had slipped into the church and climbed the belfry. When a police officer arrived at the church and asked for an explanation, Conant informed him that hometown boy Carlton Fisk had hit a game-winning homer in the World Series.

"Hell," the officer responded, "if I had known that, I would have come and helped you!"

The story was humorous, even charming. It was, Dylan supposed, a real-life fable to townspeople of a certain age. His father had been 11 years old the night of the Fisk homer, an age when sports feats assumed an importance—especially to boys—that dwarfed all other accomplishments. Patrick had told the story of the bells of St. Luke's more times than Dylan could remember. The game had begun on a Wednesday night, October 21st, a school night. Virtually the entire population of Charlestown was still awake early Thursday morning when the game ended. Patrick, who couldn't sleep after watching the telecast, was in bed when the bells began to toll. He never forgot that and—in Dylan's view—couldn't stop talking about it.

If I have to hear that story about the fucking church bells one more time, I'll blow my OWN brains out, not some redneck dealer's.

After being one step from being Tapped for membership in one of the most important secret societies at perhaps the most prestigious institution in the world, Dylan had found himself sitting at a desk in his father's dealership. Patrick wasn't happy he was there. Dylan *certainly* wasn't happy to be there. He despised the bullshit Let-me-talk-to-my-sales-manager-and-see-if-we-can-make-this-deal game.

He was sitting at his desk, surfing the internet, when his cellphone rang. Seeing the unknown number on the screen he almost didn't answer, but then thought, *What the hell, might be someone that wants to buy a car.* He picked up.

"Dylan Riordan, Riordan Buick, Chevrolet, Cadillac. How can I help?"

The voice, with a trace of mirth, asked, "Is this the Dylan Riordan who got pissed at me at Rudy's Bar on Chapel Street when I played him that Aerosmith song?"

Dylan was silent for a second. When realization set in, he exclaimed "Min?!?"

Dylan's thoughts instantly went back to that night in New Haven. Both he and Min had come from their disciplinary hearings. They were drowning their sorrows, coming to grips with the fact that their days at Yale were numbered. After several drinks they disclosed to each other, in some detail, what they had done to put themselves in this position.

Min recounted how Beau Tinker had laughed at him at the 50-foot range and how he'd pointed his rifle at him in retaliation.

"Sounds like he was a real jackass...had it coming." Dylan sipped his beer.

Min nodded sullenly. "It will cost me dearly. I'm sure I'll be sent back to China." After a beat he asked, "So, what brought you to the Executive Committee Room?"

It must have been the alcohol that led Dylan to unburden himself to a stranger. He told Min how he'd been contacted by two of Yale's societies. How one, Mace and Chain, had requested he meet in Sterling Library. And finally, how he'd taken the elevator down after the meeting feeling almost giddy.

"Then that goddamned blonde from Delaware got on when it stopped on the fourth floor. We'd been looking at each other in psych classes for over a year. I knew she wanted me. I just, well, let nature take its course. I mean, I barely kissed her...had her in my arms, sure, but she fucking freaked out... started screaming at me. She was still screaming when we got down to one and the doors opened. And, of course, there was a security guard right there. Come to find out Glynnis...her name was fucking *Glynnis*...was from one of the richest families in Delaware. She was a legacy...fourth generation Yale. She called her daddy, bitched to anyone who would listen —that was pretty much everybody—and really put the screws to me. I got Me-Too'd...canceled."

Min listened without comment.

Dylan summarized. "So, no Mace and Chain for me...no Fence Club. No Yale. I'll never be an Eli. I'm out on my ass...all because of 30 fucking seconds on that elevator." He reached for his beer mug.

Finally, Min spoke. "Don't you mean because of 30 *non-*fucking seconds on that elevator? You said nothing really happened."

161

Dylan's mug stopped halfway to his lips. He eyed Min for several seconds before a wide grin appeared on his face.

"You're quite a smartass, aren't you Min?"

It was a half hour later, after more beer, more bitching, and a conversation that even touched on the sentimental, that Min began to fiddle with his phone. Dylan soon took notice.

"Texting a girl, Min, or giving your parents the bad news about coming home?"

Min shook his head. "Neither. Just looking for a song that might cheer you up. Ahhh, here we are." He touched the screen with his index finger and turned the phone to his new friend.

Dylan recognized the song immediately. It was recorded over a decade before he was born but it was performed by a legendary Boston-area band, so even twenty-somethings knew it.

It was "Love In An Elevator" by Aerosmith.

Dylan burst out laughing.

"You really *are* a smartass, aren't you Min?"

They clinked mugs.

Min grinned. "Gānbēi."

Two years passed before Dylan took Min's call at his desk.

"Yes, my friend. This is Min. I have a...proposition for you."

CHAPTER NINETEEN

Who in the hell DESIGNS these things?

Willie was inside the traffic circle. The Sentra moved in fits and starts as he attempted to follow Dylan's Range Rover Evoque through Troy. He had never liked the damn things. He seemed to yield unnecessarily then pull into the flow of traffic at exactly the wrong times. For all his intelligence he would have a difficult time explaining how they function to a person who was unfamiliar with them.

I can't even explain what I'm trying to do right now. Am I trying to drive THROUGH the circle?...drive AROUND it?...PAST it?

A driver behind the Sentra laid on his horn. Brakes squealed. Willie felt his blood pressure rise. His shoulders tightened.

Screw it!

He pressed the accelerator and shot through to the other side, nearly sideswiping a black pickup truck whose driver had pulled into the circle from the right after seeing the Sentra come to a complete stop inside of it.

Willie exhaled in relief as he saw Dylan's Range Rover Evoque edge back into the street ahead of him.

Out loud Willie exclaimed, "When in doubt, go YOLO!"

As he fell back in behind Dylan and followed him out of Troy, Willie reflected upon how the acronym for *You Only Live Once* had come to define the track his life had taken since he met Dylan and Min.

Willie had been a nerd growing up in Providence, Rhode Island. He read extensively, mostly history, sometimes thrillers or mysteries. He was the first person in his high school anyone could remember playing Puzzle Rush, a game on Chess.com that combined the satisfaction of solving puzzles with the intensity of blitz chess. He scored extremely well on the aptitude tests that measured a student's readiness for higher education.

Willie may have actually been *too* intelligent. Or, at least, he thought he was. He tended to believe that he knew better—about almost everything.

When the time came to choose a college Willie selected Brown University, which was located right there in Providence. Being close to home was not a factor in his decision. The university being a founding member of the prestigious Ivy League certainly was. But it was Brown's acclaimed Open Curriculum that was the primary draw.

Willie saw that Brown's website posed the question *What is the Open Curriculum*. The answer intrigued him.

At most universities, students must complete a set of core courses. At Brown, our students develop a personalized course of study—they have greater freedom to study what they choose and the flexibility to discover what they love.

The university encouraged students to be "the architects of their own education." This appealed to Willie. After all, who knew more about how a college experience should be constructed for Willie than Willie himself? Certainly not some college advisor sitting in an office.

He took a number of history classes, of course, but he also set off on a quest seemingly designed to acquire knowledge about obscure subjects.

After attending a party his freshman year, Willie decided it would be cool to be a craft beer snob. He saw an upperclassman holding court with a handful of other first-year students and thought, *He looks like an expert. Standing there in his flannel shirt...like a grunge-rocker.*

The fact that the man was a windbag, lording his supposed superior knowledge over a gaggle of barely-interested newbies, did not occur to Willie. He took a selection of unconnected classes with the goal of learning about yeast and fermentation. Near the end of his sophomore year he realized that, just perhaps, an Ivy League university wasn't the best training ground for a person that didn't necessarily want to be a brewer, but just wanted to *act* like one at parties.

He shifted gears, deciding that computers, which had been trumpeted as "the future" for decades, still were. He was required to take classes in the computer sciences department that were, he was convinced, below his skill level. He grew frustrated sitting in classes with freshmen and by the end of his junior year abandoned any possible computer-related degree. He was left with history. He'd continued to take classes in that discipline each semester and he found that it was the only subject in which he would have enough credits to graduate in four years. As graduation neared, he began, belatedly, to investigate his prospects in the job market. He was discouraged to learn that a career in historical research, which he might find interesting, barely existed. No, the Smithsonian wasn't looking for a newly-minted Brown University graduate to walk in and assume a supervisory role. Most distressing, his undergrad degree was a Bachelor of Arts. This meant that he wasn't technically qualified to even teach high school history. For that he would've needed his degree to be in Educational Studies with a concentration in history.

Not QUALIFIED? How the hell am I not qualified to teach high school fucking history?

He could go back to school and earn a Master's degree in history, which would allow him to apply for college teaching positions. But this would take at least two more years and after completion he would be at the lowest rung of the ladder in a history department *if* he was fortunate enough to find an opening.

God knows where I would end up.

He already had nearly $60,000 in student debt and the prospect of paying for two more years of school before accepting a low-paying position teaching *other* know-it-all students held very little appeal. Willie had an Ivy League degree, but if he somehow time-traveled back to debate his high school self on the subject of how to get a rewarding job he wasn't sure he would win.

He was angry. He told anyone who would listen that the particulars of the different types of college degrees were never explained to him. He didn't want to admit, even to himself, that this probably wasn't true. He simply hadn't wanted to listen.

So, it was off to a job search. To see what was out there for an over-educated Ivy Leaguer with a BA who knew everything—kind of—about craft beer.

The answer was...not much.

He found himself at job fairs with graduates of low-end public universities, community colleges, and—it still made him shudder—*high school* graduates. Opportunities were few. There were a handful of sales positions—he had no interest—a management trainee offer to sign on with a car rental company, and lastly, an opening with a private investigative firm.

His initial interview with this company, Verify P.I., to his surprise, piqued his interest. The company representative explained that the work would entail researching and following subjects. The largest clients were insurance companies who wanted to determine if disability and workers compensation claims were being faked. The next largest category of clients were men or women who suspected their spouse or partner of affairs, drug use, gambling problems, or a host of other sordid activities.

The nuts and bolts of the job were completely removed from anything Willie had ever considered as a career path. It was the location of the job that swayed him. Verify P.I. was expanding their operations in New York City. They needed people, preferably smart, inquisitive people. Willie had always thought it would be interesting to live in the city.

There was one problem—Willie hated to drive, always had. He'd just never had the desire. He lived close enough to his high school to walk. He wasn't in sports, so he had no need to drive to games or practices. He didn't date. He didn't pursue getting a learner's permit, which are available to residents of Rhode Island at age 16, until his senior year of high school. It took him three attempts to pass the driver's test. Once he did, he proceeded to sideswipe a neighbor's car with his mother's Honda CRV. At that point he lost all interest in driving and didn't get behind a wheel again until he got to Brown, where he would sometimes drive a golf cart when participating in the occasional outing with fellow students.

He was assured that—in New York City at least—this would not be a problem. The vast majority of city residents do not own vehicles. When a subject utilized public transportation, Willie could jump aboard the same bus or subway car and ride along to the same destination. If they did use a private vehicle, he could easily follow by using a taxi or ride share. This would all be covered in the training program the firm had in place for their new field agents.

Willie shrugged, thought *what the hell*, and signed on.

He subsequently learned more than he could've guessed about the depths of human nature. He learned how to spot a fake limp, which hotels were the favorite locations for afternoon trysts, and which Manhattan doormen could be bribed for information. He got detailed information on how a drug buy is consummated. He learned to spot the lookouts, the muscle that hovered nearby to ensure the seller was not ripped off, and how to identify who was actually holding the drugs. He was disgusted to discover that, at times, female sellers sometimes hid condom-wrapped tubes filled with pills, tablets, or powder, in their vagina to prevent discovery. A female employing this method was called "the purse." Willie shook his head when first learning of this but came to take it in stride.

He didn't know it at the time, but all of these experiences would be extremely useful when he came on board with Running Dog.

He was surprised when, after completing six months with the company, he was granted a permit by the state of New York to carry a handgun. Verify P.I. encouraged their field personnel to arm themselves for personal protection. Having heard all the gun control rhetoric through the media—it was hard to avoid, especially after a high-profile gun crime—he'd assumed it would be virtually impossible to obtain a permit, especially in New York. It turned out that private investigators, bail enforcement agents, and security guards were governed by a separate licensing law. Once approved, they could carry handguns as long as the maximum capacity of the magazine was ten rounds.

Willie bought a little Ruger Max 9 pistol and fired all of 20 rounds through it at a range. The first time he carried it in New York City he realized it was a detriment to doing his job. The subject he was following entered a building in Brooklyn that had a metal detector. Willie didn't want to go through the process of identifying himself at the door and displaying his credentials. He waited outside and didn't see the man for two days. The subject had left by another entrance. There were so many metal detectors in the city that it made little sense to carry the pistol. He put it back in its plastic case and forgot about it.

By his second year with the firm Willie had become a frequent customer of an Uber driver who had few qualms about breaking traffic laws in order to keep a subject in sight. Willie discovered this quite by accident one night in Manhattan's Chelsea neighborhood when a limousine he was following from the back seat of a Volkswagen Tiguan Uber passed through an intersection as the light turned red. The Tiguan was 200 feet back. Frustrated, Willie uttered "Damn."

"Want me to run the light, dude?" The driver, whose long blonde hair fell nearly to his shoulders, appeared willing.

"Can you?"

"No worries...hold on!"

The driver became Willie's go-to when trailing a subject in the city. He had the man—who was laid back and unfazed by pseudo-dangerous work—virtually on retainer. The pair exchanged numbers and Willie texted him at all hours of the day or night for rides. He was appreciative that unless the driver had another rider, he almost always came through.

One spring morning Willie's phone rang. He checked the screen and saw that it was the Uber driver. All of their previous communication had been via text. Confused, Willie answered.

"Hey Dax, what's up?"

"Hey dude, I drove a couple guys into the city from Newark this morning...I think you might be interested in meeting them."

That led to Willie's first meeting with Dylan Riordan and Min Xian. It led to a partnership that had been financially rewarding beyond Willie's wildest dreams. He had made the most important YOLO decision of his life, coming aboard with the crew from Running Dog. Together, the foursome had cut a swath through the northeast section of the country, partnering with—or taking over—heroin and fentanyl operations in "underserved" areas. There had been thrills. Willie had even used the modified putter to execute a Western New Jersey dealer who was particularly loathsome.

That was satisfying. Scary as hell...but satisfying.

It had given Willie a taste of the part of their business that was usually carried out by Dylan or Min. He did not rule out the possibility of repeating it in the future.

For now, he had teamed with Dax to form an extremely effective surveillance unit. His P.I. background and Dax's driving experience had been terrifically successful in scrutinizing and analyzing the networks they had come across. Willie was convinced that Dax had benefited from his many months chauffeuring him around the boroughs of New York City. The former Columbia student now had almost as keen an eye for drug deals as he did.

The reverse was not true, unfortunately. No part of Dax's talent in tailing another vehicle had rubbed off on him. Today was a prime example. Willie was now struggling to navigate his way through a small Ohio town with a single traffic circle while following Dylan.

Once I get this Sentra to the house, Min or Dylan will have to take over the driving. I don't want to try to find my way around out here in the country. Maybe another dealer will need taken out while one of the other guys is driving. That means that I get to...

He ended that train of thought before it became too compelling, instead concentrating on the Range Rover ahead.

CHAPTER TWENTY

It was the kind of information that could blow a case wide open. Bunker had seen it before. An apparently unrelated fact is dropped into an existing set of disjointed fragments of information and it becomes the missing piece of the puzzle that brings the whole thing together.

The mystery man's name is Eli.

There was no last name to go on. The person of interest —Bunker had come to think of him that way—had paid with cash so there was no credit card trail to chase. This could be a natural act by a completely innocent person or a deliberate move to cover his tracks. Bunker cautioned himself not to jump to conclusions. But he couldn't deny the notion that he was onto something.

I have a feeling about this guy in the pink golf shirt... and his oriental friend.

Bunker was on the way to his office in downtown Troy. He had some ideas about how to go about identifying the mystery man. Phoebe Faris, the young counter worker at Winans, had remembered the name of an obscure customer days after she'd waited on him for the for most unexpected of reasons.

Because she is DATING a guy named Eli!

Bunker shook his head, remembering her explanation.

"I remember *every* guy named Eli that orders at the store. It's a name I don't see very often. I never thought about it until I met *my* Eli six months ago...but ever since then the name really stands out, y'know?" She had paused in thought for a second then, blushing slightly, added, "Plus, it's a really easy name to write on the cups."

Unfortunately, the manager, Cledith, had been right about the quality of the video. The angle of the camera was too high to capture clear images of the two men sitting with the Shortridge brothers. If Bunker hadn't followed Garrett and Gerard to the shop that morning and watched them enter, he would've been hard pressed to identify them based on the video alone. Still, Bunker had the photo he'd taken with his cellphone and now, thanks to Phoebe, had at least a partial name to go on. He left business cards with both women and asked them to call if they remembered anything else about the men then walked quickly to his vehicle.

He made the short drive to Troy and ducked into the lot of the Miami County Safety Building, a three-story structure two blocks west of the traffic circle in the center of town. The building housed the Miami County Court of Common Pleas, the Sheriff's Office, and a number of other county departments.

Bunker parked near the rear entrance and dug out his keycard as he walked toward the door. When he was 15 feet away the door swung open and a uniformed female deputy emerged leading a working dog.

Cheerfully, Bunker called out, "Heyyy, Wild. How are you today?" His eyes moved from the woman to the dog and he lowered a hand to allow it to be sniffed. "And how are *you*, Zeke?"

The woman was Deputy Jill Kuhlman, a pretty brunette with green eyes. Smiling but feigning irritation she asked, "Amos, why do you insist on calling me that? Now some of the other deputies are starting to do it too. It doesn't even make sense."

Bunker shrugged as Zeke, a Belgian Malinois, licked his hand. "I don't know, it just came to me one day. You've heard of the Old West gunslinger Bill Hickok?"

It was her turn to shrug. "Yeah, I guess."

"Well his nickname was Wild Bill...Bill rhymes with Jill...you carry a gun, too, so...'Wild Jill.'"

Kuhlman put a hand on her hip. "That has got to be the *dumbest* damn thing I've ever heard." Still, her smile widened. There was a trace of a little sister-big brother vibe between the two.

Bunker was now scratching under Zeke's right ear. "Yeah, pretty lame, but get used to it. It's built into my software now."

Kuhlman crossed her arms. "Well, can you at least explain to the rest of the department that it's just a stupid name you made up? I think a few of the deputies are beginning to think you call me 'Wild' because I'm, well, *wild*."

Bunker stepped back from Zeke and held up his hands palms out. "Ten-four Deputy Kuhlman, Wilco." Then, "What brings you downtown, is Zeke doing the evidence room today?"

Zeke was a fully certified police working dog, cross-trained in both bomb and drug detection. He'd been instrumental in a number of drug seizures and during a traffic stop gone wrong had saved Kuhlman from serious injury when he'd aggressively defended her from a 6'4" fugitive with outstanding warrants. Both Kuhlman and Zeke received commendations.

"No, not till next week. We just stopped to check the vacation schedule. Rick and I are entering a ballroom dancing contest in Nashville in a couple months."

Bunker nodded before patting Zeke on the head and making for the door. "Better him than me...Rick's a glutton for punishment. Bye Zeke, maybe I'll see you when you come back next week."

Kuhlman turned toward her K-9 SUV. "Good to see you Amos."

Bunker grinned. "See ya, Wild."

He took the stairs to the second floor, made his way down a short hall, then pushed through the glass double doors to the Sheriff's Office. It took up half of the second floor. Bunker nodded to the uniformed deputy at the reception desk. The deputy, who was on the phone, waved as Bunker breezed past. The work area consisted of a large open space with a polished concrete floor. A half dozen cubicles were stationed throughout the area in a geometric pattern. Offices lined the walls, a few with open doors revealing occupants on phone calls or working on computers. A six-foot-wide desk with a glass top sat in the center of the open floor. It was surrounded on three sides by filing cabinets, giving it the appearance of a throne, or at the very least a command center. Considering who sat there, this was appropriate.

"Good morning Gayle. You can mark me 'In' on the In/Out Board."

Gayle DeJean shifted her eyes from one of her two computer screens and squinted at Bunker. She was 42 and the mother of two teenaged sons. Her dark-brown hair was shoulder-length and she wore fashionable amber-framed glasses. Her official title was Sheriff's Department Clerk, whose job description included processing documents, maintaining records, preparing reports, and assisting with correspondence. Her unofficial duties were too many to name.

"Well, Amos Bunker. I didn't expect to see you until this afternoon."

Amos cocked his head. "What's going on this afternoon?"

DeJean tilted her head toward the large office in the corner. "The sheriff is calling a meeting...all three of you detectives and some of the senior deputies. Two o'clock. He said he'd handle sending out the group text. I guess he didn't do that yet?"

Bunker shook his head. "Nope. He should've let you do it Gayle. If you want things done right..."

She smiled. "Something to do with the murders."

Bunker nodded. "Gotcha." He suspected that Gayle already knew more about the subject of the meeting than he would know when it ended. If there had been a "Miss Efficiency" pageant in Miami County, Gayle DeJean would win it hands down.

Hell, maybe even the whole state of Ohio.

"Will you be here the rest of the day, Amos?" She was moving the magnet next to his name from "Out" to "In."

"Depends. I have to look into some things, make some calls."

"Well, you go save the world." She waved and turned back to her computer screens before calling out, "Donuts in the breakroom."

Bunker made his way past the mostly unoccupied cubicles to a small office on the far wall. He opened the door and strode to a wood and brass freestanding hall tree—a gift from his mother—and shed his sport coat. Each of the department's three detectives maintained an office in the space. They were all furnished with utilitarian wooden desks that Bunker suspected had been purchased from IKEA. The occupants were given the freedom to decorate, within reason, in whatever fashion suited them. The hall tree represented Bunker's lone attempt at personalization, and even that wouldn't have happened if his mother hadn't insisted on commemorating his promotion from deputy to detective several years earlier.

Bunker slid behind the desk, removing the holster with its Glock from his right hip as he did so. He opened a desk drawer and placed it inside before adding the matching pouch from his left hip that held an extra magazine and a pair of handcuffs. Suitably unburdened, he started the desktop computer and removed a yellow legal pad from another drawer. He glanced at the window that overlooked downtown Troy, satisfied that the blinds were closed to prevent distractions. The door was open, keeping with office custom when rooms were occupied. When the computer screen brightened, Bunker got to work.

He first did an extensive online search of Running Dog Enterprises. Their website featured slick marketing material that focused on the many products they manufactured. It appeared to Bunker that a significant percentage of their sales involved putting custom logos on a myriad of golf-related items. Bunker was a weekend golfer himself and as he scrolled through the items he couldn't help wondering if he'd used any of these custom products. One item, the small pencils given with scorecards to players at Shelby Oaks Golf Club outside of nearby Sidney, stood out.

The printing on the side of their pencils reads, 'ERASER NOT INTENDED FOR CHEATING.' Looks just like Running Dog's stuff.

Bunker noted that one page on the site featured players on professional golf's Asian Tour that were using balls and gear that featured the company's distinctive red and white logo.

Well, they don't sponsor any American players, or even any foreign players I've heard of...but it looks like it's just a matter of time.

Bunker navigated to the website's "Contact Us" page and jotted down the international phone number as well as the firm's physical address in the city of Shenzhen and its email address. Looking further he saw that the company had a U.S. office in Newark, New Jersey. He added this information to the legal pad then printed all the pages he'd just viewed. Bunker often did this. It gave him an extra copy of the data, but he felt the act of writing pertinent facts with his own hand helped his retention.

He dialed Gayle DeJean's extension with the desk phone and waited for her to pick up.

"Gayle, I'm printing some information out there on the bizhub. Can you pull it off and hold it for me? I'll grab it later."

Assured by DeJean that she would set the copies aside, Bunker hung up. As soon as he got a dial tone, he punched in the phone number listed for the office in New Jersey. After three rings he heard a male's recorded voice.

"You have reached Running Dog Enterprises. No one is available to take your call right now. At the sound of the beep please leave a message and we will respond as soon as possible. Your call is very important to us."

Bunker hung up without leaving a message. He swiveled back to the computer and brought up Google Earth. The Newark address was in the 700 block of Broad Street not far from the city's center. It appeared to be a seven-story building, no different from those on either side. Bunker tried the number a second time, again got the recording, and decided once more to not leave a recording.

It's possible they're swamped with calls. I'll try again in a few minutes...try to get a person on the line.

He decided to place an international call to the company headquarters in China. Again, he reached a recording but this time it had an interactive component designed to allow the caller to select his language and the department he wished to connect with. Bunker selected English and then pushed 'o' to be connected to the operator. He was greeted by a woman's voice that betrayed very little accent.

"Good evening, Running Dog Enterprises, how may I assist you please?"

Bunker thought, *Good evening?* It hit him, *There's a time difference...what time would it be there?*

He nearly verbalized the thought. Instead he stated, "Hello, I'm calling from the United States. I'd like to speak to someone familiar with your employees in this country."

The woman paused. Bunker, sensing the operator might function as a gatekeeper, something common in American businesses, followed up.

"I'm a member of law enforcement here in the states...I just have a few questions." Then to cushion his request with a pleasantry, he put a light tone in his voice. "What time is it there? I'm sorry, I've probably called at a very inconvenient time."

She answered, "It is 11:35 p.m. Friday here sir."

Bunker checked his wall clock. *It's 10:35 a.m. here, still Friday. They are...13 hours ahead of us.*

"Oh wow, then it *is* a bad time."

The operator assuaged his concern. "No, not inconvenient at all. We maintain the phones around the clock. Many of our customers are international and call at all hours. This is a courtesy many businesses in China provide for overseas clients." She continued, "But I'm afraid only our sales desks are staffed after hours and on weekends. There will be no one available in personnel. Would you like to leave them a voicemail?"

Bunker said that he would, thanked her for her help, and waited for the voicemail prompt. He left his name, title, and cellphone number, asking for a return call whenever possible. He briefly considered asking about a U.S. employee named Eli but dismissed the thought.

No sense tipping my hand too much.

The next thread to follow was to track down who lived at the house outside Urbana that the Range Rovers had driven to after the meeting.

Were these guys visiting someone there? Could Running Dog own the house?

He discovered that the owners were in Canada visiting family. Bunker was able to locate them at their daughter's house outside Montreal and they confirmed that they'd rented the home via Airbnb. He asked for details on the occupants. The couple remembered that the renter was a company, not an individual. They agreed to dig up the information and call back. Bunker suspected he might know the identity of the company. He thanked the couple. After disconnecting he drummed his fingers on the desktop. As he did so his cellphone vibrated indicating a text. He picked it up.

Staff meeting 2:00. Conference room. Please confirm.

Bunker smiled.

Sheriff Hollis finally got around to sending out his group text.

Bunker typed, ***Got it.***

He spent the remainder of the morning gathering as much information as possible on the two Range Rovers he'd witnessed in the Winans parking lot the day the two strangers met with the Shortridges. He pulled up the registration information from the Departments of Motor Vehicles in both New York and Connecticut. He recorded the plate numbers on the legal pad and sent print instructions to the bizhub. He was about to call Gayle again to have her gather the copies when he shifted gears.

She's probably busy. The bizhub is on the other side of the cubicles, so she has to stop what she's doing to go after them. I might as well get off my lazy butt and get them while I'm waiting on the couple in Canada to call.

He walked out of his office and made his way to the bizhub, an office copier on steroids manufactured by Konica Minolta that featured multiple drawers housing blank paper in several different styles and sizes. He retrieved his copies from the unit and rifled through them as he walked absentmindedly to Gayle's desk to pick up the pages that she'd gathered earlier.

"Right there, Amos." Gayle pointed to a folder on the corner of her desk. She backed away from her computer screen and adjusted her glasses. "I'm going to run out and grab lunch. Would you like me to pick up something for you?"

Bunker realized that it was past noon. He was waiting on a call from the vacationing couple in Canada. With the meeting scheduled for 2 p.m. he might not have time to get out of the building.

"Well, I don't want you to go to any trouble."

She waved a hand. "No trouble. I have to go out to pick up some colored paper before the Sheriff's meeting. I was planning to pick up something to eat anyway."

Bunker knew that colored paper meant that Sheriff Hollis was gearing up for a department-wide investigation. He liked to assemble documents from his investigators in different colors: red for reports from Pappy Karabin, the senior detective; grey for Bunker; and blue for Cody Simon, the most junior member of the investigative staff. Bunker suspected that the sheriff had chosen grey as his color because of his hair.

"Which restaurant are you going to?"

"I was thinking Chipotle."

Bunker reached for his wallet.

Beats the hell out of stale donuts.

Bunker took the last bite of his burrito an hour later. The couple had called back with the information on the Airbnb. The house had indeed been rented to Running Dog Enterprises.

Okay, exactly WHAT are these guys from a Chinese manufacturer of golf products doing? Renting a house in the country...meeting with Garrett and Gerard...hmmm.

As he sat contemplating there was movement at his door.

"Hey Amos, the sheriff wants to get started a few minutes early. Looks like everybody's here."

It was Cody Simon, a tall, athletic man with a quick smile. He'd been a multi-sport star athlete in high school and a college baseball player until a series of injuries ended his athletic career. After graduating from Wright State University, he joined the Sheriff's Department. He made detective after just five years as a deputy by showing initiative and an eye for detail. His quick promotion rubbed a few people the wrong way. This included not only a couple deputies with longer service time, but Pappy as well. Bunker liked Cody. They were both sports fans, often discussing happenings in football, baseball, and—least interesting to Bunker—basketball.

Bunker couldn't stomach the extra steps that referees allowed players to take without dribbling. He and Simon once got into a quasi-heated argument on the subject. The younger detective maintained that this was just a natural evolution of the game. Bunker believed that traveling could be called on virtually every possession.

"Let me ask you something Cody. If the same leniency was applied to sprinters in the Olympics and they were allowed extra steps out of the blocks before starting the timer, what do you think the world record would be in the hundred-meter dash? Five seconds flat?"

Simon shook his head and said simply, "Christ, Amos... you and rules."

"If you have them, you stick to them."

The three detectives joined four senior uniformed deputies—two male, two female—and the sheriff in the conference room. Sheriff Robin Hollis was a balding 52-year-old with a thick mustache and a pleasant face. Though he had the look of a favorite uncle, Bunker knew him to be an effective administrator with a solid background in the trenches. Like Bunker, Hollis had spent time as a deputy on patrol. Their service on the roads of Miami County overlapped for two years. Bunker had witnessed Hollis handle tough cases and dangerous perpetrators. He understood that the Sheriff's affable manner helped him get elected, but he knew there was a serious law enforcement official behind the smile.

"Thanks for carving out some time for this, people. As you might've guessed, the purpose of this meeting is to bring everyone up to speed on the recent murders in the area. The Ohio Bureau of Criminal Investigation put a rush on their examination of the bullet that killed Garrett Shortridge. It matched—with a 90% probability, a similar .22 caliber bullet taken from another victim in Urbana several days ago.

There was murmuring. Heads turned to each other as a single thought passed through the room.

Serial killer?

"We're working with Champaign and Shelby Counties... sharing information. Champaign reports that a person of interest"—he checked a report that he held in his hand—"Kevin Turner, is unaccounted for. Here's what I need; Pappy, I want you and Simon to work this hard. Turner needs to be located pronto. Gayle has put folders together that include all the information we have on this guy." He pointed to a stack on his desk. "She has included contact information for the detectives running point on this in the other two counties. Feel free to contact them directly but keep me up to speed. I want to be updated daily on anything new."

He turned to Bunker but spoke to the entire room.

"Amos is clarifying details of the Shortridge brothers' movements in the days before their murders. Everyone in the room knows that Garrett and Gerard have been suspected of selling illegal narcotics for some time. I don't want to leave a stone unturned. It's possible that someone other than Turner is involved."

He nodded to Bunker then turned to the deputies.

"Turner has been driving a beat up 20-year-old Chevy pickup truck since he got out of prison. It's registered to his

181

sister. Urbana PD has interviewed her, and she claims to have no idea where he *or* the truck are…Says if we find them, she wants the truck back, but we can keep Turner."

One of the male deputies chuckled.

"Your packets will include a list of all of his known relatives and friends. Some of them live in our county. I want regular drive-bys of these places. Get the info on the truck to everyone on your shifts. If you spot him call for backup. Assume he'll be armed…and with something bigger than a .22."

He gestured to the folders. "Take one and familiarize yourself with the details. Detectives, get a short summary of what you've done—and what you plan to do—to me before you leave here today. Questions?"

There were none.

"I'll be here for a few more hours if you think of one. The cubicles are open if you deputies want to drop anchor here while you're reading. Everybody has my number. Let's find this guy."

The group filtered out as most of the deputies found a cubicle and began to review the file on Turner. The detectives returned to their respective offices. Bunker spent 20 minutes on the computer recapping the steps he'd taken so far. These included the surveillance he'd done at the coffee shop the day the Shortridges met with two unknown subjects, his tracking of the men to a house near Urbana, his subsequent interviews with the staff at Winans, and the efforts he'd made to contact Running Dog Enterprises. He assumed that Sheriff Hollis would overlook the fact that he'd strayed into Champaign County when he followed the Range Rover to the rental house.

Considering what's happened since that morning, maybe it's not such a bad thing to bend a rule every now and then.

Even though the act of leaving his jurisdiction may have paid dividends, Bunker's inclination to follow rules and regulations was still top of mind.

He had just started on the report when he heard a single knock on the door frame. He looked up to see Pappy Karabin.

"Hey Amos, I hear you'll be moving your mom into StoryPoint."

Dana Bunker's issues had been an open secret in the department for some time. Bunker had to request time off to tend to her more than once.

"Yeah Pappy. It should be sometime in the next week or so." Bunker was surprised. In the years that he had worked alongside Karabin, the senior detective had almost never discussed subjects that had to do with a colleague's personal life.

"Well, if you need any help with that, give me a call."

Bunker managed, "Uh, okay Pap, thanks. I appreciate that."

Karabin tapped the door frame twice and turned in the direction of his office.

Bunker thought, *Well, what do you know?*

He wrapped up the report and emailed it to the sheriff. It was nearly 4 p.m. and he thought he would check on his mother on the way home. He retrieved his holster and cuffs from the drawer and attached them to his belt. As he reached for his sport coat his eyes fell on a file folder on the corner of his desk. It was the paperwork he'd been putting off for more than two weeks. He sighed and sat back down.

Better just tackle this now. It's going to get really busy for at least the next few days. Might as well spend ten minutes now and knock it out.

He had opened the envelope when it arrived on his desk and dropped it on his to-do pile. He'd subsequently received a reminder in the mail. He dug out the original letter. It was a standard request from the state for background information. This one was from the foster and adoption program. They directed their requests to law enforcement departments and personnel that had contact—either positive or negative—with applicants. Information returned to the program was kept on file and could be accessed by private adoption agencies. Bunker had completed a half dozen of these requests in his time as a detective.

He returned to the computer and entered the web address provided in the letter. It would take him to the page that was specific to these applicants. He hit "enter" and waited. He saw the screen change and stared at the first line.

BACKROUND REQUEST FOR APPLICANTS:
Hull, Paul M.
Hull, Lauren R.

Bunker's brow furrowed.

CHAPTER TWENTY-ONE

Dylan punched the garage door opener and waited as the door at the rental house rose. He saw that Min had moved his Evoque inside. When the door came to a stop, Dylan pulled his SUV in next to its twin. He got out and watched as Willie came up the driveway in the Sentra. He walked to the car as it came to a stop and waited for Willie to emerge.

"How did you like that traffic circle?" He asked the question with a slightly mocking tone.

Willie tried to sound bored.

"Zero stars...would not recommend."

Dylan laughed.

They entered the house through the garage, Willie carrying his travel bag. They found Min staring into the refrigerator with one hand on his hip.

"Hello comrades, welcome back to our humble home." He stared at Willie with an exaggerated look of surprise. "Tell me William, did you actually *drive* here from Dayton?"

"Of course I fucking drove here!" It came out almost as a snarl. "Why the fuck does everybody give me shit about driving?"

Dylan's and Min's eyes met. Both struggled to suppress laughter.

Min raised his hands. "Whoa, big boy. Calm yourself." He shifted gears. "I'm hungry. I think I will order food from the Chinese place in Urbana. Interested? I'm thinking orange chicken and spring rolls."

This got Willie's attention. "Now you're talking."

The food was delivered 45 minutes later from a restaurant called Great Wall. The three men ate in the television room while lounging on chairs and a couch. The television was tuned to a cops and robbers movie.

Dylan stared at the restaurant's logo on the bags.

"Hey Min, have you visited the Great Wall? I mean, the real one in China, not the restaurant in Urbana."

Willie's fork, laden with fried rice, paused halfway to his mouth. He snorted.

Min frowned at Willie and turned to Dylan.

"I have not. It is over 2,000 kilometers north of Shenzhen. That is"—he squinted and looked at the ceiling—"maybe 1,300...1,400 miles. Too far to travel."

Willie spoke around a mouthful of chicken.

"You *do* realize where you are right now, right? It's not exactly a hop, skip, and a jump from your hometown."

Min nodded as he broke a spring roll in half.

"Yes, my friend, but I'm here on business. That's different." His eyes wandered to the flat screen on the wall and recognition flashed in his eyes. "Oh, I've seen this movie. It is..." He paused, trying to remember.

Dylan spoke up. "*Heat*. Good flick. De Niro, Pacino. Really good flick."

The threesome watched in silence as the De Niro character and his gang prepared for a robbery. It seemed like as good a time as any to discuss their own business.

Dylan selected a spring roll of his own and turned to Willie. "Tell us more about the people who will be taking over for Shadow and the Shortridge brothers."

Willie nodded. "Okay, Shadow had a couple relatives selling for him. Basically, street level. One is a kid in the local high school who, I guess, is moving a good deal of drugs to other students. All kinds, a little coke, a little meth, pretty much anything Shadow could get his hands on."

Dylan swallowed. "The kids are basically playing Russian roulette, doing any drug that's available."

"Yep, like those parties we went to when *we* were in school. You know, everybody steals a vial of pills from their parent's or grandparent's medicine cabinet...the pills get emptied into a basket and mixed together then every kid swallows one...or two or three."

Dylan nodded, memories of a few high school parties swimming into his mind.

Min looked from Willie to Dylan. "You actually did that?"

Willie smiled. "It was before I got into craft beer."

Min shook his head. "You Americans are fēng diān... *fucking* fēng diān."

Both Willie and Dylan laughed. They had heard Min use the Chinese words for crazy in the past, though not quite with this level of emphasis.

Willie liked to spar verbally with Min.

"Oh, *we're* crazy. I suppose you're completely normal... out there shooting everyone in sight."

Min's mouth twitched. "I believe we have all joined that club. Some of us are simply more willing."

The three men sat silent for a few seconds, each contemplating his own level of contrition. The level was not particularly high in any of them. They, and the fourth member of their group, Dax, shared a number of traits. All four were either an only child or a first-born male. All received an inordinate amount of attention and coddling for most of their lives. Though they viewed themselves as high performers, their accomplishments as adolescents—with the exception of Min—generally fell short of their potential. The Chinese "Little Emperor" culture came with a certain level of expectation. This no doubt motivated Min to achieve the sustained level of performance that helped him earn the Sanyu Scholarship.

In the case of the three Americans, the environment was different. Yes, their parents expected success—and were certainly disappointed when their son's Ivy League glory turned to humiliation—but the level of cultural standards was much higher for Min. It was not until he came to America that his motivations changed. Now all four shared common inclinations; get rich, take what is rightly theirs, kill if necessary.

They saw others as insignificant—human smoke. Beings that swirled around them, waiting to be walked through or blown away. All four men were—despite their internal assertions to the contrary—psychopaths to one degree or another. On one level they didn't even see themselves as criminals. They hadn't created the opioid crisis or the forces driving it. They had simply swept into these areas of rural

America and made the loose network of dealers more effective. They didn't commit crimes, they co-opted less effective organizations...absorbed them. They were doing what Ivy Leaguers had done for generations; applying a higher level of expertise to an already existing undertaking. They were not unlike Theo Epstein, a Yale graduate who, at the age of 28, was hired as the general manager of the Boston Red Sox. Epstein produced near-immediate results when the Sox won the 2004 World Series, their first title since 1918.

The foursome was confident that they simply had a better way of doing things. They also had a skewed sense of morality.

It was a deadly combination.

"Anyway, the second relative is a cousin. He has a factory job. Sounds like both of them easily moved whatever inventory Shadow was able to scrounge up for them. Obviously, we don't care about the other stuff, but they should be able to move a dozen of the loaded balls a month...maybe two dozen."

The "other stuff" Willie was again referring to was cocaine, amphetamines, marijuana, or any of the other non-opioid substances commonly supplied by dealers. The Ivy Leaguers only cared about their product—extremely potent carfentanil. They knew that people who were hooked on opioids, whether it was after first using a prescription version or something obtained from an illegal source, experienced extremely uncomfortable symptoms when they went too long without their next fix. These included: muscle aches, stomach cramps, diarrhea, nausea and vomiting, excessive sweating, shaking, chills, and even yawning. The condition had a name: dope sickness. Individuals who reached the point of being dope sick would do almost anything to get their next dose.

Dylan asked a question. "Are these people going to be able to work with stuff as potent as ours? I mean, the Shortridge brothers had an operation with their own pill presses. How are Shadow's people going to process our goods for sale?"

Willie shrugged. "They say it won't be a problem. They say they have plenty of PPE gear left over from COVID. They'll cut up the carfentanil and mix it by hand with tranq." He was referring to xylazine, a powerful sedative approved for veterinary use. The combination of the two substances had proven to be lethal in many instances.

Dylan's eyes widened slightly. "Jesus."

Willie responded. "Ought to thin out the herd a bit, don't you think?" He chuckled.

Dylan allowed a smile at the bad joke. He turned to Min. "The golf bag is ready?"

Min was watching the movie. He answered without taking his eyes from the screen.

"All ready, boss. Putter cleaned and loaded, drug balls in the big right-side pocket, regular Running Dog balls on the left side. The cut-open ball in plastic is in the small center pocket on top."

"Counting that one, we have a total of three dozen drug balls left, correct?"

"Yes, yes, correct." Min appeared to be slightly annoyed. He glanced at the remote as if considering turning up the volume.

"Okay, Willie, call your contacts in both groups. Set up meetings. I want to have everything lined up with both of them by the end of the weekend so we can move on. The quicker we leave this area, the better. I think we should give the cut ball to Shadow's people."

Willie nodded. "Give them a taste of what's coming their way?"

"Exactly. The Shortridge people, if they're as professional about the process as it sounds, we probably leave them an uncut ball or two as a goodwill gesture. Let them know they can use a Dremel or, better yet, a table saw to remove the covers. They can take it from there. Both groups should be placing orders with us for full boxes as soon as they sample the wares."

Willie speculated, "If we get something going with Dr. Mahmud in Dayton, we're going to go through our stash pretty damn quick."

"Yeah, that means a trip back to Newark by Dax to grab more stock from the warehouse, or at least partway to meet one of our people making deliveries."

Running Dog maintained a small cadre of couriers working out of the Newark office. They were responsible for picking up cash payments. Occasionally they delivered the illicit balls which, typically, were shipped via one of the express package delivery companies.

"Speaking of the former Lion, we need to talk to him to see if anything's moving with the doc."

Willie smiled at the mention of his running mate. Dax had been kicked out of Columbia University. He, like his companions, had a complicated history with his former school. Dylan, Min, and even on occasion, Willie, would refer to Dax as if he were the mascot of his former university.

Dylan turned back to his orange chicken. "Okay, let's get this set up as soon as we're finished eating."

Min, eyes still locked on the screen, seemed not to have heard Dylan.

"Really good shootout scene here, guys. That Val Kilmer is a badass in this movie."

Willie used his burner phone to call Shadow's cousin. The man worked second shift at his factory job and would be at work that night so Willie set up a Saturday meeting. When he spoke to the man who ran the Shortridge pill press operation he was told that a meeting could be fit in Sunday, but "not until after church." Willie rolled his eyes, agreed on a time, and ended the call. That done, he yawned and headed for the stairs.

"Guys, I'm beat. I was up late with Dax last night and did the early meeting this morning. I'm taking a nap."

Min looked up as the movie broke for a commercial. "Yes, go sleep. You are becoming a *gōngzuò kuáng*—a workaholic." He spotted the travel bag in Willie's hand and had a thought.

"Did you bring your little Ruger pistol?"

Willie eyed him suspiciously. Min, a rifle aficionado, had given Willie grief in the past about the compact size of the Ruger.

"Yeah, why?"

Min hopped out of his chair. "I think that model is made to accept a red dot sight. I was just in a gun shop buying a sight for my rifle. I'm curious, can I look at it?"

"Knock yourself out." Willie dug into his travel bag and fished out the black plastic case. He handed it to Min.

"When was the last time you cleaned it?" Min opened the case and examined the pistol, which rested on foam padding with an extra magazine.

Slightly embarrassed, Willie answered, "Uh...never. I shot it at a gun range a few times when I bought it a couple years ago. It's pretty much been in the case ever since."

Min, like many gun owners, was a fanatic when it came to the cleaning and maintenance of his weapons. The look he gave his companion exhibited a combination of dismay and disbelief. He shook his head.

"I will clean it too...go sleep."

Dylan spent 15 minutes on the phone with Dax. He learned very little. The doctor, Mahmud, had spent the entire day so far at his office. Dax sat in his Range Rover in the parking lot scrolling on his phone.

"I'm still here. Nothing unusual. Just a stream of patients. You know, I think I'm getting pretty good at picking out the users. They look kinda paranoid when they get out of their cars...always checking over their shoulders."

Dylan brushed the comment aside.

"Yeah, just let me know if you spot the courier. You said he was expected in today." He checked the time. "Looks like the drop won't happen until after the office closes." He was about to add that this meant the delivery would be at the doctor's house or a remote location but decided against it.

Dax knows what he's doing. He's spent enough time with Willie watching these people that he'll figure it out.

"Well, just make sure your gas tank's full. No telling how far you'll be following him back to his home base when he leaves." Dylan needed to know if they were dealing with a major player.

"Already topped off."

After the call Dylan checked in on Min and found him at the dining room table cleaning a pistol.

"That Willie's?"

Min nodded. "Yes, he says he hasn't cleaned it since, I suspect, he did his last sit-up."

"Ha! That long, huh?" Dylan noticed the Running Dog golf bag in the corner and remembered his last session on the driving range. He went to the bag and unzipped a wide compartment at the bottom that was designed to act as a cooler for cans of beer or soda. Dylan kept foam practice balls there as well as the SureFit adjustment tool for the driver. The tool was tucked inside a small bag with a drawstring at the top that also hid a handful of .22 short rounds that could be fitted into the putter. He removed a handful of the balls and the tool before plucking a few tees from the pocket above. He tucked the SureFit and the tees into his shorts. He then slid his driver from the bag.

"I'm going out back to hit some practice balls...going to tweak the set-up of my driver."

Min was squirting oil on a cleaning patch. He did not look up from his task.

"Okay...I wish you Fu—good fortune."

Dylan was amused. He wasn't sure if Min was trying to be sarcastic.

The backyard of the rental house was expansive. Dylan guessed it was 200 feet deep. It was surrounded by a five-foot wood fence whose slatted construction gave the house and rear patio a degree of privacy.

Should be plenty of room to hit practice balls and keep them inside the fence.

He teed up one of the balls then stepped back and took a few easy practice swings to warm up. He then set up over the ball and unleashed a smooth swing that sent the ball arching toward the rear of the property. He repeated this with the remainder of the balls before walking to the back of the yard.

Not bad. Could still use more draw.

He gathered the balls. One had come to rest a few feet from the fence. When he retrieved it, he stopped and looked over the fence at the farm fields beyond. He was looking west across a field that sprouted rows of a low green crop. State Route 36 was off to his left. Dylan watched the desultory traffic creep past for a few seconds before turning and tossing the balls on the grass. After hitting all of them back toward the house he walked in the same direction.

Now, to get more draw do I adjust the head of the driver to the left or the right?

He couldn't remember. It had been a few months since he'd tweaked the set-up. He used the SureFit to adjust it both ways, hitting a series of balls that kept him moving from one end of the yard to the other. Once he figured out which direction the head need to be adjusted, he experimented with the number of increments he needed to go in that direction to achieve the ball flight he was looking for. Next, he made swings that generated different heights of ball flight to gauge the effect of the adjustments.

I think I'll keep the driver and practice balls here when Willie leaves so I can keep working on this...really dial it in.

It was a time-consuming process. Dylan found his thoughts wandering back to the present situation with the rural opioid networks. He had been thinking for some time that it would be beneficial to have their own people to put in place with the organizations after they'd been co-opted.

People that can move in as soon as we take over and get ready to move on to the next target area. We should put in place a kind of junior executive training program. They roll into a place like Urbana or Troy, stay until everything's cooking, then follow us to the next burg. We already have couriers working out of the Newark office that pick up payments. Have to get word to Mr. Chu in China about this.

Dylan, as often happened when he was swinging a golf club, had lost track of time. He sent another half-dozen foam balls on their way to the fence when he had a thought.

Maybe I should pull a dozen regular Running Dog balls out of the bag and hit drives over the fence into the field. I sure as hell won't walk all the way out there to pick them up. I'll just leave them there. I don't really give a rat's ass if Farmer Jones doesn't like it. It'll give me a truer read on ball flight and—

The burner phone in his pocket vibrated. He stepped to the patio and leaned the driver against the house. He dug out the phone. It was a text from the informant with the Miami County Sheriff's Department.

It began; ***Most of force is looking for a man named Kevin Turner in connection with the murders.***

Dylan smiled with satisfaction before reading on.

But one detective is tasked with looking at other possible suspects. He witnessed you meeting with the Shortridge brothers at Winans. Has run your plates. He is looking at Running Dog. Just wanted to warn you. This guy can be very effective.

Dylan felt a chill run up his back.
FUCK!

CHAPTER TWENTY-TWO

Saturday morning found Dax Devereaux sitting behind the wheel of his Range Rover. He was parked on Peachcreek Road, a few miles southwest of the Home2 Suites hotel in the Dayton suburb of Centerville where he and Willie had stayed for several nights. Dr. Mahmud lived in one of the several dozen four-unit buildings—Dax wasn't sure if they were considered apartments or condominiums—that populated the web of streets that coiled through the immediate area.

It was a few minutes after 7 a.m. Though Dax was limited to just four hours of sleep the night before, he was pleased, no, damn near delighted, to get them. For much of Friday night it looked like he would be stuck in the Range Rover, attempting to stay awake while watching for Mahmud. After following the doctor home from his office to his place on Peachcreek, Dax spent nearly two hours watching and waiting. At 7:45 p.m. Mahmud left his residence, driving right past Dax's Range Rover.

There was no doubt it was the doctor. He drove a Mercedes sedan whose shade of red, Dax decided, could surely be perceived by even the most severely color-blind. Dax and Willie had been locked onto the car since coming to the Dayton area. Despite operating without Willie's set of eyes on Friday, there was little danger that Dax, working solo, would lose the Mercedes.

He trailed Mahmud, generally heading west, for less than ten minutes before entering an area that featured mostly commercial buildings. Mahmud signaled and turned into the parking lot of what is euphemistically known as a gentlemen's club. Many would term it a strip club. It was a box-shaped single-story concrete-block building with no windows visible from the street. Dax was able to deduce the nature of the business from its name—Lust. A Ziebart auto undercoating shop was next door. Dax remembered what Willie had said when they first noticed this.

"Nice. You can take care of your lust and your rust at the same time."

This was the fourth night that Mahmud had visited the club since the Ivy League pair began to watch him. They had taken turns entering the building on the other occasions. Willie had gone in once. Dax—who liked the ladies—twice. They witnessed Mahmud passing clear plastic vials to other patrons on two occasions. He accepted money in return but at no time did they see him receive anything that looked remotely like a drug shipment, either inside the club or in the parking lot. For the most part he ogled the women, all of whom appeared to be less than half his age.

On Friday night Dax elected to stay in the Range Rover in the Lust parking lot. He recognized many of the vehicles as belonging to regulars and decided none of their drivers could be Mahmud's source. He also didn't want to take a chance of Mahmud recognizing him. Dax was relieved when the doctor emerged from the club a few minutes before 1 a.m. and drove straight home. He decided to return to the Home2 Suites for a few hours of shuteye before picking up surveillance again in the morning.

Now, after a 6 a.m. wake-up call, a shower, and a quick stop for gas where he also grabbed a couple Celsius energy drinks, some beef sticks, and a Snickers, Dax was parked again on Peachcreek Road, hoping to witness Mahmud's next score. Two different sources had told Willie and him that Mahmud was expecting a shipment any day.

Better be pretty freakin' soon. We can't stick around forever waiting to see if this dude is our next target. Dylan seemed a little weirded out on the phone yesterday.

Dax had taken a call from Dylan while following Mahmud Friday night. Dylan explained that a detective from Miami County was sniffing around. He—Dax guessed it was a he—had apparently seen Dylan and Min meet with the Shortridge brothers not long before their demise. The information came from their source inside the sheriff's office.

"We're gonna try to firm things up this weekend with both these networks. We'll give you a day or two to see if

196

Mahmud is tied in with one of the big players. If not, he's the next target. But if he is..."

Dax knew that meant they would vamoose, check out. They would bypass Dayton and move on to the next area in Dylan's master plan. That meant Kentucky. Dax knew they would definitely skip over Cincinnati, 50 miles south of Dayton, and move back into a rural area.

The sun was soft Saturday morning. Sipping from a can of Celsius, Dax watched as a pair of joggers made their way past his Evoque. He could see the Mercedes in the parking spot in front of Mahmud's unit.

Damn, that thing is red.

Dax idly searched the Mercedes website to find the specific name of the shade.

Patagonia red.

He sighed, resigned to the fact that his foreseeable future would be determined by the designs or impulses of an unscrupulous doctor who was probably sleeping in. It was difficult to stay alert. It made his mind wander to obscure subjects—like the appropriate name of the shade of red on a Mercedes.

It was tempting at times like these to bury his head in his phone. He could, if given the opportunity, kill an hour—or two or three—by simply bouncing from one inane social media post to the next. He also knew that this was an excellent way to lose track of his subject. Even worse, it could keep him from noticing the approach of a police officer who may have been notified of a suspicious man by a nosy neighbor. Dax had found a way to adjust his mental settings, allowing half his brain to stay focused on observation and the other half to reign free.

Willie called this Dax's "zen state."

As the morning sun inched upward, Dax allowed a portion of his mind to wander. This time it pulled him back to his hometown.

Springfield, New Jersey was located some 20 miles west of New York City. Dax and his younger sister were born and raised there. Their father worked in senior management for a number of companies. He had a track record of success in turnaround situations. He was brought in to trim the fat from companies that were preparing to sell. Once the necessary changes were put in place—making a business more attractive to buyers—he was paid a large bonus. He would then choose from a number of new suitors and move on. To some in the media he was known as a "serial CEO," to others, a "hatchet man."

Dax's mother enjoyed charity work. She was on a number of boards, most of which were based in New York City. A few were in Newark, which is situated midway between Springfield and the Big Apple.

Dax had little oversight as a teen. His father joined a local golf course and Dax took full advantage. He played several times a week in the summer months. He became a good player but, to his father's dismay, also came to have an overdeveloped sense of entitlement. He mistreated staff in the pro shop, argued with other members, and belittled greenskeepers.

Seemingly not content to cause his parents grief by his actions at the course, he doubled down by constantly complaining that the Devereauxs weren't members of the *real* club in the area.

Baltusrol Golf Club, located in Springfield Township a few miles from the Devereaux home, was a private 36-hole club that was founded in 1895. It had been the site of seven U.S. Opens and two PGA Championships. In 2014 it was designated a National Historic Landmark. The club took its name from the oddly-monikered Baltus Roll, a farmer who lived on the land during the early 1800s. Roll was murdered on the property in 1831 by two thieves who believed he'd hidden a small treasure in his farmhouse.

Baltusrol was one of the most famous golf clubs in the world. Jack Nicklaus won two U.S. Opens there—in 1967 and 1980. It is also one of the most exclusive. Initiation fees are reported to be $150,000, with an additional yearly dues fee in the $20,000 range.

The expense, combined with his son's temperamental behavior, was more than enough to convince Dax's father to pass on any attempt to join Baltusrol.

Dax rebelled. He began to run with the wrong crowd. There was a series of arrests. At first the offenses were minor: shoplifting in the mall, vandalizing cars, and underage drinking. But soon, expensive items began to disappear from the clubhouse lockers where the Devereauxs were members. Dax was identified as the thief when another member saw his own driver for sale on eBay. He selected the "Buy It Now" option, sent the payment, and was astonished when it arrived at his house three days later bearing the return address of his neighbors down the street, the Devereaux family.

This was the last straw for Dax's father, who gave his son an ultimatum—"Straighten the hell up, *Keenan*. You're out of options. You're about to be trimmed from the fucking payroll. You know, I rightsize organizations for a living. Maybe it's time we downsized here at home too."

Dax decided discretion was the better part of valor. He buckled down in his final year of high school and was accepted at Columbia. This was due primarily to three factors: a high-priced attorney successfully getting Dax's police record as a minor sealed, an excellent SAT score that was partly the result of private tutoring, and letters of recommendation from business associates of his father—associates that didn't want to be rightsized themselves.

Columbia University is the oldest institution of higher learning in the state of New York and the fifth oldest in the United States. It is located on Manhattan's Upper West Side. In its storied history, Columbia has produced a staggering collection of high performers. These include: four U.S. Presidents, ten Justices of the Supreme Court and over 100 Nobel laureates. It has also turned out 33 Academy Award Winners and over 100 Pulitzer Prize recipients, and, most noteworthy to Dax, 53 living billionaires.

Columbia was the first university in the U.S. to grant the MD degree. Critical research and planning for the

Manhattan Project—the program that developed the atom bomb during World War II—also took place there.

Columbia University has seen an astounding variety of wondrous achievements by its students. Like any college, it is also home to the mundane. Students oversleep and miss class. They eat the wrong food. They drink too much. And sometimes they are careless with their personal possessions.

It was this last phenomenon that caught Dax's attention in the first semester of his freshman year. He noticed a door propped open down the hall from his second-floor room in John Jay Hall—one of four dormitories that housed freshmen. Dax stuck his head inside, saw no one, then checked to confirm there were no witnesses in the hall. Seeing none, he helped himself to a small glass piggy bank that was partially filled with change. It was stupid, impulsive, and incredibly risky.

It was also the start of something that consumed him.

Dax began to steal at every opportunity. At first, he roamed John Jay exclusively. After a few weeks, he expanded his activities to the three other freshman dorms: Carman, Furnald, and Wallach Halls. The most common items he stole were small electronics such as laptops, tablets, and cellphones. He knew these had a "Find My Device" feature so he rarely kept them for more than a day. He'd noticed a crude printed handbill on a campus bulletin board that displayed the words, *BUY, SELL, TRADE...I DEAL IN GADGETS...NEED A DEVICE?...HAVE ONE TO SELL? CALL ME...*

Dax made a call and, after a feeling out process, learned that the man would pay cash for his booty—no questions asked.

Dax had a fence.

Life was good for two months. Dax scoured the freshman dorms on a daily basis. He came to think of the stolen goods from these forays as a "harvest." He quickly expanded his activities to other buildings. There were 21 libraries in the Columbia system, 16 of which were located on main campus. Dax scouted these buildings, generally while wearing a COVID mask. He carefully noted the location of security cameras and chose his victims accordingly. Restrooms, where no cameras were permitted, were a productive hunting ground. He was initially amazed at the number of times another student would leave a backpack or computer bag on the sink counter or the floor outside a stall when using the facilities. He came to expect it.

Columbia allowed freshmen to keep a vehicle on campus. Dax took advantage of this. His parents had given him a brand-new Volkswagen Tiguan SUV as a graduation present, partly as a reward for curtailing his thefts during high school. Every few days he drove it over the Harlem River to a small house in the Bronx not far from Yankee Stadium and exchanged the stolen devices for cash. The fence was happy to pay for credit cards and jewelry as well.

Dax, of course, kept any cash that he'd been able to steal. When he made off with a bag or backpack, he generally found a private area, quickly rifled through it, and kept the items he could sell. The remaining contents, and the bag itself, were discarded. On rare occasions he would keep the odd item for personal use.

This would prove to be his downfall.

Dax was in his dorm room on a Thursday afternoon watching Fast & Furious 6 on his personal laptop. He was a major fan of the franchise and had seen the original and each sequel several times. The movie was nearly over. Dax planned to bolt from the room as soon as the final scene ended. Two stolen iPads and a purloined Samsung Galaxy cellphone were inside an unzipped backpack on the floor next to his chair. His fence in the Bronx was expecting him in an hour. Dax had just picked up the devices that afternoon and planned to unload them quickly.

Wonder how fast I can get there if I drive like Paul Walker in the movie.

He was streaming the audio to a set of wireless Skullcandy earbuds so he wouldn't disturb his roommate, an international student from Toronto. The earbuds worked beautifully. Dax saw them unattended on a desk at the Health Sciences Library two weeks earlier. They were black, with miniature peace sign decals affixed to the exterior. He had nonchalantly laid a jacket over them, bent to tie a shoe, then gathered them with the jacket and made his way out of the building. He tried them out that night and decided to keep them. They were worth more to him than the 30 bucks the fence would pay.

There was a knock at the door. Dax looked at his roommate expectantly. The movie, after all, was near its end and he didn't want to pause it.

The roommate sighed, got up, and opened the door. A member of the campus police stood outside. Behind him was a pixyish young woman with pink hair. She stood on her toes and strained to look over the policeman's shoulder. She held a cellphone in her hand and her eyes darted from the interior of the room, to the phone, and back again.

"This has to be it!" She said the words with a high-pitched voice.

Dax's roommate, confused, asked, "Can I help you?"

The policeman spoke. "We're looking for some missing earbuds."

Skullcandy, Dax would later learn, had recently introduced products with tracking technology. He was wearing one of the first sets.

The woman shouldered her way around the officer and thrust a finger at Dax, a furious look on her face.

"There they are, see? The peace sign decals...I put them on there!"

Dax stood and removed the devices. He had the volume turned up on the movie and the sound of a car crash poured from them into the room. He thought fast.

I just found them...I was going to turn them in to lost and found but wanted to try them first...make sure they were working.

His roommate spoke first.

"I think he's been stealing stuff. I don't know for sure, but...check that bag." He pointed to the backpack on the floor with the stolen electronics. Four sets of eyes stared past the open zipper.

Dax, who had given his roommate $500 early in his spree to keep his mouth shut, looked at him with contempt and spoke in a conversational tone.

"You damn Canuck bastard."

Dax was dismissed from the university. He avoided jail time by cooperating with the NYPD. He identified the fence in the Bronx. He also made restitution to a number of the victims, draining the bank account he'd built up for months.

Though his father hired an excellent attorney, he was disgusted with his son. Dax also found that his mother, who was generally much more lenient with him, had cooled considerably. Dax learned that she had been quietly asked to leave two charity boards after revelations about her son made the news.

Dax was back at home, but it was a very uncomfortable existence. Eventually an agreement was reached; Dax would move out. He would find a suitable apartment, get a job, and get back on his feet. His parents would provide a monthly stipend and allow him to keep the Volkswagen SUV.

Though he would've preferred to move back to New York City, the expense of housing there made it out of the question. Dax found a small apartment not far from downtown Newark. The stipend would pay the rent, but just barely. He would need a job to make ends meet.

Dax acquired a fake ID that said he was 25 and began to drive for Uber. He found that he enjoyed it. He drove riders all over the Newark-New York City area. He made money, met interesting people, and—he couldn't help himself—kept any items the riders happened to leave in his vehicle. He had worked at this job for nearly three years, not quite ever getting the urge to go back to college, when he first met Willie.

Dax remembered that first ride with his future partner. He'd accepted the ride request and arrived at the 86th Street subway station near Central Park where Willie was waiting. The destination was an apartment building in Chelsea. When they arrived, a limousine was parked in front of the building. A man emerged from the building entrance and ducked into the back seat of the limousine.

"Uh, hey man," Willie began, "sorry to do this, but is there any way you can follow that?" He pointed at the limo. "I'll make it worth your while."

Dax thought, *What the hell.*

He disregarded the posted speed limits, rushed through a few yellow lights—one or two may have been red—and cut off a semi to reach an exit on the Jersey side of the George Washington Bridge. The pair followed the limo to its destination, an inexpensive hotel in Fort Lee.

Willie didn't forget. He searched for Dax in his Uber history two weeks later when he again needed to get somewhere in a hurry. Soon he was calling Dax directly and scheduling rides. Some were open-ended, with Willie asking Dax to follow another vehicle.

Dax picked Willie's brain, asking about the private investigative business. Neither of them had close friends. They found themselves opening up to each other, discussing their backgrounds. They had common ground; they felt the world owed them.

A few months after meeting Willie, Dax picked up two riders from John F. Kennedy International Airport, a frequent occurrence. Both men had small suitcases and wore golf shirts with embroidered logos. One had Asian features. The second man pulled a golf travel bag in addition to his suitcase.

Dax hopped out of the SUV and opened the rear hatch door. As he put the luggage inside, he realized each piece bore the same logo that was on the men's shirts—Running Dog Enterprises.

"Hey, are you guys with Running Dog? Kind of a new player in the golf market, right? I've used those balls."

The man with Western features nodded.

"Yeah, good company. We plan to really make some noise."

Dax saw the man look at his Asian companion and smile.

The destination was an office building on Broad Street in downtown Newark. Dax found the men open to conversation, which was not always the case in a ride share situation. They introduced themselves as Dylan and Min on the way into town.

"So, you've used the balls...what do you think?" This from Dylan.

Dax answered. "What's not to like? Cool logo...priced right. You know, I'm an Uber driver so I'm not gonna spring for Titleists."

Min leaned forward. "You are young for an Uber driver, yes? Are you also in college?"

Dax frowned, remembering his time at Columbia. "Not anymore...bad experience."

After an awkward few seconds Dylan, apparently trying to change the subject, asked, "So, you play a lot of golf?"

Dax eased the Tiguan around a stalled car. "Used to back in Springfield. Don't play so much now. It's expensive, y'know?"

Dylan inquired, "Springfield? New Jersey? You ever play Baltusrol?"

Dax shook his head. This was another sore subject.

Dylan pressed on. "Just curious, you seem to be pretty good at this job, why is your rating only 4.7?"

Thinking about it later, Dax was never quite sure why he answered candidly. Maybe the entire conversation had helped shift his mindset away from the polite banter he normally kept up with talkative riders.

"Honestly? It's because a couple riders have accused me of keeping stuff they forgot to take out of the vehicle."

Min jumped in.

"What kind of stuff?"

Dax looked at him in the rearview mirror. "An iPad... maybe a purse."

Min grinned. "Did you? Keep them, I mean?"

Dax thought, *What the hell.*

"I might've." He grinned back.

In the mirror he saw Min turn to Dylan, raise his eyebrows, and nod.

Dax pulled himself back to the present when he noticed movement. Dr. Mahmud stepped from his front door and walked to his Mercedes. He wore light brown khakis and an untucked button-down white shirt. He carried a leather valise, which he tossed onto the passenger seat before sliding behind the wheel.

Okay...casual clothes—check. A little satchel that can hold the goods—check. Looks like it's game on.

Mahmud pulled away from the complex and headed west at a leisurely pace. Dax followed, careful to keep other vehicles between his Range Rover and the Mercedes. For several minutes it appeared that Mahmud was again heading for the gentlemen's club.

Geez dude, get a life!

Mahmud, to Dax's relief, drove past the street that led to Lust and continued for another mile until he reached I-75. When he jumped onto the southbound ramp, Dax followed. Thirty minutes later Mahmud signaled and pulled into a rest stop. Dax followed him in. They were near Monroe, roughly 25 miles north of Cincinnati.

Dax guided the Evoque into one of the diagonal parking spaces, watching as the Mercedes rolled slowly past several vehicles, making its way to the far side of the lot. Finally, Mahmud pulled into a space next to a grey minivan. The doctor got out of his car. He had the leather valise in one hand. Dax sipped the last of his Celsius and watched the front passenger window of the van lower. He realized that the driver was a woman.

His source is a chick? Interesting.

Mahmud casually lifted the valise and handed it through the window. A minute later it was offered back to him. He took it, said a few words to the van driver, and turned to the Mercedes with a smile on his face.

Dax was not close enough to hear them but whispered an imagined conversation to himself.

"Nice doin' business with you. Don't spend it all in one place."

The Mercedes backed out, followed by the van. Both headed for the merge lane that would return them to the highway.

Okay, Mahmud will probably get off soon and head back to Dayton with his stash. Let's see where the mystery woman goes.

As Dax expected, the red Mercedes got off at the next exit. The van—Dax noted that it was a Chrysler Town & Country—continued south. Minutes later it merged onto the I-275 beltway that encircled Cincinnati, moving southeast. The van traveled partway around the city before leaving I-275. Still moving southeast, the van, with the Range Rover in tow, followed a series of smaller state highways. They wove through hilly country, crossing the West Virginia border.

After an hour Dax unfastened his seat belt, unzipped, and, raising his upper body off the seat just so, was able to urinate into the empty Celsius can.

Ahhh. I'm good for another couple hours.

He tore open the Snickers with his teeth and took a bite. As he chewed, he mulled over the situation.

Sure looks like we're headed toward the Heroin Highway. If that's the case, the drugs are almost certainly coming from an organized gang, one of the big players.

The Heroin Highway was Interstate 81. It ran from New York in the north to the edge of Tennessee in the south. Drugs and cash flowed in both directions. Gangs operating in eastern seaboard cities accessed the highway and used it as a main artery for distribution. The FBI considered a 50-mile length between Chambersburg, Pennsylvania and Winchester, Virginia a particularly bad stretch.

Dax thought that a woman driving an anonymous minivan might be an excellent combination to move drugs in a targeted enforcement area.

Helluva lot smarter than a biker with saddlebags full of ecstasy or meth.

Dax had all but decided he had a longer drive in front of him when, three and a half hours after leaving the rest stop on I-75, the Town & Country got off the highway at Parkersburg.

Stopping for gas? Food?

It was neither. The van made a series of turns before entering a development with two-story homes configured around a man-made lake. When it pulled into a driveway, Dax eased the Range Rover to the curb a couple hundred feet back. He reached into the console and withdrew a small pair of binoculars.

The van was inside the garage now. The woman, a blonde wearing sunglasses with lenses the size of drink coasters, exited. She was talking on a cellphone as she raised the rear hatch door. Dax saw boxes inside. He focused on words printed on the sides. They were nonsensical.

What the hell?

Then it hit him.

They are the names of prescription drugs.

Dax had once read a story on one of his favorite websites, mentalfloss.com, that two women in Chicago come up with all the odd names for prescription drugs. They worked for USAN, the United States Adopted Names program. Though the names appeared to be random to the general public, Dax had learned that there were actually strict guidelines. Certain letters were chosen—or avoided—for specific reasons. The letters "X," "Y," and "Z" often appear in brand names because they give the drug a high-tech sounding name. Conversely, "H," "K," "J," and "W" aren't used or are difficult to pronounce in certain languages so are avoided.

Those boxes are sample cases...She's a pharmaceutical drug rep, selling her samples. Somehow, she's gotten around all the limitations put on company reps since the opioid crisis blew up. I doubt she can accumulate enough to keep Mahmud happy.

Mahmud was not dealing with one of the cartels. The Ivy Leaguers could definitely co-opt him next.

CHAPTER TWENTY-THREE

On Saturday, Paul and Lauren attended the memorial for Bean Grissom. It was held at a Baptist church on Dayton's north side. They arrived a few minutes before the ceremony began and saw Gatewood in the parking lot with members of his family.

"Good of you to come, Sticks." Gatewood clasped Paul's hand and gripped his shoulder in a half-embrace. Lauren hugged Gatewood's wife, Roberta. Both women, in their role as wives of Air Force Combat Controllers, had attended more ceremonies for those taken before their time than they cared to remember. They held the hug for several seconds.

The Dowdells' youngest son, Henry, stood respectfully to the side, a somber look on his face. Lauren disengaged from her hug with Roberta and approached him. She opened her arms and he stepped forward. Henry smiled and reached for her, though his melancholy eyes betrayed his mood.

"Vida and Billy weren't able to get away."

Gatewood stated this matter-of-factly, not in an apologetic tone. The Dowdells' daughter, Vida, piloted Army V-280 Valor tilt-rotor aircraft. She was currently in Amarillo, Texas. William was an F-16 pilot on his first duty assignment at Shaw Air Force Base in Sumpter, South Carolina. Both the Dowdells and the Hulls took for granted that the needs of the military often superseded family concerns.

Roberta added, "But we'll see him soon, right?" She studied her husband.

Gatewood nodded. "Yeah, Adelia has picked up speed. Billy's squadron will be leaving Shaw any day. They're headed to Wright-Patt until it's cleared the East Coast."

He was referring to the tropical storm in the Atlantic. It had stalled northeast of the Bahamas for two days but had increased strength and was now moving toward the lower Atlantic states. It had also acquired a name—Adelia—from the World Meteorological Organization. The fact that it began with the letter "A" identified it as the first such storm of the season. Adelia currently had sustained winds of 70 mph, putting it on the verge of hurricane status.

Paul nodded. "So, you have to be pretty swamped at work, right?"

"Yeah, we have to make arrangements for all the planes that will come in from the coastal bases. Finding spots for them is not the biggest issue. We have to increase security to protect them. My people are scrambling, but—" he turned to look at the church.

Paul finished for him. "But you were able to make time for this."

Gatewood nodded.

The group made their way toward the church. Henry turned to the Hulls.

"It sure is nice of you folks to come here for this."

Paul deflected the comment. "It was the right thing to do. We enjoyed watching you and Bean play in high school. You two were quite a receiving combination. The Wayne Warriors were a handful."

Henry nodded somberly. "Yeah, until he got hurt."

Gatewood reached the door and held it open for the group. Paul was last in line. He hesitated and leaned in toward his friend.

"So...was it really fentanyl?"

Gatewood nodded. "One hundred percent." He looked past Paul to see if anyone was within earshot.

"He took prescription oxycodone after his knee surgery. Got hooked. When the prescriptions ran out, he started buying it on the street. He apparently ratcheted up to more and more powerful stuff." He paused. "It's a damn shame."

"It sure as hell is."

Paul and Lauren were silent most of the way home from the memorial service. After several minutes, Paul spoke.

"Pretty bad, huh?"

Lauren turned to him. "That poor family. The mother... it was just so heartbreaking."

Paul nodded. After a few seconds he stated, "You know, there is always a chance that we could find ourselves in a position like that if the adoption process works out. Are you sure you want to go forward with it?"

Lauren's face showed resolve. "Absolutely, no matter how bad things might get, it'll be outweighed by the good."

Paul smiled. "Agreed."

They drove another mile in silence before Paul spoke. "You're gonna be a great mom."

They had intended to ride on the bike path near Troy Saturday after the service, but rain washed out their plans. They decided to put off the ride until the next day. Paul checked out the bikes and added air to their tires in the garage while the rain beat down outside. They made popcorn and started *Landman*, a series by the creator of *Yellowstone*, one of their favorites. They were hooked immediately, watching three episodes before turning in.

Sunday dawned a beautiful day. Paul started the coffee and then ducked into the home office. He opened the closet and retrieved the drone that Lauren got him for Christmas from its shelf. The drone looked exactly like the type of object that Chappy would damage so Paul stored it in a spot that wasn't accessible to the cat.

I know Lauren loves him, but Chappy is a damn menace.

He tinkered with the controller, refamiliarizing himself with its features. Satisfied, he plugged in the battery to top off its charge before returning to the kitchen. He found Lauren there, slicing cantaloupe and strawberries.

"Morning Paul, getting the drone ready?"

Paul opened a cupboard and selected his favorite mug. It was Air Force blue with block lettering that proclaimed, "THE 24," a reference to his former unit, the 24th Special Tactics Squadron.

"Yep, all set. The battery should be ready in less than an hour...shouldn't need much juice. I'm thinking we set the altitude high enough that it can fly well over any of the trees along the path. It has a collision avoidance feature that keeps it from running into objects but that slows it down. I don't think it will keep up with us if it has to dodge many trees."

Paul planned to set the drone on its "Follow Me Mode," the active tracking feature that tasked the unit to follow a subject automatically. No manual adjustments were required by the person with the controller. He'd used this feature several times on solo rides, but never when biking with Lauren.

Paul poured coffee into his mug and began to fill a bowl with fruit. "Uh, I have to ask again. How much did you *pay* for that thing? I mean, it has all those bells and whistles...the battery lasts 45 minutes, which is much better than a lot of the drones I've seen online. It even has a hi-res camera."

He'd asked about the price a couple times. His Christmas gifts to Lauren were a new pair of her favorite running shoes and a gift certificate for a spa day. He suspected the drone cost much more and felt bad about it.

Lauren sat down on a stool on the far side of the kitchen's island. She raised her own mug with both hands, her elbows on the counter, and took a small sip before regarding him with an amused smile.

"Get over it Paul. It was a gift. I'm just happy you're using it. Besides...you can make it up to me next Christmas." She winked.

Paul laughed. He'd had an interest in drones for some time, though he didn't remember ever mentioning it to Lauren. Drone technology had become an increasingly significant component of modern warfare. Most Americans had heard of the large aircraft-sized versions like the MQ-9 Reaper. They fit into a category known as unmanned aerial systems—or UAS—and were capable of carrying a significant munitions payload. They were controlled remotely, often by operators on another part of the globe, by the utilization of satellite links. These drones took off, completed a mission, and returned to their base.

Less well known were the U.S. military's handheld versions. Army and Marine Corps units were becoming more adept at using them while deployed. Paul remembered talking to members of the 82nd Airborne Division's 3rd Brigade Combat Team, the first Army infantry brigade to be issued pocket-sized drones. This was in Kandahar in 2019. The drones were Black Hornets, miniature craft that resembled a helicopter and were just a few inches long. One of the 82nd's sergeants told him they weighed less than two ounces. The 3rd Brigade used them to support foot patrols, scanning for ambushes.

Small drones were used by both sides in the Russia-Ukraine war. The Ukrainians developed increasingly effective versions of lethal "kamikaze" drones that were used to dive into Russian tanks and personnel carriers. Paul saw the drones as a component of modern war. He hadn't used handheld drones during his combat deployments to Afghanistan or Iraq as a Combat Controller, but he was aware that the U.S. Air Force had developed models in this class. The RQ-11B Raven weighed less than five pounds, had a wingspan of four and a half feet, and could stay aloft for 90 minutes. Air Force security personnel used them overseas to help protect air bases. Their capabilities were light years beyond the drone that Paul found under the tree Christmas morning, but, he noted, each of the Ravens cost the USAF $260,000.

Even though Lauren spent too much on mine, pretty sure it was less than $260K.

Paul was aware that militaries across the globe were scrambling to come up with defenses against drones. The U.S. Army was fielding a handheld mechanism called the Dronebuster, a jamming unit that severs the connection between an enemy drone and its controller. There were others: the Bal Chatri, the Modi Device, the DroneGun Mk4, and the Smart Shooter. All were anti-drone devices developed to help ground forces counter this new type of warfare.

It's not getting any easier for our people out on the battlefield.

Lauren brought him back from his thoughts. "So, what do you have planned after the bike ride? Busy week coming up?"

Paul closed an eye and looked to the ceiling. "Zoom calls again with Mike and Marge tomorrow. The thing in Chicago is stalled a bit. We're supposed to hop on with a network of grocery stores from Illinois in the morning to try to get some of the brands that Jasper Spirits reps into their stores."

Lauren was confused. "Wait, you can work directly with grocery stores to get liquor on their shelves?"

Paul nodded. "Illinois is one of the few states that allows the sale of spirits in grocery stores."

Lauren eyed him suspiciously.

Paul held up his hands. "No kidding."

When the drone's battery was fully charged, Paul packed the unit in its case and slipped it inside a black nylon backpack. He intended to record video on a six-mile section of trail that ran between Troy and Tipp City, the next town to the south. The Hulls lived north of Troy. They planned to bike to town on county roads. Once they cleared the downtown and residential areas, they would launch the drone and have it follow them along the Great Miami River Recreational Trail.

Lauren was in the garage sliding water bottles into holders on both bikes. Like her husband, she was dressed in biking gear with a high visibility neon green jersey. Paul joined her, twisting his upper body to adjust the fit of the backpack as he entered the garage.

"Got your phone set up?"

She nodded and pointed to her bike's handlebars where her cellphone was secured in a mount designed for that purpose. "Yep, all set."

They set off for town. Lauren insisted that Paul lead, noting that the backpack hid his green jersey. She trailed so drivers approaching from the rear would have a clear view of hers. They held their positions once they reached the city limits and picked their way through town. They accessed the bike path a few blocks from the heart of downtown and followed it along the river. Paul braked to a stop two hundred yards after pedaling past Miami Shores Golf Course. Both he and Lauren stood, straddling their bikes. Paul removed the backpack and went to work on the drone, removing it from its case and extending its arms.

Lauren had seen some of the videos Paul made with the unit, but this was the first time she'd actually seen him operate it. She knew that he'd worked with extremely complicated communication and targeting gear as a Combat Controller and had no doubt when she purchased the drone that he would master its operation. She watched with growing curiosity before interrupting.

"Whoa, whoa, whoa...slow down. Show me how this thing works." She removed her sunglasses and dabbed at perspiration on her brow.

Paul grinned. "You got it, Warrant Officer Hull." His fingertips brushed against his bike helmet as he gave her a mock salute.

The drone was white, just 12 inches square, with rotors at all four corners. The camera hung near the center. Paul finished locking the arms into place and handed it to Lauren. He then removed the controller from the case.

"So, first I turn this on." He nodded at the controller before engaging a switch. An electronic beep emanated from the unit. "That blinking light on the drone means we have a good link."

Lauren turned to the drone and saw a green light flashing steadily.

"We need a clear takeoff point." He examined the immediate stretch of bike path and the positions of trees on either side. "How about right over there?" He gestured at a clear spot a few yards away.

Lauren dismounted her bike and walked it to the side of the path where she leaned it against a small tree, while holding the drone carefully. She walked to the spot Paul had selected and, after checking in both directions to make sure there were no approaching bikers or joggers, bent to place the unit on the asphalt surface. When she stepped back, Paul engaged the controller and he and Lauren watched as all four rotors began spinning rapidly.

"Okay, now I select the proper mode," Paul made an adjustment on the controller as Lauren stepped to his side, "and *voila*, we're in business." The small display screen on the controller lit up and showed a close up view of the asphalt that was directly below the drone's camera.

Lauren smirked. "*Voila*?"

Paul smiled and toggled one of the controller's two joysticks. The drone rose straight up to a height of ten feet and hovered in place. He and Lauren now saw themselves in the controller's display screen.

Lauren waved at the camera while watching the screen. "Cool!"

Paul needled her. "You're like a fan sitting behind the plate at a ballgame waving toward the center field camera when a pitch is on the way. Control yourself."

She punched him on the shoulder.

Chuckling, Paul continued. "Now I go to 'Select Subject.'" A green box appeared around Paul's image on the screen, then jumped to Lauren's image. "You'll have to move so that my figure is the only one on the screen. Then I can lock on...it's in its object detection phase."

Lauren stepped back several feet.

"That's good." Paul watched as the box again appeared around his image then pushed the button that locked in the camera. "Now to raise it to the proper altitude." He worked a joystick and the drone rose steadily.

Lauren returned to his side and divided her attention between the climbing drone and her and Paul's shrinking forms on the controller screen. A pair of joggers approached from the direction of the golf course and stopped when they reached the Hulls.

"Gonna film as you ride the path?" This from one of the joggers, a lean, bald man in his sixties.

Paul turned to him. "Yep, just about ready."

"I guess we'll be in your video then." The man began to jog south. His partner, a man of a similar age with a full head of grey hair, followed. But not before adding, "Let me apologize in advance for the tremendous glare that will reflect off his head." He pointed toward his running buddy.

The bald man feigned outrage. "Thanks a lot, Bob."

They disappeared around a bend in the path.

Paul's attention was back on the screen. "Okay, that looks about right."

Lauren put her sunglasses back on as she squinted at the sky. "How high is that?"

"Should be just about 300 feet."

Just as professional golfers and military snipers can fix on an object in the near distance and accurately estimate its distance, Combat Controllers—who call in aircraft to make low passes or strafing runs—are adept at gauging altitude. There were indicators on the controller's display screen for both air speed and altitude, but Paul didn't think either were particularly accurate. He fell back on his own experience.

Lauren leaned in to look at the display. "Oh wow, we're really small." She waved her arms as she continued to view the screen. "I look like an ant down there." She looked back at the drone. "Down here...whatever. You can see the bike path for what, a hundred yards in each direction...two hundred?"

"Something like that. It's more than high enough to clear all the trees on the path and I don't want to go much higher. The FAA has a regulation saying 400 feet is the max. I don't particularly want to find out what the penalty is for going over."

Paul had rigged small bungee cords to his handlebar to accommodate the controller. He strapped it down and hit the record button. A blinking red light appeared showing that the feature was engaged.

"Lights, camera, action. Let's roll!"

They set off, Paul again in the lead. Lauren rode to one side and inched toward him every few seconds to glimpse the screen.

"Looks like you can even see wet spots ahead on the path from last night's rain. Oh, there are the two joggers. We'll be coming up on them soon."

When they reached the joggers, Lauren dropped back behind Paul, seemingly content to enjoy the scenery from the ground rather than on the display screen with its bird's eye view. They pedaled along at 15 to 17 miles per hour, a pace that was not too strenuous but, if maintained for a sufficient distance, was enough to provide a good workout. The stretch of trail from where the drone was engaged to their destination was just over six miles. Paul hoped to get to Tipp City, turn back, and return to the start point near Miami Shores Golf Course before terminating the flight. He calculated that they would reach the battery's 45-minute limit at about the same time.

Riding almost always had a soothing effect on Paul. He cruised along, occasionally sipping from his water bottle, and allowed his mind to wander. For a few minutes he found himself worrying about the delay in the adoption process. It obviously worried Lauren. Paul hoped it would be resolved soon and they could take the next step in the process. Halfway to Tipp City, he stole a look up at the drone and his thoughts turned to something completely different.

Paul had a vague idea for a book. It would be a thriller. He even had the title—*Time Drone*. The story would involve a high-tech company that invented a drone that could be launched in the present before transitioning to a predetermined time in the past. The drone would have a finite dwell time due to limited battery life and extreme energy demands. Like Paul's unit above the bike path, the drone would be able to record video. It would hover above an area, transport to another time, and materialize at the same geographic spot. It would then record video before returning to the present.

Imagine launching from Gettysburg National Cemetery and going back to noon on November 19, 1863 to record Abraham Lincoln giving the Gettysburg Address. Or almost exactly 100 years later, November 22, 1963, to the Texas School Book Depository in Dallas at 12:30 p.m. when JFK was assassinated. What would those videos be worth?

Could scholars pinpoint the exact location of Jesus on a specific day so he could be recorded?

Paul thought it important that the drone be launched from the exact location where a historic event occurred.

I mean, it would be completely unbelievable that the drone could take off in one location and appear in another.

Realizing the concept was no more far-fetched than his time travel premise, he laughed out loud.

"What's so funny?" Lauren accelerated to pull abreast and cocked her head.

"Uh nothing...I'll tell you later."

They arrived at a park on the outskirts of Tipp City in just under 22 minutes. They made a U-turn in a parking lot that adjoined the path and turned back. Paul turned to Lauren.

"All good?"

She gave him a bright smile. "All good."

The problem with the book idea, Paul mused as he pedaled, was how to go about doing it. He didn't know how to structure the story. He wasn't sure how to edit it. Who would proofread it? How the hell would one go about getting the damn thing published? And, most important, would anyone even want to *read* it? These problems, he realized, were probably insurmountable. Still, the idea continued to float through his mind.

The developers of the Time Drone would have financial motivation...hoping to sell the videos. But criminals would get involved. Maybe the government. Maybe OTHER governments. They would try to use the thing to change history. Maybe put a weapon on it. Might not even need a weapon. People just SEEING the thing overhead might be enough to change history. Abe could be starting the Address; "Four score and seven years...Hey what in blazes is that thing up there?"

He was smiling, his mind back in time, when Lauren called out.

"Oh look! A deer on the path. No, two, three of them!"

Paul braked and focused on the figures ahead. The deer stood in a line 200 feet away. They had come out of the trees on the right side of the path and stopped, perfectly centered. Their heads were turned toward the Hulls. The only visible movement was the occasional twitch of their white tails.

"They're beautiful, Paul!"

Paul had the presence of mind to look down at the drone's display screen and realized they would have a video record of the encounter.

Lauren exclaimed, "Oh, there they go. Something must've spooked them."

Paul looked up in time to see the deer disappear to the left through a gap in the trees. He saw Lauren pedaling past him, moving toward that spot.

"C'mon Paul, let's go see where they went."

Paul followed her to where the deer vanished and eased his bike off the path to get a better view. He realized that there wasn't just a gap in the trees here, but a wide dirt trail that ran to the west. Paul could see the trail intersect with railroad tracks a hundred feet away. The tracks, he knew, paralleled the bike path. There appeared to be a large grassy field on the other side of the tracks.

Lauren seemed disappointed. "Aww, they're gone. Weren't they pretty?" She turned to Paul and saw that he was pointing at the drone overhead.

"We can still watch them. Come look."

Lauren, straddling her bike, shuffled to his side. They could make out the deer on the display screen. They were on the other side of the railroad tracks, hidden from Paul and Lauren's line of sight by the trees. The camera on the drone captured them as they grazed in the field.

"Oh, that's so cool. Wow, you would never pick them out if you didn't already know they were there." Lauren watched the screen for nearly a minute until Paul interrupted.

"Better get moving...battery is getting low."

Paul walked his bike back to the asphalt path, noticing a small metal sign on its east side. It was brown, the color usually reserved for historic sites. This drew Paul's attention as he made a point to visit as many such locations as possible.

I've ridden this path dozens of times. How have I missed this?

He angled his bike until he could see a white arrow on the sign pointing in the direction the deer had run. With another step he could read the entire sign.

Oh, interesting. I didn't realize we were so close to that place.

CHAPTER TWENTY-FOUR

It was a productive weekend for Dylan, Min, and Willie. A meeting was arranged with Shadow's people for Saturday afternoon. Much thought was put into the location. Over a bowl of cereal at the Airbnb that morning, Dylan expressed his concerns.

"We have to think about this. I'd like to get this out of the way as soon as possible. Today...the earlier the better. I don't want to wait until tonight. Has to be a neutral location. No way you guys are walking into some house these people pick out."

Dylan had decided that Min and Willie would attend the meeting while he waited for an update from Dax on the situation with Dr. Mahmud. He also expected to communicate with his source in the Miami County Sheriff's Office on their investigation.

Min leaned against the kitchen counter, his eyes on the toaster. He turned to Dylan.

"I'll take Willie's pistol. We will be," he searched for a word, "vigilant. These people will be more interested in money than vengeance. They want the drugs. We have seen it before."

Since embarking on their venture, the men had been pleasantly surprised at the lack of malice shown by dealers who took over for a murdered superior. The replacement was almost always aware that their boss was meeting with a possible new source for potent opioids. They had to know—or strongly suspect—that one of the Ivy Leaguers had pulled the trigger. Yet, so far, none of the substitutes had displayed threatening behavior when it came their turn to negotiate. Their desire for the product—and the money it would bring—superseded a craving for revenge. Still, Dylan remembered the University of Michigan study on the culture of honor.

We're out here in the sticks. Only a matter of time before one of these characters decides to take his pound of flesh.

Dylan slowly shook his head. "We're not taking any chances. We have too many balls in the air. We have to get things in place with Shadow's replacements...do it quick, but safely. Then we take care of the Shortridge network tomorrow and move out of the area."

Min's eyebrows furrowed slightly. "Balls in the air?"

Willie sat across the table from Dylan. He spoke through a mouthful of Cap'n Crunch cereal.

"It means we have a lot going on right now...too many variables. I agree with Dylan. Let's do this right, pick a good spot."

Min held up a hand in a sign of acceptance. "Okay, we choose a safe location...but I'm still taking the pistol." He smiled.

The metallic sound of the toaster ejecting its contents drew Min's attention. He turned to see the tops of two Pop-Tarts appear. His smile widened.

Mmm...brown sugar cinnamon!

Min's mother made him breakfast every morning in China. It usually consisted of a traditional dish such as rice congee or wheat noodles. But occasionally she would fry dough sticks and dip them in a mixture of cinnamon and sugar. The Pop-Tarts reminded him of this.

They discussed possible sites, discarding most of them immediately as being either too visible to witnesses or so secluded that they invited trouble. Min and Willie would be taking some of the golf balls, including the one whose cover had been removed to reveal the carfentanil inside. Shadow's cousin, or even the high school student that helped him sell the drugs, could be tempted to rob them.

Willie spoke up. "What about that old school building right down the road?" He gestured with a thumb in the direction of Urbana.

Dylan sat back in his chair, looking thoughtful. The small village of Westville was located a mile east of Country Road on State Route 36. A brick structure stood on its western edge. Dylan agreed that it appeared to be a school, though he hadn't paid it much attention the several times he'd driven past.

Min spoke. "I do not believe it is a school. There is a sign out front, maybe two signs. It might be a business."

Dylan stood and walked to the sink. He placed his empty bowl inside. "Well, it's only a mile away. Let's go check it out."

It wasn't a school. Not anymore, at least. The building was on the north side of Route 36. It was a large, two-story edifice of more than 20 rooms. A bell tower rose above its front face. The steps leading up to the front entrance were less than 50 feet from the road. A pull-in parking area was visible in front of the building. The spaces bracketed a rectangular frame of railroad ties that bordered a raised bed of shrubbery and flowers. A large white sign stood in the center of the rectangle. It read: *Renewed Strength Church—Christian Learning Center, Day Care, and Pre-School.*

Min drove his Range Rover. He turned in just past the sign and parked. He looked at the face of the building.

"This is a church? It is a very different design than others in America."

Willie leaned forward from the back seat and peered up.

"Pretty sure it was a school at one time. Lots of times these non-denominational churches take over buildings that were built for other purposes. I see some lettering up there... can't make it out from here. Let's check it out."

The three men exited the Range Rover and stood near the front steps. An arched window with a green frame was set into the building directly above the front door. Above the arch they could see a two-foot-wide concrete rectangle with lettering pressed into its face.

WESTVILLE PRECT
18 SCHOOL 91

Dylan spoke. "You're right. It's an old precinct school, whatever the hell a precinct school was."

He turned to survey the surrounding area. There was a large parking lot to the west of the building. Dylan wondered if it had once been utilized as a playground. He wasn't sure, but he didn't think automobiles would have been used in great numbers back in 1891. A semi rumbled by as he turned to view the east side of the property. A rambling, olive-green, two-story house stood just feet from the edge of the church's asphalt lot. It was the first in a line of a dozen similar homes that ran the entire modest length of the village. A corresponding line of homes stood facing them on the south side of Route 36. Dylan noted a bronze marker with brass patina lettering standing between the church lot and the olive-green house.

He turned back to his colleagues. "Well, today is Saturday. That should mean no services at the church until tomorrow."

Willie nodded. "And the day care would be open just Monday through Friday." He turned toward the road and watched a pickup truck cruise past. "Sporadic traffic...not what they would want if they're trying to ambush us."

Dylan rubbed his chin. "Houses close, but not *too* close. We could set up the meet in the big parking lot on the west side." Both he and Willie turned in that direction, not noticing that Min had wandered off.

Dylan continued. "The downside is that this place is only a mile from our Airbnb. We don't want them paying us a visit after the meet."

Nodding, Willie agreed. "So, we get here early, wait for them...when we leave, we drive through Westville, east...away from our rental. Take some country roads on the way back to our place. It should be easy to see if they try to follow."

"Makes sense. Min, what do you—" He turned to see their colleague standing in front of the bronze marker. "Hey Min...what the hell?"

Min stood in front of the marker, reading. He raised a hand to fend off the interruption and concentrated on the text.

HARVEY HADDIX

Baseball great Harvey Haddix was born on September 18, 1925 and grew up on a farm south of Westville. He attended School until March 1940 and played his first organized baseball at this site. Entering Major League Baseball in 1952, he played for the St. Louis Cardinals, Philadelphia Phillies, Cincinnati Reds, Pittsburgh Pirates, and Baltimore Orioles in a career that lasted until 1965. In 1959, while with Pittsburgh, he pitched what some believe to be the greatest game ever pitched in baseball as he hurled 12 perfect innings against the defending champion Milwaukee Braves. He lost the game by a score of 1-0 in the 13th inning. A three-time All-Star and Gold Glove Award winner, he won two World Series games in 1960, including the deciding Game 7, while playing with Pittsburgh against the New York Yankees. He died on January 8, 1994 and is buried in Clark County.

Min stood back, shaking his head.

An elaborate marker celebrating an obscure baseball player. Yet, there was nothing honoring the bodyguard of George Washington. America can be very strange.

Back at the house, Willie called Shadow's replacement and set the time of the meeting for 3 p.m. Rain was expected shortly after and the timing seemed right. Dylan instructed Willie to make a special request.

"Tell him to bring some of their pills for us. We'll make it more than worth his while by giving him one of the carfentanil balls. We need some of their finished product for our informant."

As a matter of policy, the Ivy Leaguers never operated while possessing the street version of an opioid. But when rewarding an informant, it was common for them to acquire some from a dealer.

After using his burner phone to set up the meeting, Willie volunteered to don the protective suit and remove the cover from another of the loaded balls. They would be giving the one that Dylan had worked on to Shadow's cousin. It would be beneficial to have a second one available for the meet the following day with the people—a married couple who operated a farm—who would inherit the Shortridge network.

While Willie worked on the ball in the garage, perspiring in the suit, Dylan hit foam practice balls with his driver in the backyard. After twenty minutes, Min walked outside. He was eating a peanut butter sandwich. He watched as Dylan made a series of fluid swings, launching the colored foam balls toward the back fence.

After striking the last ball, Dylan turned.

"Want to take a few swings?" He held out his driver.

Min held up the remainder of his sandwich. "Go ahead. I'm eating."

Dylan walked toward the back fence while speaking over his shoulder.

"You're going to have to work on that swing, Min. You're an Associate Director of Business Development for Running Dog. People expect you to be a player."

It was a subject they had discussed in the past. Dylan believed every member of the organization should have a working knowledge of the game. Dax was a good player. Willie enjoyed the game, though mainly for the opportunity to drink beer and drive a golf cart, which could generally be steered across open fairways not cluttered by excessive traffic or complicated by obstacles like roundabouts. Min, on the other hand, had little interest in the game.

Dylan gathered the balls near the back fence and began to stroke them back toward the house. He liked the flight of the balls that he was seeing as they left the driver. After hitting the last ball, he walked back toward the patio in thought.

I just might have the right setup on this driver. Sure looks like I might be getting the right amount of draw. Hard to tell with limited flight foam balls. Well, there's one way to know for sure.

He had removed a box of regular Running Dog balls from the golf bag and laid them on the patio table. He made his way to it and picked out one of the sleeves.

"You're going to hit real balls here?" Min asked the question with a trace of amusement.

Dylan stuck a tee in the ground and placed one of the balls on top. "Sure, why not? That's just an open field out there. Can't hurt anything."

Min shrugged and pushed the last of the sandwich into his mouth. He watched as Dylan took two practice swings then addressed the ball.

Thwack!

The swing was smooth and powerful. The ball streaked over the fence and flew straight out over the field for well over a hundred yards before its trajectory altered slightly to the left. Both men watched until it descended and disappeared below the top of the fence.

"How about that shit, Min?" Dylan had held his follow through and stood in perfect balance with the driver now pointing toward the house.

"Impressive. It curved to the left...that was intentional?"

Dylan bent to tee up another ball. He straightened and winked at Min. "Yeah, that's called a draw. You use it when you're playing a hole with a dogleg to the left. Or when you need to hook a shot around a tree, or...are you sure you don't want to take some swings?"

Min shrugged. "You are persistent. Okay, I'll try again."

Dylan reviewed the grip, the stance, and the desired swing path with Min. He talked him through each step, reminding his associate of the almost mystical feeling that can come over a golfer when he makes a good swing and the ball comes off the clubface properly.

"There's nothing like it, Min. It's better than sex."

Min eyed Dylan doubtfully, but shrugged again. "Okay, many in my country love this game. You, obviously, do too." He set up over the ball, taking care that he mirrored the overlapping grip style that Dylan preferred. He closed his eyes and visualized a fluid swing that made solid contact. After drawing in a breath, he exhaled slowly.

Behind him, he barely heard Dylan whisper, "You got this."

Min swung the club. The bottom of the driver struck the ball and sent it screaming toward the back fence. It struck the wood surface two feet above the ground and shot back toward Min. It passed between him and Dylan and struck the rear of the house before bouncing across the patio into the backyard.

Dylan stared down at the ball, attempting not to laugh.

Min glared at the ball before tossing the driver to Dylan. "Stupid fucking game."

Min and Willie took the Sentra to the meet with Shadow's cousin. They arrived twenty minutes early and Min parked in the center of the large lot west of the former school. They scanned in all directions, looking for threats, but saw none. They sat, watching light traffic stream past.

"He'll be driving a blue Honda Accord." Willie had the passenger window down. He leaned against the door to get as close as possible to fresh air. The orb of carfentanil was on the floor behind him. It was inside a sealed, clear plastic bag that was, in turn, tucked into a black trash bag, but Willie was uncomfortable being around the substance once the protective cover was removed. He was well aware of its potency.

"Does this man have a mysterious nickname like his cousin Shadow?" Min rolled down his own window.

Willie snickered. "Not hardly. He goes by 'Wood-Man.' His name is Steve Woodruff."

"Very imaginative."

The Accord rolled into the parking lot at 2:55 and steered tentatively toward the Sentra. A dark-haired man in his forties was behind the wheel. As the Accord drew abreast, Min and Willie saw that the man was alone. He appeared nervous. Min sensed this immediately.

He is afraid. He knows we eliminated his cousin.

Min smiled.

The deal was completed in minutes. Min opened his door, creating a shield to prevent a clear view from vehicles passing by. He retrieved the trash bag and opened it, revealing a small white-grey sphere inside the second bag. He turned his body to face Woodruff and swung his legs out of the Sentra to extend the bag toward the Accord. Woodruff saw the drug, smiled, then saw the Ruger Max 9 on the seat between Min's legs. The smile disappeared.

Still holding the carfentanil bag, Min uttered, "What happened to your cousin is unfortunate. Of course, you will make no mention of us to the police, yes?"

His eyes still on the Ruger, Woodruff swallowed.

"Of course."

Woodruff accepted the bag, then watched as Min held up two golf balls before dropping them one at a time to the asphalt. The first bounced as expected. The second did not. He quickly grasped how the carfentanil was getting into the country.

Min could sense the greed.

Woodruff asked, "How much can I get?"

They reached an agreement. Woodruff could keep the bag and its contents. He passed a pill bottle to Min that was full of tablets. He then asked for another dozen balls, saying he was happy to pay $500 dollars for each one, but he would like the covers removed.

"We'll have to do some planning to figure out how to process these things. It would really help us out. I'll pay extra and I can have the cash for you Monday."

Min turned to Willie. Both men knew Dylan wanted to leave the area as soon as possible. Willie shrugged. Min turned back to Woodruff.

"Okay...deal."

On Sunday morning Dylan drove the Sentra to Piqua. It was a clear, breezy day, the rain from the previous evening had moved out of the area. He'd spoken to Dax while Min and Willie were meeting with Woodruff.

"I really think Mahmud's source is a mom-and-pop operation. Well, actually it's just a mom operation."

He went on to explain that a pharmaceutical rep from West Virginia was selling pain medication on the side. Dax was on his way back to Dayton from Parkersburg.

"So how do you want to handle this?"

Dylan told him he would send Willie back to Dayton Monday morning.

"We're wrapping up things with these networks over here. Call Mahmud on your burner and set up a meet as soon as possible. Monday would be great. The quicker we get out of Ohio, the better."

When Dylan spoke those words on Saturday, he expected to be out of the Airbnb on Sunday. That was no longer the case. Min and Willie's agreement to remove the covers on another dozen balls for Shadow's cousin meant he would be staying another day.

"Are you still pissed?" It was Willie. He was riding in the passenger seat, again with the window down.

Dylan stared straight ahead. "I'm not pissed."

"Oh, you're pissed. We could tell as soon as we got back to the house."

"I'm over that now."

After speaking to Dax about Mahmud and his source from West Virginia, Dylan exchanged texts with the informant. There had been no new developments in the investigation. The prime suspect in the killings, Kevin Turner, was still missing. Most of the personnel working the case were off for the weekend. This included the detective that was looking into the Running Dog connection. The informant had provided his name: Amos Bunker.

"I'm good with the deal you made. I still want to get out of the area before the rental agreement on the Airbnb expires next Saturday, but staying until tomorrow, or even Tuesday, shouldn't be the end of the world. Besides, since you and Min made the deal, you two get to process those dozen balls."

Willie sighed.

Both men were silent for a few minutes. They were three miles from Piqua. Willie turned to stare out his open window at the fields beyond. A crop that was low to the ground —he thought they were soybeans—filled many of the fields. Corn, most of it a couple feet high—accounted for the rest. Farmhouses were spaced irregularly, often isolated from the neighboring properties. Willie looked at the next house ahead on the right and imagined what it might be like to live there, so far away from the Eastern cities that he and his colleagues preferred.

I think I might need to take daily painkillers if I had to live here.

As they passed the house Willie noticed an odd sight standing in front of a corn field just beyond. It was a stone disc, about three feet in diameter. It was mounted vertically on a stone base. Willie had seen these discs before. They were millstones, used for centuries in gristmills to grind wheat and other grains. He saw that words were engraved on this one. Before the Sentra passed by, he was able to make out the first several words: "THE DILBONE MASSACRE, IN MEMORY OF HENRY AND BARBARA DILBONE WHO WERE KILLED BY THE INDIANS..."

Willie craned his neck to look back but could read no more. He'd gotten the gist.

For Christ's sake, they commemorate massacres here.

His thoughts were interrupted by Dylan.

"Tell me about this couple we're meeting."

Willie turned from the window. "Gladly."

"What?"

Willie shook his head. "Nothing. So, it's a husband and wife; Jon and Grace Geigerling. They run an organic dairy farm a few miles north of here on Snodgrass Road."

"Beautiful word, Snodgrass."

"Isn't it though?" Willie smiled and continued. "They sell eggs, vegetables, some apples, pumpkins at Halloween, like that."

Dylan nodded.

"Their farm is also a herd share."

"What the hell is a herd share?"

Willie looked at the sky.

"Well, it's basically an entity that is set up to sell raw milk and cheese where it's otherwise illegal. See, customers—or members—pay a fee to become part owner of a cow. Since they are technically owners, they are then legally permitted to pay a separate 'boarding fee' for each gallon of milk or block of cheese."

Dylan furrowed his brow. "So, it's basically just to dodge the regulations?"

"Yes."

"What people will do to make a buck."

The irony of Dylan's comment was not lost on Willie. "Anyway, the Shortridge brothers set them up with a couple pill presses. They're in a building behind the farmhouse. Dax and I followed Gerard there one night and peeked inside. The presses are about the size and shape of a butcher's meat slicer. They're on a large table with two apple presses used to make cider and an actual meat slicer which, I guess, is used to process the meat from cows that are slaughtered."

"So, the pill presses blend in?"

"Yeah, real well. Looks like the Geigerlings can crank out thousands of pills in a relatively short time. There's a workshop on the property that should allow them to cut open the balls fairly easily. They have three kids...I wouldn't be surprised if they were put to work helping somehow. The Shortridges had three or four people selling for them—they'll be needing product—and word on the street is the Geigerlings have signed up members in the herd share who aren't particularly concerned about the high nutrient levels of raw milk, if you know what I mean."

"They just want the pills."

"Bingo."

They reached Piqua at 10:30 a.m. and passed over I-75, turning right at a Speedway gas station. As they passed the Speedway, they noticed a Cracker Barrel Old Country Store restaurant on the left. A steady stream of vehicles—apparently fresh from church services—trickled into the parking lot.

Dylan continued past those businesses, heading north, and cruised down a narrow road that descended into a large secluded clearing. This was Hollow Park.

They were 15 minutes early. They saw one vehicle in the park, a Ford minivan. Three young children—two girls and a boy—romped in a nearby playground in their church clothes while their parents stood next to the van.

"That's them."

Dylan pulled next to the van and switched off the ignition. He got out and opened the trunk before walking toward the couple.

"Are you the Geigerlings?"

The woman, a blonde with an expressive face, thrust out her right hand while gesturing to her family with the left.

"We're the Geigerlings." She smiled exuberantly.

Dylan decided the smile was a couple clicks short of maniacal. "I'm Dylan. That's Willie. I know you've been talking to him on the phone." He nodded to his partner, who had lifted the Running Dog golf bag from the trunk and stood it next to the van.

The husband stepped forward. He was a tall, lanky man with dark-rimmed glasses.

"I'm Jon, good to put a face to a name."

Willie unzipped the top center pocket of the leather bag and withdrew two balls. He demonstrated the difference between their bounces when dropped.

Dylan checked the park for watchers, saw none, then removed a clear plastic bag from a side pocket of the golf bag. He turned it so the couple had a good view.

"This," he said, "is what's inside one of those balls."

The Geigerlings stared at the contents with fascination.

Grace turned to her husband.

"Jon, get the money. Let's make this deal then get to Cracker Barrel. There's going to be a line."

CHAPTER TWENTY-FIVE

The Hulls returned home from their Sunday morning bike ride before noon. While Lauren showered, Paul took the drone to their office and downloaded the video of their ride to his laptop. He was careful to keep the door closed so Chappy couldn't enter and offer his particular brand of assistance. The cat made his presence known by pawing at the door, an exercise that was as persistent as it was annoying.

"For God's sake, Chappy, give it up!"

His words did not deter the feline. Their only effect was to inspire him to add a periodic meow to his efforts.

Paul did his best to ignore Chappy and concentrated on the video. He watched the first few miles of the ride. It was captivating to view their recent experience from this perspective.

Very cool. The drone is really steady at this height.

He fast-forwarded the video until the turnaround point and continued to skip ahead until the point where he and Lauren had seen the deer.

Oh, nice. Once you know they're there and you're looking for them, you can see their approach from the east, watch them stop on the path and look at us, then run over the railroad tracks and graze in the field to the west.

There was a knock at the door and Lauren called out.

"The shower is all yours. I'll start lunch."

Paul made a mental note to play the video for her later.

After lunch, Lauren ran errands in town. Paul spent nearly three hours detailing his pickup truck. It was a black 1989 Ford XLT Lariat. Since he'd taken the job with Jasper Spirit Consulting, Paul had few chances to drive the truck. It remained parked in the driveway while Paul traveled in his Pilot and Lauren drove her Jeep Grand Cherokee. The Lariat was decidedly the third vehicle at a residence with a two-car garage. It stoically endured Ohio's winter snows and summer storms. Often weeks went by without its engine being started.

There were times when visitors stopped at the house and the space occupied by the Lariat might've been put to better use.

But Paul loved the truck. It was like an old friend, one that shared common memories. The Lariat was a bit more than just a truck to Paul. Two years earlier it had served him well in a perilous situation. Paul wouldn't forget. Lauren knew this and, although she might have been tempted, never came close to suggesting that Paul sell it.

They went out to dinner at Agave & Rye near the traffic circle in downtown Troy, a fantastic casual restaurant that specialized in tacos. When they returned home, Lauren made a FaceTime call to her mother in New Mexico, something that was developing into a bit of a Sunday evening ritual. Paul retreated to the office and started to prep for his work week.

He realized that his mind was wandering. Instead of concentrating on the liquor distribution regulations set in place by the state of Illinois, Paul found himself staring uncomprehendingly at his computer screen. His mind was elsewhere. He couldn't get Bean Grissom's death out of his thoughts.

How the hell had this happened?

He picked up his phone and dialed Gatewood, who picked up after the second ring.

"Hey, Sticks. How you doing?" He sounded fatigued. Paul could hear people talking in the background.

"I was just sitting here thinking about Bean." He sighed. "Can't get over it...a 20-year old kid. Thought I'd check in with you, see how everybody's doing at your place."

"Hold on, let me close the door."

Paul heard the faint sound of a door closing and the voices in the background disappeared.

"Sorry about that. I'm back."

"Hey Woody, if you have people over there, I can talk later."

"You're good. I'm not at the house. I've been at the base all day...could use a break."

Paul remembered that Wright-Patt was about to become the temporary home to dozens of East Coast military aircraft and that Gatewood was neck-deep in the logistics.

"How's it coming there? I haven't checked the news today. What's the latest on the storm?"

Gatewood gave him a quick summary. "Adelia is now officially a hurricane...expected to make landfall late Tuesday, early Wednesday. She's tracking more westerly now and is projected to hit somewhere north of Jacksonville and slide up the coast as she moves inland. We start receiving planes tomorrow morning. We had some Falcons here from the 180th but we sent them back to Toledo. We've shut down training flights for the Moose and parked them. The runways and airspace here are about to get busy."

Paul knew that the Falcons were F-16s. The specific unit Gatewood referred to was the 180th Fighter Wing of the Ohio Air National Guard. Their home base near Toledo was much smaller than Wright-Patt. Paul also recognized the unofficial nickname—Moose—of the massive C-17 cargo aircraft that called Wright-Patt home. Officially known as the Globemaster III, the C-17 was 174 feet long and had a wingspan of 169 feet, 10 inches. The only larger cargo plane in the U.S. inventory was the C-5 Galaxy.

He allowed himself a smile, remembering something he'd learned about the C-17 during his days as a Combat Controller. The nickname was derived from the sound that emanated from the plane's pressure relief valves during refueling. It resembled the call of a female Moose in heat.

"And Billy? Are you still expecting him?"

Gatewood seemed to perk up. "Yes, his squadron is the second one due in on Tuesday. Looks like he should make it home for dinner that night. Roberta's already cooking. Too bad he'll miss Henry. He's on his way back to Lexington now. He's hitting the weight room hard in the off-season, plus he's assigned to help with new recruit visits that start tomorrow morning."

The mention of Henry brought Paul back to the purpose of his call.

"I hope Henry's hanging tough through this thing with his buddy. It's just hard to believe that a kid like Bean died from fentanyl."

Gatewood responded. "We stayed at the memorial late... got into a conversation with some of the other families there. This opioid thing is more widespread than you might think. Sounds like people from all walks of life are hooked. They're goin' about their day-to-day business just like us, but the entire time they're lookin' for their next fix. You and I are damn lucky we're not with them."

Paul knew that Gatewood was referring to their respective injuries. Both men had been prescribed their share of pain killers. Gatewood after the IED blast in Iraq that cost him his lower left leg, and Paul after the parachute landing that damaged his right one. Both men were given Percocet, which contains oxycodone, a powerful opioid. Paul remembered Woody visiting him at Womack Army Medical Center at Fort Bragg.

Sounds like Woody and I both dodged a bullet.

Paul found it difficult to return to his work material after the call. He turned to his laptop and typed *opioid crisis* into the search box of his browser. As he suspected, the results were virtually limitless.

Most accounts agreed that the root of the problem went back to the mid-1990s when the powerful agent OxyContin triggered the first wave of deaths linked to the use of legal prescription opioids. Purdue Pharma—whose name had nothing to do with Purdue University—was a pharmaceutical company headquartered in Stamford, Connecticut that manufactured OxyContin and other pain medicines. They used aggressive marketing tactics to increase the use of these drugs. Purdue sales representatives enticed doctors to prescribe the pain medicines by offering them paid speaking engagements and all-expenses-paid vacations under the guise that they were attending pain management seminars.

Three brothers: Arthur, Raymond, and Mortimer Sackler, owned Purdue Pharma. Arthur died in 1987 and his share of the company passed to his brothers, who oversaw the growth and dissemination of painkillers.

Purdue's promotion of its synthetic opioid medications was aided by decisions made by well-meaning organizations. In December of 1995, the U.S. Food and Drug Administration, which is responsible for protecting public health and ensuring the safety and efficacy of drugs, approved the use of OxyContin. At about the same time the American Pain Society introduced its "pain as the fifth vital sign" campaign.

At the time, there were four patient vital signs recognized by the medical community: body temperature, pulse rate, respiration rate, and blood pressure. As a result of the campaign, the Veterans Health Administration adopted pain as the fifth sign. It soon became an accepted tenet in the medical field.

Soon, doctors were vilified if they didn't prescribe a potent painkiller—usually an opioid. There were instances when physicians faced legal charges if they didn't do everything possible to alleviate pain. Most doctors considered it an easy choice to send a patient home with a prescription for 90 OxyContin tablets rather than recommend another course of action that would draw criticism. Add the incentives they were being plied with by Purdue and others, and it became a foregone conclusion that patients would become opioid users if they complained of pain.

Many patients quickly figured this out. They reported a wide variety of hidden pains that could not be disproved. The "quick fix," all too often, was another prescription. Often, patients complaining of kidney pain, for example, were given a prescription for Dilaudid, another synthetic opioid. A high percentage of these patients became dependent on the drugs and the "dope sick" phenomena of drug withdrawal took hold as users needed more and more doses to stave off the negative symptoms.

Purdue Pharma was later shown to have fraudulently described OxyContin as less addictive than other opioids—something that millions who had taken the drug could've identified as false.

When users were unable to acquire the drugs legally, they turned to the street. Illegal sales of codeine, heroin, morphine, hydrocodone, and fentanyl spiked. These drugs were provided in many forms by unscrupulous dealers. Their methods of ingestion included: snorting a powder, swallowing a tablet, injecting a liquid, and wearing a saturated patch.

Foreign players rushed in to provide accessible sources of these substances. Russia, Mexico, and China were believed to be a few of the big players but there were undoubtably many others.

An entire industry of anti-opioid products was created. There was medication that blocked the effects of the drugs, personal protective gear necessary for the handling of them, and a number of devices invented to detect them.

The Sackler brothers were billionaires, but many paid for it with their lives. By 2023 there were over 86,000 annual opioid overdose deaths in the United States.

Mortimer Sackler died in 2010, Raymond in 2017. Purdue Pharma filed for bankruptcy in 2019. Purdue was eventually ordered to put $6 billion in a trust to be used to pay the claims of opioid creditors, victims of addiction, hospitals, and municipalities.

Paul checked the time and saw that he'd been reading about the crisis for nearly two hours. Synthetic opioids, he realized, had left a path of devastation across the United States. He stared at his computer screen, seeing the final page he'd viewed in his depressing, self-guided tour of the sordid history of opioids in America. It listed some of the victims who lost their lives to this family of substances: Prince, Tom Petty, Michael Jackson, and Whitney Houston.

Bean Grissom is on that list now.

CHAPTER TWENTY-SIX

Min Xian worked the Dremel tool around the curved surface of a golf ball. He wore the yellow DuPont protective suit. He could feel a bead of sweat collecting on his right eyebrow. He squinted in an effort to free it from its position, hoping it would release and drop to the bottom of the mask. He knew from experience that if left undisturbed, the perspiration would almost certainly find its way to the surface of his eye, causing him to pause his task and step out of the garage to the backyard to remove the mask.

The drop wouldn't budge. Min sighed and switched off the Dremel. He brought the back of his gloved right hand to the clear plastic face shield and carefully pressed it to his eyebrow. The perspiration was transferred to the plastic. This created a splotch that blurred his vision somewhat but would allow him to continue his work uninterrupted.

What do the Americans say? "The lesser of two evils."

Min wore earbuds and was listening to a playlist on his iPhone. It was lying on the workbench inside a sealed plastic bag to prevent contamination from the carfentanil. Next to the bag stood the nasal spray bottle of naloxone. He was cutting open his third ball of the evening, one of the six he'd committed to after Dylan and Willie returned from making the sale to the Geigerlings.

It is only fair, I suppose, that Willie and I were assigned this task. We made the agreement with Shadow's replacement—Woodruff—to provide this service. Still, I wish I had worked on my half dozen first.

Min had forgotten how freely his colleague perspired. Willie toiled for nearly two hours in the closed garage on his six balls. He worked during the 80-degree heat of the afternoon after returning from the Geigerling deal with Dylan. Despite the suit airing out while the men ate dinner, its interior was still moist when Min put it on. He frowned, remembering the unpleasant feeling.

Back to work.

Min turned on the Dremel and leaned back toward the vise that gripped the ball. As he worked, an up-tempo song by the Chinese alternative band New Pants began playing through his earbuds. His head bounced up and down to the beat. After loosening the vise often and turning the ball slightly each time, Min was able to complete the cut. He then used a pair of needle-nose pliers to remove both hemispheres of the cover. He dropped them into the garage wastebasket that he'd situated near the workbench. He reminded himself for the third time that day to remove the trash bag when he'd finished and seal it. He and his partners would dispose of it in a random public trash receptacle before leaving the Airbnb.

Min then used a putty knife to scrape the thickened gel of odor counteractant directly into the wastebasket. When the core was completely exposed, he carefully placed it in a separate plastic bag where it joined eight others. Min then selected another ball and placed it in the vise.

When I finish with these, we will have just 14 more balls to sell. A dozen of them may go to the doctor in Dayton. We will also have a drug ball that still has its cover—Dylan likes to drop one when meeting with dealers to show they don't bounce normally—and one with its cover removed to display its contents. We will need more very soon.

The New Pants song ended. It was followed by the mellow opening notes of "Hotel California" by The Eagles.

Min smiled as he began work on the next ball. "Hotel California" was not only one of his favorites, it was extremely popular throughout China. Min couldn't explain it. The song, released back in 1976, was a staple at parties and karaoke bars in his home country. Many Chinese parroted the words despite not speaking English.

Min applied pressure to the Dremel, attempting to push through the ball's tough dimpled surface. Once the initial penetration was made, the Dremel's 420 Cut-Off Wheel could more easily bite into the remainder of the cover.

Min put together a mental checklist of things he wanted to cover with Willie, who was upstairs packing his gear. He knew that Willie planned to go to sleep early tonight since he was leaving Monday morning to return to Dayton.

One: I must make sure he leaves his Ruger pistol. I want to have it when I deliver the 12 cut balls to Woodruff. Two: Go over the set-up of the leather Running Dog golf bag that he is taking; regular balls in the large left pocket, uncut drug balls in the right, one regular ball and one uncut drug ball in the top center pocket, putter is loaded, extra rounds in the drawstring bag in the bottom center pocket. The single drug ball with its cover removed is also in this bottom pocket, wrapped in plastic.

Unable to easily write down these points while wearing the protective suit, Min committed them to memory. If Willie left in the morning before Min was awake, he would be up to speed.

Min listened as "Hotel California" reached what he considered its apex: the double solo performed by guitarists Don Felder and Joe Walsh. Felder begins the solo before Walsh takes over. At the end, the two talented artists harmonize with their instruments, playing together.

Min's head rocked slowly from side to side.

Ahh, that Joe Walsh...also a badass. Though perhaps not as much as Val Kilmer in Heat.

He grinned and ground away at the cover of the ball. When the song ended it was followed by another old song by an American artist that was also strangely popular in China—"Country Roads" by John Denver. It was the favorite American song of his friend, Yang Wei.

I need to remember to tell Yang next time I see him that this rental house is actually located on Country Road. He will be amused.

Yang was now a Lieutenant in the Chinese Navy, officially known as the People's Liberation Army Navy. He was assigned to the Type 055 guided-missile destroyer Nanchang. He and Min had last seen each other when Yang was home on leave, a month before Min returned to the United States as an employee of Running Dog Enterprises.

It was Yang who shed light on the true nature of China's attitude toward the United States. They had been at a KTV in Guangdong, drinking and listening to karaoke. Yang, slightly inebriated, leaned toward Min and declared, "We are going to defeat them. Not just economically, but militarily...in the Pacific."

Yang spent the next 20 minutes sharing information with Min that clarified a number of things.

Before Min first traveled to America, after winning the Sanyu Scholarship, he attended a series of mandatory meetings. Most of these were designed to prepare him for life in a foreign country. He would be representing China and, Min supposed, the officials wanted to give him every chance at success.

One meeting was different. Min was summoned to the local office of the public security bureau, the government agency responsible for issuing passports. His photograph was taken, and he was told that his credentials would be processed in an expedited manner. He was taken to a small room to wait. Upon entering the room, he found a man waiting for him.

"Sit down, Min."

The man explained that Min would be expected to act in China's best interest while at Yale. The expectations went beyond performing well academically.

"You do, of course, believe that Taiwan should be returned to mainland control, correct?"

Taiwan was situated just 100 miles off the coast of southeastern China. It became a Japanese colony in 1895. When Japan lost World War II, China took control. At the time, a decades-long conflict also raged in China between Mao Zedong's Communist party and nationalist forces under General Chiang Kai-Shek. The communists prevailed in 1949 and Chiang and his allies fled to Taiwan. They referred to the island as the Republic of China, or ROC. The communist mainland, officially the People's Republic of China, or PRC, considers Taiwan a wayward province that must return to communist control.

The man—Min came to believe he was part of China's state security apparatus—did not wait for an answer. "Our country has many ways to collect intelligence on the United States that can help us gain the upper hand. You will be in a position to contribute to this, Min. Keep your eyes and ears open."

He went on to explain that Min could help his country by picking up facts on any number of subjects. He mentioned something called TRAM, which seemed to have something to do with the American Navy's missile capabilities.

"Perhaps you meet someone at Yale who mentions their father works in the defense industry on this system. We would like to have the name of this person. Or you may hear something about projects that seem obscure. An American company in Vermont, for example, is working on a system to collect urine from fighter pilots during long missions. Did you know that? There are any number of subjects that interest us."

The man slid a card across the table that displayed a printed phone number.

"You are expected to represent China in more ways than one when abroad. Contact us at this number with anything useful."

Min accepted the card, thinking, *they want me to spy while I'm at Yale? I'm supposed to pick up information on how American pilots piss?*

Min never called the number. Once he got to Yale his priorities changed, eventually leading to his dismissal. A week after returning home he was summoned back to the public security bureau, where he met the same man. A 30-minute discussion ensued. Min realized it was a debriefing. The man was not judgmental about Min's humiliating experience in America, he was simply probing for useful information. Min felt shame that he could provide none.

It was not until the night in the KTV with Yang that Min fully understood the nature of his meetings with the man from state security.

"It will be a missile war, Min." Yang narrowed his eyes for emphasis. "The Americans will be fighting a great distance from their home country. The Pacific Ocean is vast. Their weapons will be launched from forward-deployed ships and from planes based in Japan and Guam. The ships have a finite number of missiles. The land-based planes will be in the air for hours just to reach the battlespace."

Min peered at his friend, attempting to follow along.

Yang continued. "You see, a significant number of our missile assets are land based. They are not just on the mainland, but on our island bases, including those that the Americans mockingly refer to as the 'Great Wall of Sand.'"

Min, like most Chinese, understood that his government had created artificial islands far from the mainland in a disputed area known as the Spratly Islands. Dredging operations had gathered millions of tons of sand, which were pumped onto coral reefs. Fantastic amounts of concrete were added. The end result was a string of seven military facilities that boasted airstrips and were bristling with offensive and defensive missile batteries. During Min's time at Yale he learned that Americans, and apparently most of the rest of the world, believed this building program violated international law. This was a revelation to Min, who had accepted the assertion from his government that it was a necessary and just measure against foreign aggression.

Yang sipped from his bottle of Tsingtao beer before carrying on.

"In effect we have created unsinkable aircraft carriers with these artificial installations. The Americans have their own carriers—which are formidable—but we can eliminate them. One method is to fire swarms of land, sea, and air-launched missiles at once. The Americans possess excellent anti-missile weapons, but they cannot match the number that we can throw at them. They will be overwhelmed, and they know it. Our intelligence agencies have learned that their sailors have a name for this—getting 'gang banged.' My ship, the Nanchang, will play a role in these attacks."

He smiled proudly, then went on.

"We can also strike them with our larger DF-21D and DF-26 ballistic missiles. They are fired from hardened silos or mobile launch vehicles on land. These missiles travel at Mach 10—ten times the speed of sound, or two miles a second. The 21 has a 1,000-mile range and can reach targets well east of Taiwan. The 26 can reach Guam, 2,000 miles from the mainland."

Yang looked over his shoulder and leaned in toward Min. He lowered his voice.

"The Americans are not convinced that these weapons, which reach heights beyond the earth's atmosphere, can return to the surface and strike a moving target. Our engineers and scientists have developed guidance systems that achieve this. Do you see what this means? An American carrier can be sunk, or at least damaged to the point that it cannot launch aircraft, by a single weapon. We possess carrier-killer weapons and, with the DF-26, Guam-killers."

Min tried to absorb this information. His thoughts went back to the meeting with the man from state security.

He asked, "What is TRAM...and why are we interested in trivial facts like how American pilots collect urine?"

Yang's eyebrows rose. He seemed impressed by the question.

"TRAM is the American's Transferrable Reload At-sea Method. You see, once an American naval vessel expends its missiles, it must travel to a base to be reloaded. This is time-consuming and extremely inefficient in a shooting war. TRAM is a system they are trying to implement that will allow them to rearm at sea. But we have an answer for this. We will concentrate attacks on their supply chain. They rely on a small number of large, unarmed supply ships that are operated by civilian employees. They no longer have what was known as their Military Sealift Command. If we sink just one of these ships it will be the equivalent of sinking an entire convoy of World War II supply ships. We will also target their tankers. Though many of their warships—particularly the aircraft carriers—are nuclear powered and, in military slang, operate by 'burning neutrons,' their aircraft run on jet fuel, which must be transported to them. An American carrier battlegroup carrying out wartime operations will burn through this fuel in just three days."

Min nodded slowly. "And the urine collection?"

Yang explained. "The American land-based fighter aircraft will travel much further to reach the battlespace than they have been accustomed to in past conflicts. They will require multiple instances of refueling and their pilots will be severely taxed. These planes were not designed with all of the," —he searched for a word—"necessities that are required by this type of warfare. The pilots will need to piss. In the past they have simply avoided drinking fluids before a mission. Pilots would be dehydrated by the time they reached their targets where, I might add, they would be met by Chinese fighters that are at least their equal. They must drink, and they must piss. The Americans have not faced a peer-level foe on the battlefield since World War II. We are interested in anything they design to help them fight this type of war."

Yang paused to take a long sip of his beer before continuing.

"You see, Min, we desire the reunification of Taiwan for two reasons. One, of course, is political. The island is part of China. The second is just as critical. TSMC—Taiwan Semiconductor Manufacturing Company—is far and away the largest producer of a specific type of microelectronics in the world. These are the logic chips that are built into most of the devices that facilitate modern life. I'm speaking of computers, cellphones, even smart refrigerators. And, yes, weapons."

Min appraised Yang, amazed at his former schoolmate's grasp of concepts Min hadn't considered.

Yang seemed to read his mind and smiled.

"TSMC accounts for over 90% of the world's production of these chips—some estimates say it is as high as 98%. Microelectronics are the new oil, Min. Modern nations must have them. There are no substitutes, no secondary suppliers. The Strait of Taiwan is the new Persian Gulf. If we defeat the Americans—and we will—we will control the chips. We will bring America to its knees. We do not have to invade Taiwan and ravage the island. We must simply engage their protectors —the Americans—and neutralize them. They will not be able to sustain combat operations on a long-term basis. In effect, our conflict with the Americans does not need to result in their overwhelming defeat, just a stalemate that blunts their influence in this region."

He raised his bottle of Tsingtao in a toast.

"Gānbēi!"

Min tapped his bottle against Yang's and watched as the lieutenant in the Chinese Navy dismounted his barstool and walked unsteadily toward the men's room.

The conversation with Yang had added perspective to Min's thought process. He contemplated. *Does everyone know these facts? Am I ignorant of China's true relationship with the Americans?*

Min had the offer from Mr. Chu at Running Dog to assist in an undertaking that would weaken the United States. Until speaking with Yang, his motivations about whether to proceed were primarily financial. Realizing that conflict with the U.S. was inevitable, his decision to participate was reinforced.

He was infatuated with America and its freedoms, but he loved China.

The John Denver song ended and was followed by Michael Jackson's "Beat It." Min paused his work for a second.

That's right, I have several American songs in a row on this playlist that are popular in China.

He resumed his work on the golf ball, remembering his recommendations to Mr. Chu on how to implement the drug project. He convinced Chu that an American needed to be in charge, at least nominally. This would make it much easier to do business in rural parts of America. Min believed that Dylan Riordan, after his dismissal from Yale, could be convinced to come on board. He was correct. Dylan was certainly motivated by the prospect of making money, but he also felt that his rightful status as an American elite had been taken from him. He held a grudge.

Dylan was named the Managing Director of North American Business Development. He showed a talent for traditional business dealings, implementing the courier system for delivery of drug balls to co-opted networks as well as a number of other procedures. He coordinated this with a long-time Running Dog official named Zhou Yan, who managed the company facilities in Newark. He also showed a talent for something less traditional; he was more than willing to personally execute dealers that stood in the way of the organization. Willie and Dax were of a similar mindset. All of them, Min included, had believed themselves deserving of an anointed status. All had somehow been unjustly denied their rightful place in the world. Given a second chance, all four were willing to be ruthless to take what was theirs.

Min had done well in recruiting assets for Mr. Chu's enterprise.

An hour later, Min completed the cleanup from the work in the garage. The protective suit and gloves were spread on the back patio, where he had sprayed them down with a hose. The garage was open, airing out. The processed drug balls were inside a sealed bag and hidden in a toolbox, where they would stay until Min delivered them to Woodruff the following day.

Min entered the house and saw Willie standing over the leather golf bag. He had unzipped the top pocket and was peering inside.

"Let me assist." Min proceeded to review the setup of the bag's pockets.

Willie yawned. "Got it. I left the Ruger in your room."

Min nodded. "You've spoken to Dax?"

"Yeah, we might not be able to meet with Mahmud until Tuesday. He has a meeting after work tomorrow night that he doesn't want to miss. Believe it or not, it's with a community group looking for solutions to the opioid crisis. Dax thinks he's just trolling for new customers."

Min laughed. "In China we would say that is fěng cì."

"If that means *ironic*, then you would be right. I'm heading upstairs. I want to look at different ways to get back to Dayton on the navigation app on my phone."

Smiling, Min guessed, "You don't want to drive through the traffic circle in Troy again?"

Willie adjusted his glasses. "No fucking way."

CHAPTER TWENTY-SEVEN

Bunker drove his Malibu north on I-75 toward Piqua on Monday morning. He'd gotten an early start to the day, stopping at the office at 6:45 a.m. He checked voice messages and emails, hoping to see anything that would contribute to the angle he was taking in the Shortridge murder investigation.

Still nothing from Running Dog Enterprises' office in New Jersey. I'll give them a couple hours to respond this morning, then rattle their cage if they ignore me.

He then spied the letter on the corner of his desk from the state foster and adoption program. Before leaving the office Friday he'd gone online and provided the information requested on Paul and Lauren Hull. He sat back, trying to convince himself that he'd done the right thing.

Two years earlier a criminal had come to the Midwest. He was referred to by law enforcement as Glenn Smithson, though this was almost certainly not his real name. In fact, to Bunker's knowledge, his true identity was never established. What was known was the man had been a skilled hacker, believed to have committed a series of crimes both within the United States and internationally. These included murders in Belize as well as an area in rural Indiana.

Bunker strongly suspected that the Hulls were victims of some of Smithson's crimes. He also suspected—but couldn't prove—that the couple was instrumental in Smithson's death. It was this belief that guided Bunker as he completed the "Additional Information" section of the state's adoption form. Bunker remembered what he wrote.

Though both subjects have served with distinction in the military, I find it necessary to make mention of some troubling concerns. It is my belief as an experienced law enforcement official that Paul, and perhaps Lauren as well, are comfortable going outside the law if they feel it benefits them. I have my doubts that this quality should be rewarded, particularly when the future of a child hangs in the balance. I believe your waiting list of hopeful adoptive parents almost certainly includes safer candidates.

Bunker stared at the ceiling, considering what he'd typed. Was it fair to the Hulls? Smithson had been the most high-profile criminal to visit Miami County since 1927 when, during a bank robbery in Piqua, John Dillinger shot the brother of Sheriff Frank Mathews. Still, there were laws for a reason. If Hull did what Bunker suspected, he should answer for it—and certainly not be rewarded for it in the adoption process.

Bunker sensed activity outside his door. He looked through his open doorway and saw Pappy Karabin and Cody Simon moving past the cubicles toward their respective offices.

Looks like we all had the same idea this morning—get an early start.

Karabin noticed Bunker's open door and veered away from Simon. He leaned on the door frame and fixed his eyes on Amos.

"Anything new on those people from the golf company?"

Right to the point. Good morning to you too, Pappy.

"Nothing concrete. I expect to talk to company representatives in New Jersey this morning. In the meantime, I have a couple leads to run down. I was just getting ready to head out."

Karabin nodded. "Okay...the quicker you can wrap that up, the better. We can use all the help we can get tracking down Kevin Turner. We're putting on the full court press now that everyone's back from the weekend."

He made a fist and was about to rap on the door frame, something that was beginning to annoy Bunker, before asking, "Oh, yeah, how's your mom?"

Bunker fought to keep his eyes from narrowing.

256

Again with my mom? What gives?

"Uh, hanging in there. I helped her box up things most of the day yesterday. Good days and bad, you know?"

Karabin nodded. "Gotcha. Let me know if I can help."

RAP-RAP

He was gone.

Bunker allowed his eyes to narrow. He turned off his computer and pulled the door shut before making his way through the cubicles. He saw Gayle DeJean entering the office. This told Bunker it was just before 7 a.m. Gayle was always on time. She smiled at him.

"Good morning, Amos. Looks like you're heading out. I'll get the coffee going right away if you can wait a few minutes."

Bunker shook his head. "I'll pick up something on the road. I'm heading up toward Piqua...taking my personal vehicle today so the easiest way to reach me will be on my cell." He hesitated, then asked, "Anything I need to know before I roll? Sheriff Hollis isn't in yet."

DeJean sat her purse on her desk and closed one eye.

"I just saw Deputy Kuhlman in the parking lot. She'll be doing the walk-through with Zeke Wednesday morning. I'll be sending a text this morning to all of the detectives. If you have anything that needs tidied up in the room, better get it done."

By "the room," DeJean meant the evidence room. Several months earlier it was discovered that the contents of three vials containing morphine tablets had been tampered with. The tablets were replaced with aspirin. This cost the county prosecutor a conviction and launched an investigation that bore no fruit. Sheriff Hollis tightened the restrictions on the room, adding extra security cameras and reducing the number of personnel authorized to enter to four: him and his three detectives.

An additional safeguard was put in place. Twice a month, Zeke, the detection dog, would be walked through the room. If he didn't indicate toward an evidence box that was supposed to hold drugs, it would signal another problem for the department. So far, Zeke had accounted for all the contraband.

"Nope, I'm good. Okay, mark me 'Out.' Have a good day, Gayle."

Now on the highway, Bunker formulated his plan for the rest of the morning. The day before the Shortridge brothers were killed, Bunker had followed two Range Rovers from Winans coffee shop in Piqua to a house in Champaign County. He had not yet discovered the drivers' identities. He was becoming more and more convinced that they were involved in some way.

I need to go back and check out that house. Maybe I can get a better look at those guys...pick up some information. First, I'll stop at Winans and grab a coffee...see if the staff has anything to add.

As he drove, Bunker's thoughts drifted to Pappy Karabin. The senior detective seemed to be going out of his way to show interest in Bunker's mother.

Seems out of character. I don't remember him asking about her at all in the past and now twice in just a few days? And he's really pushing me to move on from the Running Dog angle in this investigation. Hmmm.

Pappy's inquiry had done more than stir Bunker's suspicious nature. It prompted him to remember his time with his mother on Sunday. It had been a bittersweet day. The act of packing up her possessions was every bit as difficult as Bunker expected. The apartment at StoryPoint was relatively spacious but would not come close to housing all the accrued possessions of a lifetime. Most of his mother's things would remain in the house for the time being. Eventually, he supposed, a fair amount of it would be sold or put into a storage facility. Deciding what made the cut for the move was depressing.

But certain things stirred memories that brought smiles to both Amos and Dana.

"Mom, why the hell did you keep my old peewee football trophies?"

Dana, who was having a so-so day, perked up. "Well, Amos, I used to throw a football with you so you could get better, remember? I guess I always thought of those trophies as, well, half mine." Her smile, for just a few seconds, made her look 20 years younger.

Minutes later, going through photographs, she came across a shot of Amos with a pretty brunette. They were embracing, standing in front of a Christmas tree.

"Oh look. There's a picture of you and Sarah. She is such a nice girl." A look of confusion appeared on her face, one that Bunker often saw at the onset of a mental slide. "What ever happened..." She trailed off.

Bunker reached for the photo. It was taken the previous Christmas, just a few weeks before he and his fiancé had parted ways.

Sarah Craycraft was a nurse at a Dayton hospital. They met at a barbecue hosted by mutual friends near the Dayton International Airport in June. It was the weekend of the Dayton Air Show and the friend's house was close enough to the action to offer excellent views without fighting the crowds. They exchanged numbers and found themselves swept up in a whirlwind courtship, something that neither of them expected.

Both were single, both a stone's throw from 40—Bunker just beyond, Sarah not quite there—and both seemingly satisfied with their unattached status. This changed quickly. They were just months away from their May wedding date when Bunker's hardline stance on procedures showed itself.

It was not the first time. There had been arguments over trivial things like ordering items in restaurants that weren't listed on the menu—"You should never do that, Sarah; they print these menus for a reason." But the deal-breaker came out of Sarah's revelation that she wanted to keep her last name—with a hyphen attached—after they were married.

"Are you kidding?" Bunker was incredulous.

Sarah became defensive. "What's wrong with that?"

Bunker took a deep breath and let it out slowly.

"Well, lots of things. For instance, which name comes first, Bunker or Craycraft? Is it Sarah Craycraft-Bunker or Sarah Bunker-Craycraft? And what about our kids?"

"What *about* our kids?" Sarah was getting angry.

"Well, let's say we have little Johnny Bunker-Craycraft, or, sorry, little Johnny Craycraft-Bunker. His name won't fit on the back of his football uniform properly, it'll take him longer to learn to write his name than other kids, doctor's offices and hotels will file his records under the Bs instead of the Cs—it'll be a pain in the ass for him to check in...I mean all *kinds* of things get screwed up."

She looked at him disdainfully, but he continued, undeterred.

"And here's a big question, what if Johnny marries someone that thinks the same way you do? Will they become Mr. and Mrs. Johnny Craycraft-Bunker-Trapino? Or Mr. and Mrs. Johnny Trapino-Craycraft-Bunker? I mean, where does it end?"

He stared at her, genuinely wanting to know the answer. He found out.

"Right here, Amos. It ends right here." She removed her ring, handed it to him, and walked out the door.

He stared at the photo. "Do you mind if I hold onto this, Mom?"

She looked back at him blankly.

Bunker got off at State Route 36 and pulled into the Winans lot. From his vantage point he could see that the manager, Cledith Roosa, was working the drive-thru window. He took his place at the end of a line of vehicles and waited his turn. After placing his order—a large black coffee and a cinnamon roll—through the outdoor menu board, he pulled to the window.

"That'll be $6.75 please...Oh hello detective! Good morning, nice to see you!"

Cledith was upbeat, cheerful.

She's so bubbly she's damn-near effervescent. Is she always in a good mood?

Bunker remembered an old quote attributed to Abraham Lincoln when the Civil War was not going well for the Union. Their most prominent generals had lost a series of battles. This came to an end when General Ulysses Grant's forces won a battle in Tennessee. Critics of Grant derided him as a drinker. Lincoln supposedly said, "Well, I wish some of you would tell me the brand of whiskey that Grant drinks. I would like to send a barrel of it to my other generals."

Bunker had no idea if the story was true, but he was beginning to believe he should consider starting his mornings by switching to whatever Cledith was having.

"Good morning, Cledith." He handed her a ten and asked. "Anything new on the two men we talked about last week?"

Cledith opened the cash drawer and retrieved his change. "No, sorry detective. They haven't been in today. I worked Saturday and they didn't show then either. Phoebe is filling in at another Winans for a few days, so she hasn't been here." She handed him his change before gathering his order.

"I'd like to get copies of the pictures I took of them to you for your staff to look at. Do you have a problem with that?"

Her smile remained bright. "Not at all, I'll have them posted behind the counter. It should give our people a good way to compare faces."

Bunker accepted the coffee cup and small bag.

"Thanks again, call me at any time if they show up. I better get moving so you can get back to work."

Bunker made his way back to State Route 36 and headed east. He figured he would make it to the house outside Urbana in 15-20 minutes. The fact that he would again be just outside of his jurisdiction brought a sad smile to his face.

I wonder if Sarah would be impressed that I'm pushing the boundaries a bit...coloring outside the lines.

He then remembered the multi-jurisdictional nature that the investigation had assumed and decided he probably wasn't overstepping his authority by pursuing leads in Champaign County.

Well, so much for the thought that I'm turning into a rule-breaker.

Bunker sipped his coffee, his thoughts in the past as he accelerated out of town. His mind was occupied as he passed the first road a mile east of Piqua. He barely noticed a grey Nissan Sentra that was waiting to turn as he cruised past in his Malibu.

Willie slowed in his rented Sentra as he neared his turn, a left onto a two-lane road a mile outside of Piqua. A car was approaching from the west, so he came to a stop and engaged his left turn signal. He stole a quick look at the navigation app on his phone.

Troy-Sidney Road.

Willie wasn't concerned about the name of the road, just that it would provide a route to Dayton that prevented him from negotiating that damn traffic circle in Troy. He'd plotted a course the night before that avoided the traffic near the I-75 interchange at Piqua and allowed him to duck onto the highway a few miles later before he reached Troy.

The car drew near. As it sped past, Willie saw that it was the same nondescript shade of grey as the Sentra.

A Malibu? The best color for a surveillance vehicle—at least that's what the instructors at Verify P.I. always said.

Willie made the turn and accelerated. There was no traffic on this road, so he relaxed. He pushed the radio button and poked at the preset stations until a Talking Heads song came up.

If Dylan was here, he'd be trying to find Howard Stern.

He'd driven nearly two miles on this road before he saw a stop sign in the distance. It was at this instant that he had the thought that occurred to virtually everyone who had already embarked on a trip—*did I pack everything?*

Willie took his foot off the accelerator and allowed the Sentra to coast toward the intersection. He saw headlights off to the left, the first vehicle he'd encountered since turning off Route 36. He resisted the urge to look over his shoulder to check his gear.

When I get to the four-way stop I'll double-check everything.

The Sentra rolled to a stop. Willie squinted as the glare of the vehicle to the left bounced up and down. It was still a couple hundred yards from the intersection. He turned to check the back seat and confirmed that his travel bag was there, next to the leather Running Dog golf bag.

Perfect...remembered everything.

As he removed his foot from the brake pedal and pulled away from the stop sign, he had a thought.

Wait, did I leave the top pocket unzipped on the golf bag?

The thought disappeared, replaced in an instant by first panic, then resignation, as he heard the terrible scream of braking tires.

The intersection was a two-way stop.

CHAPTER TWENTY-EIGHT

Bunker approached Country Road 15 minutes later. When he'd followed the Running Dog Range Rovers there the previous week, he'd been more intent on keeping them in sight than making a close examination of the surroundings. This trip was different.

He remembered that the street itself was basically a stretch of asphalt—less than a mile long—that had houses on either side and ended in a cul-de-sac. Mature trees stood in every lot, giving the development the look of a narrow island situated in a sea of corn and soybean fields. Bunker peered at it as he drew closer, the houses becoming easier to make out through the trees.

Kinda reminds you of a stream that cuts through farm fields—trees growing near the banks with cleared land beyond as far as you can see.

Bunker turned left onto the paved lane and drove slowly north, gliding past well-kept homes. Most were two-story designs on large lots. The substantial number and size of the trees contributed to a sense of privacy. Less than a half-mile after turning off of Route 36 the Malibu neared a small roundabout.

Bunker's eyes were on the house as he eased through the roundabout. He could see one of the Range Rovers in the driveway. He accelerated slightly as he reached the far side of the circle and continued north but kept his speed below 30 mph as he approached the house. It was on the left, the second house past the roundabout. Bunker gazed at it with a look of practiced disinterest as he passed by.

The Range Rover in the driveway has New York plates. That's the one the Asian man—probably Chinese—was driving. That means the one with Connecticut plates is either in the garage or not currently at this address.

He continued north until he reached the cul-de-sac then turned back. Halfway back to the Airbnb he pulled to the side of the asphalt and put the Malibu in park. The physical characteristics of the neighborhood did not lend themselves well to surveillance. There was one way in and one way out. There was no reason to be on the road unless you lived there, were visiting, or delivering something. Any strange vehicle pulled to the side of the roadway would draw attention. Fortunately, it was past the time that people working away from the house would've left for their place of employment. But Bunker was aware that he would likely draw the attention of anyone still inside the handful of houses in his immediate area as well as any random local resident who might drive past on the way to run errands.

Kids are out of school for the summer. A lone male pulled over in a car will not be looked upon favorably once Johnny or Suzy comes outside to shoot baskets or kick a soccer ball.

Bunker sat in the Malibu watching the house. There was no activity. Twenty minutes in, he saw a garage door south of the Airbnb open. A few minutes later a woman in a bikini top drove out on a riding mower. She traced a path along the borders of the ample front yard before settling into an out and back method that left a diagonal pattern. Bunker watched, imagining that he could smell the cut grass.

A half hour later a car approached from behind. It was obviously coming from one of the houses between Bunker and the cul-de-sac. He watched it draw near in his side mirror. It slowed perceptibly as it drew abreast, and Bunker saw the woman behind the wheel give him a look that was equal parts apprehensive and judgmental.

Well that didn't take long. Nothing blows a stakeout quite like a nosy neighbor.

Bunker decided he should be grateful that he lived in a rural area where, for the most part, the general public was willing to pick up the phone and call the authorities when something looked out of place. He'd heard too many stories of city-dwellers walking past a crime in progress and not bothering to report it.

I should probably call the Champaign County Sheriff's Office and let them know I'm here. For all I know, one of their deputies is already on the way here, answering a call about a suspicious grey-haired man parked on the street.

Bunker was reaching for his phone when it vibrated, indicating an incoming text. He checked the screen.

Deputy Kuhlman and K-9 Zeke will be conducting an inspection of the evidence room this Wednesday at 8 a.m. Please make sure all current evidence boxes are in order and any new evidence is properly processed and stored before that time. Also, a reminder to turn in a report to Sheriff Hollis at the end of the day on the progress of your investigation.

Bunker saw that the text came from Gayle DeJean and went out to him, Pappy Karabin, and Detective Simon. The sheriff was also included in the group text. Bunker sent a response acknowledging the message and was about to dial the Champaign County Sheriff's department number when his phone vibrated again. This time it was a call. He looked down to see a number in the 973 area code. At first, he thought it was from a local caller. The predominant area code in this part of Ohio was 937. Then he saw that two of the digits were reversed.

That's a Newark, New Jersey number. Has to be from Running Dog.

Realizing the call might take some time, he made a quick decision. He started the Malibu and put it in gear.

I could be sitting here on the phone with Running Dog when a deputy shows up and knocks on my window. I have to take this call. Better to leave the area while I'm talking and swing back afterward. I can turn onto State Route 36, drive while I'm talking, and pull over if I need to. If one of the Range Rovers leaves the house while I'm gone, I may still see it when I double back.

Bunker eased the Malibu onto the road surface and steered toward the roundabout. As he did so, he opened the console and pulled out a notepad. He glanced toward the Airbnb, still seeing no activity, and reached for the phone.

"Detective Amos Bunker."

"Good morning, detective. This is Zhou Yan with Running Dog Enterprises in Newark. I am returning your call from Friday."

The man's voice now flowed through the Malibu's speaker system as the call was transferred from Bunker's handset to the vehicle itself. This freed Bunker to jot J-O-E Y-A-N on his notepad as he steered through the roundabout and headed toward Route 36. The man on the other end of the conversation had an accent. Bunker decided he'd better ask for the proper spelling of the name.

"Do you mind spelling your name, so I have it correct in my records?"

"Certainly, detective. It is Z-H-O-U Y-A-N."

Bunker was momentarily confused and was silent for a beat. He'd intended to clarify the spelling of the man's last name, thinking it could possibly begin with a 'J' rather than a 'Y.'

The man added, "In China, the name Z-H-O-U is pronounced 'Joe.'"

"Ahh, thank you."

Bunker reached the end of Country Road. He had to make a decision. If he turned right, he would be driving back toward Piqua. Urbana was to the left. He supposed it was a toss-up what direction the men in the Airbnb would turn if they left the development. Bunker's plan was to drive while he spoke to the Running Dog representative then turn back to the house. If one of the Range Rovers departed while he was talking, he would see it when he turned back—if he chose correctly.

A left takes me deeper into Champaign County. Justifiable...but not my territory.

He turned right.

"Mr. Yan, I'm trying to get in touch with a couple men who I believe are employed by your company. Both are currently in Western Ohio. One man is, I believe, Chinese. The other is an American. Both appear to be 25 to 30 years old."

Yan was silent for a few seconds before responding. "Hmm, that physical description matches any number of our employees. Our corporate headquarters and manufacturing facilities are located in Shenzhen, China. We employ hundreds of Chinese. A number of them are in the United States with work visas. And the description of the American is, well..."

Bunker cruised through St. Paris. He was aware that his description of the man he thought of as Eli was vague.

"I believe his name might be Eli. Can you tell me if you have an employee with that name?"

The question was again met with a short silence. Finally, Yan spoke.

"Detective, can I ask the purpose of these questions? Have these men done something wrong?"

Bunker began to detect some resistance.

it's interesting he is just now getting around to asking that question.

"Certainly. We believe these men may be able to assist our department with an investigation." He tried to downplay their involvement. "We have reason to believe that they may have seen or heard things that appeared to be inconsequential at the time but may clarify some things we are looking at."

"So they are potential witnesses?" Bunker thought he recognized a hint of relief.

"Very possibly...can you check the name—Eli?"

"One moment, please."

Bunker heard the sound of keystrokes coming through his speakers. His pen hovered over his notepad. Seconds passed. He saw the village of Lena ahead and took note of a semi tractor-trailer rig pulled to the side of the road. The trailer was bright blue. The words *Woeber's Horseradish Sauce* were printed across its length. Bunker felt himself growing impatient.

"I'm sorry, detective. We have no employee named Eli."

Bunker tapped the pen on the notepad several times.

"Okay, how about some variation of the name? Maybe Elijah…or Elias?" He jotted the names on the pad absentmindedly.

"I will check."

More keystrokes. Bunker was now a mile west of Lena and was making an effort to remain patient. After more than a minute the keystrokes ceased.

"No results, detective…sorry."

"What about a previous employee? Someone still in your files?"

Yan sounded almost apologetic. "I checked. We've had no employee by that name."

Bunker concentrated.

"Okay, let's try another angle." He flipped a page on the notebook, revealing the plate numbers of the two Range Rover Evoques. "I'll read off two license plate numbers and I'd like you to tell me what employees are driving the vehicles, Okay?"

Yan again hesitated before responding.

"I will be happy to check the plates, but I'm afraid we do not always keep records of which employees are driving a particular vehicle on a particular day. Our business can be very…fluid."

Bunker recognized "the runaround." He'd been on the receiving end of it more times than he could count.

Christ, I'm almost to Fletcher.

He ran a hand across one side of his face and took a deep breath.

"Just try, please. I would appreciate it."

He read the numbers and again heard the keystrokes. After another full minute, Yan spoke.

"Yes, both vehicles are registered to Running Dog Enterprises."

"And?"

"And as I suspected, neither are currently assigned to a specific employee." Yan injected a bit of guilt into his tone. "Perhaps we are violating an American regulation by not keeping such records? If so, let me apologize. I can assure you we will, how do you say...*tighten up* this oversight in the future."

Bunker felt a combination of irritation and validation. Yan was doing everything possible to appear cooperative while remaining evasive. This was not altogether uncommon for employees of corporations. In Bunker's experience, these people chose their words wisely, not wanting to say something that could be construed as an admission of wrongdoing. This felt like something more.

He forced himself to smile so that his words conveyed no hint of annoyance.

"Thank you, Mr. Yan. You've been very helpful. Please contact me if you think of anything that could assist our investigation."

Yan's contented voice floated from the car's speakers.

"But of course, detective...but of course."

Bunker stabbed the "End Call" icon on the Malibu's touch screen display. He let his eyes drop to the notepad before flipping its pages. He'd gathered no concrete information that furthered the investigation. Experience told him, however, that he was on the right track. He focused on the road ahead, trying to orient himself.

Damn, I'm only a couple miles from Piqua. Better get back to the Airbnb.

He began to search for a spot to turn around when movement in the distance caught his eye ahead and off to his left. He focused and realized it was a helicopter. It was descending slowly. Bunker's head pivoted from the helicopter to the road ahead and back again multiple times in quick succession.

That helo is blue. That means CareFlight from Miami Valley Hospital.

This was the Level 1 Trauma Center in Dayton that served a number of surrounding counties. Bunker knew this meant, in all likelihood, there had been a serious accident. This seemed to be confirmed seconds later when he glimpsed vehicle emergency lights in the area.

Better see if I can help.

Bunker approached the scene minutes later. There were several emergency vehicles in the area, dispersed around an intersection. Bunker slowed as he neared the activity, seeing a female uniformed deputy in an orange vest holding up both hands to stop his progress. He saw that the CareFlight helicopter had set down in a bean field just northwest of the intersection, its blades spinning. A stretcher was being loaded through an open side door.

The Malibu crept forward. He saw a frown appear on the deputy's face. Bunker rolled down his window and stuck his head out.

"Hey Paula, looks like a bad one." He nearly shouted the words so they could be heard over the din of the helicopter.

The deputy lowered her hands as a look of recognition replaced the frown.

"Oh, hey Amos." She walked up and leaned on the side of the car, matching Bunker's volume level. "Yeah, pretty bad. Looks like a guy in a little Nissan pulled out in front of a fuel truck...got T-boned."

Bunker got out of the Malibu and surveyed the area. He and the deputy stood on Troy-Sidney Road, about 200 feet from a stop sign. An intersecting road, Loy, ran east and west just beyond the stop sign. Bunker was familiar with Loy Road from his days as a deputy on patrol. He'd also worked a stolen motorcycle case nearby as a detective. Traffic on Troy-Sidney had to stop. Traffic on Loy did not.

"Is the driver going to make it?"

A doubtful look came over the deputy's face.

"Looks pretty iffy. The Piqua Fire Department folks had to work over half an hour to cut him out. They used the Jaws of Life. Paramedics did what they could, but it's up to the trauma unit now." She tilted her head toward the helicopter, dipping her grey Smokey the Bear-style hat.

Bunker nodded. He counted no fewer than eight emergency vehicles clustered near the intersection, including two fire trucks and a separate water tanker. There was also a tow truck.

"What was the fuel truck hauling?"

"Diesel," replied the deputy. "He was out making deliveries to farmers. Sure looks like he didn't do anything wrong—came up to the intersection doing 55, maybe 60—but the other guy just pulled out in front of him. A couple state troopers are down there, doing accident reconstruction. We're turning away traffic from all four directions. The fire trucks are here in case of fuel leaks from the tanker or if fire breaks out. So far, no leaks."

Bunker nodded and was about to ask another question when the pitch of the helicopter's blades changed. He and the deputy saw that the side door was closed and all personnel on the ground had backed away. The helo—Bunker remembered it was a Dauphin—rose for several seconds before banking slightly and heading south. All eyes squinted at the sky, watching it disappear.

Her voice now back to a normal level, the deputy asked, "You want to take a look?"

Bunker appeared non-committal. It looked to him like the accident scene was well staffed and he hesitated to insert himself into an investigation when his presence could be a hindrance.

"Well, it looks like all the bases are covered here, Paula. I was actually just about to—"

"Detective Bunker? Hey, Detective Bunker!"

Bunker turned toward the intersection to see a tall deputy walking toward him. He recognized the man as Deputy Adam Fatkin, a Kentucky native who had been on the force for three years. Despite his lack of experience, he was well thought of and seemed ticketed for advancement. Bunker strode toward Fatkin, meeting him halfway.

"Glad to see you, detective. You might be able to help us out."

Bunker cocked his head. "How so?"

Fatkin removed his hat and wiped his brow.

"I think we have the scene pretty well secured. The state boys are finishing with their measurements and pictures, J.D.'s Towing came up from Troy and will be hauling away the

Sentra, and an outfit from Sidney that handles big rigs will be here any minute to get the fuel truck out of the ditch." He gestured toward both vehicles that were involved in the accident. The truck had large red letters across its silver tank. They read SCHAFER OIL CO. Fatkin continued. "The fire crews will stay until the fuel truck's gone, then spray down the area."

He began to walk toward the accident scene and Bunker followed. "And we've identified the injured driver. He's from Rhode Island and the Sentra was a rental. We have his wallet and his cellphone. We'll begin reaching out to his family ASAP."

An ambulance was parked near the intersection. Paramedics were talking to a tall man with reddish-grey hair wearing work clothes. The name above his breast pocket read "Randy." He was obviously the truck driver and had apparently refused a trip to the hospital. He sat on the rear step of the ambulance, staring expressionlessly at the Sentra.

Bunker and Fatkin reached the intersection and angled toward the wrecked vehicles, careful to stay out of the way of the troopers. Pieces of metal, plastic, and glass were strewn across the road surface. The Schafer Oil truck was in the ditch on the south side of the road, canted slightly to the left. Bunker saw that skid marks trailed the truck into the ditch. He turned and saw the marks started well before the intersection.

Bunker had worked scenes like this when he was a deputy and knew they could be complicated.

"Nice work, deputy. I'm not sure I can add anything to what you've done."

Fatkin stopped twenty feet from the mangled Sentra. Bunker drew up beside him and they stared at the wreckage. The Nissan had apparently spun after being struck and had slid for over 100 feet before ending up off Loy Road on the north side. The entire front left section of the car was caved in. It was further mangled by the operators of the Jaws of Life. Bunker saw that both the side and front airbags had deployed —for all the good they could do in a crash that was this violent —and blood was visible inside.

Fatkin spoke. "It's really not about managing the scene. It's about handling personal belongings of the driver."

Bunker turned to him, confused.

Fatkin continued. "See, the truck driver won't be cited. The Sentra driver is at fault, but he probably won't pull through. His phone and billfold give us everything we need to contact his next of kin. But he had some gear in the car that needs to be safeguarded. I was thinking the evidence room back at the department might be a good place to store it. But Sheriff Hollis has that new policy in place. Only certain people can enter the room, and..."

Bunker got it now.

"And I'm one of them." He smiled. "Glad to help, deputy. Where's the gear?"

Fatkin seemed relieved. "It's down there, laid out on the other side of the car." He led the way down to the wreck and stepped behind the trunk.

Bunker avoided looking directly into the front seat of the Sentra. In his years as a member of the Miami County Sheriff's Department he'd seen more serious accidents than he cared to remember. He no longer possessed the morbid curiosity that seemed to be a fundamental trait of witnesses to tragedy.

Fatkin reached the far side of the Sentra and pointed toward the ground. "There it is. Looks kinda expensive."

Bunker trailed Fatkin around the wreck and looked fixedly at the objects on the grass on the other side. The first item was a nylon bag. It no doubt held paraphernalia that a traveler would deem necessary. The second item, however, stopped Bunker in his tracks.

It was a white leather golf bag with red lettering and a familiar logo—Running Dog.

Son-of-a-BITCH!

CHAPTER TWENTY-NINE

Dylan checked the time and saw that it was not quite noon. He planned to ride along with Min for the exchange with the man—Steve Woodruff—who had taken over for Shadow. Min set the meet for 1 p.m. at the former precinct school in Westville.

Sounds like this Woodruff guy wants to do the deal before his shift starts at the factory.

Dylan was fine with this. After the exchange he and Min would return to the house and pack up. They would be leaving the Airbnb several days earlier than originally intended. The plan was to join Dax and Willie in Dayton and, hopefully, expedite the next deal—this one with Dr. Mahmud—before leaving Ohio.

Maybe for good, Dylan thought. *Things here have gotten complicated.*

He still had time to hit more practice balls in the backyard. He'd removed the Titleist driver, the foam balls, and a handful of tees from the Running Dog golf bag before Willie left. Today he was working on hitting a fade. He was near the back fence, methodically striking balls back toward the house. Before setting up over each ball, he concentrated on three key swing thoughts.

Align feet and shoulders left of target...Move ball forward in my stance...Open the face of the driver slightly.

Dylan drew the club back and felt it coil smoothly overhead before he unleashed a swing that, he knew, looked effortless. The practice ball—this one was orange—flew toward the center of the patio before tailing to the right and bouncing off the house.

Dylan grinned.

Nice. Ben Hogan himself couldn't have done it better. When—not if—I get to play Augusta National, that's the shot I'll use off the tee on number 15. I'll bet I can birdie that—

His phone vibrated in his pocket. He checked the screen and froze.

One of your people was in a bad accident. Careflighted to Miami Valley Hospital in Dayton. FYI Bunker has R.D. golf bag that was removed from the car.

It was from the informant. Dylan struggled to process the information.

Willie hurt? Had to be him. CareFlighted? They only do that if it's life-threatening.

His mind skipped completely over any concern for his associate's health.

Can he speak? What will he tell them? And the cops have the bag?!? That goddamned Bunker again. Have they found the carfentanil? How the fuck could Willie let this happen?

Dylan made an effort to remain calm. He ran through the possibilities. An already problematic situation had just taken an exponential leap.

Are we now the main focus of their investigation? If they found the drugs we must be. That means we have to pull the plug on everything and get the hell out of Ohio immediately.

He composed a text.

Has bag been examined?

He realized the informant was savvy enough to recognize that this question prioritized Dylan's concerns. Willie's wellbeing was secondary. The bag was more important. It must contain something that could connect Running Dog Enterprises to serious crimes. Though Dylan's question served to confirm this, he sent the text anyway. The informant obviously knew they were supplying drugs and had mentioned the golf bag for that very reason.

The three-dot typing awareness indicator appeared on Dylan's screen. He paced the patio as he waited and leaned his driver against the back of the house. Finally, a message appeared.

Bag is standing in Bunker's office. No unusual activity. I believe it was removed from accident scene to protect personal belongings. Also a small nylon travel bag here.

Dylan breathed a small sigh of relief. Maybe the situation could still be managed without pulling the plug on their operations.

We're so damn close to wrapping up things with Woodruff and Mahmud. If we can get that bag back before they take a close look at it, we're good.

Another text appeared on the cellphone's screen.

Bunker will store bag in evidence room for safekeeping.

Dylan read this and was mulling over possibilities when he again noticed the three dots. The screen changed.

FYI, drug dog will be brought into evidence room Wednesday morning for regularly scheduled inspection of seized contraband.

Dylan read the text and flinched, realizing what it meant. He ran a hand through his hair.

We have to get that bag back before Wednesday. That goddamned Bunker! He's the only person investigating us, and HE ends up with the fucking golf bag. Goddamn it Willie...We need to take a hard look at Bunker.

He quickly typed another text.

Will need personnel records on Bunker ASAP.

279

Thirty seconds later a response appeared.

I can get you hard copy today. Can trade for more stuff. Regular meeting place. 2pm.

Dylan peered at his phone. By "more stuff" he knew the informant was demanding opioids.

These goddamned drug people.

Bunker sat in his office and scrutinized the golf bag in the corner. Its fine leather, he knew, set it apart from standard bags. It was constructed with the same quality and craftsmanship as those carried by the caddies of touring professionals. The head covers on the fairway woods were made of matching leather. The uniform colors of the bag had just one exception—the cover on the putter's head was yellow and the words "Breakfast Ball" were stitched on top.

When he and Deputy Fatkin retrieved the bag from the ground outside the wrecked Sentra—after Bunker got over the shock of seeing the Running Dog logo—he'd noticed that there was no driver in the bag. He thought that odd and examined the rear seat of the vehicle to see if it had been thrown from the bag on impact. The driver wasn't there, but Bunker's glance into the front seat confirmed what he'd suspected—the crash was probably not survivable.

It was tempting to look inside the bag. Bunker thought there was a chance that it held secrets that could further the investigation into the recent murders. The top pocket was actually unzipped but appeared empty when he pressed on it. The side pockets both seemed weighted down but were zipped shut. Bunker drove from the accident scene with both the golf bag and the smaller nylon carry-on in the back seat of his Malibu.

It would be so easy. Just pull over somewhere and spend a few minutes going through the damn thing.

In the end his inclination to adhere to procedure won out. He had no search warrant. The driver's identity had already been established by the deputies on the scene. Even though Bunker could later argue that he was just trying to confirm the identification, he knew in his heart that wouldn't be the truth.

Rules are rules.

He drove directly to the office from the accident scene rather than doubling back to the Airbnb. He knew the house was difficult to watch without being noticed and realized he'd been away from it for so long that he could've missed the departure of the men inside. Once he agreed to transport the belongings from the crash site, he determined there was no reason for delay. On the way to Troy he decided to take another path in the investigation. He would begin to phone neighbors near the rental house to see if he could pick up information. This could be done without tipping off the occupants of the Airbnb. He felt the risk was low that a homeowner would alert the renters of his inquiries.

When Bunker walked through the double doors of the sheriff's office with the travel bag in one hand and the golf bag hanging from the opposite shoulder, he felt several sets of eyes.

Gayle DeJean looked up from her computer screen and did a double take.

"Well this is certainly a new one, detective." She gave him a sardonic smile.

Bunker nodded without smiling. "Hi Gayle. These things belong to the victim of an accident near Piqua. The responding deputies asked me to safeguard them until the victim can reclaim them...or, I guess, until the next of kin asks for them."

DeJean suddenly understood the situation.

"Oh...sorry to hear that. I didn't mean—"

Bunker waved away her apology.

"Forget it, Gayle. Mark me 'In,' huh? And, hey, can you contact the Champaign County Sheriff's Office and ask them for help? I need cell and home phone numbers for anyone living on a road named Country Road, west of Urbana."

"Sure, Amos."

Bunker strode through the cubicles on his way to his office, turning slightly every few feet to allow the golf bag to fit through the narrow passageways. Ahead, he saw Sheriff Hollis and detectives Simon and Karabin staring at him through their open office doors. All three men stopped what they were doing and moved to their doorways.

"Bunker, what in the hell are you doing?" Karabin pronounced 'the' as 'thee.'

Again, Bunker went through the explanation. He saw the expression of all three men change. Finally, the sheriff spoke.

"I heard about that wreck. It sounds like there's no doubt the driver of the car was at fault. Damn shame about the truck driver. Heard it was Randy Schafer. I know him...he delivers fuel oil to my place. He's a good stick. Something like this weighs on your conscience...even when you did nothing wrong."

Bunker allowed a small smile at the term "good stick." It was something he only heard from people over the age of 50.

Karabin spoke. "Isn't that the company you're investigating?" He was pointing at the red Running Dog logo on the side of the leather bag.

Bunker nodded. "Sure is. The driver of the Nissan had it in his back seat."

Pappy turned to Simon. The younger detective met his eyes and uttered, "What are the odds?"

Now sitting in his desk chair, Bunker stared at that same red logo.

Just what in the hell is going on with this company?

Before leaving the crash site, Bunker learned from Deputy Fatkin that the driver of the Sentra was William Pace Wylie and there were indications he was employed by Running Dog Enterprises. Fatkin promised to let Bunker know if this was confirmed. Bunker stood and stepped to the bag, pausing with his hands on his hips.

"Better get you secured."

Bunker carried both bags down a short hallway to the evidence room. There were two cameras mounted on the ceiling. They captured images in front of the door from different angles, ensuring anyone entering the room would be recorded. A card scanner was built into the door a few inches above the knob. Bunker sat the bags on the floor and withdrew a key card from his wallet. He slid the card—magnetic strip down—into a slot in the reader and heard the door's lock release. He turned to the cameras and gave a small wave before opening the door and pulling the bags inside.

The room was unspectacular, 12 feet wide and 20 feet deep. The far wall was bare. Shelves lined the other two. Bunker noted that barely a third of the shelf space was being utilized, the other two-thirds were empty.

The designers of this room may have overestimated the amount of space required for evidence in a rural county.

One side of his mouth curled up in a smile. He saw a couple flat screen TVs with white tags attached. One shelf held a number of video game systems—mainly PlayStations and Xboxes—also with white tags. On the left, Bunker noted a half dozen shoebox-sized plastic bins. Lids were tightly attached and held in place with a seal of security tape that ran the entire circumference of the bins. The tags on the bins were red. Bunker eyed them without expression.

The drug inventory.

Bunker knew that months earlier, the seal on a bin exactly like these had been sliced open and someone had tampered with three vials of morphine tablets. At that time, the only video camera trained on the door of the evidence room was some 30 feet away, and it had mysteriously malfunctioned. A furious Sheriff Hollis had the two cameras installed over the door a few days later and began an investigation that had yet to identify a suspect. In response, the sheriff limited access to the room to himself and his three detectives. Bunker shuffled to the far wall and stood the golf bag in the corner. He laid the nylon travel bag on the floor next to it. After locking the door on his way out, he returned to his office, where he was met by DeJean.

"I just received this from Champaign County." She handed Bunker a printed sheet of paper showing names and numbers. "It's the list of contact numbers and addresses you asked for."

Bunker accepted the paper and glanced at a wall clock, seeing that it was just past noon. "That was fast."

"They pulled the information from the emergency contact list. These are just the cellphone numbers. Home phone numbers will take longer."

Bunker nodded. He knew that Ohio counties maintained lists of cellphone numbers that allowed texts to go out during emergencies. This was often done in missing person situations.

Bunker removed the Glock and holster from his belt, laid them on his desk, and settled in to make calls. He was interrupted twice over the next 45 minutes—once by Pappy Karabin and once by Detective Simon. The two visits brought Bunker up to speed on the search for Kevin Turner, the person of interest in the shootings. There had been a break in the case. Turner's Visa card had finally been used. It happened at a gas station in Nelsonville in the southeastern part of the state. Karabin and Simon were coordinating search efforts with the sheriff and police departments in Athens County.

Bunker's calls generated little information. It seemed that the occupants of the rental had kept to themselves. He detected concern from a few of the neighbors who wondered why a law enforcement official was asking about renters in their immediate area. One woman, Julie Knotts, complained about the owners of the house.

"I told the Martins it would cause problems if they started renting out that house. But that damn Barney wouldn't change his mind. He's stubborn as a mule. We need to change the zoning laws here, or whatever, to prevent houses on this street from being rented."

"Yes, ma'am."

"Can you help with that?"

Bunker rubbed his temple.

"No ma'am, you'll have to work through your local officials."

The one bit of interesting information he picked up was from a woman who lived two houses away from the rental. Her name was Cindy Lybeck and she reported that her son rode his bike past the house a few days earlier and saw what he described as "a man in a spacesuit in the garage" when the outer door went up.

"But you have to understand, Andrew has a very active imagination...he's eight."

Bunker continued to make calls, often having to leave voicemail messages. Occasionally he received return calls. When his cellphone rang at 1:15, he assumed it was one of the neighbors. He checked the screen and was surprised to see the caller was J.D., the owner-operator of the tow truck that removed the Nissan Sentra from the accident scene outside Piqua.

"Hello, this is Bunker."

"Hello detective. J.D. here. Would you happen to be at your office?"

"I would."

"Good. I was hoping to catch you there. Listen, I took that wrecked Sentra out to our lot on the edge of town. After I unhooked it, I took a look inside. Not snoopin'...just wanted to make sure nothin' was left inside, y'know?"

"Sure, sure." Bunker made an effort to use a tone that put J.D. at ease. He was a former mechanic in the U.S. Army who now owned the towing business as well as an auto repair shop. He had an excellent reputation.

"And I saw a couple things on the floor of the rear seat. Must've been thrown under the front seats in the accident and slid out when I hooked up the car. I left the Sentra at our lot, but I was able to stretch my arm through the busted rear window and reach the floor. I'll be comin' past your parking lot in ten minutes. Any chance you can meet me out there?"

Bunker furrowed his brow.

"Yeah, sure J.D. See you out there in ten."

He hung up and stared out the window, wondering what J.D. could possibly have found. He knew that Deputy Fatkin had checked the car. It had seemed to Bunker that he had been very thorough. Bunker stood and reattached the holster to his belt. He flipped off the light and stepped through the doorway, noticing a lack of activity. The other offices were dark. He made his way to Gayle DeJean's desk. She finished a phone call and turned to him.

"Need something, Amos?"

"Actually, yes. Can I have the log for the evidence room? I need to make an entry."

DeJean removed a binder from a drawer and handed it to him. She reached for a second drawer. "What color tag do you need?"

"No tag. I'm just storing the accident victim's belongings there." He scribbled his signature in the designated box and looked around. "Quiet...where did everybody go?"

DeJean accepted the binder back and returned it to the drawer.

"The sheriff left a half hour ago; said he could be reached on his cell. He didn't say where he was going, but that's not unusual for him. Detective Simon went to lunch 20 minutes ago, and Pap—uh, Detective Karabin just left. He's meeting with someone that might provide background information on Kevin Turner."

Bunker nodded.

DeJean continued. "I might be ducking out to grab another late lunch. Can I get you anything? Chipotle again?"

Bunker checked his cellphone for messages and slipped it into his pocket.

"No...thanks for asking...but someone's swinging by to meet me outside in a few minutes. After we talk, I'll just hop in my car and grab something. Go ahead and mark me 'Out.'"

She smiled and gave a little wave as Bunker turned toward the door.

Five minutes later Bunker pushed open the door leading to the parking lot on the east side of the building. He squinted in the bright June sunshine and shaded his eyes. At almost the same instant a tow truck appeared a block away. Bunker walked to the sidewalk and waited a few seconds for it to reach him. As the truck came to a stop, it made a screeching sound.

Bunker leaned into the open passenger window and, with a grin, said, "Better take this thing somewhere and get those brakes looked at."

J.D. matched Bunker's grin.

"I just might know a guy." He winked.

As Bunker watched, J.D. reached into the console and withdrew something. He stretched his closed fist toward the window.

"Like I said, detective...they must've rolled out from under the front seat."

Bunker reached in with an open hand and felt something drop into his palm. He withdrew his hand and saw he was holding two golf balls.

Both had Running Dog logos.

CHAPTER THIRTY

Dylan approached Troy on State Route 55 in his Range Rover Evoque. He couldn't help feeling somewhat exposed. He knew that the detective—Bunker—had witnessed him driving away from Winans in the SUV the previous Monday. Dylan would feel more confident about a daylight meeting with the informant if he was driving something less conspicuous. But he decided it couldn't be helped. The rental car that Willie was driving at the time of the accident was gone. The Evoque was his only option.

After learning of the accident during the text exchange with the informant, Dylan allowed for the possibility that the situation wasn't as serious as it appeared. Those hopes were dashed less than a minute after receiving the informant's final text when Dylan—standing in the kitchen of the Airbnb and talking with Min—took a call from Zhou Yan in Newark.

"What the hell is going on out there? I received a call from a detective in Ohio asking for information about two Running Dog employees—obviously you and Min from his descriptions. He had the plate numbers of your vehicles. Then, minutes later, Willie's mother calls. She was extremely upset... tells me a deputy called her—again, from Ohio—to say that her son was in a serious car accident...that his condition is grave. Is this true?"

Dylan had to admit it appeared Willie had indeed been in an accident. He told Zhou that an informant had contacted him to say Willie had been flown by helicopter to a hospital in Dayton.

"Will he live?"

Dylan hesitated before admitting that he didn't know.

Zhou asked another question.

"If he does, will he talk to the police?"

Again, Dylan hesitated.

"No...no way. Not Willie."

He realized he sounded more confident than he felt. The words seemed to mollify Zhou somewhat.

"So you believe the situation can be managed? What about the detective...this Bunker?"

Dylan responded. "He is acting alone. His department is focused on another suspect, and another theory of the case."

Zhou seemed to brighten.

"Then we can continue to be evasive with him, as I was today. You move on from the area and he is left grasping at smoke. He can be...ignored, disregarded."

Dylan sighed. "He can't be ignored...he has the golf bag."

Zhou was well aware of the bag's significance and what was likely inside its pockets.

"You must get that bag back!"

Dylan respected Zhou. The man had been instrumental in selecting the specific maritime shipping route that Running Dog's products—including the loaded golf balls—took to Newark. Rather than a faster, more direct route that took 35 days, Zhou selected one that took an entire week longer. After departing China, a ship transited half the globe, passed through the Suez Canal, and reached Newark before continuing down the East Coast of the United States to Charleston, Savannah, and Miami. It was a journey of nearly 14,000 miles and less expensive than the quicker route. Dylan learned that it had the added advantage of port security contacts that Zhou had made during his varied career in exporting—contacts that might look the other way for a price.

Zhou had also selected the storage facility in Newark that housed Running Dog's products, keeping the drug balls in a secure area accessible only to him.

Though Dylan liked to impress opioid dealers with the fact that his organization brought the carfentanil into the country by the pallet, the reality was that they were still going through the first shipment of 18,000 balls. The second pallet was en route now from the production facility in Shenzhen. Zhou, no doubt, was anxious as he waited for the pallet to reach Newark safely. The last thing he needed was the discovery of the missing golf bag's contents.

After speaking with Zhou, Dylan called Dax to inform him of the developments. The one-time Columbia student focused on Willie's accident and seemed shaken by the news.

"How bad is he? Will he make it? Where is he now?"

The questions came at Dylan in quick succession and seemed to confirm something he'd suspected—Dax and Willie had formed a bond. They'd known each other longer than Dylan and Min knew either one. Willie's dislike for driving meant the two men spent a significant amount of time together when surveilling drug networks. Dax was obviously affected by the news.

"All I can tell you is it's bad and they've flown him to a hospital in Dayton. Are you still at the Home2 Suites?"

"Yeah, I was waiting for Willie...figured we'd grab lunch together. The meeting with Mahmud is supposed to be tomorrow night. Should I—"

Dylan interrupted. "Don't cancel it. We need to get him on board as soon as possible." He hesitated before delivering more bad news. "See, Willie was bringing the Running Dog bag."

Dax was silent for several seconds as he processed what this meant.

"So where the hell is it? Are we fucked?"

Dylan let out a short breath.

"No, not completely. It's in the Miami County Sheriff's Office, but—"

"*What?*" Dax was apoplectic.

Dylan attempted to calm him.

"They haven't opened it yet. They're storing it in a holding area until it's claimed by Willie's family. I'm working on a plan to get it back. I'm meeting with the informant today to get more information." He paused. "It's that goddamned Bunker again, the detective that's been dogging us...he's the key. I need a way to get to him. We can still come out golden."

Dax sounded doubtful.

"You sure we shouldn't just bolt?"

Dylan fought to keep his cool. The situation—Willie's status, the loss of the golf bag, and the juggling of multiple deals with illegal opioid networks—was complicated. Dylan believed he could navigate his way through it. He needed everybody onboard.

"No, not yet. I need you to find out where Miami Valley Hospital is located and get over there. See what you can find out about Willie. Tell them you're a family member—maybe a cousin. Min and I will work on getting the bag back. Plan on meeting Mahmud...you might have to go solo."

Dax seemed assured.

"Got it."

Dylan was now inside the Troy city limits. He checked the Evoque's GPS display and saw that his destination—an address on Adams Street—was a few blocks away. Dylan had considered the situation for the entire drive to Troy. A part of him was amazed that the golf bag hadn't been examined. It made no sense. Natural human curiosity would seem to be reason enough to peek inside. The fact that the driver—Willie —was involved in a serious accident made it more likely. Yet there was no indication that the investigation into Running Dog's activities had intensified.

Apparently, the Miami County Sheriff's personnel— with the exception of the informant—are honest to a fault.

Dylan and Min had discussed the possibility that the rendezvous could be a trap. After careful consideration, Dylan dismissed it.

We know the informant was accepting pills from the Shortridge brothers in exchange for providing information on investigations. Dax and Willie made contact to set up the same arrangement with us. For today's meet to be a setup, that would mean all the previous activity was part of a sting operation—very unlikely. No, this is someone that could've shut down the Shortridge operation months ago but has decided the free pills are more important.

After that discussion, Dylan sent Min to the former precinct school for the exchange with Woodruff. He then prepared for his own meeting.

Can't forget to take the vial of pills.

As he approached his destination, Dylan shot a quick glance at the Evoque's console where he'd stashed the vial. He slowed and engaged his left turn signal, then waited for approaching traffic to pass by. He turned his head to survey the building. It was an expansive facility whose exterior was primarily light brown brick. The center section was a monolith-like block of concrete, perhaps 40 feet high and 80 feet wide, that was dotted with windows and a number of wide glass doors. Red, three-dimensional script letters were mounted near the top of the concrete, spelling out *Hobart Arena*.

When the traffic passed, Dylan wheeled into an entrance drive and past a large LED display sign that stood near the sidewalk. The sign's frame bore the name of the arena in the same red script. The screen was lit with the message: REO SPEEDWAGON...JULY 15. Dylan pulled past the sign and turned into a large, mostly empty, parking lot on the right side of the building. He saw a handful of vehicles parked near a side entrance—apparently staffers of some sort—but no sign of the informant's vehicle. This did not surprise him as he was more than ten minutes early for the 2 p.m. meeting. He steered to the far side of the lot and backed up against a parking block near a shade tree. From this vantage point he would see any vehicle entering the lot. Dylan checked the sky—storms were in the forecast—saw no sign of rain and rolled down his front windows.

Hobart Arena was a 3,782 seat multi-purpose arena that opened in 1950. It had hosted minor league hockey, the Harlem Globetrotters, professional wrestling, and trade shows. Numerous musical performers appeared there, including 21-year-old Elvis Presley on November 24, 1956. It was built on a floodplain on Adams Street, just north of the Miami River, which flowed through the center of Troy. The high bank of an earthen levee stood between the river and the arena's parking lot.

Dylan sat nervously, the rear of the Evoque pointed toward the levee. He was in a fairly secluded spot but was well aware that the Miami County Sheriff's Office was just a few short blocks away, across the Adams Street Bridge.

I have to admit, it's pretty ballsy to arrange illegal drug transactions this close to a building where your entire department works.

Minutes later, Dylan watched as a dark blue Chevy Suburban turned off of Adams Street and entered the lot. It was the vehicle that he'd expected. It pulled slowly past the cars of the staffers before its driver spotted the Range Rover. It turned in Dylan's direction and rolled hesitantly toward him, finally coming to a stop next to the Evoque. The two SUVs faced opposite directions, so the driver's side windows were just a few short feet from each other.

Dylan watched as the Suburban's window lowered. He peered at the driver.

"Hello Gayle."

A nervous smile appeared on Gayle DeJean's face, then quickly disappeared.

"You're Dylan?"

He nodded. "Thanks for meeting on short notice. Forgive me for getting right to the point, but I don't want to sit here any longer than necessary. Do you have the file?"

DeJean nodded and reached for something on the passenger seat. She came up with a manilla envelope and held it where Dylan could see.

"Did you bring the..." She left the word unsaid.

"Yeah, right here." He patted the console. "First, I have some questions."

DeJean looked nervously over a shoulder, then focused on Dylan. "Okay, I thought you might...your two guys I met with said you're the boss...well, they didn't really say that, I just got that impression. I know about bosses. They want all the facts." She gave another brief smile.

Dylan appraised DeJean. She had dark brown hair and wore a pair of expensive looking glasses. She looked exactly like the photo Willie surreptitiously snapped of her when he and Dax witnessed her meeting Gerard Shortridge in this very parking lot nearly two weeks earlier. A few days later they arranged a meeting with her, and she selected the same site. She appeared to be intelligent and—despite nervously checking her surroundings every few seconds—seemed comfortable with the location. Willie's impression of DeJean was that she was hopelessly hooked on the painkillers and would do just about anything to maintain a consistent source.

Willie's exact words were, "She has the look of someone who's taken a drive down the Dope Sick Highway and never wants to travel that road again."

Dylan spoke. "Give it to me straight...can you get that golf bag out of the building?"

DeJean closed her eyes and shook her head.

"No...no way. Only four people can get into the evidence room. Other people—me included—had access at one time but, uh, some drug evidence came up missing and the sheriff clamped down. Now it's just him and the three detectives. They have key cards...there are security cameras, a sign-in sheet...it's pretty regulated."

Dylan held her eyes for a beat before she looked away. He was fairly certain he knew who was responsible for the disappearance of the evidence room drugs.

Okay, she can't get the bag. Even if she could, we would still have the other problem—Bunker. He's already looking at us and if the bag disappeared, he would make sure we become the focus for the entire department. Eventually they'll realize the other suspect they're looking at for the murders is a dead end. We need to get the bag back AND deal with Bunker.

"Okay, let's see what you have in the envelope." He reached his hand through the window.

DeJean again checked the surroundings before bringing the envelope up to her chest.

"And...the stuff?"

Dylan looked at her closely, noticing for the first time that a thin film of perspiration coated her forehead.

She's hurting.

His hand disappeared back inside the Evoque. When it reappeared, it held the vial. DeJean's face betrayed a brief flicker of relief. They made the exchange.

Dylan slid two printed pages from the envelope. A photo appeared near the top of the first page. He stared at it, seeing the face of a man with light grey hair.

So this is Bunker.

Dylan had wondered if he would recognize the man as someone he'd seen in the last week. Bunker had obviously been investigating him and had been close enough to gather some information. But the face on the page was not familiar. He began to scan the sheet for details.

"So, I have to get back, but how is this going to work with the Shortridge brothers gone?"

Dylan looked up from the personnel file to see a questioning look on DeJean's face.

Jesus, the pills I just gave her should last weeks but she's already trolling for her next batch. She's got it bad.

"We've got that covered. New people are already in place. I'll have them contact you to set up regular deliveries."

Again, DeJean's face showed relief. She actually closed her eyes and exhaled, as if a weight had been lifted from her shoulders.

Dylan continued. "But this is a two-way street. We're going to need things from time to time."

DeJean smiled and nodded. "Sure, I understand." She put the Suburban in reverse and prepared to pull away.

"Hold on there." Dylan's voice had a hard edge. "I have more questions."

DeJean's smile vanished. She put the transmission back in park.

Dylan continued to scan the personnel file. He spoke without looking at DeJean.

"Tell me about this dog."

She was momentarily confused, then responded.

"Zeke? Well, he's amazing. They have a lot of money invested in him. He can detect drugs *and* explosives which, I guess, is pretty uncommon. They use him to check school lockers when a kid calls in a bomb threat...that kind of thing. But mostly he and his handler, Deputy Kuhlman—Jill—are used to detect drugs. They're really careful with him because some of the stuff out there," she paused for the briefest of seconds to glance at the vial in her hand, "can be dangerous to the dog. They only bring him in to check the seized drugs in the evidence room a couple times a month...I guess to limit his exposure."

Dylan nodded. He was aware that detection dogs took rapid, deep breaths when they found drug odors. Substances like heroin powder could easily be disturbed into light clouds that a dog might inhale. A number of detection dogs had suffered overdoses, with a few being saved by the quick use of opioid antagonist drugs designed to be used on humans. He made a mental note to pick up more bottles of naloxone nasal spray.

Probably ought to have one in every vehicle.

Dylan was aware of the danger of the pure carfentanil. He realized that he and his colleagues may be getting a bit too comfortable when working with the balls.

DeJean interpreted Dylan's silence as an invitation to continue. "When Zeke smells the drugs, he just sits and stares at the location."

Dylan looked up from the file. He remembered the stories of trained dogs being used in the Running Dog facility to see if the loaded balls were detectable. Some dogs are trained to react actively when they discover a substance. Usually this is manifested by the dog making a digging motion. Other dogs alert passively and act exactly in the manner DeJean described.

Zeke sounds like the real deal. He is damn sure to sniff the coverless ball in that golf bag, even though it's inside a plastic bag. He'll probably alert to gunpowder residue on the putter, too. If they take it apart, they'll discover the firing mechanism. Ballistics can match it to several murders. We'll be cooked. The golf bag absolutely has to be out of that room before Wednesday.

He exhaled. "Okay, I have some questions about Bunker."

DeJean looked uncomfortable. She liked Amos and had no desire to bring harm to him. Still, she needed the pills.

"Is he married...have kids?"

"Uh, no. He's single, no kids."

"Girlfriend?"

DeJean's unease increased. She realized that she felt a slight sense of relief after giving her answer.

"No, no girlfriend. He was engaged at one time, but something happened, I guess, and that fell through."

Dylan frowned. "Any family nearby? Anyone at all?"

DeJean swallowed. "Well, his mother lives here in town...he's really close to her." She felt a quiver of dread as soon as the words left her mouth. She quickly added, "But she's about to go into a nursing home. She has some kind of dementia."

Dylan returned his focus to the personnel file and ran an index finger down the first page until he found a heading for emergency contacts. He found Dana Bunker's name, address, and phone number. He smiled. An idea was forming in his mind.

"Okay, Gayle. You should hear from the people who are taking over for the Shortridges in a few days. Thanks for the information." Dylan turned his attention to the Range Rover's navigation screen.

DeJean realized she was being dismissed. Her eyes moved from Dylan to the vial of tablets. She closed her eyes as a wave of shame swept over her. She pushed it away and shifted the Suburban into reverse.

Dylan finished punching Dana Bunker's address into his navigation system and looked up as DeJean's Suburban pulled away, halted, then turned toward the parking lot's exit. As it pulled away, Dylan noticed two stickers on the SUV's rear window. Both read *DAYTON CLASSICS*. Under one was the name "Brady." Under the second was "Cody."

Dylan watched as the Suburban turned onto Adams Street.

Even soccer moms.

Plum Street was just a few blocks north of Hobart Arena, across the Adams Street Bridge. Dylan noted that there were two routes to get there but one would take him past the sheriff's office. He selected the second route and found himself rolling down Plum five minutes later. It featured two-story brick homes on mid-sized lots dotted with large trees.

Dana Bunker's house blended with the rest of the neighborhood. A brick step below the front door led to a narrow sidewalk that curved to a driveway on the left side of the house. The driveway was coated with black asphalt sealer and was just wide enough for one vehicle. It ended at a small garage—also brick—that sat several feet beyond the left rear corner of the house.

Dylan rolled slowly past the house, observing as many details as possible. He pulled into a driveway several houses away and reversed his route. He noted that Dana's house seemed curiously isolated, despite its proximity to neighbors. He decided the trees had something to do with this.

Okay...there's a Ring doorbell on the front door. Not sure if it has a view of the driveway. Maybe another one on the back door, can't tell from here. The back of the house looks pretty secluded—trees guard it from three sides.

Dylan pulled to the curb. He saw how it could be done. He needed to confirm that Bunker's mom was in the house. DeJean mentioned that she was supposed to be moved to a nursing facility. He searched for her contact information on Bunker's personnel file and found a number next to "Home Phone." He dialed.

The call was answered after four rings. A hesitant voice answered.

"Hello?"

Dylan listened for a while then smiled as he hung up.

Dylan picked his way through residential streets, heading generally south. He selected Min's name from the favorites on his cell phone's contact list and dialed. Min answered on the first ring and immediately launched into a summary of his exchange with Steve Woodruff.

"It went well. He had all the cash. He was very happy to get the...inventory. I believe he will be a very popular man. What is the joke in America? He could run for mayor."

Dylan brushed aside the comments.

"Okay, that's good, that's good. Listen, we have a job to do. We have to act fast—tonight. I'll be back at the rental in an hour or so. Order a pizza and have it delivered. I need you to get some things ready." He dictated a short list.

Min listened without questioning. He knew he would hear the specifics in person later and avoided asking for details over an open line.

Dylan wrapped up the call as he drove south out of Troy. A minute later he reached his destination and turned in, past a sign that read: *WACO Museum & Aviation Learning Center*. The cluster of buildings that he'd noticed days earlier were directly ahead. He was more interested in the area beyond. He entered a parking lot on the right side of the complex and drove slowly through it, checking the terrain beyond. A grin formed on his face.

Oh yeah, this is the spot. Now...where can I buy a flower arrangement?

CHAPTER THIRTY-ONE

Bunker returned to his office in the middle of the afternoon. He sat a Diet Coke and a bag containing a turkey sub on his desk before removing the Aker holster holding his Glock. He settled heavily into his chair.

"Ow, dammit!"

He felt pain near his groin and was momentarily confused. He reached to touch the spot and quickly assessed the problem. The two golf balls that J.D. had given him were still in his right front pocket. They'd apparently shifted position as he took the steps to the second floor. He dug them out of his pocket and carefully placed them on the desk. He guessed that the balls may have been in the unzipped top pocket of the golf bag and had been dislodged during the crash. He adjusted them so the red Running Dog logos were facing him.

Bunker removed the sub from the bag and unwrapped it, leaving the paper underneath. He took a bite and sat back in his chair, keeping his eyes on the logos.

Running Dog is connected to these murders somehow...I can feel it.

He checked his email and found nothing of importance. He'd received a return call from one of the neighbors on Country Road while his sub was being made. The employee—Subway called them 'Sandwich Artists'—was asking Bunker what kind of cheese he wanted when he took the call. Trying to be as professional as possible, Bunker listened to the caller in silence as he pointed to his preferred cheese. The "Artist," Bunker now realized, misunderstood. This was how his sandwich ended up with pepperjack instead of swiss. Bunker frowned, swallowed the first bite, then disassembled the sub and tossed the offending pepperjack into his waste basket.

The office was quiet. Gayle DeJean was out, as were the other two detectives. Bunker noticed a light in Sheriff Hollis's office when he'd walked in and heard him speaking on the phone. This reminded Bunker that he had to put together a daily report on his progress in the investigation before leaving the office for the day.

Bunker spent the remainder of the afternoon doing follow-up calls and working on the report. Although his gut told him the Running Dog connection was the key to solving the murders, he realized that he had little tangible evidence in his update. Late in the afternoon he was able to speak on the phone to Deputy Fatkin, who was communicating with the staff of Miami Valley Hospital in Dayton.

"Any update on William Wylie?"

Fatkin's response was concise.

"Critical condition. The docs are being cautious because of HIPAA, but it sounds like he's in a coma...multiple fractures on the left side of his body—pelvis, femur—also the skull. There seems to be a number of internal injuries. I'm just speculating here, but his ribcage took a helluva shot. I wouldn't be surprised if they cracked and ripped up a lung... maybe even damaged his heart. I've seen it before."

Bunker agreed with this possibility. He'd spent time as a deputy working accident scenes and was well aware of the damage this type of crash could inflict.

Fatkin continued. "I'm told the victim's parents are on their way from Rhode Island. There were no direct flights from Providence to Dayton, so they won't get here until sometime tomorrow after a layover at Washington National." He paused. "We'll see what they want to do about the personal items from the rental car."

Bunker thought again about the bags in the evidence room. It was getting more and more tempting to disregard policy and examine their contents. He dismissed the thought.

"What's your read on this, Deputy...will Wylie make it?"

Fatkin gave a short pause before answering.

"Pretty damn doubtful."

It was nearly 5 p.m. when Bunker closed his office door. He'd turned in his report and spoken to both Simon and Karabin, who had returned to their offices late in the afternoon to complete their own paperwork. The three detectives shared their progress. Bunker learned that Kevin Turner's credit card had again been used. This time it was to purchase two tickets from a business called Hocking Valley Scenic Railway that operated train rides for tourists through the picturesque foothills of the Appalachian Mountains, an area known for cliffs, gorges, and waterfalls.

Karabin elaborated, "We were hoping he bought them for a ride in the next few days, but the tickets are for a trip in October to view fall foliage. So we know where he'll be on October 4th, for all the good that does us." He paused and narrowed his eyes. "Are you getting anywhere with that other angle?"

Bunker had to admit that things had stalled. "I spent the afternoon on the phone...didn't come up with much."

"Might be time to drop it, Detective."

Bunker walked past Gayle's desk on his way out of the office. She'd just shut down her computer and was fishing her keys from her purse.

"Have a good night, Gayle. See you tomorrow."

"You too, Amos." DeJean watched Bunker walk out the door before murmuring quietly.

"Take care of yourself."

Bunker decided to visit his mother on the way home. He knew that she hadn't been eating regularly and decided, despite having eaten a late lunch, to pick up food. He made the short drive east on Main through the traffic circle and parked in front of K's Hamburger Shop, a restaurant that was established in 1935. He entered under an art deco neon light that read "EAT," and emerged 15 minutes later with two chocolate malts and a bag containing burgers and fries.

Okay, not the most nutritious food in the world, but if she hasn't eaten today at least it provides calories.

He drove the Malibu to Plum Street and parked in the driveway. He walked to the front door with his hands full and used a knuckle to engage the Ring doorbell. As the distinctive three-note tone rang through the house, Bunker turned on the stoop and casually observed the street. When the door hadn't been answered thirty seconds later, he rang again. Glancing through the trees to the west he saw dark clouds forming and remembered storms were in the forecast.

Bunker turned back to the door and tried to peer through one of the small windows on its side. He was beginning to get concerned. He had just sat the food on the stoop and was digging for his keys when he noticed furtive movement at the edge of the window. He rapped softly on the door.

"Mom, open up. It's me...Amos."

When the door eased open Bunker saw immediately that his mom was having a bad day. She appeared nervous and looked over his shoulder to the street beyond.

"Come in...hurry!"

Bunker frowned and walked inside.

"You okay, Mom?"

She closed the door and locked it before turning to him.

"It's happening again. They're back! Phone calls... people spying on me from the street...it's not safe!"

Bunker regarded her and recognized the same wild look in her eyes he'd seen many times in the past few months.

Shit.

It took several minutes to convince her to sit and eat. He picked up the handset on the counter and scrolled through its call history.

"There's just one call here from an odd number, Mom. I'm sure it was just a spam call." He glanced at the answering machine and saw there were no voicemails. "I wouldn't worry too much."

"When I answered there was someone on the line...they just listened for a while then hung up on me."

"Just a wrong number...or a telemarketer that didn't engage quick enough. Sometimes that happens. You pick up a spam call and it's silent on the other end. I think they use an autodialer and have so few people answer the phone that they're not ready to talk when someone actually picks up."

He could see that she was unconvinced. He was relieved when she finally settled down and ate most of her meal. When he left an hour later the sky had darkened and the first drops of rain had begun to fall.

"See you tomorrow, Mom. I'll be by in the morning to help clean out the attic. I'll stop for donuts."

Dana looked warily past the open door before meeting his eyes. She seemed a bit more at ease.

"Thank you, Amos. You're a good boy."

An hour later Min's Range Rover turned onto Plum Street. He was at the wheel. Dylan sat in the passenger seat wearing a ball cap and a waterproof golf jacket. The rain had come down in fits and starts for the last 20 minutes, with each resurgence being marginally heavier than its predecessor.

"It's up there, Min. On the left. Let's do a drive-by and get a good look."

Min nodded and steered south on Plum. The Range Rover's wipers glided back and forth on their low setting. The cloud cover was sufficient to activate the Evoque's automatic headlights. They cruised past the house and were gratified to see there were no vehicles in the driveway or parked on the street in front.

As they passed, Dylan asserted, "Looks good. I see a light on through one of the downstairs windows. I say we do it just the way I laid it out earlier."

He was referring to the conversation the men had at the Airbnb when Dylan returned from his trip to Troy earlier in the day. He believed Bunker's mother, with her health issues, was probably no longer driving. Her vehicle—if she still owned one—would be safely tucked away inside the detached garage. Any vehicle parked in the driveway or in front of the house would've been driven by a visitor, hampering their plan.

Min offered an opinion. "I agree. We know she is there. The phone call confirmed that. She must be alone. I will drive around the block and approach from this same direction."

Dylan had placed a second call to Dana Bunker's home phone a few minutes earlier and again hung up when he heard her answer.

As Min steered the Evoque through the residential area, Dylan prepared. He slipped on rubber gloves before zipping shut the jacket and pulling its hood over the top of his ball cap. He checked the jacket's front right pocket to make sure the envelope was there. Then he twisted in his seat and retrieved two items: first, a can of black spray paint and second, a floral arrangement in a blue vase.

Min flicked a glance at his partner and cracked, "I will hate to see the flowers go. They make this vehicle smell so fresh." He grinned.

Dylan ignored the comment. He'd purchased the arrangement at a small flower shop a few blocks from downtown Troy. His requirement was that the display needed to be large enough to obscure his face when he approached the door on Plum Street. The counter attendant mistook his scrutiny of the available choices as the indecisiveness of a confused shopper. She asked a number of questions about the occasion and the recipient. Dylan deflected the questions and selected the blue vase, which held—the attendant happily added—cream roses, white Asiatic lilies, and something called purple statice.

"Oh that is a wonderful choice. It's perfect to cheer up someone in the hospital...or as a gift for that special someone?" This last part came out as a question.

Dylan simply smiled, ignoring the mini interrogation.

The attendant took the hint.

"Cash or charge?"

Dylan stared at the flowers.

They're also wide enough to easily hide the face of a kidnapper.

"Cash."

The Range Rover completed its trip around the block and approached the target house. It looked exactly as it had minutes before. Min turned into the driveway and continued along the side of the house, turning off the SUV's headlights as he neared the garage. He put the transmission in park and reached below the seat where he'd stashed a roll of duct tape and Willie's Ruger pistol. He saw that Dylan was already out of the vehicle and muttered, "Zhù nǐ shùnlì"—*I hope it goes well.*

Dana Bunker sat in a recliner staring at the TV. *Antiques Roadshow*, a program she usually enjoyed, was on with the sound turned low. She'd had a bad day. The visit by Amos had helped her rally a bit. The food he'd brought also seemed to give her a boost. Before he left, he made sure she took some medication. She had now reached the point where she at least *realized* she'd had a bad day. It was—she'd come to understand—the first stage of a return to her normal self. She always felt a degree of relief when she floated back from the darkness and confusion. At the same time, she was frightened. She couldn't control the slide, no matter how hard she tried.

I'm afraid it's happening more often. Is it happening more often? I'm losing touch with...what is the word...reality.

Her mind seemed to operate in a trance-like state. She found it difficult to connect thoughts and concepts like she had done her whole life.

So frustrating!

She feared she'd become a tremendous burden for Amos.

Such a good boy. He works so hard.

A tear ran down her cheek and she dabbed at it with an index finger. She stared at it, confused.

What?—

The three tones of her Ring doorbell rang through the house, causing her to flinch.

What is that? Is there danger?

Her mind seized upon thoughts from earlier in the day. There were phone calls. Men stalking her. The ringing continued.

ding-ding-DING...ding-ding-DING

She stood.

It's the doorbell. Have they come for me?

She shuffled to the front door and pulled a corner of the curtain away from a small window at its side. She peered outside.

Nothing.

The tones began again.

ding-ding-DING...ding-ding DING

The back door. Someone must be at the back door. Wait. Amos showed me how to see outside on my cellphone.

She returned to the chair and reached for the phone on the small wooden stand next to it. She preferred to speak on her home phone, but Amos had given her an iPhone two years earlier. She used it to play solitaire and, in situations like this, to access the doorbell cameras. She picked up the phone and automatically touched her thumb to the indented circle at the bottom, not quite sure why. The screen brightened and half a page of app icons appeared. Her finger hovered over the solitaire icon—she supposed out of habit—then pushed the blue symbol next to it labelled "ring."

Doing a little better now. Starting to figure things out.

She watched as split screens appeared. The top view showed Plum Street. The bottom screen was black.

ding-ding-DING...ding-ding-DING

That darn bell! Must be the back door. Something wrong with the camera.

She made her way back through the kitchen and cautiously approached the door. She noticed a bag from K's Hamburger Shop on the table.

Where did that come from? Did I have K's?

There were no curtains on the window of the rear door, so Dana stopped a few feet away and focused. She saw the form of a man and began to panic, then realized he was holding an arrangement of beautiful white flowers. The man pressed an envelope to the window. She stepped closer and made out a few handwritten words—*To Mom, From Amos.*

Dana smiled and reached for the doorknob.

CHAPTER THIRTY-TWO

Bunker lay sprawled on his couch, mechanically cycling through channels on his flat screen TV with the remote. He changed out of his work clothes as soon as he returned from his mom's house and now wore sweats and a well-worn hoodie that featured the logo of the St. Louis Blues hockey team. He'd hoped to mow the grass after work, but the rain had taken that out of play. He checked the time and saw it was 7:39. He continued to click through the channels until he came across an old episode of *Star Trek*. It was the original version of the series with William Shatner as Captain Kirk and Leonard Nimoy as Mr. Spock. He saw that it was the episode that featured Ron Howard's younger brother Clint, who plays an alien named Balok.

Bunker was a bit of a Trekkie, though certainly not to the extent of the loonies who attended the conventions. He remembered watching reruns as a kid and favoring the episodes where the characters used their phasers to battle villains. He was a typical boy, he supposed. Much more into the gadgets and action than the moral lessons the show offered.

He pushed the information button to see the name of the episode: "The Corbomite Maneuver, Original Air Date 1966."

Bunker smiled as young Howard—he looked to be seven or eight years old—spoke to Shatner.

It's amusing that every single alien in that series spoke English. I mean, couldn't they at least have added a plot device that said the crew was equipped with a universal translation tool that allowed them to communicate with a Romulan or a Klingon? They have every other gadget—

A tone sounded from his cellphone indicating an incoming text. He lifted it from the couch and turned it to view the screen. The message was from a number he didn't recognize. The screen showed that an image was attached. He would ordinarily delete something like this without opening it but saw the accompanying text.

Detective Bunker, important info here related to your current investigation.

He eyed the message and felt his eyebrows rise slightly.
Has to be from one of the neighbors on Country Road. New information? Could be a break.

He opened the attachment and stiffened. It was an image of his mom. She had duct tape over her mouth and her eyes had a look of panic—one he'd never seen.
What the hell?!?

Now standing, he began to type a response, then stopped. Instead he called the number. It was picked up after the first ring. A man spoke.

"That got your attention, didn't it Detective Bunker?"

The voice sounded in control.

Bunker fought to keep his composure.

"Who is this? Where is she?"

"No names, Amos. Just a guy on the phone...a guy that needs something. You can get it for me. Interested in making a trade?"

Bunker was pacing.

"What?!? What are you talking about? Listen, if anything happens to my mom—"

The voice grew cold.

"What? If anything happens to her...what? Are you threatening me?"

Bunker took a breath.

"No...just...let her go. Where is she? I'll come and get her."

"It's not going to be that easy, Amos. You can get her back, but as I said, I'll need something in return."

"Money? How much? I have some savings, I..." Then he understood.

The text said this had something to do with an investigation. That can only mean one thing.

"The golf bag. The goddamned golf bag." It came out as a statement, not a question. Bunker knew.

"Now you're getting it. You have my bag in the evidence room. I need it back and you're going to get it for me."

Bunker was confused.

"How did you—"

"How did I know it's in the evidence room? I know a lot of things, Amos. I know only four people can get inside that room and you're one of them. I know that a drug detection dog will be inside the room Wednesday morning. I know that you're not married, have no kids, and you and your fiancé split up. That leaves mom as my best bargaining chip. How am I doing...pretty accurate?"

Before Bunker could answer, the man continued.

"I know everything that's going on inside your office. And here's more bad news for you...I also have a source in the FBI. If you try to get them involved, you'll never see your mom again, got it?"

Bunker tried to process this information. The mention of his breakup with Sarah struck a nerve, but the revelation that this man had sources inside law enforcement—inside *his department*—was stunning.

"I said GOT IT?"

"Yeah, got it." Bunker forced himself to concentrate on the conversation and push away the emotion.

"Okay, this is what you're going to do. I need you to go into the office tomorrow and remove that bag from the evidence room. Call me when you have it. Then, tomorrow night we'll meet and do the exchange—I'll let you know where. Do NOT bring a weapon to the exchange. Is that clear?"

"Yeah, it's clear."

"Good. That's all for now. Remember. If you try to pull something, mom is gone."

Bunker sensed that the man was about to hang up.

"WAIT!"

The man paused. In an annoyed voice he asked, "What? What is it?"

"I need to know that she's alive."

The voice was dismissive. "You saw the photo. That's proof that—"

"That's proof of nothing. It shows that she was alive when the picture was taken. I need to know that she's alive now."

The line was silent for a few seconds as the man apparently considered the request. Bunker heard some distortion. It sounded as if a microphone was being covered. He then heard the man's voice again, appearing more distant.

"Take the tape off her mouth."

Bunker strained to pick up any sound. He thought he heard a short ripping sound, followed by a single word—"Oh!"

Bunker knew.

Mom...that's Mom!

The connection became clearer and the man's voice reappeared.

"Say hello to your son."

Bunker pressed the cellphone tighter to his ear.

"Go ahead, it's okay. Say hello."

A tentative voice spoke his name.

"Amos?"

Bunker closed his eyes, then blurted, "Mom are you okay?!?"

The man's voice came back.

"There...satisfied?"

Bunker felt anger wash over him.

"Look you son of a bitch, if you hurt—"

"Whoa, whoa, whoa. Hold on there. I'm not sure you're getting it, detective. You're not in charge here. You *will* do what we're asking or...well...things won't end well for Dana here." He paused to let his words sink in before adding, "Get that goddamned bag tomorrow and call me. I'll expect to hear from you by 9 a.m."

The line went dead.

Bunker slid open a drawer on his coffee table and searched through miscellaneous items inside until he found a pen and a pad of paper. He needed to get his thoughts in order and felt there was no better way than to get them down on paper.

At the top of the page he wrote *Source?—Informant?*

Below that he jotted three names: *Pappy Karabin, Cody Simon, Sheriff Hollis.*

He stared at the list for a few seconds before adding two more: *Gayle DeJean, Deputy Fatkin.*

He spent the next several minutes writing short sentences under the names.

Has access to personnel records.

Knows location of golf bag.

Knows about breakup with Sarah.

There were several others. In the end, the exercise did little to reduce the number of candidates. The possible exception, he believed, was Fatkin. Bunker did not believe the deputy knew about his breakup. That left four possibles. Midway through his task it struck him that Pappy, Simon, or Hollis—if they were the informant—could simply remove the bag from storage themselves. He then realized that it wasn't a coincidence that he—the only detective working the Running Dog angle in the murders—hadn't been targeted solely for his access to the room.

This guy wants to get rid of me, not just get the bag back.

The thought was chilling. Not because he might be singled out for elimination, but because of what it meant for his mom.

If he takes me out, no way Mom comes out of this alive.

He went back to the notepad. What did he actually know about the people on his list?

Detective Simon seemed smart, capable. A former athlete. Could he be involved in this? What would be his motivation?

Money, of course.

Pappy was a respected investigator, but difficult to read. He seemed distant, aloof.

He's been different lately...asking about Mom...trying to get me to move away from my investigation.

313

Sheriff Hollis had moved to the area at a young age. He'd been an Air Force brat; his father having served for many years. The family had lived near several bases before finally settling near Wright-Patt. Hollis was more of a political animal than the rest of the names on the list combined.

That alone opens up several possibilities for corruption.

And Gayle, though she didn't have access to the evidence room, compiled the daily reports for the sheriff and could therefore view the progress of the investigation.

Plus she definitely knows about my breakup with Sarah.

Bunker reviewed the notes and shook his head.

My lean would have to be Pappy. Could he really be involved in this?

He decided there was no way to determine the informant based on the information he possessed.

I have to proceed as if it's any of them. I'm on my own. If I confide in the wrong person, the kidnapper will find out. He mentioned having a source in the FBI. Going to them would be the natural next step in a situation like this. But if I do—and the kidnapper finds out...

Bunker didn't finish the thought, knowing how such a scenario might play out for his mom. He had a thought and scribbled another note at the bottom of the page.

Two Perpetrators.

The caller had asked a second person to remove tape from his mother's mouth.

The identity of the traitor in his department was still undetermined, but Bunker suspected from the moment the caller began speaking that he knew who was involved in the kidnapping.

It's those two guys I saw meeting with the Shortridge brothers last week...the guy in the golf clothes—Eli?—and the Asian man—he has to be Chinese. They're connected to the murders. Probably committed them. They're definitely kidnappers...and there's something in that damn golf bag that's made them desperate—and dangerous.

Bunker stood and paced again. He concentrated on his notes while he reviewed the phone conversation.

What did I miss?

Reaching his small dining room, he tossed the pad on the table and took a seat. Bunker slumped forward and put both elbows on the table. He rubbed his temples with his fingertips, deep in thought. The rain had picked up and occasional gusts of wind directed it more forcefully against the kitchen window. Slowly, understanding came to him.

They're going to kill us—both of us. They want the bag and they want to blunt my investigation of Running Dog. They've been killing people at out of the way locations— Garrett and Gerard Shortridge at Wesley Chapel Cemetery— Shadow Donald at that novelty loaf of bread in Urbana...who knows how many others there might be.

Bunker considered his options. He saw only one.

I have to go after them...get Mom back myself. They must have her at that house on Country Road.

Bunker was relatively familiar with the location, having been there twice, once when he followed the Range Rovers from Winans and a second time when he briefly parked down the street from the rental house and watched for activity.

I'll have to go in after her.

He ran through several scenarios of how it might play out. There could be a gunfight. People could be killed. He decided if it came to that, he would answer for it later. First, his mom needed to be freed.

No telling what kind of shape she'll be in. I'll probably have to carry her. So, I drive there, go in after her, get her to my car and drive out? The car needs to be close.

Ideas were appearing to Bunker in quick succession. He disregarded some and considered others. One thought swam into his head and threatened to override all others.

She tried to tell you she was being watched. You ignored her.

He pushed this accusation away—time to deal with that later—and returned to his train of thought. He could think of no way that a rescue of his mother could be pulled off alone.

315

I'll need a second person. Someone to drive the car.

He couldn't trust anyone in his department. He didn't dare go to the FBI.

He would need someone capable. Someone willing to do what was right, even if it was technically outside the law.

He thought back to the paperwork he'd worked on Friday, the background information for the state's adoption program.

I think I know someone.

CHAPTER THIRTY-THREE

"This is ridiculous. What kind of a sick, twisted individual thinks something like this is appropriate?"

Paul Hull sat at his dining room table staring at the disarray in front of him.

Lauren giggled. "My mom, remember?"

She sat in a chair next to him, their shoulders nearly touching. Spread out on the table in front of them were a thousand puzzle pieces, virtually all of them displaying some shade of green.

"I've always liked your mom...maybe I need to reconsider."

"Paul!" Lauren gave him a playful punch on the shoulder.

He frowned. He had a puzzle piece in his hand. His eyes flicked from it to the upturned box that showed the scene they were trying to reproduce.

"No one gives a present like this to someone they love. You give a puzzle like this to someone you're trying to drive insane. Maybe I've misjudged her all these years."

He turned the puzzle piece upside down, shrugged, and laid it back on the table.

Lauren giggled again.

"It's been in the closet since she gave it to me for my birthday last year. You saaaiiid that I get to decide what we do tonight before you leave for Illinois tomorrow."

"Well, yeah. But I thought you would pick out a movie, or maybe walk barefoot on broken glass. You know, something fun...not this."

She punched him again, this time a little harder.

Paul's on-again, off-again trip to Illinois was back on. He'd thought that the morning Zoom call with the representatives from the grocery store network would tie up all the outstanding loose ends. But some of the pertinent points

317

that the clients touched on involved how products were displayed in stores with different floor plans. They presented pictures on the Zoom feed and even a couple videos, but Paul— and Mike and Marge McClary, who were also on the call—still had questions.

It was Marge that finally made the decision.

"Paul, I think we need to send you up there."

Paul understood. Video calls were useful, but sometimes only an in-person meeting gave you a full grasp of the situation.

Paul explained to Lauren that he would be gone for two days and she accepted the news impassively. Her only request was that she got to choose how they would spend the evening.

"Let's do a puzzle tonight."

Paul was bewildered.

"Okaaay...I didn't see that coming."

Now, nearly an hour into the project, they'd assembled little more than the outline of edge pieces. Here and there a cluster of two or three connected pieces rested, waiting to be fitted into their proper place. The remaining 850-odd fragments were spread across the table.

Paul squinted at the image on the box.

"She couldn't find something more sensible? Like puppies or," he considered, "maybe a castle? Yeah, a castle would be good."

"Too easy. Besides, I like this one. Mom did well."

Paul shook his head.

"Seaweed...a one thousand-piece puzzle of a bed of seaweed. Every piece is the same!"

Lauren smiled, concentrating on the shapes.

"Shush. Give me some help, here. Whatever doesn't get done tonight will be left for me to do the next couple days while you're gone."

"No way this puzzle gets finished in less than a week. Chappy will have a field day with these pieces. He'll be slapshotting them across the kitchen all week. There'll be pieces under the refrigerator. Think how frustrating that will be—you spend a week on this thing, and you can't finish it because a few pieces are missing. We should just quit now... save all that frustration."

"Mom thought of that. She sent me one of those puzzle mat thingies that lets you roll up and store the part you've completed. Back to it, Master Sergeant."

Paul sighed.

"Yes ma'am."

They worked in silence for a few minutes, the sound of the rain becoming more noticeable. Occasionally, a peal of thunder rumbled through the house.

"Kind of cozy, isn't it?" Lauren asked the question without looking up, absorbed in her task.

Paul had turned a number of pieces upside down, speculating that it might be easier to find shapes that fit properly. He fixed his eyes on them with a growing feeling of exasperation.

"What?...Cozy?"

She nodded. "Yeah, reminds me of when I was a little girl and the electricity went out. Mom would get out a puzzle or a board game and light candles. We'd set at the table and make a night of it. Once, the lights came back on and Mom turned them all off until we finished the game." She paused.

Paul glanced up from the puzzle and looked at her admiringly. He realized that she was sitting with one leg bent and tucked under the other, something she often did while reading or talking on the phone.

Lauren continued. "You know, sometimes it's simple things like this that kids remember." She paused again, this time for several seconds, before turning to him.

"Paul, why do *you* think we haven't heard from the adoption program? Something must've gone wrong with the background check. What could—"

The doorbell rang.

Bunker decided before taking any action with the men in the Airbnb that he needed to assess exactly what happened at his mom's house. He quickly changed out of his sweats and

319

pulled on blue jeans and work boots. He threaded his belt through the loops and clipped on the Aker holster and Glock. The leather holder containing his cuffs and extra magazine went on his opposite hip. He threw on a black windbreaker that bore the logo of the Miami County Sheriff's Department.

Who knows, it might come in handy to have the logo visible.

He snatched his keys from the kitchen counter and hurried out the door.

Five minutes later Bunker's Malibu turned sharply into his mother's driveway, its headlight beams sweeping across the front of the house. Bunker ran to the front door, his right hand on his holster. He jabbed the doorbell and, as the tone sounded, rapped forcefully on the door.

"Mom...mom, open up...Mom!"

He leaned into the small side window and shielded his eyes with his hand. He could see the blue glow from the TV wash over Dana's recliner. There was no sign of her. He pushed the doorbell button a second time and, without waiting, hurried back to the driveway and around the side of the house, pulling up his hood as he went. The Malibu's headlights shone on him as he ran and cast a frenzied shadow on the detached garage.

Bunker turned the corner and stopped. The rear door to the house was open. He drew the Glock and approached in a crouch. Any lingering hope that his mom hadn't been taken had dissolved.

Rain was slanting through the doorway, saturating a small welcome mat inside. As Bunker neared the opening, he noticed an object on the concrete pad just outside the door.

Mom's cellphone.

Bunker let the Glock lead him through the doorway, stepping carefully past the mat and onto the slick tile floor. He swung the pistol from side to side, now sure that she was gone, but driven by his training. It wasn't until he reached the TV room that he again called out to her. As expected, there was no answer. He holstered his Glock and walked back through the kitchen.

The rear doorbell camera should have a recording.

Bunker stepped through the door and bent to pick up the phone. As he stood, he turned his head toward the doorbell. His eyes narrowed. Black splotches covered the entire casing of the doorbell as well as an area surrounding it.

They spray painted the camera. Shit!

He had hoped to confirm that he was dealing with the two men from the coffee shop.

Maybe they were recorded just before the camera was covered.

Bunker knew the four-digit code his mom used to activate the phone's features. He tried to pull up the home screen with no success.

Completely dark. Most likely rainwater got to it. Gotta get going.

He pulled the sleeve of his windbreaker over his right hand, then used one covered finger to pull the door shut. Again, his training had kicked in, compelling him to preserve evidence. As he turned toward the Malibu, lightning flashed overhead, illuminating low forms Bunker had rushed past earlier. They were a few feet from the door. Bunker stepped to them and crouched. He saw a white flower—a lily. It had apparently been stepped on and ground into the asphalt driveway. Next to it was a flat, white rectangle. He focused and saw handwritten words, blurred from the soaking rain.

To Mom, From Amos

In had been nearly two years since Bunker had encountered the Hulls. Their house had been burglarized on the same day that Lauren's car was broken into in the parking lot of Kettering Health, where she worked. Bunker had walked through the house with Paul and—though nothing seemed to be missing—noticed a few things that stood out. One was the display of photos on the wall of the home office. They showed Paul with other soldiers that—despite the smiles on their faces—still managed to appear no-nonsense. Another was the little Ruger .22 rifle that leaned in the corner of a closet in the master bedroom.

Days later the criminal known as Smithson—the man Bunker believed responsible for the break-ins—was found shot to death. He was riddled with bullets—from a .22.

Smithson's crimes were of such magnitude that most of the effort put forth by investigators focused on them, rather than his own death. Law enforcement officials ran up against a series of dead ends. The case remained open. Bunker never had a solid reason to look hard at Hull and he suspected that if the man was involved, he was too canny to be caught.

Bunker learned that Paul was an Air Force Combat Controller. He'd had to research what this meant and was suitably impressed by what he discovered. There were only a few hundred CCTs on active duty and they were some of the most highly trained and deadly individuals the United States military had to offer. Hull, in fact, had taken it to an even higher level. He was part of the 24th Special Tactics Squadron —the elite of the elite. The unit's members worked with the Navy's SEAL Team Six and the Army's Delta Force. They took on the toughest missions in the toughest environments. Bunker suspected that if Paul wanted this Smithson character to go away, he was more than capable of making it happen.

Still, thought Bunker as he walked up to the Hulls' front door in the rain, the possibility—Amos thought it was a *probability*—that this had occurred had always stuck in his craw. Bunker believed in rules—laws. What Bunker suspected Hull of doing was not to be admired.

But he's exactly the kind of man I need right now.

He rang the doorbell.

Paul answered the door. He saw a man in a Miami County Sheriff's Department rain jacket. His first thought was that there had been a car accident on Polecat Road in front of their house. He looked past the man and saw only darkness on the road. Then he looked back at the man's face.

He saw desperation.

What the hell's going on?

The man spoke.

"Mr. Hull, I'm Detective Amos Bunker with the Sheriff's Department. We met a couple years ago when your house was burglarized."

Paul stared at the face, letting his eyes travel up to the tuft of light hair peeking out from under a hood.

"Oh, sure Detective, I remember. Come in out of the rain." He stepped aside.

Bunker entered. He looked past Paul and saw Lauren, who stood from her chair and was moving tentatively toward the door.

Paul stepped back to give Bunker more room.

"What can we do for you, Detective? Was there an accident?"

A bitter laugh escaped from Bunker.

"No...no accident. This is much worse. I'm not sure where to start."

"Maybe you better come sit down."

It took ten full minutes to lay it out. Bunker explained the murders, the different paths of the investigation, and the car accident that resulted in him coming into possession of the golf bag. He emphasized the fact that someone in the department was cooperating with the kidnappers and that going to the FBI was problematic. Finally, he recounted the details of his mother's kidnapping and her physical condition. He sat at the kitchen table with both Hulls. At no point did he consider asking Lauren to leave the room. What he would be asking her husband to do would affect her. A few minutes into his narrative, Lauren moved to the counter to put on a pot of coffee, paying close attention the entire time.

"And you say some of the murders were committed with a .22, but not all?" Paul leaned forward, watching Bunker intently.

"That's right, Gerard Shortridge was shot with a 5.56 round from a distance. The .22 head wounds were up close—lots of gunshot residue." Bunker leaned back as Lauren sat a mug of coffee in front of him. He caught her eyes and immediately felt ill at ease for referring to violent acts in an almost casual manner.

"Uh, sorry Mrs. Hull."

"Don't be. I've heard this kind of thing before...and you can call me Lauren."

Bunker looked from Lauren to her husband. It struck him that Paul's combat experience would've exposed his wife to many things that never touch most people.

This is not an average couple.

Bunker took a deep breath. He'd reached the difficult part—the point where he would ask Paul to put himself in danger and assume the risk of criminal charges. He exhaled and brought his eyes to Hull's. To his surprise, the former Combat Controller spoke first.

"You need my help."

Bunker stared at him, dumbfounded. "Uh..."

Lauren examined Bunker over her coffee mug. "He's right, isn't he?"

"I was hoping...well...I'm not asking for him to go into the house with me. I just need someone to take me there and, if things go well, to drive me and my mom away as fast as possible."

Paul understood.

"You can't do a one-man rescue of a person that's being held by more than one kidnapper, particularly if the hostage will need assistance moving. If your mom is not ambulatory—for any reason—there's a good chance she'll need carried out. It sounds like there is a better than average chance of this. She's probably being restrained and there won't be time to free her in the heat of the moment. Also—excuse me for being, uh, *indelicate*, it sounds like her diminished capacity could keep her from assisting."

Bunker's expression showed resignation. He nodded.

Paul nodded back. "I assume you're armed? There is a high probability of a gunfight."

Bunker patted the side of his windbreaker, indicating a pistol on his hip.

Paul continued. "You obviously need to surprise them... get the jump on the first guy and take him out. You need to get to the hostage quickly to shield her. Do you have a ballistic vest?"

Bunker realized he'd driven to Hull's house without considering the vest. Luckily, it was in the trunk of the Malibu.

"I have one...it's in the car."

Paul sipped his own coffee and stared into the middle distance. Bunker watched in silence, trying to imagine what was going through Hull's mind.

He must be wondering why I've come here and laid this mess at his feet...why I picked him. Does he know what I suspect him of doing two years ago? Is he offended? Who the hell can help me if he kicks me out of his house?

Paul broke the silence.

"Can you pull up a view of the kidnapper's house on Google Earth?"

Bunker pulled out his phone and tapped the screen. Outside, lightning flashed, and the accompanying rumble of thunder rolled through the house. Seconds later he handed the phone to Hull and pointed to a spot on its screen.

"That's the house."

Paul accepted it and manipulated the view, alternately zooming in and out. He spoke under his breath.

"Hmm, a single access road...large lots, a fair number of trees." He tilted the screen toward Bunker and indicated a spot with an index finger. "What's this feature?"

Bunker squinted. "It's a roundabout, a small one. I have no idea why it's there. There's no intersecting east-west road, so I don't see a reason for it being there."

"It was probably the original cul-de-sac at the end of the road...they extended the road north and added more houses... just kept the round shape and added some landscaping to the center of the circle."

Bunker cocked his head.

Damn, I didn't think of that.

Paul searched the overhead shot with a practiced eye.

"There are no vehicles parked on the side of the street... I'm assuming it would stand out if you did that?"

Bunker nodded. "Yeah, I tried to surveil from the street during the middle of the day. Pretty much every place that has a view of the house is exposed. I was thinking about parking out on Route 36 and walking in to the rear of the house. There's a fence around the backyard. I could come in there." He leaned toward Paul and pointed to a large field behind the houses on the west side of Country Road.

Paul frowned. "No, too far. That's a half mile in the dark. We used to do ops like that all the time with night vision devices, but it's not an option here. Plus, that field is nothing but mud with this rain. No, I think we can use this roundabout as a drop-off point. It has trees on two sides and should give a bit of cover."

Bunker couldn't help but notice Hull had used the word *we*. He felt a twinge of optimism, his first since the phone call with the kidnapper.

"The rainclouds are blocking the moonlight—there's a three-quarter moon tonight—and the rain itself will make someone moving through the neighborhood harder to see."

Bunker thought, *Of course...he's done stuff like this before. But he knows the current phase of the moon?*

Paul finished his coffee and set down his mug.

"We're going to need to move fast. In my experience, the quicker a rescue force acts, the better...it's more disruptive to the bad guys. We'll take my vehicle—they may have seen yours." He stood. "I need to change clothes, grab some rain gear." He hesitated.

"If I owned a weapon, I'd bring it. Sorry Detective."

Bunker watched him disappear, thinking about the .22 rifle he knew that Hull once kept in his closet.

Lauren moved toward the door to the garage.

"Paul's Pilot is full of samples for work. Let me clear out the back seat." She stopped and turned toward Bunker. "It needs to be ready for your mom." She smiled and disappeared through the door.

Bunker put his head in his hands and felt a sense of relief. This couple, this remarkable couple, was going to help him bring his mom home.

The positive feeling faded seconds later as another thought entered his mind.

These are the people I condemned in the adoption background check.

Another clap of thunder rumbled overhead. Bunker thought it sounded more distant, but he wasn't sure.

CHAPTER THIRTY-FOUR

Min regarded Dana Bunker with curiosity. He stood over her in the living room of the rental house with his arms crossed. The woman was sitting in the recliner she'd been placed in when they'd returned from Troy. Her eyes were vacant, betraying just a trace of fear.

She should be angry...terrified. Instead she is... unresponsive.

Min reviewed the events of the past few hours. Dylan had returned from his meeting with Gayle DeJean and laid out a plan to abduct Bunker's mother. They sat at the kitchen table eating pizza, working through the finer points. Less than an hour later they were both back in Troy, pulling up to the house on Plum Street in Min's Evoque.

Dylan led the way to the rear door, holding the flower arrangement in his left hand. It was positioned to hide his face from the doorbell camera. He pushed the button on the unit and peered through the flowers to the interior of the kitchen as the tones sounded. He leaned back and removed the spray paint from his jacket pocket before spraying the top half of the doorbell cover. By this time, Min stood off to the side, out of the camera's view. He held a strip of duct tape. Willie's pistol was tucked into the waist of his black jeans. Min remembered the rain beating down as they waited, and the apprehension he felt when Dylan had to ring the bell two more times.

Why was it taking her so long to answer?

Min saw from Dylan's reaction that the woman was finally approaching the door. The black paint completely coated the portion of the cover that protected the camera, obscuring its view. Dylan quickly slipped the can into his jacket, then, fumbling a bit, removed the envelope from the same pocket. Seconds after Dylan held the envelope up to the window, the door opened.

It happened quickly from there. Dylan discarded the flower arrangement while jerking open the door. He seized the woman's wrist and pulled her roughly outside. Min stepped forward and pushed the tape over her mouth before she had a chance to cry out. As Dylan rushed her toward the Range Rover, Min found the flowers and vase on the ground and scooped them up.

Min bent to check the duct tape around the woman's ankles to confirm it wasn't too tight. The goal was to restrict her mobility without doing harm. They would need her to walk when they encountered her son the following evening. They had removed the tape from her mouth when Dylan was talking to Bunker on the phone just after returning to the rental.

Min rose, satisfied that the tape on her ankles would be sufficient. Her only method of movement in an upright position, he decided, would be to hop.

I don't see that happening. It would be difficult for a person in perfect health. This woman...has challenges.

Min was conflicted. He agreed with Dylan that the kidnapping was necessary. It was their best chance to regain the golf bag and prevent discoveries that could expose their illegal activities. These discoveries would be catastrophic for Min and his associates as well as the entire Running Dog organization. It would also, Min knew, bring shame to his homeland. Still, the mistreatment of the older woman made Min uncomfortable. He'd been raised to honor his elders.

"I've left you a bottle of water...there, on the stand next to the chair."

Min gestured to the bottle, noting that the woman stared straight ahead with eyes that were wide, yet still managed to look weary. He'd decided to think of her only as "the woman," rather than an older individual due his full respect.

"Okay, Min. I found the spot on Google Earth."

Min turned toward the voice coming from the dining room and began to move in that direction, leaving Dana Bunker in the chair. He saw Dylan sitting at the table, focusing on the screen of his cellphone. Min took a seat, sliding Willie's pistol aside and pushing the empty pizza box toward the vase and flowers on the far side of the table.

Dylan angled the phone so that Min could view the screen.

"Here is a view of the area. It's south of downtown Troy. Here, let me zoom out so you can see the exact location." He pinched the screen, causing structures and features to shrink.

Min concentrated on the screen.

"So that is Troy at the top, and the field is down there, correct?" He used his index finger to point first to the top, then the bottom of the screen.

Dylan nodded. "Yes. You can see that if you drive south out of downtown Troy on Market Street, the museum buildings are ahead on the left. Even though it's still considered Market Street, the area is basically rural."

Min held up a finger and then lowered it to point toward the living room.

"Should we be discussing this where we can be overheard?"

Dylan gave a contemptuous sniff. "Do you really think she's in any condition to spoil our plan? Or, for that matter, to even comprehend what we're saying? She's in even worse shape than DeJean led me to believe."

Min lowered his hand. "I must agree."

Dylan continued.

"There's a paved parking lot at the front of the property, near the entrance. There are four or five buildings clustered behind the parking lot." He worked the screen, magnifying the buildings. "I'm guessing some of the planes are inside, probably other exhibits, stuff like that."

"And the name of this place is the WACO Air Museum? Isn't Waco a city in Texas? Why is this museum in Ohio?" Min was truly curious.

Dylan waved a hand.

"Don't know. Doesn't matter. It's just an out of the way museum for old airplanes—biplanes, actually. I was stopped in traffic in front of the place last week and saw one of the planes flying over. Classic looking...old school, you know?"

Min looked at him with an expression of incomprehension.

"Not important." Dylan again manipulated the cellphone's screen. "What matters is the layout of the place. Behind the buildings, to the east, is a grass airstrip. It runs north and south, just like Market Street in front of the buildings. But this," he swept a finger across the screen, causing the view to shift, "is the key element."

Min saw that Dylan had focused on the parking lot at the front of the property. A dirt and gravel trail, apparently just wide enough for a single vehicle, appeared on the lot's southern fringe. It continued south, paralleling Market Street for some 200 yards, before encountering a line of trees. At this point the trail curved left—to the east—and followed the tree line a similar distance before disappearing in another line of trees east of the airfield.

Min saw that the trail, and the trees next to it, appeared to define the southern boundary of the airstrip.

"That is...some type of maintenance road?"

Dylan shrugged.

"Could be. The biplane I watched came in low from the south, cleared the trees and the trail, and touched down in the grass. All I know is that area can be accessed by vehicles and it's isolated. And look at this." He pinched his thumb and index finger on the screen, expanding the view of the museum complex and its surroundings.

Min saw it immediately.

"Ah, an entrance to the highway—I-75—is a short distance away."

Dylan grinned. "It can't be more than a half mile from the museum entrance. We do what we have to do, get the bag, and jump on the highway. We hook up with Dax 20 minutes later in Dayton, then bolt for Kentucky."

Min felt he had an adequate understanding of the basics of the plan but had questions about the specifics. Unlike Dylan, he had not viewed the area—and he would be expected to make the shot. He found that Dylan's manipulations of the phone screen made it difficult to keep all the physical features of the WACO site in perspective.

"One moment."

He stood and walked to the kitchen, pulled out drawers, and sorted through the contents. He returned holding a black Sharpie. Before sitting, he slid the pizza box and flower arrangement back to his side of the table. He lifted the box lid and propped it against the flowers, then began to draw.

"So, this is Market Street." He drew a straight line across the bottom of the open box lid. "Here is the parking lot, and above it, the buildings." He started to draw outlines of the structures, then stopped and simply wrote "WACO" in block letters. "Here is the trail...and this," he gestured to the large, unmarked area above the block letters, "is the airstrip." He turned to Dylan for confirmation.

Dylan nodded and reached for the Sharpie.

"Up here is a raised area of ground—maybe bulldozed earth from when the airfield was carved out." He drew a horizontal oval near the top right corner of the lid. "It's overgrown with high weeds, small trees, like that. You will be waiting there."

Min studied the lid. "And you will meet Bunker where, exactly?"

Dylan circled a spot on the right edge of the lid, midway between its top and bottom. The line representing the maintenance trail was inside the circle.

"I'll have him come here. We'll let him know that a sniper rifle is aimed at him. I'll have his mom, with a knife to her throat. I make him sit the golf bag on the ground and back away. I walk her to the bag, pull away the knife, and have her keep going toward Bunker. While they have their little reunion, thinking my knife is no longer a threat, I detach the putter head from its shaft. You pop Bunker with the rifle, and I use the .22 on Mom. No witnesses. End of story."

Min stared at the lid, trying to visualize the sequence.

Dylan continued. "I checked, and once this storm passes, clear skies are expected all day tomorrow. There'll be a three-quarter moon, pretty good light...and you have that low-light scope." He paused. "You can make the shot, right?"

Min pointed at the oval at the top of the box lid then shifted his finger to the spot Dylan had indicated for the exchange. "How far is that?"

"Maybe 100 yards." Years of hitting approach shots at golf course flagsticks had made Dylan an excellent judge of distance.

Min smiled confidently. "Méi wèn tí"—no problem.

Dylan grinned. "That's just a little sand wedge for me... for most golfers it would be pitching wedge distance. I—."

He stopped in the middle of the golf analogy and his face clouded over.

"Oh shit!" He pushed away from the table and stood quickly.

Min felt a stab of panic. "What, what?"

Dylan stepped toward the door to the garage and spoke over his shoulder.

"I just remembered that I left my driver outside when DeJean texted me about Willie's wreck and the missing golf bag. It's still out there in the rain...god-*dammit*! I paid nine hundred bucks for that thing!"

Min watched him disappear through the door then burst out laughing.

CHAPTER THIRTY-FIVE

Dylan rushed through the garage to its rear door and stepped into a driving rain. He looked to the patio and his heart sank. The driver wasn't visible.

Where the hell is it? Didn't I lean it against the house?

Lightning flashed overhead, illuminating the entire backyard. Thunder rolled over the countryside. Dylan caught sight of an object on the patio near the house's foundation. Shielding his face from the rain, he stepped onto the patio and hurried to the spot. As he approached, he was relieved to see the driver. He stooped to pick it up, then noticed the white leather Running Dog head cover a few feet away.

Damn, I forgot to put the cover back on. The driver didn't just get soaked, it probably got scratched up too when it was blown over.

He bent again and snatched the head cover, turning his body slightly to avoid the worst of the rain. As he stood, another bolt of lightning lit up the sky. Dylan flinched. Then, in his peripheral vision, he caught movement.

Across the patio, the gate to the fence was swinging slowly inward. Dylan could just make out the top of someone's head as it moved cautiously toward the opening.

Dylan dropped the driver and head cover and rushed back to the garage.

Paul and Bunker wasted little time. Minutes after leaving his dining room to change clothes, Paul returned. He wore trail shoes, olive drab pants, and a dark t-shirt. He was pulling on a black Gore-Tex jacket.

"Can you describe the two men that have your mom?"

Bunker nodded. "I can do better than that. I took a picture of them the morning the Shortridge brothers were killed." He scrolled through his phone and searched for the image.

Lauren returned from the garage and stood next to Paul. Together, the three of them examined the shot. Lauren was the first to speak.

"One of the men is Asian?"

Bunker nodded. "Yes, Chinese...at least I think he is. I can give you the full story of the connection these men seem to have with this Chinese company, Running Dog."

"Save it for the drive." Paul reached into a basket on the counter and grabbed his keys. He turned to Lauren and met her eyes. "I'll call you as soon as I can."

She leaned into him and rested her head on his chest as they embraced. "Come back."

Bunker stood uncomfortably a few feet away, feeling like a voyeur. *I have no right to involve them in this.* His unease was punctuated by another thought.

They must've had these moments before...all of Paul's combat deployments...does it ever get easier for them?

Bunker decided it didn't. He watched as the Hulls kissed, then Lauren turned to him.

"Go get your mom, Amos."

Paul drove the Honda Pilot. The Hull's house was north of Troy, making the drive to the Airbnb just over 20 minutes. On the way Bunker recounted as many details as he could remember about his phone calls to Newark as well as the conversations he had with the neighbors on Country Road.

Paul handed his phone to Bunker and instructed him to make sure each man's number was in the other's device. To their mild surprise, they discovered the numbers were already in the contacts, a result of the dealings they'd had two years earlier when the Hulls had been burglarized.

They settled on a strategy. They would drive past the house and continue to the cul-de-sac. This would give Paul his first look at the property and allow both men an opportunity to look for details that could affect their plan. Once back past the house a second time, Paul would slow going around the roundabout and allow Bunker, now wearing his ballistic vest under his jacket, to jump out. The detective would then spend several minutes—the specific length of time was not set—watching the house and the rest of the neighborhood. Five minutes before making his entry into the house, he would text Paul.

After dropping off Bunker, Paul would continue south to State Route 36. He would need an inconspicuous spot to park that was a short distance away. He told Bunker he knew of a church in Westville—a former school—less than two miles away. As soon as he received Bunker's text, he would rush to the house, pull in the driveway, and help get Dana Bunker into the SUV.

"Open the glove compartment, Amos. There's a folding knife in there. You might need it to cut through restraints."

Bunker did as he was told and found the knife—an expensive Gerber—and removed it. He glanced at Hull, who kept his eyes focused on the road.

This guy knows what he's doing.

When they were just three miles from Country Road, Paul called Lauren and gave her a rundown of the plan.

"I want you to look up the phone number for the Champaign County Sheriff's Department. If you haven't heard from us by"—he glanced at the clock and saw it was 9:42 p.m.—"10:45, call them and have them get to the house. Amos is texting you the address now." He sighed. "I guess that's it."

Lauren paused, then added, "First There, Paul."

He repeated the phrase back to her, "First There."

It was the motto of the Air Force Combat Controllers.

Minutes later the Pilot passed through the roundabout and approached the target house. A grey Range Rover Evoque was parked on one side of the driveway.

Bunker craned his neck. "That one has New York plates. That's the one the Asian man was driving. The second one must be in the garage."

Paul steered to the cul-de-sac at the road's end and started back. "Lights are on...curtains pulled."

Bunker could feel his pulse rate increase. He touched the butt of the Glock on his hip. He managed, "Yeah."

They passed the house a second time. The only noise in the Pilot was sound of wiper blades sliding back and forth across the windshield. Lightning struck somewhere, providing the neighborhood an instant of daylight. A moment later a second bolt followed. The men concentrated on the house, oblivious to nature's strobe effect.

Paul guided the Pilot back to the roundabout and braked partway through the curve.

"I'll be at the church lot in two minutes. Remember... text me five minutes before you hit the house. I'll come fast and go straight to the driveway."

Bunker nodded.

Paul continued, "Remember your training...eyes on front sight...shoot straight. Good luck, Amos." He held out his hand.

Bunker shook it, set his jaw, and was gone.

Two minutes later Paul backed into a parking space in front of the Renewed Strength Church and Christian Learning Center on the edge of the village of Westville. He left the Pilot's engine running and propped his phone on the dash so he wouldn't miss Bunker's text.

It was an unusual situation for Paul. In the military, as part of the Joint Special Operations Command, he was typically "on target" with his customer units—SEALs, Delta, the Rangers—not waiting in a support capacity. He was an active participant in the operation, engaging in a gunfight, or—more likely—calling in airstrikes. This situation was much more passive. Reactive. He didn't like it.

I had a helluva lot more control when I was riding in on one of those Night Stalker helos with the shooters from Team Six.

He checked his surroundings and saw a few lights on in houses off to his left. As he turned his head back toward Route 36 something caught his eye. It was the historical marker that the state of Ohio had erected nearby. Paul—a history buff—had visited nearly every one of these markers within a 50-mile radius of his Troy home. This one, placed when the building was still a school, was dedicated to former Major League pitcher Harvey Haddix.

Paul couldn't read the words from his vantage point through the rain and darkness, but he didn't have to. He knew that Haddix, who grew up in the area, had pitched perhaps the most famous game in baseball history, losing a perfect game in the 13th inning. His Pittsburgh Pirates fell 1-0 to the Milwaukee Braves.

It led to one of Paul's favorite stories. Haddix was barraged by congratulatory and conciliatory telegrams after the game. One, from a fraternity at Texas A&M University, simply read, "Dear Harvey, Tough Shit."

Paul laughed. The memory had broken the tension. Minutes later he received the expected text from Bunker and put the Pilot in gear.

Bunker watched the target house from behind a tree on the edge of the roundabout after Hull drove off. There was just one house between him and the Airbnb, but the lots were large, and in these conditions, it was nearly impossible to gather intelligence from this distance. He made his way slowly north toward the house.

If I'm walking near the pavement when a vehicle drives past, sure as hell they will stop. I can't have that.

He also knew that if he moved up close to the intervening house he risked being discovered by its inhabitants. Luckily that house had a number of trees in the front yard. Bunker picked his way from tree to tree, keeping his eyes on the target house the entire time. The rain did not let up. Bunker was grateful that he'd worn the windbreaker. His head was covered by the hood of his St. Louis Blues sweatshirt—for all the good that did. It was soaked.

He reached the last tree in the lot and eyed the house where he believed his mom was being held. An image of her in her diminished condition appeared to him and his temper flared.

If these son-of-a-bitches have hurt her—
He shook his head. No time for that.

339

Concentrate!

Bunker peered through the darkness and saw that a five-foot-high wooden fence surrounded the backyard. A gate was on this side, just 30 feet from Bunker's position.

That's my way in.

He had decided to approach from the rear. Virtually no one locked the door from the inside of their house to their garage. There was typically a door at the rear of the garage. Bunker planned to enter the backyard and move to the rear door. If it was unlocked, he would be in the garage. If the rear door was locked, he was confident he could break a pane of glass in this storm without being detected, then let himself inside the garage. From there it was a simple tactical building entry.

Piece of cake, right?

Bunker smiled ruefully. He had never discharged his weapon while on duty—other than in training. He wasn't sure he was up to the task.

Hull could do it. No doubt in my mind.

Before making for the gate, Bunker dashed to the front corner of the house. He wasn't sure, but he thought there was a gap in the curtains behind one of the front windows. He duckwalked behind shrubs in front of the house, feeling parts of them tug at his clothing. His boots, already saturated, became heavy with mud. Finally, he was under the window. He looked up and saw there was a sliver of light. Rising slowly, he peered inside.

There was his mom. She was sitting in a recliner, her eyes open. Her ankles were duct taped together and rested on the extended footrest. Her hands were unbound and rested at her sides. From the look in her eyes, she was in one of the down periods of her Lewy body dementia.

She was having a bad day.

Bunker fought to push down a growing rage. He caught movement behind his mother and shifted his view. He saw two men sitting at a dining room table. They were intent in conversation. An open pizza box was visible on the table. It was the Chinese man and the American that Bunker thought of as Eli.

They're eating pizza while Mom is taped up in the next room?

Again, he fought to stay under control. His mother's life depended on it. He felt for the knife in his front pocket.
It would be needed to cut through the duct tape.

No matter what happens, Paul has given me a chance.

He paused. *Paul.*

Bunker retrieved his phone and ducked behind a shrub. He used his upper body to both hide the light coming from the device and to shield it from the rain.

He composed a short text—**5 minutes**—and hit send. Bunker slowly worked his way to the corner of the house, freezing in place behind another shrub when a car passed by the house. He reached the corner and squinted down the side. It was open, no vegetation. He unholstered his Glock and rose slightly, preparing to dash to the rear gate. Lightning flashed overhead, causing him to hunch his shoulders reflexively.

Gotta move.

Bunker started for the gate, quickly realizing that the mud on the bottom of his boots was hindering his movement. Reaching the gate, he looked between two wooden slats. He saw a patio constructed of stone pavers. Four aluminum and fabric swivel chairs surrounded a patio table near the center of the paved surface. He could make out a door on the far side.

Bingo...that's how I get into the garage.

Bunker pulled the knife from his pocket and opened the blade. He spent several seconds scraping mud from his boots, then wiped the blade on his jeans and returned the folded knife to his pocket.

Time to go.

There was a black handle on the outside of the gate. Bunker gripped it and tugged. Nothing.

Has to be a latch on the other side.

He stood on his toes and reached over the gate. His hand searched for the latch. Finding it, he slowly eased it open, limiting noise. Bunker pulled at the handle and the gate cracked open. He slowly widened the opening, hoping the deliberate pace would prevent the hinges from squeaking. When the opening was wide enough, Bunker started through. He frowned as another bolt of lightning flashed, then a thought struck him.

I can use the thunder to mask any noise from closing the gate.

He did just that two seconds later when the sound boomed from the clouds. He pressed his entire body through the opening and latched the gate during the short duration of the thunder.

Bunker crept across the patio, hunched under the windows, his Glock leading the way. He noted a golf club on the patio surface and dismissed it as unimportant. He reached the door and gripped the knob.

If it's locked, I'll have to smash the window and reach inside. End of subtle approach. I'll have to move fast after that.

He turned the knob.

Unlocked!

Bunker took a breath and moved into the dark garage. The second Range Rover was parked inside. The door to the house was three strides away with a single concrete step in front. He approached, feeling certain that it would be unlocked. He believed he would find a kitchen on the other side, with the dining room visible just beyond. The men were there, possibly armed.

I have the element of surprise. I can get on top of them. I may not even have to shoot anyone. I have a set of cuffs to detain one. The other...I'll improvise. Once I get to Mom, I cut the ankle tape and go out the front door. Paul will be there.

He decided that he'd twist the doorknob rapidly and move through it as quickly as possible. No slow turn that's used in movies for dramatic effect. He took a deep breath.

Here goes.

Amos Bunker quickly twisted the doorknob with his left hand and flung the door inward. He burst through, looking over the front sight of his Glock.

Dylan stood in front of the dining room table with Willie's Ruger pointed at Dana Bunker's temple.

He'd charged through the garage entrance door to the kitchen in near panic.

"Min, get your rifle! Watch the front door!"

Min sat at the table, a mirthful expression still on his face as he thought of Dylan's driver in the rain. The expression froze on his face. "What?"

Dylan rushed past him and entered the living room, moving to the recliner.

"Someone's coming through the back gate! Gotta be Bunker...or someone with him. I'll get the woman. Leave the pistol and get your rifle. Watch the front door. There could be more of them."

Min immediately dashed for the stairway, brushing past Dylan. He reached the post at the bottom of the stair railing and used it to catapult himself up the steps.

Dylan grabbed Dana Bunker by the shoulders and pulled her roughly to her feet. She made a single sound.

"Oh!"

He disregarded the panic in her eyes as she stood unsteadily, unable to keep her balance with the tape binding her ankles. Dylan dragged her to the dining room table and reached for the Ruger with his free hand. His left arm was across her chest. He turned her to face the door to the garage then reached the pistol around the right side of her body so he could grip it with both hands. He pulled back the slide to seat a round in its chamber and flipped off the safety.

Dylan touched the barrel of the pistol to Dana Bunker's temple and waited.

Seconds later he heard Min's voice as he rushed back down the stairway.

"I have the rifle!"

"Watch the front door!" Dylan turned in time to see the door to the garage quickly swing open and a man emerge. Rainwater dripped from his black jacket. Strands of white hair clung to his forehead under a hood sodden with moisture. Both hands gripped a pistol that pointed in Dylan's direction.

"Amos?" The voice was Dana Bunker's.

Dylan saw the man's expression change slightly.

"Drop the gun, Bunker." Dylan's head poked out from behind the woman.

Amos kept his Glock pointed in Dylan's direction.

"I can't do that. Let her go."

"Well, I don't see you carrying my golf bag, so that's not happening. When I get the bag, you get mom." He tilted the Ruger slightly, as if gesturing at Dana.

Min's voice came from the living room.

"There is a vehicle outside...in the driveway!"

Dylan frowned and tightened his grip on the woman.

"Who the fuck is that, Bunker?"

Amos was silent.

"Who is it? Another cop?" Dylan pushed the barrel of the pistol harder into Dana's temple.

Amos spoke. "No, not a cop. Just a friend."

Dylan's voice went up an octave.

"Who the hell told you to bring another person into this?"

Min backed into the living room; his rifle directed at the front door. He turned to take in the intruder, then spoke.

"The driver isn't getting out of the vehicle."

Dylan turned his head toward Min, concentrating on this new information. When he did, Amos looked past him to the table beyond. He saw a flower arrangement, partially hidden by the open pizza box. White lilies, identical to the one he'd seen near Dana's back door, made up part of the display. As his eyes returned to the kidnappers, he saw scribbling on the pizza box. He made out one word—WACO.

Dylan's eyes narrowed and refocused on Amos's face. "So he's, what...your getaway driver?"

"Something like that...let her go."

Dylan thought quickly.

"This is what's going to happen. You'll tell us your friend's name, then you will walk out the front door and drive

344

away. You will go to the office tomorrow and get the golf bag. I will contact you with instructions for the exchange. We will still meet tomorrow night. Now, who is he?"

"Don't worry about him."

"Too late for that, Amos. You brought him into this, not me. His name?"

The detective hesitated. "Paul Hull. Ex-military. He's not a cop."

Dylan scowled. "I don't think you understand the situation. You *do not* talk about this...to *anyone*...if you want her back." He shifted his eyes toward Dana's head as he spoke the last few words.

Bunker simply nodded.

Dylan shuffled backward, dragging Dana, to give her son room to pass through to the living room.

Bunker kept his Glock trained on the man's right eye as it peeked at him from behind his mother's head. He shuffled past and into the living room where he saw the Chinese man. The man was swinging his rifle from the front door to Bunker, and back again. Bunker faced the two gunmen and backed to the door, reaching back for the knob. It struck him that he'd left muddy footprints all the way to the door.

Bunker cast a last look at his mother as he turned the knob, then heard a final instruction from her captor.

"Oh, Amos...tomorrow you will bring Paul Hull, ex-military, along to our exchange."

CHAPTER THIRTY-SIX

Bunker had been involved in hundreds of fact-finding conversations during his time in law enforcement. These included interrogations of suspects, refereeing domestic disputes, and testifying at criminal trials. He didn't think that he'd ever been part of an exchange that was quite as thorough as the one he was involved in on the way back to Troy after the incident at the Airbnb.

Paul wanted to know everything; from how Dana Bunker was being restrained to details about the kidnappers. He asked Bunker to try to recall every word spoken in the house. The questioning allowed Bunker to focus on something other than the anguish he felt over leaving his mom behind.

"Tell me about the weapons you saw."

Bunker concentrated. "The American—Eli—had a nine millimeter pistol...one of those compact models...a Ruger, I think." He recalled the sight of the pistol being pressed against his mother's temple and shuddered.

"And the other guy...the Chinese?"

"He had..." Bunker forced himself to recall every detail. "He had a black rifle...carbine length...a ventilated barrel with small, modern-looking optics on top—not a traditional scope."

Paul mulled it over. "Would you say it fired 5.56 rounds?"

Bunker saw what Paul was implying.

"Yes...absolutely." He turned to Paul. "That has to be the rifle that killed Gerard Shortridge."

Paul nodded. "My guess is the Chinese man was the shooter."

They drove on. The lightning had diminished significantly, and the rain had subsided to the point that Paul had switched the Pilot's wipers to intermittent mode.

"Think, Amos...what else can you tell me about the inside of the house."

Bunker closed his eyes, attempting to relive the experience.

"Well...when I looked through the front window I saw Mom in a recliner in the living room...the men were sitting at the dining room table, eating pizza...when I made it inside the garage I saw the other Range Rover...I—wait a minute."

Paul turned his head slightly and glanced at him. "What?"

"They weren't actually eating pizza. There was a pizza box on the table, and it was empty...but the lid was propped up. I could see that someone had drawn on it...almost...Yeah! It looked like a map. And I saw one word written on it— WACO."

Paul immediately recognized what the word referred to by the way that Amos had pronounced it—"*WOCKO.*" He knew that most outsiders—and a high percentage of locals— pronounced the word as they did the city of the same name in Texas.

Paul reviewed the facts. "So...let's think this through. They want to meet us tomorrow night to trade your mom for the golf bag. They have a rifle that could've—probably did—fire the round that killed one of the Shortridge brothers. And they are drawing a map that includes the word WACO—probably the museum and airfield area south of Troy."

"That seems to sum it up."

Bunker's face was impassive as realization set in.

The men arrived at Paul's house minutes later. Lauren met them at the door. Paul had called her on the way home from Country Road to give her a condensed report of the events at the rental house, but she was eager to hear the entire story. While Bunker recounted the details, Paul hurried to his office. Minutes later he returned, carrying a laptop computer.

"I think I have something here that will be useful."

Bunker looked at Lauren. She shrugged.

Paul opened the computer and navigated to a file that bore the title "Bike Path with Lauren—Deer." He clicked on the file.

The threesome watched as the video started. The screen showed an aerial view that featured trees and farm fields. Few structures were visible. A sinew of narrow pavement could be seen, running from the bottom of the screen to the top.

Slightly puzzled, Lauren asked, "The drone video from our bike ride?"

"That's right." Paul confirmed Lauren's speculation but kept his attention on the video. He used the cursor to advance the video progress bar several times.

Lauren turned to Bunker. "That's us down there." She pointed to two bikers moving in line along the path as the video progressed. "Paul recorded with a drone camera as we rode the bike path between Troy and Tipp City." She turned back to the screen, still confused.

"Okay, getting closer." Paul removed his hand from the keyboard and leaned back. "This is when we reached Tipp and then turned around to ride back to Troy."

Lauren and Amos looked at each other. Lauren shrugged. Minutes later Paul leaned into the screen and moved the cursor over the video's pause symbol.

"There!" He clicked on the symbol and the video froze. He pointed to a spot on the bike path. The image showed that the riders—Paul and Lauren—were no longer in line but were now side by side.

"That's when we stopped to watch the deer, right?" Lauren regarded Paul, still unsure of the video's significance. "I don't see—"

A trace of a smile appeared on Paul's face.

"Okay, here are the deer." He indicated small brown figures grouped on and around the path in front of the bikers. "They came from the right—east—and watched us, then moved in the opposite direction."

Paul restarted the video and the deer began walking west, off the bike path. They moved through a break in the trees and crossed a double railroad track before reaching a dirt path. They continued on the path for several yards, apparently content to utilize a feature created by humans, before veering to their right and spreading out.

349

Paul paused the video again and pointed to a spot near the bike path.

"You can't see it from this perspective, but there is a sign right there that reads 'Historic WACO Airfield and Museum.' An arrow points in the direction of the railroad tracks, exactly where the deer went when they left the bike path. This area," he made a circular motion with his finger over the field where the deer stood frozen, "is part of the WACO airfield."

Bunker stared intently at Paul.

"Wait, you're sure?"

Paul nodded. "Yeah, I stood with my bike ten feet from the sign. I remember being surprised we were that close to the WACO complex. There are trees on both sides of the bike path. When you're riding, your view of what's on the other side of the trees is limited. I've visited WACO...and I've ridden the path dozens of times. I just never associated one with the other."

Bunker turned back to the screen.

"So, the drawing the kidnappers had on the pizza box corresponds to the area we see on this screen?"

Paul nodded. "I think so...at least in part. The drone's view that we're seeing shows the area from the bike path to... say...a hundred yards or so on either side. We don't care about the ground east of the bike path. But that area to the west just might be where the exchange takes place tomorrow night."

Three sets of eyes returned to the laptop's screen.

Lauren suggested, "Paul, play the video from this point. I remember standing next to you on the bike path for a few minutes, watching the deer on the drone's display screen that was attached to your handlebars. Maybe we'll see more of the property."

"Good idea." Paul started the video again and they watched. This time their eyes examined the landscape, rather than focusing on the deer. As the creatures slowly roamed across the terrain, the view from above shifted slightly as the hovering drone was apparently affected by gusts of wind.

Bunker spoke. "I could just make out the corner of one of the WACO buildings for a second on the edge of the screen."

"Yeah, I saw it." Paul backed up the video and stopped it when it reached that point. "This appears to be the most comprehensive view. If they've picked this location, there must be a reason. Maybe we can figure it out if we scrutinize every part of the airfield and its surroundings."

Bunker agreed. "Worth a try...seems like our best shot. Let me pull up the area on Google Earth on my phone. The view won't be much different but maybe we will pick up something we didn't notice on the drone feed."

They studied both screens for several minutes. The satellite view on Bunker's phone had the benefit of showing all of the buildings on the property.

Paul looked closely and determined the kidnappers probably wouldn't want to chance a meet near the structures.

"Too well lit...too close to the street out front."

Bunker pointed out the trail that ran from the museum parking lot south before curving east and skirting the end of the airfield.

"Look, that trail cuts all the way across the property. When it gets close to the trees along the railroad tracks it narrows." He shifted his eyes back and forth between the screens. "The trail actually runs through the trees, crosses the railroad tracks, and intersects with the bike path."

Paul added. "That's where the deer entered the field."

The attention of both men was now on the trail.

Bunker speculated. "If a vehicle drove far enough along that trail, it would be impossible to see from the road."

Paul was about to agree when Lauren pointed to the laptop screen and spoke.

"Why is that area along the edge of the airfield a different color than the rest of the field?"

The men eyed the sector she indicated. They saw an oval-shaped space that ran along the east side of the airfield. It was green, contrasting with the yellowish hue of the grass that covered the airfield itself.

Paul squinted at the laptop screen. Bunker turned to his cellphone and enlarged the area.

Bunker said, "It's an elevation...looks like it's covered in weedy vegetation and small trees." He turned to Paul.

The former Combat Controller spoke.

"Excellent location for a sniper."

CHAPTER THIRTY-SEVEN

Sunlight fought to penetrate the Airbnb on Country Road Tuesday morning. The storms of the night before had moved on and clear skies were expected for the next few days. Dylan and Min kept the curtains drawn to prevent a random discovery of their hostage.

Dana Bunker sat at the dining room table, staring blankly at the bowl of Honey Nut Cheerios and milk in front of her. She'd spent the night in an upstairs bathroom. Before locking the door for the night, Dylan tossed in a blanket and pillow. He then removed the duct tape from her ankles so she could use the facilities. He left her there, without comment. Now, at the table, her ankles were again taped.

Dylan dipped a spoon into his own bowl and managed to capture the final three Cheerios. The incident the night before had rattled him.

I should've anticipated Bunker's play. I knew he'd followed us here from Winans the morning Min and I met with the Shortridge brothers. He's a cop—a detective. DeJean warned me that he was capable. He came close to ruining everything. If I hadn't gone out in the rain and spotted him...

He gazed at the three Cheerios, suspended in his spoon on a thin layer of milk. Bunker, he realized, came to the house prepared to do anything to free his mother.

He could've killed us.

The thought of being the hunted unnerved Dylan. He had always been the hunter. He would not let it happen again. Bunker, he realized, could not be underestimated again—especially if he had recruited a confederate: this man Paul Hull. Dylan would contact Gayle DeJean this morning and give her the license plate number of the Honda Pilot that was in the driveway the night before. He wanted to make sure that Bunker was telling the truth about who was driving.

Dylan's reverie was broken by Min, who came down the stairs and made his way to the dining room.

"I spoke to Dax...told him about last night. He is... apprehensive." Min glanced at Dana before turning back to Dylan. "He thinks we should leave now."

Dylan frowned. "We're not going anywhere without that golf bag. It would mean the end of the entire enterprise. Right now, we still have a chance to rectify the situation."

Min was standing a few feet behind Dana. "Okay...how do we proceed tonight with a second man involved...this Hull? The putter gives you just one shot. If I eliminate one of the men, you have a single bullet for the other. What about..." He nodded toward Dana. "Do you simply take Willie's pistol?"

Dylan shook his head. "Can't take the pistol. I want them to believe I'm not a significant threat to them. Psychologically, they will believe your rifle is their biggest concern. They'll know how difficult it would be to eliminate three moving targets in the dark from a distance...and they will certainly be planning to move once she," he cocked his head toward Dana, "returns to them."

Min looked thoughtful. "Okay...then what about the third target?" His eyes shifted to Dana. "Do I take a second shot from distance? *She* could be moving at that point."

Dylan smirked. "I'll still have the knife."

Bunker was up early. He'd slept fitfully, unable to get the image of his mom out of his head. He made coffee and sat at the table with the notepad he'd used the previous evening. He reviewed his notes, reliving the night's events. He still couldn't be sure of the identity of the informant but now completely dismissed Deputy Fatkin as a possibility. He drew a line through his name and turned to a blank page. He began to jot down details of the plan he and Paul had devised late last night. Bunker heard both sides of Paul's phone conversations as the former Combat Controller placed calls with his phone on speaker.

Bunker smiled, remembering the series of calls Paul made. His first was to his boss, Mike McClary. Paul explained that he had to cancel a work trip to Chicago the next day and that he would explain later. McClary, apparently reading

Paul's tone, accepted the news without question. The next call was to a man named Gatewood Dowdell and occurred after 11 p.m. Dowdell had answered without preamble; "I know you can tell time, Sticks...so this better be important."

The plan had been finalized in less than an hour. Bunker was impressed with the concept and astounded at the willingness of strangers to take significant risks to help recover his mother.

The Hulls suggested that Bunker spend the night at their house. Bunker begged off, saying he had a lot to do at the office and wanted to get an early start. He didn't mention the main reason for turning down the offer. It was the phrasing Lauren used.

"It doesn't make sense to go home this late. You can shower here and put on some of Paul's clothes...there's a bed in the nursery—uh—spare bedroom."

Bunker winced, remembering again the assessment of the Hulls that he'd sent to the adoption program. He'd likely created the lone obstacle to them being approved. He would remedy this situation today, knowing that after tonight he may not be around to do so.

He made it to the office a few minutes after 7 a.m. He immediately went to the evidence room and used his key card. After entering, he stood just inside the doorway with hands on hips and glowered at the golf bag. Its front section faced him. He imagined the head on the red dog logo turning to him with a menacing smile on its face.

What is the significance of this damn thing?

Bunker strode to the far side of the room and slid an arm through the bag's shoulder strap. He bent to the travel bag on the floor next to it and lifted it with his opposite hand. He made his way to his own office after securing the evidence room door.

He placed the smaller bag on his desk and reached for the zipper. Technically he still was not authorized to search its contents. He decided to close his office door, something he almost never did when inside.

Rules are becoming less important to me at this point.

He stepped to his chair and automatically reached for his holster, remembering as he did that he'd left it and the Glock with Paul as part of their plan.

The contents of the small bag were ordinary: a shaving kit, dirty laundry, a couple t-shirts with ironic sayings on the front, a folded pair of Dockers, and a flannel shirt. Bunker spent ten full minutes examining the bag.

Nothing. Not that surprising, I guess. Eli didn't ask for it back. He only seems to care about the golf bag.

Bunker adjusted his gaze. The bag stood in front of his desk, its white leather looking extravagant. A striking image of a red dog, its legs extended as if sprinting, was visible—also in leather—on three sides. Briefly, a question occurred to Bunker —*what would something like this cost?*—but he dismissed it as unimportant.

He dragged the bag behind the desk and began to pull the clubs out one at a time. The heads of the fairway woods were protected by head covers made of the same white leather as the bag. Smaller versions of the red dog logo appeared on each cover. He removed the yellow cover from the putter and saw a blade-style head that, though somewhat heavy, was far less exotic than many models currently on the market. Bunker also removed each of the Ping branded irons. Once all the clubs were out of the bag, he used the flashlight feature on his cellphone to scrutinize the interior. Finding nothing unusual, he returned all the clubs to their places, vaguely remembering that he'd seen the driver on the patio the night before.

Bunker turned his attention to the pockets. The one at the top front of the bag was already unzipped. Bunker theorized that the two balls that the tow truck driver—J.D.— had given him had come from there. He turned to look at them on his desk for a second, then directed his attention back to the leather bag. He systematically searched the remainder of the pockets, finding little more than a number of golf balls bearing the Running Dog logo still in packaging as well as the normal detritus that any golfer carried. This included tees, ball markers, and small brushes used to clean the grooves of clubs.

This changed when he came to the wide cooler compartment at the bottom of the bag. Bunker removed a black plastic bag that was balled up. He eyed it for a second before setting it on his desk. He dug deeper in the pocket and pulled out a number of foam practice balls in various colors. He continued to search and felt his fingers close around a plastic bag with odd shapes. Removing this, he was astounded to see that, in addition to holding a tool used to adjust the head of a driver, it held a handful of small bullets.

They were .22 shorts.

This is the caliber that killed Garrett Shortridge...and Shadow Donald...Who knows how many others? They must have a pistol. The shots came from up close. Paul and I will have to assume that they bring the pistol to our meeting tonight.

Bunker stared at the bullets.

Are there fingerprints on the cartridges? If so, they could possibly tie these men to murders.

Bunker considered keeping the .22s. In the end, he decided not to.

They probably wouldn't be admitted in court as evidence because this is an illegal search.

Bunker's natural inclination to adhere to regulations was still there but he could feel it ebbing.

He turned his attention to the black plastic bag. He carefully opened it and found a second bag—this one clear. It held a small, off-white orb.

Bunker had seen more than his share of illegal drugs in his day.

Oh shit.

He hurried from his office, trying not to attract attention, and made it to the supply closet, which was down the hall from the evidence room. He removed a fentanyl/opioid PPE kit, a fentanyl test kit, and a bottle of water. He rushed back to his office, barely acknowledging Gayle DeJean, who had arrived at work and was waving at him somewhat sheepishly from her desk.

Bunker closed his door, locking it this time. He opened the PPE kit and donned a respirator, rubber gloves, and safety glasses. He then opened the fentanyl test kit and removed a small plastic cup with graduated lines on the side. He poured a small amount—15 milliliters—of the bottled water into the cup.

Bunker picked up the plastic bag holding the orb and opened it. He used a thin wooden strip that came with the kit to scrape a small amount of material from the orb while it was still inside the plastic bag. He then tilted the bag so the scraped fragments dropped into the plastic cup. Bunker quickly resealed the orb, wrapping it inside both plastic bags. He returned his attention to the cup, seeing that the scrapings were partially dissolved. He used the wooden strip to swirl the water until no trace of the scrapings were visible.

Okay...test strips next.

Despite wearing a respirator, Bunker found himself breathing shallowly, already suspecting what the test results would show.

He tore open a packet holding test strips. They looked exactly like some of those used for home pregnancy tests. Bunker removed a strip and held it in the solution for ten seconds. When it was withdrawn, Bunker balanced it on top of the cup. It would take 60 seconds to get a result.

Bunker knew the test detected fentanyl and 11 fentanyl analogues, or variants. Some were worse than others. Carfentanil, he knew, was easily the most potent. It was a binary test, meaning the result would either be positive or negative. Bunker watched the second hand on the wall clock as it made a complete sweep.

This has to be the reason Eli and his Chinese partner want the golf bag back. The Shortridge brothers were dealers...Shadow was too. The round glob is valuable enough to them that they'll kill for it.

The second hand reached its starting point. Bunker looked at the strip. One red line appeared on it.

Positive!

He looked at the plastic bag on his desk, now knowing that it held a potent synthetic opioid.

What the hell do I do with that?

He decided to return it to the cooler compartment where he'd found it, reasoning that the kidnappers may want to verify it was inside the golf bag as a precondition to releasing his mom. He did so, then slid open his office window to allow the space to air out.

Hell, this stuff might be so powerful that Zeke will still sniff it when he comes in tomorrow.

The thought gave him pause.

That's why they're so desperate to get the Running Dog bag tonight! They know about Zeke's walk-through tomorrow. The informant told them about it.

Bunker carefully placed the cup with the dissolved drug solution into his desk wastebasket. His rubber gloves followed. He then removed the trash liner and tied it shut.

Have to get this stuff out of the building.

He slung the golf bag over his shoulder before removing the safety glasses and respirator. Picking up the trash liner, he exited his office. He pulled the door shut and made for the front door. He noticed lights on in all of the other offices but avoided eye contact with anyone as he crossed the workspace. Gayle was on the phone. He noticed her eyeing the golf bag as he pushed through the door.

Was she the leak?

Bunker tried to work through it as he took the steps to the rear entrance. Whoever was informing the kidnappers—Bunker now knew that in addition to kidnapping and murder they were involved in drug trafficking—was deriving some benefit. A steady supply of opioids for personal use would explain it. Gayle was a mother of two with a steady job and, as far as he knew, a stable marriage. Though the general public might not consider her a likely candidate to be hooked on such a substance, Bunker knew it happened to people in all walks of life.

What about the others in the department? Pappy Karabin's recent interest in Bunker's mom seemed even more suspicious now. Detective Simon, Bunker knew, had at least one surgery to correct a sports injury. Could he have gotten hooked on prescription medication like Bean Grissom? Bunker couldn't dismiss the possibility. And Sheriff Hollis couldn't be ruled out. What did Bunker know about the man's personal life?

Very little. Hollis rarely spoke about anything that wasn't work related. Searching his memory, Bunker could think of just one example. Hollis once mentioned that he frequently visits the National Museum of the U.S. Air Force at Wright-Patterson Air Force Base. His father was a plane mechanic in Vietnam. He had worked on F-4 Phantom fighter-bombers with the 8th Tactical Fighter Wing, commanded by Robin Olds, a legendary combat pilot. Olds shot down 12 German planes in World War II and was still deadly in Southeast Asia over two decades later. Sporting a non-regulation handlebar mustache, Olds, by then a colonel, downed four enemy MiG fighters over Vietnam. Sheriff Hollis said his father helped paint red stars on the colonel's F-4, one for each victory. The sheriff, in fact, was named Robin after Olds.

Could be any of those four people.

Bunker decided that he had to continue to act as if all four were the informant. He reached the ground floor and made his way to the parking lot, first securing the golf bag in the Malibu's trunk, then tossing the trash liner in the nearby dumpster.

Upon returning to the second floor, he saw that Gayle was off the phone.

"Good morning, Detective Bunker."

"Hi Gayle. Can I get the evidence room log? I need to sign out the personal effects from the accident victim."

DeJean nodded. "Sure." She produced the log and watched him enter the appropriate information. Bunker noted that she avoided eye contact and made no comment about the removal of the items. He finished with the log and headed toward his office.

"Thanks, Gayle."

"Sure...sure, Amos."

Halfway to his door Bunker saw Detective Karabin coming from the break room, a cup of coffee in hand.

"Hey, Amos. Big break in the Turner case."

Bunker turned, "Yeah?"

Pappy drew near. "Yeah. He used his Visa to pay for pizza last night. Athens County ran it down. The pizza joint delivered to a house outside Nelsonville. They're gearing up to hit the place later today. Looks like we'll get our man."

Bunker feigned enthusiasm.

"That's great, Pappy. Let me know how it goes down."

"Will do." Karabin strode to his office.

Bunker worked in his office until early afternoon. For the first hour he wore the respirator and kept the door closed. He emailed the state foster and adoption program, adding an addendum to his initial negative submission on the Hulls. This time he was effusive in his praise, reporting that his previous concerns were preliminary and that "new evidence has come to light that makes any negative assessments of Paul and Lauren Hull, and their suitability to care for an adoptive child, null and void." He followed this up with a phone call and, after waiting on hold for several minutes, reached the case worker that was in charge of the Hulls' application. They spoke for several minutes before the call ended, with Bunker doing his utmost to vouch for the couple.

If that doesn't move them to the top of the list, I have completely lost my touch when it comes to bureaucrat-speak.

He allowed himself a small smile. It faded quickly.

It's the least I can do for them.

Bunker opened the door, while leaving the window open. He then spent another hour typing up a detailed synopsis of everything he'd learned about Running Dog and the two kidnappers. This included every aspect of his mother's abduction, his failed attempt to rescue her, and the opioid and .22 bullet discoveries he'd made that morning. When he'd finished, he made a copy. He used the small printer in his office rather than the bizhub out in the main office.

If something happens to me tonight, I want to leave a trail of breadcrumbs for the rest of the department.

He slid the copy into a large envelope and put it in the top drawer of his desk. It was now early afternoon. He wanted to get home, coordinate with Paul, and wait for the call from the kidnappers.

He stood and automatically searched his desk for his holstered Glock before again remembering he hadn't worn it to the office.

It would be great to get in a nap before things go down

—

"Ouch! Dammit!"

He'd bumped his thigh on the corner of his desk. The impact moved the heavy wooden unit a full two inches. Bunker watched as a number of items on the desktop shifted, including the two Running Dog golf balls he'd received from J.D. The balls rolled to the side of the desk, evading Bunker's reflexive grasp. He watched as they fell to the polished concrete. One bounced 18 inches and continued toward the corner.

The second ball struck the floor with a dull thud and barely rebounded. Bunker stared in fascination.

Hel-lo.

CHAPTER THIRTY-EIGHT

The call from the kidnappers came at 3:37. Bunker had just finished working on the golf ball with the deadened properties in his garage. He carried a PPE kit in his Malibu and utilized it while cutting through the tough Surlyn dimples of the ball with a coping saw. He worked with a small bottle of naloxone nasal spray nearby, though he had doubts that he would recognize the effects of an overdose in time to self-administer the inhibitor. After removing the cover, he discovered a layer of a sticky, goo-like substance whose function was not evident. He carefully scraped it away. The remaining core was a twin of the orb that had tested positive earlier in his office.

They're smuggling dangerous synthetic opioids into the country inside golf balls!

Bunker carefully sealed the deadly core of the ball inside two layers of plastic and placed it in the trunk of the Malibu, all the while thinking of the Running Dog logo balls that filled the pockets of the leather golf bag. He tried to imagine the magnitude of the problem.

How many of the balls contain drugs? How long has this been going on?

He could only guess at the answers. It was apparent to Bunker that he had just scratched the surface of an enormous drug operation, one that seemed to be international in nature. The string of connected murders proved that those involved were willing to do anything to facilitate and expand their activities.

And these people have my mom.

The call came from the same phone number that Eli used to send the picture of Bunker's mom after she'd been taken from her house. Bunker suspected it was a burner phone.

"Hello, this is Bunker."

363

The man on the other end got right to the point.

"Eleven o'clock tonight. Bring the bag. No weapons, got it?"

Bunker responded. "Where?"

"I said *no weapons*, is that clear?"

"Yeah, no weapons." Bunker fought to keep his composure.

The caller—Bunker recognized Eli's voice—continued. "I better not see that Glock pistol you had last night, got it?"

"Got it."

"That goes for Hull, too. By the way, we checked to see if you were lying when you gave us his identity. You were a good boy and told the truth. If you keep following directions, you will get your mom back. If not...well..."

Bunker knew that the most obvious way for Paul's identity to be checked was by running his license plates. This would've most likely been accomplished by someone in the sheriff's department contacting the Department of Motor Vehicles. It was another example of the connections the kidnappers seemed to have.

"So you and Hull will show up tonight wearing nothing but shorts and t-shirts. I'll need proof that you're not armed and the only way to be sure of that is to make sure you have no place to hide a weapon."

Bunker's anxiety level was climbing. He had not yet learned the location of the exchange. If he and Paul had guessed right, they had a chance to save his mother, turn the tables on the kidnappers, and possibly unravel the entire Running Dog operation. If they guessed wrong...

Bunker didn't want to consider it.

The instructions went on.

"We will meet at the WACO Museum south of Troy...Do you know it?"

A wave of relief washed over Bunker. He allowed a smile to momentarily cross his lips, realizing Eli had incorrectly pronounced the name of the museum with a long A, as in the city in Texas.

We were right!

"Yeah, I know it. You take Market Street south out of town."

"You and Hull get there at eleven o'clock. Not a minute before. We'll be watching the area all night to make sure you don't try to play the hero and ambush us. We get a sniff of something like that and your mom pays for it. Got it?"

Bunker was growing tired of the threats but had to avoid provoking the kidnapper.

"Yeah, got it."

"You'll see an unpaved lane on the south side of the parking lot. Turn off your headlights. Follow the lane until you see my vehicle. I'll show you where to park. I'll have your mom. We make the trade and go our separate ways."

Bunker was now sure that the kidnappers planned to kill him, his mother, and Paul. They could not allow living witnesses who could identify them.

"Oh yeah, Amos...my associate will have a rifle trained on you the entire time. You saw it last night. He'll be hidden... and he's an excellent shot."

Bunker sensed the air of superiority coming through the phone connection.

"See you tonight, Amos. Eleven o'clock...sharp."

The call ended.

Bunker immediately called Paul.

"We were right. It's WACO." He repeated the kidnapper's instructions.

"Gotcha," Paul acknowledged. "See you tonight. Everything on my end should be in place soon. I'll be at your house around 10. Try to get some rest."

Min followed Dylan's Range Rover around the traffic circle in downtown Troy. It was 10:20 p.m. and the heat of the day—it had reached 87 degrees—had subsided as darkness fell over western Ohio. Min drove his own SUV, a clone of Dylan's. He wore his customary black jeans and t-shirt, which, on this night, were more than merely a statement of his identity. The clothing would allow him to easily blend into the darkened landscape as he waited to take the shot. He reviewed the past few hours in his head.

He and Dylan packed up all of their possessions at the Airbnb. With the exception of Min's rifle and Dylan's Titleist driver, everything fit in the two small suitcases that they traveled with. Min walked to the driveway and stored his suitcase inside his Evoque. Dylan's suitcase, the rifle, and the driver went into the rear cargo compartment of Dylan's SUV in the garage. The men would be leaving Min's vehicle at a drop site—a small used car lot south of the WACO property—before he transferred to Dylan's.

They made a token effort to meet the needs of Bunker's mother, asking her several times if she needed to use the bathroom. She did not verbalize an answer—she still wore a vacant look on her face—but twice she nodded. Both times Min removed the tape from her legs and escorted her. She ate very little, finally finishing most of a bowl of microwave oatmeal that Dylan had found in the pantry late in the afternoon. She slept in the recliner for nearly four hours afterward.

Around noon, Gayle DeJean texted a photo of a computer screen showing information from the DMV. Dylan was on the phone with the Home2 Suites where Dax was staying—he and Min would need a room for the night—when it reached his phone. It revealed that Bunker was telling the truth about Hull's vehicle being in their driveway the previous night. Hull was 51 and had a clean driving record. The page included a driver's license photo. Dylan gazed at it for several seconds, committing it to memory. When they met tonight, Dylan wanted to make sure that it was Hull that showed up. If a different man accompanied Bunker, that meant that there was still another loose end to tie up.

Dax called after lunch. His meeting with Mahmud was set for 8 p.m. at Lust, the gentlemen's club. Mahmud called him earlier during his own lunch break to confirm that the meeting was still on. Dax took this as a good sign.

"I think he's more interested in doing business than he let on earlier."

On a whim, Dax asked the doctor to see if he could use his connections to learn more about Willie's condition.

"It probably violates every rule in the book, but he said he would see what he could do. He hinted that there's someone at Willie's hospital that he's, uh, done business with."

Dylan commented, "I don't think Mahmud is exactly Mr. Ethics."

Dylan placed his call to Bunker just after 3:30. He gave explicit instructions, stressing that no weapons were to be brought to the exchange. Though Bunker seemed compliant, Dylan remained wary.

This guy's a cop...and the other guy was in the military. We can't take any chances...have to get right on top of them.

Dylan and Min ordered Chinese from the Great Wall restaurant and had it delivered for a late dinner. Dana was kept in the downstairs bathroom until the delivery driver left. She sat on the floor, her back against the vanity, with the same blank look she'd shown since they had pulled her from her doorway. After Dana was returned to the recliner, Min fixed a bowl of steamed dumplings and fried shrimp—finger food— and offered it to her. Again, it was met with the same flat expression.

Watching from the dining room table, Dylan asked with a smirk, "What's the Chinese word for zombie?"

"Jiāngshī." Min couldn't help himself. He joined in Dylan's laughter.

They left the Airbnb for the last time at 9:45 and headed toward Troy. Dylan led the way. Duct tape secured the wrists and ankles of Bunker's mother, with a separate strip covering her mouth. She was on the floor of the back seat and was covered by an extra bedspread that Min had found in an upstairs hall closet.

A few minutes before reaching Troy, Dax called again.

"Mahmud is in."

"Excellent." Dylan pumped a fist as he drove.

Looks like things are starting to go in the right direction.

Dax continued. "He wants the first shipment as soon as possible—by the Fourth of July at the latest. He says he knows people who can process the raw stuff and turn it into usable product. He didn't say who they were, how they'll do it, or what the final product will look like but—"

Dylan finished for him. "But we don't care."

Dax agreed. "We do not." Then he sighed. "He had some other news."

"Spill it."

"Willie isn't going to make it. Mahmud's connection says it's one hundred percent. They're planning to harvest his organs...either tonight or tomorrow. His parents are at the hospital. They're freaked."

Several thoughts and emotions swam through Dylan's head. He was silent as he considered.

I should get with Zhou...have him divert Willie's share of the payments.

The venture with Running Dog had never been just about money for Dylan. He sought to prove that he was an elite, a top performer, that he could be just as ruthless as anyone that the top institutions in the country had ever produced.

But—he reasoned—if there was extra money to be had, why not make his claim?

His next thought was more abstract.

Willie was an organ donor? Hmm...you think you know someone...At least we don't have to worry about Willie being a loose end.

After clearing the traffic circle, Dylan dialed Min. He'd decided to not tell him about Willie, reasoning that negative thoughts and emotions could affect his concentration and possibly hinder his ability to make the shot tonight. Dylan glanced at his rearview mirror and could just make out his colleague's face as he answered.

"Yes?"

"The museum is up ahead on the left. I'll pull into the parking lot and make a wide turn. Follow me in. Look for anything suspicious."

"Got it."

Thirty seconds later Dylan turned in at the sign in front of the complex. He wheeled to the right and crossed the parking lot as Min followed, slowing momentarily as he reached the point where the dirt and gravel trail began. He then executed a wide turn to the left. The beams of his headlights spilled out to the airfield beyond before tracking across the buildings. Min's lights traced the same path a few seconds later. There was no sign of activity. No vehicles were evident. Dylan nodded in satisfaction and steered back to the entrance.

Less than a minute later, both Range Rovers pulled into the used car lot. It was located to the south, less than a quarter mile from the I-75 entrance ramp that was part of their escape route from the WACO property. Dylan drove to one side of the lot and spotted a gap between two cars. He rolled down his window and pointed. Min's Evoque glided into the space.

Min jumped into the passenger seat of Dylan's SUV and turned to look behind the seat. The blanket completely concealed their hostage.

"Did she give you any trouble?"

"Not a bit." Dylan shook his head. "You're a good traveler, aren't you, Dana?" He half-turned his head to the rear, then grinned at Min. There was a slight movement under the bedspread but no noise.

They returned to the museum. This time, after turning into the entrance, Dylan turned off the headlights. Pale moonlight illuminated the property, allowing him to find the trail. Once off the asphalt surface of the parking lot, the Evoque swayed slightly from side to side as it progressed along the uneven surface. They rolled south at a crawl for most of a minute until the trail curved to the left at a line of trees. Dylan eased through the turn and they continued eastward, the flat, grassy surface of the airstrip ahead to their left.

Min gazed ahead. Another tree line lay in the distance, running right to left. He knew the elevated position where he would be stationed was somewhere in the gloom. From this angle the rise, covered in dark vegetation, blended in with the trees beyond. As the Range Rover continued east, the feature took shape.

Min spoke. "I see it."

Dylan verified Min's observation.

"Yeah, that's it...let me get another hundred yards or so closer."

They drove on. The Range Rover had now reached the edge of the airstrip. The featureless expanse of the landing area disappeared into the murky distance to the north. When Dylan determined that the Range Rover had reached the proper spot, he braked. It was obvious from this vantage point that the rise of ground on the runway's eastern edge was not a natural feature. It looked like something created by skimming a straight edge across a child's sandbox. It was 150 feet long and 15 feet high. The vegetation on its surface appeared to be dense.

Dylan surveyed the elevation.

"Yeah, I'd say that's sand wedge distance."

Min sniffed. "For you."

Three minutes later Min was gone. He'd retrieved his P-15 Minuteman rifle and marched off in the direction of the rise.

Paul arrived at Bunker's house late. It was nearly 10:15. Already on edge, Bunker had paced in his front room and watched for Paul's SUV. He checked his phone frequently, looking for text messages or missed calls. He saw only a group text from Sheriff Hollis, informing all the recipients of a mandatory meeting in the office tomorrow at 8 a.m.

They must've located the other suspect—Kevin Turner —in Nelsonville and figured out he had nothing to do with the murders.

When the Honda Pilot arrived, Bunker opened the door and welcomed his associate—a man that he was beginning to think of as a friend.

"Everything alright?" He stared at Paul, half expecting to hear that their plan had fallen apart.

Paul gave him a reassuring smile as they entered the house. Like Bunker, he wore shorts and a t-shirt.

"All good. The timing was tight. On paper, this kind of thing looks easy. In practice...well, the logistics can be pretty damn difficult."

Again, Bunker was conscious of the lengths Paul had gone to in order to assist a man he hardly knew.

They sat in the living room and reviewed the plan. Paul revealed a new wrinkle. Bunker stared at him incredulously.

"You're kidding...is that possible? At night?"

Paul grinned.

"Oh, I think it is."

Dylan checked the time on his phone: 10:52.

He had turned the Range Rover around after Min departed. The SUV now faced west, toward Market Street. He wanted to be ready to make a quick exit if anything went wrong. If all went as planned, Min would return to the vehicle after the targets had been eliminated.

After Min left, Dylan spent several minutes alone in the Evoque with Dana Bunker but hardly gave her a thought. He reviewed the plan, looking for holes. The only possibility, so far as he could see, was that Bunker and Hull would try to ambush him somehow. It was a legitimate concern, especially considering the events of the previous night. Dylan had Willie's pistol in his hand, having retrieved it from the glove compartment. He still planned to lull Bunker and Hull to complacency at the exchange, holding only a knife, but he'd be damned if he'd be taken by surprise again before then.

If Bunker or Hull thought they were going to catch him off guard before the planned meet, they would be sadly mistaken. The pistol would go directly to Dana Bunker's head.

On Market Street a vehicle slowed and turned into the museum entrance. It angled toward the parking lot.

Right on time.

Bunker drove the Malibu through the lot and switched off his headlights. He eased onto the trail and drove slowly, focusing on the path in the pale moonlight. Next to him, Paul strained to see evidence of Dana and the kidnapper.

"There they are." He pointed to the east.

Bunker turned and saw a shape in the distance. Seconds later the Malibu reached the curve in the trail and began to move directly toward the shape. As they drew near, they saw that it was, as expected, a dark grey Range Rover. Two figures, one behind the other, stood next to the vehicle. Once the Malibu crept to within 40 feet of the Range Rover, the identities of the figures were clear; the kidnapper stood behind Dana Bunker. His left hand gripped her arm, his right was near her throat.

Bunker was silent. He stared at his mother. She looked haggard, exhausted. Her wrists were duct taped. A separate strip covered her mouth.

"That son of a bitch. If he's hurt her—"

Paul interrupted. "Easy, Amos. I need you to focus."

Bunker nodded, his eyes still on his mom.

The kidnapper snapped an arm in the direction of the airfield. When he did so, the blade of a long knife glinted in the moonlight. Both Paul and Bunker saw it.

Bunker repeated, "That son of a bitch."

Paul directed, "He wants you to pull off the trail and park in the grass."

Bunker guided the Malibu off the trail, his face taut. The car bumped along for thirty feet before Paul spoke.

"He's waving...stop here."

Dylan watched as the two men got out of the car and stood side-by-side, facing him. He was relieved to see that the second man was Hull.

No surprises...excellent!

He walked Bunker's mom a few steps toward them and stopped.

"Where's my bag?"

Bunker answered. "In the trunk."

"Get it."

Dylan pulled Dana closer and pressed the flat side of the knife's blade against her neck. It was a 10-inch carving knife that he'd taken from the Airbnb. He'd examined every knife in the butcher block holder on the kitchen counter and selected this one. There was more than one reason. First, it was intimidating. Bunker and Hull were sure to focus their attention on it. Second, and more important to Dylan, he believed the length of the blade would allow him to draw it across Dana's neck and avoid having her blood spurt onto his hand.

Dylan had killed many times—always from up close with the modified putter head—but he'd remained unsoiled. He had no desire to have actual blood on his hands.

Bunker opened the driver's side door and pulled a lever to release the trunk. He walked to the rear of the vehicle and pulled out the bag before closing the trunk.

"Bring it toward me, both of you," Dylan ordered.

Bunker lifted the bag and, with Paul to his left, took several steps toward the kidnapper.

"That's far enough. Set it down. Remember...there's a rifle aimed at you right now."

Bunker lowered the bag and stood it on the ground. It leaned to one side and he repositioned it. As he did so, Dylan pulled a small Maglite from the front left pocket of his golf shorts. He increased the pressure of the knife blade against Dana's neck to maintain control. He turned on the Maglite and shined it on the two men to his front.

"Pull your shirts up and turn around slowly. I want to make sure you're not armed."

Bunker and Hull complied. Both had raised a hand to shield their eyes, but Dylan knew it was too late. The Maglite's beam served more than one purpose. In addition to verifying that the men brought no weapons, it would disrupt their night vision for a few moments, helping to obscure Dylan's actions.

"Looks like you were good boys. Now move back."

Bunker and Hull backed partway to the Malibu.

"Stop there." Dylan turned his attention to the golf bag, its white leather nearly phosphorescent in the pale light.

It's all there...including the putter.

He used a knee to prod Dana forward, stopping when they reached the bag.

"You have your damn bag, now let her go," Bunker demanded.

Dylan brushed his lips across Dana's ear.

"Go to your son."

Dana hesitated, then took her first step toward salvation.

CHAPTER THIRTY-NINE

Min Xian watched through the Romeo Red Dot sight mounted to his rifle. There was enough ambient light to make the shot without the device. With it, the task would be simple.

Min was lying in a prone shooting position on top of the rise of ground. He'd walked directly toward the feature when he left the Range Rover, fixing on a small sapling that rose a few yards from its center. He used the sapling as a guide and marched across the low grass of the airstrip, holding the rifle at his waist.

I should buy a sling for the rifle. It would be much more convenient.

The ground was still soft from the previous night's rain. Min could feel it give in spots as he made his way toward his destination. A light scent of alfalfa hung in the air. Stars overhead in the cloudless sky provided a spectacular backdrop to the three-quarter moon. Reaching the base of the ridge, Min picked his way up its slope. He nearly lost his balance at one point but was able to right himself and continue to the top. Once there, he surveyed the area and selected a relatively flat spot 20 feet north of the sapling. He settled into his shooting position. In his black shirt and jeans, he would be invisible to anyone in the field below.

He'd watched through the sight as the sedan entered the museum's parking lot and made its way along the trail to the Range Rover. He saw Dylan get out of the vehicle and open the rear door. The dome light was on and Min saw Dylan lean inside and make quick motions with his arm.

Cutting off the ankle tape.

Dylan stepped back. Min saw Dana Bunker tentatively emerge from the vehicle. Dylan closed the door and moved with the hostage to the front of the Evoque to greet the newcomers.

He watched as things unfolded exactly as Dylan had planned. Bunker and Hull retrieved the Running Dog bag from the trunk of the car and approached Dylan and the woman. Min found himself straining to hear the conversation, but the distance was too great. He suddenly realized that he'd tuned out the background noise. It was the sound of crickets.

It was a good omen.

Bunker saw the kidnapper whisper something into his mother's ear before roughly tearing the strip of duct tape from her mouth. She flinched but kept her eyes straight ahead. Bunker saw that she was looking at him. A trace of recognition seemed to flicker in her eyes. She walked in his direction. Bunker focused on her face, failing to notice the kidnapper's actions behind her.

Dylan slowly lowered the knife and repositioned it so he had the use of both hands. He reached for the putter and deftly removed its head cover. He then manipulated the hosel, uncoupling the putter's head from its shaft. He heard the satisfying click of the trigger as it snapped in place.

He was ready. Min would fire any second. Dylan was less than ten feet from Bunker and Hull. The woman had crossed half the distance in between. This was Min's cue. Hull was closest to Min's position. He would die by the rifle's bullet. Dylan would quickly step forward and shoot Bunker with the .22. He would fire at center mass, incapacitating the detective. He would then use the knife on the woman and, if necessary, her son.

He began to raise the putter head.

Min watched the woman step away from the golf bag. He saw Dylan's hands find the putter. Min carefully adjusted his rifle to the right, placing the red dot in the sight's reticle onto the center of Paul Hull's head. He took a deep breath and began to let it out.

The pain was intense. He felt it on the right side of his body, high on his ribcage. Min was instantly aware that the origin of the pain was external. Something had struck him with enough force, he sensed, to break bones. He felt himself rolling to the left, instinctively curling into a fetal position. He released his grip on the rifle and screamed.

Sebastian "Scrabble" Tzortzakakis, the former Army Ranger, dropped his Hoyt compound bow to the ground, quickly rose from his knees, and rushed toward the shooter. The bow was one of several he owned. He'd chosen it for the night's task because its length—34 inches—made it shorter than the others. He had rightly assumed that the more compact size would be an advantage when maneuvering to his hide site.

Scrabble took a call the night before from Paul, explaining the situation.

"I think we know where this thing is going down. If we're right, we've found a way to get someone to the area where the sniper will set up. We need someone who can get close to the guy and take him out. Someone capable. Know anyone that fits that description?"

Scrabble smiled. "Do we want to kill him?"

"No, we would prefer to take him alive. That avoids a murder charge. My partner on this is in law enforcement. We figure the cops will overlook roughing up the guy—especially if the rest of his crimes come to light."

"Well...that still might be fun." Scrabble paused.

"I'm in."

The method used to get Scrabble to Ohio was ingenious. Paul's longtime CCT buddy, Gatewood Dowdell, was in the midst—in his capacity with the security force at Wright-Patt—of coordinating the influx of military aircraft from the East Coast as Hurricane Adelia barreled toward landfall.

The Air Force's 165th Airlift Wing was based at Savannah Air National Guard base. The unit flew C-130 cargo planes. Eight of the planes were the most recent variant, the C-130J-30 Super Hercules. All eight of these flew to Wright-Patt on Monday. A few of the older C-130H Hercules models had not yet left. They were scheduled to depart early Tuesday, just beating the storm. Gatewood pulled a few strings and secured a spot on the last plane for the former Ranger.

Although Scrabble lived near Savannah, he still had to scramble to grab his gear and jump through hoops at the base before getting on the plane. He brought along a little surprise —his Hoyt Concept FX bow. It was an exotic looking contraption with wheels and pulleys that could propel an arrow at a speed of over 330 feet per second. Scrabble had mastered its use over hundreds of practice hours. He'd placed highly in national competitions. Along with the bow, Tzortzakakis carried a target arrow that featured a blunt rubber head that flared out at its tip to create a larger striking surface. It was typically used for target shooting into tree stumps. The rubber kept the point from penetrating. But Scrabble knew that some hunters used them on small game. The arrow killed by shock, not by penetration.

He had always wanted to carry a bow on a real mission. Now he had his chance.

When he arrived at Wright-Patt, Paul and Gatewood were there to meet him. Scrabble got off the plane wearing woodland camo pants and a dull green shirt with the logo of the Windjammer, an Isle of Palms, South Carolina bar.

Paul bumped fists with him.

"Lookin' good, Scrabs. What's with the bow?"

Scrabble simply smiled.

They finalized the plan. Sunset was at 9:04 p.m. Paul drove his Pilot—carrying both his and Lauren's bikes—with Scrabble to Miami Shores Golf Course at dusk. They parked in the same place the Hulls had on the day they made the drone video. Paul led the way south on the path, riding Lauren's bike. Scrabble followed on Paul's, his bow and target arrow strapped to his back. Their pace was slow as darkness fell. When they reached the sign that pointed out the location of the WACO field, they hid the bikes. Both men crept through the trees until the elevated area of earth came into view.

Paul spoke. "Okay, you got it from here."

Tzortzakakis nodded.

"Shouldn't you have brought more than one arrow?"

Scrabble touched the pancake holster on his hip. It was Bunker's Aker model, and held the Glock. The detective had left it with Paul, who had passed it on. Scrabble was to fire three quick shots into the ground once the sniper was neutralized.

"I'll still have this. Besides...I'll only need one arrow." He grinned.

Once Paul left, Scrabble slowly made his way to the rise and scaled it from the east. He had no way of knowing if the sniper was already in position, so he took his time, stopping several times to listen. At last he neared the top and peered over, careful to not rise above the peak and silhouette his body against the sky where an adversary might see it. Visibility was excellent—he'd operated overseas in far worse—and there was no sign of another human.

Some time later, two identical SUVs entered the parking lot near a group of buildings on the far side of the airstrip. They circled the lot slowly before leaving. Minutes later one of them returned. Scrabble watched as it drove along the trail. Soon after it stopped, a lone figure made its way across the field in the direction of the elevation. The figure carried a rifle.

Scrabble watched as the man reached the slope and crashed upward through the brush. He shook his head at the sniper's lack of fieldcraft. Eventually the man with the rifle settled into a shooting position. Scrabble was more than 100 feet to the man's right. Over the course of the next ten minutes, he crept to within 60. The dampness of the vegetation made the task relatively easy.

Scrabble and the sniper watched the action unfold below from separate hides as Paul and Bunker arrived. Scrabble concentrated on the sniper—an Asian—as the situation progressed below. Once Bunker's mother began to walk away from the kidnapper, the sniper's posture changed. Scrabble sensed the man's tension and rose to his knees. The bow and arrow were poised as Scrabble aimed for the sniper's ribs.

The shooter took a deep breath.

Tzortzakakis loosed the arrow. He dropped the bow and sprinted for the shooter as a scream rent the night. Scrabble pounced on the man, kicking the rifle aside. He then drew the Glock and fired three shots into the brush.

Paul watched Dana Bunker move away from the kidnapper. He heard Amos's concerned voice.

"Mom, are you okay?"

Dana continued toward Amos, the beginning of a smile forming on her face.

Paul tensed, preparing for action.

It will happen now.

The scream pierced the night, coming from Paul's left, exactly where he'd expected it. He took a step toward the kidnapper and saw the man's hand rise from the top of the golf bag.

Bunker heard the scream. He saw his mom's expression —which had begun to revitalize for the first time in two days— cloud with confusion.

Three quick gunshots rang out.

Dylan recognized the scream immediately—it was Min. Something had gone terribly wrong. He'd believed Hull was a split second away from taking a bullet. Dylan was raising the modified putter to fire at Bunker. The scream changed everything. Dylan hesitated for a beat, unsure of his next move.

He heard the gunshots.

It's all gone to hell! It was Bunker and Hull? They played us! How...?

Dylan saw both Hull and Bunker step quickly toward him, one on each side of the woman. The putter was up now.

I have one bullet!

Dylan chose his target and squeezed the trigger.

CHAPTER FORTY

He sat in the small room, staring at nothing—and everything. A life had ended, snuffed out by a heartless criminal. Memories of that life would live on with those fortunate enough to have been touched by it. But he knew that memories were fleeting. Many were already difficult to elicit. As time passed, he supposed, it could become easier—or harder.

Amos Bunker's mother was gone.

His mind replayed the events again and again, as if discovering something significant in the sequence might allow him to alter the result and save his mom.

Bunker flinched, remembering the report of a pistol at the instant that their plan was achieving success.

Seconds before, a scream had echoed across the field, having originated from the elevation where Paul's friend had been posted. This was followed by three gunshots, the signal that Tzortzakakis—the former Army Ranger—would give to convey the sniper was down. Amos had just recognized a trace of his mother's true self in her eyes. She was coming to him.

And then the shot.

How had it happened? I checked the golf bag. There was no gun. The kidnapper—murderer—wore shorts and a golf shirt. Could he have hidden a small .22 pistol in a pocket? He must have.

Bunker saw the next part of the sequence in great detail. He feared it would haunt him for the rest of his life. Confusion on his mother's face as she collapsed forward. Bunker rushing to catch her, not yet fully processing what had happened. Paul coming to their aid. The confused expression on Dana's face—inches from his—being replaced by one reflecting pain. Her final words to him as she faded to unconsciousness.

"Amos, you're a good boy."

Bunker now closed his eyes and buried his face in his hands. A tear ran down his cheek, taking him by surprise. He'd thought all his tears had been drained over the last few hours.

He'd lowered Dana to the ground and, with Paul's help, searched frantically for an entry wound. She wore a dark blouse, making it difficult—even in the moonlight—to detect a bloodstain. Paul, obviously trained to some extent to deal with gunshot wounds, gripped the back of Dana's collar and ripped it open, exposing her back. They saw it then, an evil little hole to the left of her spine, a few inches below her neck. Paul immediately began to apply pressure and turned to Bunker.

"We have to get her to a hospital!"

Bunker stood and glanced at the Malibu. He saw movement out of the corner of his eye and turned to see the Range Rover racing away from them.

The kidnapper—murderer—was gone.

Bunker sped to the hospital in downtown Troy, his pulse racing, as Paul sat in the back seat, desperately applying pressure to Dana's wound. The Malibu ran every red light and swerved into the emergency entrance drive of Kettering Health just three minutes after leaving the WACO airfield.

The bullet pierced Dana's left atrium and lodged behind her breastbone. She was still alive when they arrived and was rushed into surgery. Twenty minutes later it was over.

Dana Bunker was dead.

The next few hours were a blur. Law enforcement—both the sheriff's department and the Troy PD—were notified of the incident. They scrambled, sending representatives to the crime scene as well as the hospital to interview Amos and Paul. They put out an APB on a Caucasian male in his late twenties or early thirties driving a grey Range Rover with out of state plates. Sheriff Hollis arrived with Detective Karabin. Bunker asked to speak to the sheriff alone. The story had to be told. Even though Hollis was one of four people that Bunker believed could be working with the criminals, he decided to gamble and confide in him.

After a scowling Karabin stepped out, Bunker began.

"Someone in our department is working with these people."

Hollis shot him a grim look.

"I know...it's Gayle."

Bunker was stunned. Not that Gayle was the informant, but that the sheriff knew.

"We just found out this afternoon." He glanced at his watch and saw that it was now past 2 a.m. "Make that yesterday afternoon. I've been working with Pappy on this ever since the drugs in the evidence room came up missing. Let me get him back in here and we'll explain it."

Hollis had been furious when the opioids were stolen. He summoned Karabin, the senior man in the department, and put in place a series of measures. Some, like the addition of cameras to record the comings and goings at the evidence room, were overt. Others were not.

"You set up tripwires," Bunker stated matter-of-factly.

Hollis nodded. "One of these was an agreement with the DMV to report any unusual requests coming from the sheriff's department."

Pappy added, "We thought one of the things a person desperate enough to steal opioids from our office might do was run plate numbers to trade for money or more drugs. Today, our liaison at the DMV let us know that Gayle requested a plate be run."

"Let me guess—it was for a Honda Pilot registered to Paul Hull."

Both Karabin and Hollis nodded.

Pappy continued. "We confronted Gayle this afternoon and she broke down, admitted everything. She's addicted, deeply in debt. Her marriage is on the rocks. She was passing information to the Shortridge brothers until they were killed. She says she was approached by strangers who knew about her agreement with Garrett and Gerard. They demanded the same arrangement. She says she had no choice."

In a low voice, Bunker breathed, "She had a choice."

Hollis nodded. "Yeah, she did. Anyway, I sent out a group text about a mandatory meeting. We were going to lay it all out to everybody in the morning."

Bunker speculated out loud. "I got the text. I figured they caught Kevin Turner in Athens County and figured out he wasn't involved."

Pappy chimed in. "Actually, they did."

Bunker eyed him. "What? They cleared him?"

Pappy nodded. "Turner's cellmate in prison has a sister. She came to visit him and met Turner. They hit it off and stayed in touch after he got out. He left home over a week ago and has been staying with her. All her neighbors vouch for him."

"True love." The sheriff shook his head.

Bunker directed his gaze at Pappy. "Tell me about the men Gayle was involved with...did she describe them?"

Karabin gave a nod. "She talked about three men, all late twenties, early thirties. All Caucasian."

"No Chinese man?"

By this time Paul Hull had accompanied several deputies and police officers back to the WACO complex where they retrieved Sebastian Tzortzakakis. They'd also placed a Chinese man—who appeared to be in great pain—in custody.

"Nope. She had first names—or aliases—for them. Her first meeting was with two men. The one she called Willie matches the description of the accident victim that was carrying the golf bag. The second man was called Dax...taller, with long blonde hair. Her last meeting was with a man in a golf shirt...dark hair...Gayle said his name was Dylan. She got the impression he was the boss."

Bunker frowned. "No Eli?"

Karabin shook his head.

Bunker stared at the wall.

That last guy sounds like the kidnapper. Same general description...certainly came off as the man in charge. Could I have been chasing him under the wrong name?

Hollis interrupted. "Anyway, we've circulated the plate number of the Range Rover to all local and state authorities.

We're compiling the information you gave us earlier about the drugs in the golf bag. This thing could be huge. We'll be contacting the Feds as soon as their offices open this morning."

A humorless smile appeared on Bunker's face.

"I would contact the DEA. The kidnapper bragged about also having an informant in the FBI."

Hollis sighed and slowly shook his head. "Thanks."

As the two men rose to leave, Bunker directed a question at the sheriff.

"So it was just you and Pappy working to find the leaker?"

Hollis nodded. "I wanted to limit the number of people who knew. We had a problem and a large list of suspects."

Bunker considered this. "Was I on your list?"

"You were, although Pappy said there was no way you were involved."

Karabin added. "You're too much of a law and order guy, Amos. If it were you, you'd also have to be the greatest actor this side of Hollywood." He grinned.

"I'm not angry about being on your list. I have to tell you, I thought either of *you* could've been the leaker." Amos looked at Karabin. "Especially you, Pappy. For the last week or so you kept asking about my mom's condition...even volunteered to help me move her."

Karabin's hand was on the doorknob. He released his grip and faced Amos.

"Well, *my* mom went into a home several years ago. It was not a nice facility...usually smelled like disinfectant and dirty adult diapers. On a good day it smelled like old people, know what I mean? I even looked it up. A chemical called nonenal—I never forgot the word—is released through the skin of older people. It can be overpowering if it's not managed. Mom's place was bad. When I heard your mom had a spot in StoryPoint, I offered to help. I know their slots don't come open very often."

Bunker didn't know what to say.

Paul and Lauren knocked and entered an hour later. Bunker was scrolling on his phone. Lauren gave him a hug. Paul waited for them to separate then handed Amos a cup of coffee.

Lauren remarked, "I spoke to our administrator—called him at home. You can use this room as long as you like."

Bunker gave a half smile. "Thank you. I was just online looking for information on funeral homes. This is going to be... overwhelming. Mom and I knew she was going downhill but we both thought there was plenty of time to make these plans later." He looked worn; the fatigue was catching up to him. He sipped the coffee.

Paul had a question.

"Uh, Amos...when I went back to the field with the officers, Scrabble handed me your Glock and holster. I'd told them that he was on the right side of this thing, so they were more interested in the Chinese guy. Scrabs had it hidden under his shirt...said he wasn't sure if you'd be in trouble for loaning it to him—especially since he fired those three rounds. He's not going to say anything about the pistol. He's still out at the site with the cops. They want him to walk through his part in this once the sun's up."

He checked the wall clock.

"That's less than an hour away. They want me there too. It sounds like they'll get your side of the story when..."

Bunker finished for him. "When I've finished with things here."

"Anyway, your Malibu was still unlocked. I put the Glock in the glove box and hit the lock."

Slightly distracted, Bunker simply nodded. The range of emotions he'd experienced in the last few hours were catching up to him. Lack of sleep contributed to this. The mention of his Glock triggered something in him.

I wish I had one more chance at that son of a bitch...I know he's gone, but I wish I had one more chance.

Dylan left the exchange in a panic.

He grabbed the Running Dog bag and sprinted the few steps to the Range Rover. He threw the bag into the back seat and jumped behind the wheel. As he accelerated away from the meeting place, Dylan looked over his shoulder. Both Bunker and Hull were huddled around the woman. He briefly congratulated himself on his choice. It had come to him in a flash. Shooting the woman was the only way to escape the airfield. Had he turned the .22 on Bunker or Hull, the other man would've come for him. Dylan had no illusions about how a hand-to-hand confrontation with either of them would've ended—even though he still had the knife.

The knife! Where was the knife?

It was in his hand when he turned from the shooting and reached for the golf bag. Had he dropped it? He had now reached the parking lot and hurried to the entrance drive. There was no traffic on Market Street. Dylan swung the wheel to the left and accelerated away from the complex. Seconds later he was passing the car lot where Min's Evoque was parked. In less than a minute he was on I-75, heading south.

He set the cruise control at the speed limit before switching on the dome light. A quick inspection confirmed what he feared.

No knife. They'll get my fingerprints!

He then realized it was worse than that. He must've also dropped the modified putter head.

They'll figure it out...run ballistics. They'll match it to the murders. How many had there been?

Dylan couldn't remember. He slammed a hand on the steering wheel.

Bunker and Hull.

Those fucking guys! They played us...They played ME! How the hell had it happened?

Dylan fought to regain control. He took stock of his situation. He had Willie's pistol. He had plenty of cash—most of the payments from Woodruff and the Geigerlings was stashed in his suitcase. He'd gotten the golf bag back. Its connection to Running Dog Enterprises should assure assistance from them.

I have to talk to Zhou. He can get me on a cargo ship leaving Newark. I'll go to China. I've proven that I'm an asset to them...they can put me to work in another part of the world.

He continued to think it through as he approached Tipp City.

Min was screaming. What happened to him? There were gunshots. Is he dead? Worse...was he detained?

Dylan decided that he had to assume the worst-case scenario. The police—if they weren't already involved—would be soon. If Min cooperated, the entire organization could go down. Law enforcement would have Dylan's identity.

Min will resist, won't he?

Dylan thought about it for a few seconds.

Eventually he'll talk...make a deal. FUCK!

Another mile slipped by. It struck Dylan that he needed to call Dax. He sighed before dialing the number. Dax answered.

"Talk to me, boss. Did it go alright?"

Dylan sighed again. "It was a clusterfuck. They ambushed us. Min is gone—either dead or captured. It was all I could do to get out of there alive."

Dax was silent for a beat.

"You're kidding, right?"

Dylan shouted into the phone.

"Do I fucking SOUND like I'm kidding?"

Dax now began to panic. "What the hell are we gonna do?"

Dylan's fingers drummed on the steering wheel. He looked at the next road sign: "DAYTON INTERNATIONAL AIRPORT 1 MILE."

"Okay...listen up."

Dylan slept in the back seat of the Evoque in the long-term parking lot at the airport. He'd carefully selected a space next to a panel van whose high profile blocked the view of the Range Rover from one direction. Dylan utilized this cover to remove the front plate—it was from Ohio—from a Ford SUV that was parked facing the Evoque. He used a dime to turn the screws. He then switched the Ohio plate for the Connecticut version on the rear of his vehicle, which he slid under his seat.

That might buy me some time.

Before nodding off, he checked to see what time the airport car rental companies opened. He had his choice of six companies that opened at 7 a.m. Dylan used a Running Dog Enterprises credit card to reserve a full-size SUV—a black Nissan Armada—from Enterprise. He curled up under the bedspread that had covered Dana Bunker and slept.

Dylan woke at 6:30 a.m. to his cellphone alarm. He retrieved some mouthwash from his shaving kit, sloshed it around his mouth, and spit it onto the parking lot surface. He'd considered driving to Dax's hotel the night before but decided against it. His Evoque, he feared, would soon be the most hunted vehicle in the state. He had to exchange it for something different. Hiding it for one night in a large lot seemed his best option.

Dylan also considered having Dax join him in the long-term lot. He also discarded this idea.

If Min is in custody, he could give up Dax. He knows about the Home2 Suites. I'll let Dax be bait. If he's still free in the morning, I'll let him hook up with me.

It was, he decided, a very practical decision.   H   e dialed Zhou's number and left a message, expecting a return call when the Newark office opened.

Dylan stowed the pistol in his suitcase before lugging it and the golf bag to the nearest shuttle bus pick up stand. Ten minutes later he was at the Enterprise counter. By 7:20 a.m. he was in the idling Armada.

God, I need coffee.

Dylan got on his phone looking for the nearest coffee shop. He was slightly surprised to see the Winans location on Miller Lane was just six miles away.

Perfect. I'll cruise past the possible meeting spot and check it out on the way to Winans. If the spot looks good, I'll call Dax. I can grab coffee and a couple scones at the shop then come back and hit some balls while I wait.

Dylan's online searching the night before had resulted in the discovery of National Road Driving Range, less than a two-minute drive from the airport. It promised to be an excellent place to meet Dax.

The men would take I-70—also minutes away—east as they made their way to Newark. It would be out of the way for Dylan to drive south to Dax's hotel. He would have to retrace his route back north. It made much more sense for Dax to come to him.

Dylan made his way to the driving range, which was little more than a small metal maintenance building with an attached office and a small asphalt parking lot. He pulled in. Dylan surveyed the area and nodded to himself.

Perfect.

He punched in the address of Winans on the map app on his phone—he had no time or desire to screw around with learning the Armada's navigation system—and set off for Miller Lane. On the way he called Dax.

"Hello?"

Dax sounded shaken.

"Hey, Dax. Are you good?"

"Good as I can be."

"Hang tough. We're getting the hell out of here. Take down this address. It's a driving range less than thirty minutes north of you. We'll meet there."

"You're shitting me...a *driving range*? You're gonna hit golf balls?"

"Have to do something while I'm waiting." He read off the address.

Dylan found the Winans, parked, and walked into the shop. It was busy. He got in line and breathed in the aroma.

Ahhh. I think I'll get one of their grande lattes with the shot of hazelnut.

Bunker was still in the small room at the hospital. He'd just completed a call with a funeral home director in Troy who, if he was excited about the prospect of unexpected business, hid it well. His cellphone rang. He automatically picked it up

390

and slid the answer icon to the right before checking to see who it was from. He'd spoken to a receptionist at StoryPoint earlier and was told that the director was not yet in her office. Bunker wanted to speak to her directly about his mom. As he raised the phone to his ear, he registered that the screen read "Phoebe Faris."

Bunker couldn't place the name.

"Hello, Amos Bunker."

"Hello, Detective? This is Phoebe Faris. I met you at Winans in Piqua. I was working there?"

She spoke the last line as if it was a question.

"Yes, Phoebe, I remember. What can I do for you?"

Bunker checked the wall clock, wondering if he should head home and get a shower. The hospital had some papers for him to sign, but he might put that off until later.

"Well, I'm filling in at another shop this week." She paused.

Bunker felt himself growing annoyed. He put some bark into his answer.

"YES?"

"Well," she seemed hesitant now, "are you still looking for that man named Eli? He's in the Miller Lane shop right now."

Bunker sprinted down the hall, nearly knocking over an orderly, and raced to the parking lot. He searched frantically for the Malibu, finally spotting it in a space near the emergency entrance. He shouted into the phone.

"Keep him there as long as you can...stall...do whatever you can. If he leaves before I get there, see what he's driving and call me back."

It was a 15-minute drive from Kettering Health to Miller Lane. Bunker made it in 10, praying all the while that he wouldn't be stopped by a state trooper. As he approached the shop, his cellphone rang. It was Phoebe.

"He's pulling out now. He's driving a black Nissan SUV —an Armada, I think. He wasn't very happy...I spilled his first drink on purpose and had to make it again."

"Great...I see him. Nice work, Phoebe." He disconnected the call.

Good girl!

The Armada was pulling out of the lot as Bunker passed by. He risked a look at the driver, hoping he or his car wouldn't be recognized.

It's him—Eli. Or Dylan. Whatever his name is...it's him.

It was the man who had killed his mother.

Bunker trailed the Armada north. It traveled at a leisurely pace on secondary roads until reaching Vandalia. Bunker stayed back, always keeping at least one vehicle between him and the murderer. On National Road he saw the Armada signal and turn into a small lot. Bunker approached and read the lettering on a small metal building.

NATIONAL RD
Driving Range

What the hell?

Bunker pulled into a dirt lane across the road from the driving range. There were no other vehicles in the parking lot. The range was apparently a 24-hour operation with coin operated ball dispensers. Bunker saw no evidence of staff on duty.

The killer rolled down both front windows then exited the vehicle holding the Winans coffee cup. He opened the rear cargo door and leaned in. He grabbed something and pulled.

It was the white Running Dog golf bag.

Bunker watched the man select two clubs and lean them against the vehicle before lowering the door. The killer sipped from the cup, seemed to frown, then removed the cup's lid and returned to the front door. He opened it and put the cup inside before grabbing the clubs and heading to the range.

Unbelievable! He killed a woman less than ten hours ago—shot her in the back. And he's going to hit golf balls?

Bunker opened the glove box. There was the Glock in its holster. He glanced back at the property.

No security cameras.

Bunker had a decision to make. He could make the arrest. It was the right thing to do—the lawful thing. Or he could cross the line—the line that existed in the space between the law and justice.

This time Amos Bunker opted for justice.

The killer was setting up to hit balls on the far side of the building. Bunker could pull into the lot and approach him without being seen until it was too late. He drove into the lot and parked next to the Armada. He palmed the Glock and stepped out of the Malibu.

Time to do this.

Bunker stepped toward the range, glancing inside the Armada at the same time.

Then he had a better idea.

Dylan stroked another perfect shot with his 5 iron. He'd paid for a bucket of 50 balls and had just hit the 40th.

Ahh, Dylan, boyo...you've still got it.

He switched to his sand wedge for the last ten balls. He knew that Dax would be there soon. It had taken forever to get his coffee at Winans, then that barista had knocked over his first cup putting on the lid.

Incompetent...just fucking incompetent.

He'd left the cup in the Armada to cool after determining—*again*—that the coffee was too hot.

He hit nine balls to four different spots on the range, all the while thinking about the next moves.

Should Dax and I toss our cellphones? The cops might try to track us through them...We still have the burners.

Dylan drug the last ball to the hitting zone with his wedge. He looked out at a wooden sign with "100 Yards" painted on it. He took his stance, let out a breath, and swung. The ball arched toward the sign, seemed to hang in the air for a moment, then descended. It made contact with the second "0."

Dylan laughed.

See that, Min—wherever you are—100 yards is a sand wedge for me.

He gathered his clubs and made for the parking lot. He saw that he still had the place to himself. He returned the clubs to the bag then got behind the wheel.

Have to talk to Zhou about getting new IDs.

He sipped his coffee, which had cooled considerably during the time that Dylan was hitting balls.

Not bad...temperature is just about right.

He took a longer pull and held the cup, not placing it back in the cup holder.

We need to get word back to Mr. Chu in Shenzhen... make sure he's aware of—

Dylan frowned. He suddenly felt exhausted. He was cold.

What the hell?

He struggled to breath.

What the hell is happening?

His body was growing limp. The latte slipped from his hands and spilled across his lap. He hardly felt it. He was floating now.

Floating away.

His eyes fell to his lap. Before they closed for the last time, he saw a damp off-white orb, somewhat smaller than a golf ball, on the Armada's seat between his legs.

Seconds before oblivion, he recognized it.

How?

He was gone.

EPILOGUE

Paul Hull drove north through the Indiana countryside on I-65. He was halfway into a five-hour drive that began before 4 a.m. He'd hoped to get through Indianapolis before the traffic of the Monday morning commute reached its peak. He'd been largely successful and now, he hoped, would have a relatively easy drive until he neared Chicago.

Paul was scheduled to attend a 9 a.m. meeting with the grocery store chain in Illinois. The meeting had been pushed back several days due to his involvement in the case in Miami County. The McClarys had called the client on the morning after Dana Bunker's shooting and informed them that Paul was helping with a criminal investigation. They were considerate, suggesting the meet be moved to the following week. Paul was grateful for their understanding and made sure he left early enough to make it to the meeting on time.

Now in lighter traffic, Paul set the cruise control and let his mind wander to the events of the previous several days. He was interviewed by local, state, and federal authorities. He walked them through the sequence of events at the WACO property alone as well as with Bunker and Scrabble. Even though Paul hadn't entered the house on Country Road, he accompanied officials to that location to review his actions on the night he and Amos attempted to rescue Bunker's mother.

Dana Bunker's funeral was held on Saturday. Both Paul and Tzortzakakis served as pallbearers. They joined members of the sheriff's department who included Pappy Karabin and the sheriff himself. It was an abbreviated graveside service, having the misfortune of taking place when the remnants of Hurricane Adelia swept through the area. Mourners huddled under the protective cover of a tent. Those who couldn't fit stood in the rain with umbrellas tilted to the southeast.

Gatewood and Roberta Dowdell were there. At one point in the service, Paul locked eyes with his fellow ex-CCT. He saw some of the same sadness he'd witnessed at Bean

Grissom's funeral a week earlier. Paul could only wonder if the death of the murderer and drug runner—now identified by law enforcement as Dylan Riordan—had given Gatewood any satisfaction.

For Amos, it had not. His mother was gone.

A reception was held in a rented hall afterward. Paul, standing with Lauren, watched Amos nod and shake hands with a stream of well-wishers. Most of the attendees that stuck around long enough to eat a piece of sheet cake and drink bland lemonade stole glances at the clock every few minutes, calculating whether they'd remained long enough to leave without appearing ill-mannered.

No one wanted to be there.

The Hulls were among the last to leave. Paul and Amos shook hands. Lauren gave the detective a long hug. Bunker, seemingly distracted, gave them a tight smile.

"I'll never be able to thank you for what you've done."

Paul managed, "I just wish..."

He didn't know how to finish.

Bunker's sad smile told Paul that he understood.

After their brief exchange and goodbye, Paul jogged through the rain and jumped into his SUV. He pulled up to the hall's entrance and leaned over to open the passenger door. Lauren stepped to the vehicle and collapsed her umbrella as she got inside. She shook the rainwater off before dropping it on the floor and closing the door.

They drove in silence, alone with their thoughts. It had been a depressing experience. Dana Bunker's death was senseless.

Paul had experienced traumatic loss many times. He knew that Dana's murder would weigh on Amos—a man Paul now considered a friend—forever. He suspected that it might also change him in some ways.

Paul knew that Lauren had similar thoughts. In a few short days she'd seemed to develop a connection to the detective, not unlike those she'd had with Paul's CCT teammates. He knew that she felt sorrow for Amos's loss. But he also knew something else.

He glanced at her as they slowed for a red light. Lauren's features still reflected the melancholy of the day but there was a trace of something else. The hint of a smile had formed at the corners of her mouth.

They had received the call Friday morning. The background check had been completed. He and Lauren had been approved by the state's foster and adoption program. They were on the waiting list.

Amos Bunker drove a sheriff's department marked SUV Monday morning. His destination was the Greenville Falls State Scenic River Area, a 92-acre recreational tract of land that featured hiking trails with scenic views. A local resident had called to complain about "weirdos" cruising the parking lot. She'd taken down license plate numbers and descriptions of the drivers and had insisted that a detective come hear her story. The location was 20 minutes northwest of Troy, near the village of Covington.

Bunker was told he could take a week of bereavement leave but he declined. Sitting alone inside his house, he decided, was the last thing he needed at this point. He would manage his grief while working. Doing his job—and doing it the right way—had always been a core component of his being. Bunker saw no reason for that to change. He couldn't deny, however, that his definition of the "right way" had evolved over the last week.

He thought back to the moments in the parking lot of the driving range. When he emerged from his Malibu, he fully intended to shoot Dylan Riordan. He would surprise the murderer, have a climactic confrontation, then pull the trigger and end Riordan's time on the planet—exterminate him. In the back of his mind, Bunker knew this would also, essentially, end his life. The bullet would be matched to his Glock. Even with a sympathetic jury he would go to prison. This realization was overcome by his rage. He strode toward his mother's killer.

Then he glanced into the rented Armada. The front windows were down. A cup of coffee with its lid removed sat cooling in a cup holder. A thought flashed into his brain. He saw a resolution that was...appropriate.

Bunker popped the trunk of the Malibu and stole a look in the direction of the range to make sure he was still hidden from Riordan's view. He quickly pulled rubber gloves from the PPE kit inside and slipped them on. He then shifted his gaze to the core of the Running Dog golf ball he'd cut open the day before. It lay there inside two layers of plastic, seemingly benign. Bunker knew better.

He grabbed the plastic and closed the trunk. Again glancing toward the range, he hurried to the Armada's driver's side door. He reached through the open window and carefully removed the coffee cup, noting the maroon sleeve with the Winans logo around its midsection. The cup was mostly full, its contents light brown. Bunker poured a small amount of coffee onto the ground to lower the level of the liquid. He then carefully removed the opioid sphere from the plastic. He held his breath. Protocol for handling such a substance was to wear a respirator. Bunker determined he didn't have time to don his. He let the orb roll from his gloved fingertips into the coffee.

After replacing the cup inside the Armada, Bunker hurried to the Malibu, removing the gloves and stuffing them into the plastic as he moved. Seconds later he was parked back in the dirt lane across National Road.

It was nearly ten minutes before Riordan approached the Armada. Bunker watched the murderer stroll unhurriedly across the lot, a look of satisfaction on his face. Riordan returned the clubs to the golf bag and got behind the wheel.

Bunker checked his watch. He had no idea to what extent the substance would dissolve in the coffee. He wasn't sure of its exact composition but knew it was a potent synthetic, perhaps even carfentanil. He saw the killer sip from the cup, seem to consider, then tilt it back for a longer swig. The odorless, tasteless properties of the substance allowed it to avoid detection. Within seconds the cup fell from Riordan's hand and his head slumped forward. The drug—apparently the key component in the whole sordid affair—had claimed another victim. The resolution, Bunker understood, was not lawful.

But it was justice.

After watching the Armada for several minutes, Bunker left the area. He called Millie, the Miami County dispatcher, and passed on that he'd received a call from a source in Dayton reporting a possible sighting of the killer. By now Dylan Riordan's identity had been disclosed by the Chinese national, Min Xian. Riordan was now a fugitive from justice and on the radar of every law enforcement agency in the region.

"I trailed him for a short time but lost him near National Road in Vandalia. He's in a black Nissan Armada." Bunker supplied the plate number.

In the end, it was a Montgomery County deputy who discovered the vehicle. He immediately requested assistance, including a HAZMAT team. He was aware that the suspect was tied to illegal opioids and had spotted the coffee-stained sphere.

Riordan's death was officially recorded as an accidental overdose, though many connected with the case believed it to be a suicide. The detached head of a putter was found in the grass where Dana Bunker was shot. It had a curious opening at the hosel. Closer examination revealed rifling inside and a trigger mechanism. The weapon was eventually linked to several murders, including those of Garrett Shortridge and Shadow Donald.

Min Xian began to talk almost immediately after officers took him into custody and away from Scrabble at the WACO location. He was in great pain, but it was obvious that he was relieved to be separated from the grinning ex-Army Ranger. He revealed the identities of Riordan and Keenan "Dax" Devereaux. He confirmed that William Wylie, the accident victim, was the fourth member of their working group. They were the lead element of an organization that had its roots in China at the direction of a man named Zhang Chu.

Though Chu was beyond the reach—for now—of U.S. law enforcement, another Chinese man, Zhou Yan, was being sought. He ran the Running Dog operation in Newark, New Jersey. Like Devereaux, Zhou's current whereabouts were unknown. Federal agents were reportedly scouring the Running Dog storage facility. Standard methods of drug detection were unsuccessful. The agents, it was said, had to resort to unpacking over a half-million golf balls and dropping them on a concrete floor to identify which might contain carfentanil.

Min was being held under a number of charges, including accessory to murder. Authorities believed he fired the shot that killed Gerard Shortridge but hadn't recovered a bullet. They were comparing test-fired bullets from his rifle to those in a database of unsolved shootings across the country, hoping for matches. Min's court-appointed attorney was arguing that his client's statements were the result of an unfamiliarity with the country's justice system, but that ploy seemed to have little chance of success. Min, still in pain with a cracked rib, was continuing to talk to investigators, content to blame as much as possible on his three associates. All four of the men, curiously, had Ivy League connections.

Law enforcement officials from every level were swarming over the Running Dog connection. Weary of battling the opioid crisis by arresting users and low-level dealers, they welcomed the opportunity to take down an operation of such significance.

Gayle DeJean took a path much different than Min. She lawyered up immediately. She was suspended from her job and remained in limbo while Sheriff Hollis and the county prosecutor deliberated on possible charges.

Though she didn't attend Dana Bunker's service, she did send flowers—a gesture that angered Bunker. He knew that she had contributed to his mother's death.

Bunker endured the blustery graveside service before welcoming visitors to the reception. He accepted their kind words with stoicism, occasionally brightening somewhat when speaking to a friend or colleague. One such instance came near the end of the reception.

Paul and Lauren Hull approached. Bunker had a connection with the couple that had developed in a few short days. It was a bond, however, that transcended its brevity. He shook hands with Paul and accepted an extended hug from Lauren, mumbling something that, he later realized, did not adequately express his gratitude.

Bunker could not look at the couple without remembering how he'd nearly wrecked their chances of adopting a child. He took consolation in knowing that his follow-up report had rectified the situation.

Now, nearing Greenville Falls, Bunker thought back to the interaction with Paul and Lauren at the reception and felt a bit of guilt. He realized that he'd almost tuned them out, his attention being drawn to the far side of the hall.

There stood his former fiancé, Sarah.

He smiled.

Maybe a hyphenated last name wouldn't be so bad.

ACKNOWLEDGEMENTS

I would not have completed this book—and by extension you would not be reading it—without the efforts of a number of people.

My daughter, Suzanne Lang, remains my go-to when it comes to navigating the many tasks required to turn out one of these books. From proofreading to editing to formatting the manuscript, she was indispensable.

Brad Beams scrutinized every word and punctuation mark. Although this examination turned up so many mistakes I was left wondering if I knew what the hell I was doing, it was exactly what the project needed.

Lauren Reneau again did excellent work creating the book's cover. I am keenly aware that I'm completely lacking in the skills to do this myself. This keeps me from taking her for granted. Thanks, Lauren—congrats again on Miss Phoebe.

The WACO Air Museum south of Troy, Ohio is one of the locations on the Dayton Aviation Trail, a collection of important and interesting sites sprinkled throughout Western Ohio. The name WACO is derived from the original name of the company—the Weaver Aircraft Company of Ohio. I have driven past the museum dozens of times over the years, always thinking I should stop and visit. After coming up with the idea for this book, I finally did. I was not disappointed.

I was fortunate enough to make it to their annual September Fly-In. WACO biplanes from all over the country add to the permanent exhibits that are on display in the museum. WACO is known in some circles as the company that designed and manufactured the gliders that were towed across the English Channel carrying troops and equipment on D-Day during World War II. The museum does an excellent job of recounting this history. But WACO originally gained fame for manufacturing beautiful biplanes in the 1920s through the 1940s. Many are still in the air today. They are flying works of art.

Put it on your to-do list. And when you're there, pronounce the name of the company as "WOCKO," you just might impress the staff.

I made a few visits to the National Museum of the U.S. Air Force to check out some things for this book. I probably could've gotten away with a simple online search to find the things I was looking for but any excuse to go to this museum is a good one. It is simply spectacular. I've said many times that I can't believe they don't charge admission. Do yourself a favor and plan a visit. You will not be disappointed.

Dan Knasel, one of the many people I know that "gets it," accompanied me on one of these visits. He had a strategy—*probably* tongue-in-cheek—for circumventing security and accessing an unauthorized area. I was hoping to see the red stars painted on the starboard side of Colonel Robin Olds's F-4 Phantom. We departed without incident and may or may not have dissected his plan over a couple of pints in a Troy watering hole on the way home.

My daughter, Suzanne, and son, Jack, gave me a small drone for my birthday when this book idea was percolating in my head. It helped fill in a gap in the plot—where Paul and Lauren ride the Miami River Recreation Trail and inadvertently video the WACO area. The sign that Paul discovers on the path that points to the WACO complex is really there. I noticed it on a bike ride of my own and, like Paul, was surprised that the secluded path was that close to the airfield. The odd rise of ground next to the airfield is also there in real life.

The book begins with an incident at the World's Largest Loaf of Bread. Yes, it really exists. It's on the property of a business in Urbana. A great friend, Joe Spaugy, was employed by the company. He invited me and a few others to tour the facility several years ago. That was a fun day. Joe is no longer with us—gone way too soon—and to simply say he is missed does not seem adequate. I'm due to stop and see you, Joe. I'll bring you a bottle of Dos Equis. Just like we used to do it on Westminster Drive.

Readers often ask me if I put myself in these books. The short answer is no. I'm not Paul, even though we have many of the same interests. But often experiences from my past find their way into the stories. There are a couple examples in this book.

In chapter three, Paul and company see a father and son posing for a photo in a Baltimore cemetery. They appear to be urinating on the grave of John Wilkes Booth, the assassin of Abraham Lincoln. As I write this in my office, I am looking at a picture of my son Jack—then about five years old—and I doing exactly that. We were not actually urinating.

I think.

And in chapter fourteen, Dylan Riordan sees a picture of Babe Ruth handing a copy of his autobiography to Yale captain George Bush on the Yale baseball field. Suzanne, a proud Ohio State Buckeye, did an internship one summer at Yale. She and I snuck onto the field and reenacted that scene. I can turn to another wall of my office and see that photo. I play the role of George Bush. Suzanne is the Babe.

So, I guess a little part of me did make it in.

Thanks for reading.

Also by Mike Van Horn

CONTROLLED FLIGHT

Paul Hull, a medically retired Air Force Combat Controller, and his wife Lauren pay an impromptu visit to an obscure historical site. It is associated with the Wright Brothers, the ingenious Dayton, Ohio pair that developed the theories and hardware that culminated in the first heavier-than-air powered flight. An occurrence at this location puts the Hulls in the crosshairs of a criminal who has no peer in the realm of cybercrime. He is evolving, becoming more like a character in the first-person shooter video games that he enjoys. Paul must pit his skills developed in the Global War on Terror against a foe that is several steps ahead of him. Events play out across a number of sites connected to Wilbur and Orville Wright.

An Eric Hoffer Book Award Grand Prize Finalist and a Chanticleer International Book Awards Finalist in the CLUE category for Suspense & Thrillers.

Also by Mike Van Horn

THE FIRETEAM

A formidable team of bank robbers has developed techniques that have frustrated the FBI. They've pulled off a series of heists across Middle America. After a particularly violent robbery they encounter Paul Hull, a former Air Force Combat Controller. This sets the stage for a manhunt for the gang's leader, a dangerous fugitive bent on vengeance. Hull's wife, Lauren, is targeted. Paul races against time to save her from a deadly adversary.

Chosen for the Chanticleer International Book Awards Shortlist in the CLUE category for Suspense & Thrillers.

Also by Mike Van Horn

NEIL DOWN: A SHOT AT IMMORTALITY

There were two separate parades for astronaut Neil Armstrong in his hometown of Wapakoneta, Ohio. The first was in 1966 after his Gemini 8 mission. The second came in 1969, a few weeks after Apollo 11, when he became the first man to walk on the moon. The first parade was dwarfed and overshadowed by the second. But in "Neil Down," a work of historical fiction, it provides Danny Hitchens critical information he uses to set up the unthinkable. Danny is a teenager growing up in a neighboring town that is even smaller than Wapakoneta. In Botkins, he is insulated from most of the factors that made the sixties turbulent. He grew up playing baseball, questioning religion, and worrying about girls and his future after high school. Danny has a great admiration for those in the space program and the military. This is heightened when his brother joins the Army and deploys to Vietnam. Danny's world is shattered by a series of tragedies. These incidents combine with his issues with religion to turn him dark and vengeful, filled with rage. He lashes out at those he perceives as slighting him. His paybacks escalate until he finds himself, in a decade of high-profile assassinations, planning the inconceivable. He will use information obtained during the Gemini 8 Homecoming parade to kill Neil Armstrong.